RITA WIRKALA

THE ENCOUNTER

COVER DESIGNED: MARCELO BASILE

TITLE IN THE ORIGINAL SPANISH: *EL ENCUENTRO*

PUBLISHED BY PEARSON, *ALHAMBRA JOVEN*
MADRID, MARCH 2011

TRANSLATED TO ENGLISH BY ELWIN WIRKALA

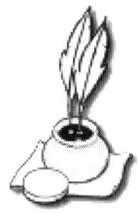

All Bilingual Press

www.allbilingual.com

All rights reserved – Printed in the U.S.A.
Copyright © 2013 by All Bilingual Press, LLC
Second Edition 2015

ISBN: 978-0-9892579-8-5

INDEX

To my husband
Elwin

And my daughters
Karen, Clarice and Elisa

who patiently and skillfully translated this book from the
Spanish original.

Where is it going so swiftly and fatigued
that weary swallow flying away from here,
soon it will find itself lost in the breeze
in search of shelter that will not appear.

Just beside my bed I'll put its nest
where we can let the season pass us by.
I'm also in the region of the lost,
Oh saintly heaven, but I cannot fly.

"THE SWALLOW" *(LA GOLONDRINA)* SONG

POEM BY NICETO ZAMACOIS (1862)

First Part

1976. Sacha Sur (Ecuador)

Huge towers belch fire over a green vastness curving toward the horizon. From far away the roof of the jungle is an unbroken, undulating surface with flare stacks jutting above it at regular intervals. Beneath them, life quivers in deathly spasms.

"Arévalo, why do you want to talk to me right now? I was just leaving."

"I took a look at the budget, sir, and I don't see any numbers for pool lining. If you don't put the sludge in storage tanks - and I haven't seen any tanks around here - or if you don't inject it back into the ground, then you'll at least need to line these pools with cement, right?"

Engineer Ruiz's sidelong glare does not intimidate Arévalo. After all, he's spent years in this business. And this new guy is just a novice with a diploma hung around his neck.

"Look, sir, I'm just an accountant, and if I mention cement it's only because I don't know of any other material to line pools with in this industry—nothing works except cement."

"We're not going to use anything, Arévalo."

"Do you mean to say that the waste is going to be dumped directly into these holes in the ground, naked? I mean…open pools in direct contact with the ground?"

From the third floor of the main building, Esteban Ruiz looks out on Sacha Sur station, a brown, steely smudge in the middle of these interminable hills of rolling green. His eyes follow the line of flaming columns, red and yellow; enormous towers endlessly blasting out burning gas day in and day out in a

1

controlled and ceaseless self-consumption. Under sun, lightning and rain, they burn with incessant fury. Ruiz observes the distortions of the violet sky through the shimmering heat, and in his air-conditioned office he feels a little shiver.

He ponders his answer, then replies,

"Come on! It's not oil. It's mud!"

"Yes, but it has benzene, right? And lead and heavy metals, as I understand. You know better than I do that these noxious wastes will permeate the soil and run off into the entire region, sir. This is the Amazon basin, and it's a fragile system, as you know.

Arévalo colors as he speaks, partly because of the uncomfortable situation of breaking protocol by addressing his superior in this way — he is talking to his boss, even if he is young— but mostly because he is just plain angry. A gringo coming to pollute his country, he thinks, is beyond unacceptable. Well... Ruiz is not exactly a gringo, he remembers, because the man is, after all, Spanish — but so what? He lives in Texas and he works for Texapetrol. Of course, he himself also works for The Company. This thought fills him with shame and he turns a deeper red.

"I'm not the one who decides this, Arévalo. They give me a budget and I do what I can," says Ruiz. "They made it clear that here in Ecuador this is how things are done, and the government in Quito doesn't butt in. We presented plans for this block, they were all approved, we were awarded exploitation rights, and that's that."

"Understood, sir. But just for your information and after this I won't keep you any longer. People live in this region, and these people use water from the rivers, for drinking, for cooking, for bathing, and there's underground water very close to the surface, with springs bubbling up here and there in the forest, and they flow into the rivers. In other words, into the fluvial system. Not to mention the rain that also washes chemicals into the tributaries."

"Look, Arévalo, before this happens, the land itself will, let's say ...clean out any remaining hydrocarbon, and the water will be pure by the time it reaches the rivers. Understand?" explains Ruiz, blinking quickly. "Soil functions like clay filters.

2

Have you seen the ceramic filters used in the country? It's the same process."

Arévalo looks at him with irritation. "Is he taking me for an idiot?" he thinks. "A toxic metal is not like an amoeba or a microorganism!"

"Don't worry," says Esteban Ruiz, while moving the accountant toward the door with a friendly hand on his back. "The jungle is powerful, and it absorbs everything and recycles everything. Nature takes care of itself!"

"Imbecile!" thinks the accountant, but he swallows hard and remains silent.

1990, Longing

Friday, June 1st, Ecuador

The young teacher puts his worn leather briefcase on the table and reminds the students that their homework was to write a composition about love. On the day he assigned the homework, he asked them, "If you had a magic nest and you could put everything you loved inside it, no matter how big, what would you put in it?" He emphasized that the students were free to fill the nest with whatever they love best.

Mario Romero, motivated by strong idealism and an altruistic spirit, arrived in eastern Ecuador from Quito a few months earlier. "The East is also a part of this country," he repeats over and over to himself.

"And aren't these little smiling faces looking up at me, yearning for learning, just as Ecuadorian as all the ones in the rest of the country?" Quichua, white, mestizo, Shuar, we're all brothers, he always tells his students.

He was somewhat disappointed when he arrived. Baeza is a provincial town offering very little in the way of cultural life. He has been assigned to a humble school on the outskirts of the village, where the jungle begins. Romero is one of three teachers, one for each classroom, each of which admits several grade levels in order to accommodate the entire student population. School materials are very limited, and reading material is pitiful. The teacher has had to send for his own books in order to offer his students more substantial learning. In spite of everything, he recognizes that his students do not lack creativity: when they found out that a new teacher was arriving, they made colored cardboard cutouts of the sun and the planets and hung them by threads from the palm roof, where the breeze keeps them in perpetual motion.

But the village is boring, he thought at first, and hopelessly slow.

However, as time passes, the teacher has begun to follow the path from the school into the jungle, where he has found a new world opening up to him like a flower. The forest has begun to release its secrets, and he is learning them.

He has learned the names of the trees and birds, and how to find amber honeycomb among the trunks dressed in vines, lichen, mosses like wavy hair; he has learned to weave hats from palm leaves bending to the humid earth as if offering their bounty.

His deep surrender to the jungle came on a day when the children took him canoeing on a silky river. The reflection of the sky, intensely blue, and of the vegetation, with its inverted image hanging from both shores like brilliant green lace, made Mario Romero feel like an astronaut drifting between two spatial planes.

He recognized, then, that the dry Andean mountains of his birthplace, with their frosty mornings, had never lifted his spirit like this, and he realized that everyone has to find his place in the world, and that here in eastern Ecuador's primordial jungle he has found his place.

That night he began his first book of poems, entitling it "The Junglenaut".

Mario Romero asks for a volunteer. He does not agree with some of his colleagues that children should be singled out unexpectedly to perform before the class, like prisoners ordered to the gallows by their executioner.

A small, slender hand rises with an air of decision.

"I'll read, Señor Romero."

"Please do, Rosa."

Radiant, the girl rises and begins to read:

My name is Rosa Epayuma. If I had a magical nest, I would fill it with books. I love books, and I want to be a writer like my teacher. In the afternoon, after we finish our chores, my granddad always asks me to read a poem to him. I mean, to read, and translate some words because he doesn't understand Spanish very well. He really only speaks and sings in Huaorani.

"Huaorani! the headhunters?" Romero asks himself. Or were they the Shuar? He makes a note to follow up on this later.

At night, Rosa continues, *when my grandma asks me to put out the lamp to save kerosene, and the crickets begin to sing, I go out to the patio and light a torch, to read under a big tree.*

He has heard about this in Quito, the teacher remembers: electricity and running water do not reach the jungle clearings. "But it's not really important," he has been told, because the Indians of the Amazon burn tree resin for light. And as for running water, well, there are many rivers. These people are happy with little," he has been assured.

Rosa continues:

If the nest were very large, I would also put my family into it, my horse, my dog, my house, and the entire little farm. My house is in the jungle, in a clearing my granddad opened with a machete for the family. It's protected. The Company doesn't come here.

"The Company?" The teacher is about to ask her to be more specific. What company is she referring to? But he does not wish to interrupt her.

But above everything in the world and the universe, I'd put my mom in there. She went to the North in a boat. It's been a year since she left. She sends money to us. That's why we have all we need in our house. But I miss her so much. Very, very much! Sometimes, at night, I feel something like a thorn sticking into my heart, and I put on a t-shirt that was hers, and it still has a little bit of her perfume, and that's how I sleep, imagining that she's with me, and I am in her arms.

Echoes of an ache, like the memory of a distant but poignant scent, graze his nerves.

....but the perfume is fading. I think I used it up breathing it in so much. I wonder if my mom's love is also getting used up. I hope she doesn't forget me, up there in the North!

Unconsciously, the teacher places his hand on his heart, as if to ward off some dormant sentiment lurking there before it wakes up and stabs him, too. Hastily, he says something to suppress it in time.

"Well done, Rosita! You've poured your feelings into the written word. That's good for you. You're an excellent writer."

"Mr. Romero" says a child, "my father is in the United States, too".

"And I have two uncles in Chicago," a girl adds.

The teacher is surprised to see several little faces eager to speak.

"Let's see... who has parents, relatives or friends in the United States?" Romero asks, with some alarm.

Thirty voices respond in unison, "I do, teacher," while thirty little hands go up simultaneously pointing toward the ceiling where the little paper planets are stirring in the air.

Friday, June 1st, California

Ernesto's suffering is so intense that he feels like he needs to learn how to breathe again. He's been sitting on the porch stairs of his house, his backpack beside him, in a near cataleptic state since arriving from school. An hour has gone by, or is it two hours? Three? Time has become an elusive reality; just an immeasurable succession of emotions.

His cat and dog are playing on the perfectly manicured lawn in front of him. The boy has been observing, with some envy, the mock battle of his pets. He thinks of himself and Carlo and their mutual hatred and disdain. He remembers with painful clarity the afternoon's episode, the enormous truth his enemy threw into his face and how it penetrated like a shard of glass — like a poison-tipped shard of glass.

From the kitchen, Esteban Ruiz calls his son.

"Carlo's mother called just now and says he's fine, but they had to give him five stitches on his head."

The man gazes at Ernesto with an intensity full of questions. The boy doesn't respond.

"Can you explain to me and your mother why you did this? Why all this violence?"

The boy continues to hang his head in silence.

"Explain, Ernesto. Now!"

"Carlo was making fun of me," Ernesto says, finally obliged to confront his father's look. "He was saying stuff to me like he always does, and I always put up with it, and I never do anything to him," says the boy with an almost broken voice. "But this time I couldn't take it anymore. I had to defend myself."

"So you lost your temper? Punched him in the face, knocked his head into a metal desk and almost killed him! And all because he was 'saying stuff to you'? Come on, Ernesto!"

"It was a freak accident. He fell badly. That part wasn't my fault."

"But you were the one who hit him. And he didn't even touch you! Legally, it's your fault. Do you understand, Ernesto, that you came close to breaking that kid's skull? Do you know that they could've shut you up in a reform school with all the delinquents in San Diego?"

Ernesto remembers the bright stream of blood running down his enemy's face like a scarlet river, girls screaming, teachers shouting, the arrival of the ambulance, the sudden panic, and not knowing where to hide himself and his shame when facing the police and his parents.

"How many times have I told you? You have to control yourself! We're not paying for the most expensive high school in this city so you can get into fights with your classmates just because they "say stuff". School is for learning, for building character, for self-control, for...."

"What did the boy say to you?" his mother interjects.

"Carlo is an imbecile. He makes fun of me, he makes me look like...he makes me look bad in front of everyone. I don't want to talk about this right now!" A wave of nausea overtakes him like a heavy sea. "I don't want dinner, either."

"Well, if you don't want to explain yourself, you'd better go to your room. Come back when you're ready to talk."

The boy goes upstairs to his room and sits on the floor, looking for something to assuage his pain.

It occurs to him that the other boy bullies him from pure envy and jealousy, because he's handsome—so he's heard—and girls always talk to him. But they won't even look at Carlo. Maybe that's what it's all about.

Or maybe Carlo is a racist.

The idea, casual at first, begins to rise as if climbing up his body, through his face, his hair, like a parasitic vine sucking vital sap from a tree.

Maybe it'd be better to go to a public school, where there are more kids like him. Or at least who look more like him.

In the kitchen his mother tries to find just the right words. She doesn't want to argue with her husband, but she can't stop herself from talking.

"Poor Ernesto. We really don't know much about him and all the things he worries about," she says calmly. "Don't be so hard on him, Esteban. I'm sure this kid Carlo makes fun of him. You know how these kids can be —they can be just plain cruel."

"I know. There are always these individuals who from childhood mold their identity by making fun of others. Maybe it's okay for Ernesto to take him down a notch or two, but not so violently. He could've killed that kid! This is serious! Don't forget, Isabel: we have even more responsibility to Ernesto that most parents have."

Saturday, June 2nd

Rosa's house is not far from the school—just a short half hour walk through the jungle. One crosses a river, climbs a hill, and there it is, with its straw roof and yellow bamboo reeds, glowing under the sun. Grandpa Caento, like many Huaorani, never sleeps through the night. Last night he got up three times, three times began to sing, and three times went back to sleep. Now he's at the riverbank, which means he's hungry.

Grandmother Umi carries a pail of water from the river to the kitchen. She pours the water into an aluminum pan blackened with soot and sets it on the fire blazing in the center of three trunks that form a Y on the dirt floor. Rosa wakes up with the crackling sound of burning logs, not far from her hammock.

As they do every second Saturday, the family gets ready to walk to the town bank to withdraw money that Rosa's mom sends her from the US. It is harvest time in the United States and Alba, living there in self-imposed exile, is spending her days squatting her way down strawberry furrows or stretching her body to pluck ripe clusters from grapevines. By working seven days a week she has doubled the number of dollars she sends, so today, everybody in Rosa's house has a smile on their face.

"Gabo, grab that red chicken for me! Enkeri, help your brother!" Umi orders.

The names of the children —Rosa, Gabriel, Enrique -and also that of Umi's daughter Alba—are Christian names, because they grew up in the protectorate of the American missionary Rachel Saint, where the Huarorani were confined at the end of the seventies.

But grandmother has also come up with, if not exactly a translation, an approximate transliteration of her grandchildren's names. For Gabriel, Gabo; for Enrique, Enkeri. They sound better that way, and roll off her tongue more naturally.

Her granddaughter, however, has remained just Rosa, because it's the name of a flower. And her daughter, Rosa's mother, always was and always will be just Alba. Alba Caento.

Hunting down a chicken, and the preparation of *ayampaco*, are part of their Saturday routine. The children race around the yard and the garden happily and wildly until one of them catches the prey, which screeches and cackles in vain and tries to escape from their hands.

"It's too bad there are no capybaras anymore," the woman says, as part of her ritual, prior to snapping the bird's neck, "and we have to make do with these chickens that get sick so easily. Too bad that wild meat is so scarce." She recalls how rare the wild animals were becoming even before native people like her were herded into the evangelical missions.

Nothing is like it used to be in the Yasuní, where she and her husband were born, Umi grumbles. The day they were told they had to leave was the beginning of a two-stage exile. First they were moved to the evangelical protectorate. Afterwards, to the farm in Baeza.

Umi didn't adapt well to the missionary protectorate, although she didn't complain. She even took to covering her breasts and using one of those brassieres given to her by the Christian women. And, though she learned to speak Spanish well, she kept her Huarorani name: Umi. Just Umi!

Her three children, Marucha, Alba and Numpa, were born in the protectorate.

At the time, she believed that their uprooting from Yasuní and transfer to the evangelical's land would be temporary and was due to some Christian charity. She did not know the role of interest groups, and only learned the truth later, when her daughter, Alba, then grown up, explained the situation to her: The Company was behind everything. The Company, needed to clear the Huao territory of its native population in order to build the Vía Auca road through the jungle and starts to operate the oil stations. Missionaries from the United States were eager to help move them, her daughter explained, because, for their part, they were interested in saving Huaorani souls. At that point she realized that their exile would be permanent.

"Save them from what?" Umi wanted to know. "From Hell, Mama", Alba would tell her, arching an eyebrow. Umi didn't care about Hell. A few others did, and became very frightened and more civilized, especially on Sundays, Alba remembered. And some began to ingratiate themselves with the American señora who gave orders there, so that they would receive benefits. Umi was never interested in these benefits, either here or on the other side of the grave. All she wanted was to go back to her beloved Yasuní and live below the majestic eye of the Jaguar watching over the Huaorani world.

Old Umi remembers the protectorate of her youth: so many people crowded into one place, and how hunting became intensive and then was exhausted. Peccaries, capybaras, tapirs and alligators were soon replaced by sugar, rice and chickens.

The woman evokes these memories of the past with irritation and discharges her disgust on the bird's neck, breaking it with one clean and efficient snap. Without the Jaguar, the natural custodian of the jungle, she reflects, things cannot go well.

Soon the air is impregnated with the smell of burnt chicken feathers.

11

"Well, at least we didn't become cripples or die like some of the Huaos, from that 'poliomilitis'. And finally we got out of the missionary's land," Umi muses, "thanks to Marucha that got us this little plot of land for the farm. And thanks to Alba and the money she earns in the North we now live here as we like. Without much wild meat, of course... and these chickens that get sick for no reason!"

"Rosita, help your grandmother!" Aunt Aepi yells. Rosa will have to learn how to sharpen the knife and cut the throat and pluck feathers, as Umi is doing at the moment. In the absence of her mother, both grandmother and aunt have been careful to educate Rosa in household tasks, because in school a girl does not learn how to be a woman.

With a rubber band Rosa ties the abundant mop of dark hair cascading over her back. Wrinkling her nose, she plucks feathers and then returns to the cabin to peruse the titles of the books lent by her teacher.

Since learning that she wanted to be a writer like him the teacher has provided Rosa with reading material - history, biographies, poetry and even children's stories he wrote. She lovingly wraps them in plastic to avoid them getting "smoked" like everything else in the house.

Having finished their breakfast of chicken soup with yucca, the women shred the chicken meat into little bits, wrap them in palm leaves and put them into a basket, which they will take to their excursion into town.

Rosa separates some entrails for the dog. She calls him with a sharp whistle and the beast, a smart and faithful animal, gallops over to her and throws himself at her feet.

Later on it's the horse's turn. She collects some straw and lifts it to his muzzle, gives him a scratch and a pat on the neck and leaves him eating to his heart's content.

The love of these two is as predictable and unconditional as the sun that rises each day, or course of the river that runs across the farm, where grandfather is now fishing.

The old man mutters something incomprehensible.
"What is it, Grandpa?"

"Fishing is bad, Granddaughter. I bet the Shuar are dynamiting upstream. Dump people, the Shuar. Ever since they got dynamite they've forgotten how to use a net. Just look at these tiny fish, will you?" he says in a weary tone. He points to some silver fish swimming below long yellow grasses bending over the water.

"Just skin and bones. Good for nothing! It's not like in our rivers back in Yasuní. The fish were so abundant there, Rosa!"

Old Caento uses his people's favorite word: abundance, that big word that in Huaorani cosmology embodies the beginning and end of existence.

He pauses.

Rosa knows what's coming.

"Yes, abundance ...until the fish floated downstream belly up," the old man laments. "It was a day after the rains. Have I told you about that, Rosita? The river turned black and red."

The image of oil-slathered fish floating belly up on a black and scarlet river always makes the girl shudder, and she grimaces with pain and repugnance. It reminds Rosa of her father, who one day traveled down another river, she has been told, and he was found all fouled with that black, viscous liquid.

Caento's adaptation to life in the evangelical protectorate was even harder than his wife's. He didn't even bother to learn to speak Spanish. And, obviously, he didn't change his name, either, but passed it on to his children so that they could use it as their clan name. That way they would have both first and last names, like white people, if that's what they wanted: Alba Caento, Numpa Caento, Marucha Caento.

He did complain. The noise from the loudspeakers — sermons were broadcast at all hours—was much too loud, he would say. And why so many prohibitions? The old man enjoys saying, with a parrot-like cackle that, for the evangelists, anything he did was "of the devil." But the worst part was when there was nothing to do after the jungle animals became scarce, because—as he never tired of explaining— they had pushed the Huaorani to violate the law of the jungle.

"And what is the law of the jungle, grandpa?" the children asked.

"Don't hunt animals bigger than yourself."

The Huao, he would explain, do not kill large animals where abundant iguanas, turtles, monkeys and birds exist. But the evangelists had called this a taboo. "Every animal that walks is for eating," they declared, because God said so in the Bible. And so the hunt had become more and more difficult in their small territory until the Huaorani were reduced to eating the soft food of white people.

"That's why we became softer, Rosa...but not whiter!"

True, in many ways the family is doing well in the farm in Baeza, even though the grandparents would love to return to Yasuní and, like all uprooted people, still dream of going back. But how to retrace a trail obliterated by dynamite and bulldozers, crisscrossed by viaducts and pipelines and cursed by the voracious hand of The Company? Return is impossible, and the family fully understands this —they understand that they were trapped in the destiny of an oil-rich jungle like innocent flies trapped in a spider web.

"Only the spirit of the Jaguar can save us from that bloodsucking spider," Uncle Numpa tells Rosa and his children. "And that spirit told me that only by copying the enemy and learning his arts are we going to save ourselves from becoming beggars. So, children, learn from the white people's books, because you're going to need what's in them!"

"Tell me, Grandpa, why do those people from The Company want so much oil? What's it good for?" Rosa asks, when she recovers somewhat from the image of her father floating on a hideous oil-polluted river full of dead fish.

"To make gasoline for their cars and buses, child. That's why they want it."

"Oh, for the cities. But we don't even have roads!"

"It's better that way, Rosa. We don't want them. The roads in Huaorani territory have only brought trouble."

This is true, Rosa thinks, because after The Company built the Auca Road, her father died of an invisible disease that eats people's spines, and her mom left for the North, leaving that enormous emptiness in her soul.

14

After spending the afternoon in the village the family comes home laden with purchases: rice, sugar and salt, seeds, chicken vaccine, kerosene for the lamps, batteries for the radio. Walking quickly up the trail to the clearing, the conversation revolves around the use of the money left over from Alba's last transfer. Grandmother insists on saving it for what she calls 'skinny-cow times'. Uncle wants to invest it in chicken wire for the coop. The children are in favor of dividing it equally before the grown-ups appropriate it for their adult projects.

Rosa is not interested. She doesn't need any more clothing or shoes or dolls because her house is bursting with presents her mother has sent each Christmas and birthday.

"Rosita, why are so quiet, child? What are you thinking about?"

"Grandpa and Grandma," Rosa said, "when can I go to the United States to see my mom?"

"Later, Rosa. Not yet. You are still a child, and going to The North is dangerous."

"Why is it dangerous?"

"Why? Well...you know, Rosita, you'd need to go with a coyote, one of those men that sneaks you in."

"Why can't I just take an airplane and go alone?"

"Because you need a visa. Written permission. And they don't give visas to people like us."

"Why not?"

"It's complicated, Rosa. You see, for us, the only way is to pay a person to take us to the other side just like your mother did. And it's very expensive."

"Mom can pay."

"It's not only that. It's a long trip and much too dangerous for a 10-year-old girl."

"Of course, they know the way," Gabriel assures her. "They take you by bus, by ship, by train, by car...even on foot!"

"They take you over the border at night," Enrique adds, "but if the U.S. Border Patrol sees you they run after you and put you in jail!"

"And if you're able to get across the border and then the coyote gets into some sort of trouble, he'll disappear and leave you all alone in the middle of the desert" says Grandmother.

"And you might get bitten by a snake."

"They might steal from you..."

"Somebody might grab you..."

"They might..."

Rosa covers her ears. Her desire to see her mother is so strong in her that it's like sickness in her heart; a heart now beating wildly, like a little swallow falling out of her nest.

Saturday, June 2nd

Violent, stridently-colored nightmares tear Ernesto and with a heavy heart, he gets himself out of bed. He would love to tell his parents how the fight with Carlo started yesterday, but either the feeling of deep embarrassment or a sense of shame —he cannot tell which—has robbed him of speech. He has never told his parents about Carlo, and has no intention of doing so today.

The fact is that the other boy has been harassing him for ages with indirect and vague, malicious, allusions. Yesterday, however, to torment him even more and to test the limits of his power, Carlo changed his strategy.

"Hey Ernesto," the boy said when the teacher had momentarily left the class, "this genetics thing is interesting, isn't it? While the teacher was talking, I thought about you. How did you turn out so dark when your parents are so white?"

"Shut up, you idiot," said Ernesto, "or I'm going to kick your ass!" and he turns back.

"Oops, I forgot. Well, there's nothing wrong with being adopted, I guess. The problem is..." and here he draws nearer to Ernesto and lowers his voice, "... not knowing who your real parents are, right? If I were you, I'd try to find out. You see, it's important to know where one comes from."

Carlo paused to let his words sink in and pour out their venom. "Who knows," he continued, "your dad might've been a wetback... Ever wondered about that? Or maybe a drug dealer... and what about your mom? Who knows?"

Although Ernesto was used to Carlo's daily bullying, yesterday's taunt was so unexpected, egregious, as if someone had stabbed iron claws into his chest and torn at his heart. At that instant an explosive mixture of blood and adrenaline rose up to his face and he felt it burning. He doesn't remember the exact moment he spun around, raised his arm, and sent his fist shooting through the air toward Carlo's face. He does not remember, either, the moment his knuckles connected with Carlo's cheekbone with such force that the other boy went down with a crash, his head bouncing off the corner of a desk. He does remember the hollow clash and metallic din of a falling body hitting the desk, and then the horror that stopped his breath at seeing blood streaming through Carlo's fingers, holding his head, wide-eyed, incredulous, and in a state of shock.

Of course he didn't want to kill him. Ernesto is sure of that. He only wanted to erase Carlo and his words, cross them out, thrust them out of his life forever.

The storm that this produced inside him abated a little, but only to give way to a new kind of pain.

Or perhaps it wasn't new, because that sensation of being rootless, of uncertain origin, always lurked in some fold of his memory and from time to time comes out to torment him. What is new is the magnitude of the desire to know, triggered by the phrase "Who your real parents are."

Someday, Ernesto promises himself, he is going to find out.

What the boy knows for sure is that one afternoon in June, 1978, someone left a baby in the doorway of a church in downtown San Diego; and that from there he was taken to a daycare at a convent, and that, pinned to the baby blanket in which he was wrapped, the nuns found a paper written in Spanish that said:

This is my baby, Ernesto. For the love of God... take good care of him.

The paper was signed: *María Moreno, de Esperanza.*

So the Someone he was missing had a name: María Moreno.

When the discovered that they could not have children they decided on another course of action. Shortly after Esteban Ruiz left Texapetrol for a new job in California a social worker brought them "an abandoned Mexican baby," which is how the nuns who received little Ernesto identified him. After an administrative waiting period, the Ruiz's adopted him. In honor of the baby's origin, and to respect his mother's choice and preserve his own name, the Ruiz's had him baptized under the name Ernesto Moreno Ruiz.

Whether out of curiosity or to prepare for unavoidable future questions, the looked for the town of Esperanza on a map of Mexico, and they soon found it, in the state of Sonora. They drew a circle around the name of Ernesto's—or his family's—village. They carefully folded the map and put it away in a drawer. Modern and well-educated parents as they were, they never hid the fact of his adoption from him, but they also didn't speak much about it as a family. Basically, they tried to maintain a balance between the duty of telling the truth, and the right to forget the matter. When Ernesto, as a boy, would ask where his birth parents were from, he always received the same information, given briefly and in a casual tone: "Esperanza, son. A village in Mexico." Of course, he knew the answers would always be the same.

But it didn't matter. It was part of his ritual. After that he would open the drawer where his mother kept his baby clothes and, when no one was looking, would lift them to his nose to see what Mexico smelled like.

It still had a slight fragrance of orange blossom.

One time, and at Ernesto's insistence, they went to the convent to ask for María Moreno. They were told not to waste time looking for her because she had been deported.

Ernesto never forgot that circle around Esperanza from the first time he was conscious of having seen it. From that moment, an insurgent force would make him climb onto a chair and take the map from the drawer to contemplate and question it. Thinking about that circle filled him with feelings of consternation bordering on anger; and yet beneath this was overwhelming nostalgia. He longed for someone who seemed ever to attract him from an unknown magnetic pole.

18

The circle on the map of Mexico turned into the self-contained, secret center of his existence, a place where his longings, for a long time, quietly hibernated.

Except that yesterday it had all blown up like a volcano.

Second Part

1995

1. Esperanza

I

1995 has been a different kind of year for Ernesto, an intense year of afternoons shut away in libraries, sleepless nights, no fun on the weekends and, finally, a marathon of passed exams. Today marks the end of these sacrifices, and the Ruiz family has opened their doors to friends and teachers to celebrate the early graduation of their son.

The year before, Ernesto had finally told his parents about his desire to travel to Esperanza, and the conversation had not gone well. He hadn't told them that this was an overwhelming desire, like a volcano that had long been seething in his chest, burning him. No, *that* he couldn't tell them. He had told them instead that he was curious about his biological family. Just that, and that he needed their written permission in order to travel.

Esteban Ruiz had raised all sorts of objections, every one of them seconded by Isabel. Having their son go out into the world looking for more legitimate parents was hurtful to them, although they didn't admit this to the boy. Instead, they used irrefutable logic: he was only 16 years old; Mexico wasn't a safe place to travel alone; he should at least finish high school before testing his wings. Ernesto remembers his father's vehemence on that day: "Your education is the most important thing right now, Ernesto. You'll have plenty of time to dig up the past later, if that's what you want. It's your right to do this, just not now. I hope you understand."

This was by no means the first time father and son had disagreed, but Ernesto had the ability to turn negatives into fuel for action. On that afternoon ten months ago, when he committed himself to discovering who he was, and when he received that resounding "no", he decided to take the bull by the horns: he would speed up his graduation to get that obstacle out of his way.

And he did just that. After all, his mind had been primed by this desire for so long that now a channel opened up into which all his thoughts flowed like tributaries rushing into a river and swelling its current into a raging torrent.

Today, Ernesto is feeling well-armed to launch the second part of his plan of attack: a high school diploma, eloquent testimony to his efforts, lies open on the table. Beside it is a letter granting Ernesto a prize in a national essay contest for teenagers. He had presented a text entitled: *Einstein, God, and Chance*. It was a daring piece of work, since the boy doesn't yet grasp the advanced mathematics underlying quantum theory. It was more philosophical than scientific. Quantum theory and its derivations (probability, chance, entanglement, symmetries, parallel universes and so forth), found fertile ground for ideas in the boy's mind, given to thoughts such as, "Who would I be if I hadn't been adopted?" and similar reflections relative to his identity and destiny.

The essay was well received by the jury and produced a pride of macrocosmic proportions in the Ruiz family, who now hope that Ernesto will be accepted by the prestigious Massachusetts Institute of Technology (MIT).

The boy, however, has other plans and, biding his time, he waits for an opening to speak with his parents.

It comes when the last guests have left and Esteban Ruiz calls his son to his office.

"Well, Son, congratulations. We've very proud of you. Not many teenagers can do what you did! And that prize... You should add it to your application for the MIT."

"I'm going to, but I didn't send the application yet. I'll do it next year."

"What? So why were you in such a hurry to graduate? To sit around for six months?"

His father's sober face makes him doubt for a moment. But then, swallowing hard, he says:

"I have other things to do."

All is quiet for a few seconds. A soft breeze wafts through the window, impregnated with the fragrance of roses, inducing in him a bittersweet sadness and pleasure —the two sides of the nostalgia that are so very familiar to him.

"You both know what my plans were and still are," the boy says, nervously.

His mother's smile freezes on her lips. His father, who had been hoping that his son had forgotten about his adolescent whims, can't help stiffening in his chair. Even the dog, sensing calamity, sits down next to the boy and pricks up his ears.

"Whatever this plan is, Ernesto, remember that you're young and impulsive."

"Listen, Dad, I told you a year ago that I wanted to go to Esperanza to look for the Moreno family. I haven't changed my mind. That's why I've been studying my ass off for a year."

The boy looks at his parents and his parents look at the carpet, as if searching in its intricate Persian design for a solution to this problem that's been creeping up and has now hit them head-on.

"I'm not going to leave you," Ernesto continued, "I just want to know who my biological parents are, if they're still alive, if I have another family; I want to know about my ethnicity, you know, and all that. I just need you to help me. Don't you think I have a point, Mom?"

"You have a point. But it's hasty, Ernesto."

"You're going to have to wait," says his father, "we're not going to let our 16 year-old travel alone in that kind of a country!"

"Seventeen in two months," replies the boy.

"If you were going to Burgos to be with your grandparents, Ernesto, or even to Bilbao," his father argues, glancing at his wife, whose Basque ancestry always brings up colorful commentary, "or to any other civilized part of Europe, things would be different. But to go to a country full of bandits, where we don't even know anyone?"

"So civilized gunmen like ETA terrorists are better than Latin American drug dealers?" Ernesto almost tells them. "Or maybe known terrorists are better than unknown criminals?" He suppresses his sarcasm, however, so as not to complicate matters. But frankly, his parents' reasoning seems ridiculous, to say the least. Pointless, as his father would say.

"Ernesto, I can go with you if you want to go so badly," says his mother. "Don't you think that's a good idea, Esteban?"

"Thanks, Mom, but that's not what I had in mind. It's kind of a personal thing."

"Well, it'll be your personal thing when you're an adult," his father says pointedly. "What's the hurry, anyway?"

"When I'm 18? What's the difference between 17 and 18? Just because I can vote doesn't mean I'll be more adult! That's ridiculous, Dad."

"Ernesto, we're not going to talk about this anymore."

"Okay, then we won't talk about it anymore!" Ernesto shouts, stomping out of the room and slamming the door behind him.

Grandpa Ruiz's portrait crashes to the floor.

More than a plan, the idea that is roiling Ernesto's brain is a thirst that needs quenching, a need to find someone to whom he can say, "We have the same blood, you and me. We carry the same genes, you and me. We're birds of a feather, you and me."

This is the fabric of his dreams.

And this urgent need sets him to devising and discarding plan after plan until he decides on a course of action.

He knows his father to be a man of immovable conviction, impossible to confront head on. He will need to come up with an imaginative solution. "The way to deal with stubbornness is to sow a seed of doubt," as Grandpa Ruiz would say, "and not to argue and bray like a donkey."

Two days later, at dinner time, Ernesto plays his final card.

"Dad, I think you're right. I'm going to put off my trip to Mexico. I have other plans now. I don't know if I told you, but last week a couple of recruiters from the Air Force went to our school to enlist students. It's not for right away—" the boy says, calibrating his words carefully, seeing that his father has almost spit out a mouthful of soup. "I have to be 18, but they say I can start training now since I've already graduated."

Ernesto places a letter with the official insignia of the United States Air Force in the middle of the table and leans back on his chair to watch his time bomb detonate.

Ruiz opens the letter. With a characteristic gesture he brushes a lock of blonde hair aside and reads in silence. For the first time the boy notices a few white hairs blending into his father's golden mane.

"Know what, Dad? There's a rumor going around about another operation like *Desert Storm*, because some people think that war was never finished, I mean, the one in '91 in the Persian Gulf. It's just a rumor, not official. But I think they need to train more guys for Special Forces, and since I like the idea of jumping out of airplanes, I'm thinking it's now or never."

After a few seconds of silence the boy says, "Did I tell you, Justin already enlisted?"

The ruse is paying off, Ernesto concludes, observing his father's serious expression. "They're taking the bait!" he congratulates himself. But his satisfaction comes undone when he sees the mournful look on his mother's face, because he knows what's going through her mind: the image of a neighbor boy who has been disabled since Desert Storm, with only a vague memory of the sun and the sand and the desert. "A tragedy," his mother has commented, when they brought him home in a wheelchair. "And a family destroyed."

A heavy silence falls between them like the ghost of Banquo at Macbeth's table. Their stomachs are tied in knots. During the rest of the dinner they don't speak of it anymore. Ernesto's father's face is inscrutable until he leaves the table.

That night, Mr. and Mrs. Ruiz discuss the matter in their bedroom.

"Ernesto is so impulsive he's capable of signing up," says Esteban Ruiz to his wife, "even though he knows that we're totally against these imperialist wars. Well... Life will teach him a lesson."

"Esteban, you always say that you're a Spaniard, even though you have an American passport. Why is that?"

"What are you getting at, Isabel? Oh. I know where you're going with this."

"Just answer the question."

"Well, you know I was born in Spain and my parents are of pure Visigoth blood. But I swear it'd be the same if I were an Italian or an Eskimo. I don't care a bit about nationality and race means nothing to me, and you know it!"

"Okay. But your identity is clear to you because you know where you're from, right? So you define yourself as Spanish. You don't say, "I'm Spanish, but who cares? Right? You say, I'm Spanish, period! Well, Ernesto doesn't have the same privilege that you and I have. His identity is complex; do you know what I mean? And don't think I like this idea of him going out to look for his other parents. It hurts me, but I don't want to be petty."

"I understand, Isabel. It's just that Ernesto is a minor. What if he gets himself in some sort of trouble? It could become a huge problem for us. Remember all those papers we had to sign when we adopted him!"

Ernesto goes to bed feeling a little guilty, with a lingering feeling of resentment, and a host of questions, more rhetorical than real: "Am I being ungrateful? Even if I am, what am I supposed to do? After all, they brought me out of that convent. Didn't they imagine that I was going to ask about my real parents? That I would have this 'wanting to know' nagging me that I can't get rid of? I swear I'll become a fighter pilot if they don't let me go".

That night the boy dreams. A fleet of warplanes are flying toward him in V formation, tearing through the sky above a desert in Kuwait with the sound of thunder. They are about to drop their bombs when all their wings begin to move flexibly, undulating like birds. Now the airplane-birds are gliding low, almost touching a field and then, in a flash, they are eagles flying away in formation, until they are lost in the sky.

When he wakes up, the dream stays with him. The perfection of the imagery surprises him in spite of conceptual errors such as the fact that eagles don't fly in formation like geese.

Still, he knows all too well that he shouldn't look for logic in dreams, but capture the symbols woven into the narrative and delivering their message from the unconscious mind. This dream is a good omen, he decides.

"When do you want to go to Esperanza?" asks Isabel.

She doesn't mention the reason for her unexpected acceptance of the idea.

"At the end of the summer," says her son, hiding his surprise. "I want to work for a few months and save up some money."

"Your father and I want to buy you your ticket to Ciudad Obregon so you can use your savings for other expenses. We don't want you to have a hard time down there."

The boy thanks her and gives her a hug, a little self-conscious from his guilt. The dog watches them with a yellow stare, then emits a mournful moan, because, for him, any hug means goodbyes and loneliness.

Ernesto waits until evening to call Grandpa Ruiz in Spain, calculating that at that hour he'll be having breakfast on the other side of the Atlantic.

The two of them have always understood each other. Ernesto has always been fascinated by his grandfather's individualism. Although he was a militant in his youth who spent time in Franco's fascist jails, he never became embittered. Instead, he became a poet.

For his grandfather's part, his adopted grandchild's mysterious past has always cast a powerful spell over old Ruiz. It is not too much to say that the true source of nutrition from which Ernesto's spirit has drawn sustenance has always been his adoptive grandfather. And the boy's receptivity has filled the old man with love.

"Foolish? Of course it's not a foolish plan," his grandfather emphatically states when the boy tells him of the trip he is planning. "I think it's a great idea, and I'll admit, I'm jealous! There's nothing more important than knowing your past to understand your present!"

"Thanks. I knew you'd approve."

"Of course I approve! Be careful, though," his grandfather adds. "When the Moors occupied Spain they used to say, *trust in Allah, but tie your camel!*"

Ernesto can almost see his grandfather arching his white, bushy brows, two inverted V's like herons raising their wings to lift off. Grandpa Ruiz always looks like this when he's announcing something important. Ernesto likes to say that Grandpa can turn himself into a bird.

He promises to be careful.

Esteban Ruiz isn't happy that his own father is encouraging Ernesto's delirious dreams, but he knows he can't do anything about it.

II

Ernesto dreams of Esperanza and of his parents. In the dream he has a confused and disappointing encounter in which the faces of people he knows superimpose themselves on the faces of people he does not know, and the expressions of happiness morph into expressions of surprise and disgust.

The boy awakens with a start as the flight attendant wakes him. She gives him a form to fill out for entry into Mexico, and he fills it in with handwriting that looks like squashed spiders.
Ernesto Moreno Ruiz... United States citizen... tourist... September 20th, 1995.

He feels cold and asks for a blanket.

A half-hour later the pilot announces their arrival in Ciudad Obregón. From the window, Ernesto sees green and ocher-colored mountains. He can feel his heart's rhythmic beating in his chest like a time bomb. Then a medium-sized city appears through an archipelago of translucent clouds floating below the airplane. Five minutes later the tires screech onto the tarmac. It is 10 in the morning.

He gets off the airplane. He goes through immigration, customs, and through the lobby. He calls home. He changes money. Everything is in order except his accelerated pulse.

Even though common sense tells him there's no reason to be nervous, he can't ignore the fact that this is not a normal trip, like the many he has made to Spain with his parents and, on occasion, by himself.

This is different. This is the culmination of desires long born, sheltered and nourished in his boyish imagination and finally taking shape in reality. For a moment Ernesto feels an impulse to return to the United States in the same airplane in which he has just arrived. He is paralyzed by the indecision he has observed in himself many times before. Perhaps indecision is not part of his nature, he muses, but the sub-product of a task imposed by his father in order to discipline his character, which, he has often heard from his parents, is impetuous.

"Today you're going to confront your history, Ernesto," he tells himself to bolster his strength.

"You're going to knock on the door of people who know who you are, and even if they don't, and even if they sic their dogs on you, or run you out at gunpoint, or take you for some ridiculous, demented fool, you're going to go forward because you have to follow your destiny. You have reached the point of no return," he repeats to himself, "and there's no turning back now!"

He slings his backpack onto his back and goes out to the street determined to face the unpredictable morning. The late-summer sun strikes his eyes with painful brightness. He sees a bus with the word "Centro" – downtown, and gets on.

"And if I don't meet anyone named Moreno?" He wonders in sudden hesitation. "What if this is all a figment of my imagination? What if it's just the nuns' dreams? Or my parents' dreams? What if this is all a gigantic mistake?"

He repeats his mantra: even if it is, there is no turning back now.

The trip is short, and soon Ernesto finds himself in the central plaza. He finds the Esperanza bus and gets on.

This downtown is not very different from any other downtown: modern buildings where modern people work, some flowers in the middle of the avenues, streets with traffic signs, well-manicured parks.

However, as the bus goes farther out he enters another reality, as if a single street separated two different countries.

The bus stops at a dusty corner to pick up passengers.

Ernesto sees rows of tin-roofed, shoebox-like houses, paint peeling from ancient plaster walls, corrugated metal roofs, sidewalks adorned with dog shit, fetid puddles, boys playing soccer barefoot in a vacant lot.

"Third World, here we come," he thinks.

He remembers how his father corrected him when he used that term: "One does not say "Third World" anymore, Ernesto. The term we prefer nowadays is "developing countries" or "emerging economies". To Ernesto it doesn't matter what it's called. To him it is the world of the poor. Of course, he has frequently seen on television suburbs blighted by poverty, but seeing them here before his very eyes, as he is seeing them now, makes all the difference in the world. Or maybe it's the smell that gives the experience this extra dimension. Smells of fried foods; sweet smells, acidic smells…

He closes the window. The bus moves on.

"Well, it doesn't matter what it's called," Ernesto says to himself, "this is the world I come from. I have to learn to love it. This is the world of my parents, my grandparents, my great grandparents - all the mestizos who came before me. Interesting," he thinks. "If I'm mestizo, if I'm part Indian and part Spanish, there's a certain symmetry in all of this: my destiny coming full circle. I have Spain from beginning to end, by inheritance first, and then by adoption. Life is so strange!"

Leaving the suburbs behind, the bus takes Route 15 heading through plains of cactus and thistle. Looking eastward Ernesto sees the silhouettes of distant mountains in faded pastels on the horizon. He keeps his nose glued to the window. Is he seeing the same mountains his mother saw as a girl? Or his grandparents? Was his father also from Esperanza? How will they receive him? It's encouraging to think that Mexican families are often extensive. There must be some Moreno who can tell him about his mother.

"María Moreno! Will you still remember me?"

III

The bus doesn't enter the village. Ernesto has to walk a long road from the highway to the center of town. In a café in front of the

Plaza he has a second breakfast. Then he enters a telephone booth on the sidewalk, because this is what his father has told him to do: consult a telephone book before beginning any investigations in the Town Hall.

He thumbs through to the M's: Mariano, Medina, Mendes, Montana, Morelia, Moreno! Once again his heartbeat picks up speed like a quickening drumbeat. He takes a deep breath, exhales forcefully to expel the specter of indecision, and dials the number. A woman's voice answers.

"Hello?"

"I'd like to speak with Mr. or Mrs. Moreno, please," he says in Spanish.

"One moment, please. May I ask who's calling?"

Although he has rehearsed this moment many times, the boy responds hesitantly, "It's ... Ernesto ... Moreno."

Then, he hears a man's voice:

"Hello?"

"Good afternoon, sir," he says, reading from notes he prepared to avoid any confused stammering. "My name is Ernesto Moreno Ruiz and I'm from the United States. I came to Mexico to find my family, the Moreno family of Esperanza. I think that you and I may be related."

His heartbeat is now drumming so loudly that he wonders if his interlocutor can hear it.

"From the United States? We don't have any relatives there. Why do you believe we are related?"

"Because my mother is from Esperanza, and her family name is Moreno."

"Hmmm, interesting. Well, come to my house so we can chat. Here's the address: Hidalgo Street, number 24. It's a yellow two-story house."

Ernesto sets off. It is hot, and small drops of sweat sparkle like little diamonds on his bronze-colored forehead. He takes some comfort in the fact that the streets of Esperanza, with their high, thin palm trees, resemble some of the streets of San Diego. This is not a large village, and in less than three minutes he is standing before a large house protected below by tall, vine-covered iron bars. Wrought-iron bars over several Spanish-style windows are also flower-entwined. Beside the large gate,

30

bougainvillea flowers encircle a sign announcing: Jorge Moreno, Attorney.

He rings the bell. A middle-aged woman in a white apron opens the door. Like his, her skin is bronze. She even has large, almond-shaped eyes like his. Could she be .... ? The boy looks at her with a hopeful expression.

"Come in. Mr. Moreno is waiting for you," says the woman in a flat voice that instantly dampens Ernesto's expectations.

In the foyer, a porcelain jar set on a round table is bursting with gladioluses. The woman opens a double glass, lace-covered door and ushers Ernesto into a large, elegant parlor. Paintings by Mexican artists adorn the walls, and an elaborate candelabrum hangs over a long wooden table. Ernesto notices several dark leather-upholstered armchairs and sofas, thick carpets on the antique wooden floor, and a well-supplied bookshelf.

A tall, bald man, of some 50 years comes into the room and extends his hand to Ernesto:

"Pleased to meet you, eh, Ernesto, right?"

"Yes. Pleased to meet you, Mr. Moreno."

"So you are a Moreno?" the man asks, peering at him over his glasses.

Under the man's pale, blue-green gaze Ernesto feels a rush of doubt.

"Yes sir," he responds, in a low voice. He wants desperately to smile and be amiable, but just now any utterance seems a heroic feat. In no way did he expect to encounter an opulent family and a man with blue eyes and alabaster skin. Still, a sliver of hope remains. Multiracial families, his racing mind reflects, often produce unexpected cases. Who knows?

"Well, take off your backpack and make yourself at home," the man says, gesturing toward an easy chair as he sprawls onto another. "Tell me how you decided to come visit me."

Ernesto tells him about his adoption and the message pinned to his baby blanket mentioning the name of the family and the village. Ending his story, the boy looks at the lawyer with questioning eyes.

Moreno crosses his arms. "We can't be your relatives because no member of our family has ever immigrated to the United States. Not one."

The two stare at each other. It doesn't take long for Ernesto to assimilate this information. He suspected it when the man entered and extended his hand, pale as mother-of-pearl. But he feels overwhelmed.

"Is there no other Moreno family in Esperanza?" Ernesto asks.

"Yes, there are several," says the man, "but they're all my relatives. We're all from the same branch and the same trunk. We've been in this village for nearly 100 years and there was never a María Moreno. If there had been, I'd know about her, because I have the family tree of the Morenos from this area."

Ernesto is silent. He doesn't know how to fit this news into the mental plan he had structured so elaborately.

"Listen, Ernesto, you should know that... there are many villages named Esperanza, here in Mexico and in other Spanish-speaking countries. It's a common name. Your mother's family may well be from another Esperanza."

Another Esperanza?

The man continues talking in a careful, patient manner:

"And there is another problem: 'Moreno' is also an extremely common surname. There are probably hundreds of thousands of Moreno's in the world. I'm sure that your parents, being Spanish, are aware of this."

"Of course, but the Moreno family in a village called Esperanza in Mexico ..." the boy responds, "this narrows it down, don't you think?"

"Did the nuns speak with your mother?"

"No. They only found me and the note."

"And did the paper say Esperanza in *Mexico*?"

"I don't know. I don't think so," he adds, somewhat panicked by the sudden revelation.

"So how do they know she was from Mexico?"

"My parents say they called me 'The Mexican baby'."

"Don't you think this could've been just an assumption?"

The man notices the concerned look in Ernesto's eyes.

"Sometimes a person receives a bit of information. The mind then compares it with its own database and it proceeds to archive it under some label. I mean, it's easy to imagine that they may have filed, so to speak, your mother in their memories as a Mexican woman just because the majority of those who cross the border are from Mexico. You see, knowing her name was María, and knowing her race, they put your mother into the same bag, so to speak. Does that make sense?"

The man ends his little speech, settles back into his chair and adds: "Hasty generalizations carry this kind of risk, my boy."

Ernesto finds himself intrigued by this line of thinking. "No wonder this guy is a lawyer," he says to himself.

"I wonder if my parents ever thought about this," the boy says.

"Well, now, they got the information from a source they considered trustworthy and they just accepted it. Don't blame your parents, Ernesto, because this kind of thing happens in the most lucid minds. It happens to all of us. Baseless guesswork!" he says emphatically. "I see this frequently in my profession."

The man, reading the mute expression of, "Now what?" on Ernesto's face, feels a pang of tenderness for the boy.

"Well, son, it's not the end of the world, nor the end of your *esperanzas*, heh heh,"[1] he says with a warm smile, "there are many *esperanzas*, and you may certainly find yours."

"To find my *Esperanza*..." Ernesto reflects, "I really don't know what to do next."

He knows he will have to make a mental adjustment, but the world seems to have become too large a place all of a sudden.

"Would you like some pineapple juice?"

"Yes, thank you."

The man calls the maid and asks for the juice and a cup of coffee for himself.

"Listen, Ernesto," Mr. Moreno continues, "you seem like a nice young man and I'd like to help you."

---

[1] A pun on *esperanza,* which means "hope" in Spanish, and *Esperanza,* the town's name.

He gets up and takes an enormous tome from the library shelf. "See this atlas? Here in Esperanza we don't even have Internet yet, but this will do for now."

The man looks at Ernesto for a moment. Ernesto looks, silently, at the gigantic atlas.

"Well," Mr. Moreno continues, "I need to go to my office, but you can stay here studying the maps. Look for other Esperanzas in the index. You'll find them, believe me. When I come back, you can show them to me and then we can come up with a plan. Here's some paper and a pen. Now please excuse me."

The lawyer goes into an adjacent room and Ernesto is alone. He was prepared for a disappointment such as, for instance, not finding his family because they died or moved out of town. He was even prepared to have doors slammed in his face. But this panorama of multiple Morenos and multiple identical names for a village is a complete surprise. He gulps his juice and then seats himself at one end of the sturdy wooden table with the Atlas before him. He begins the task of compiling a list of Esperanzas and their respective countries.

Things get complicated. In the index there are a lot of towns named Esperanza. There's even one in this very state, not very far, and there's another in the state of Veracruz. Beyond Mexico there are Esperanzas in Guatemala, Ecuador, Peru, and several in Argentina.

"All over the continent," Ernesto mutters to himself.

This seems like a joke played on him by a destiny that produces more bitterness than laughter. Ernesto considers the infinite possibilities of just one quantum particle, and he asks himself if in the relative larger dimension of one human destiny multiplicity also exists.

Whether or not it does, this labyrinth of multiple exits is overwhelming. And the proverb his mother loves to repeat, "When one door closes, a hundred others open," isn't at all uplifting. It's intolerable.

Presently, Mr. Moreno opens his office door.

"Well? Did you find your Esperanzas?"

"Yes, sir, I found all these towns," says Ernesto, holding up the list.

The lawyer makes a call. He talks to the telephone operator at La Esperanza, north of Hermosillo, and the woman tells him there's nobody in the village with that name. He calls another Esperanza in the state of Veracruz, and this time connects with another Mr. Moreno. He explains the situation. Ernesto tries to imagine the reply on the other end of the line.

"He's 17 years old, and he thinks his family is Mexican," says the lawyer ... "María Moreno ... okay, I understand ... yes, yes, thank you, and excuse the interruption, have a nice day."

The lawyer hangs up and fills Ernesto in on the call.

"This family assures me that they've also never had any relatives in the United States, and no one named María, either."

"So, another Esperanza to scratch off the list."

"Your next stop is Guatemala, then. Let's see. Oh, this is a very small town," says the lawyer, looking at the map. "There are probably no telephones there, as it's just a tiny village. Hmmm ..."

He places a call to the National Library in Mexico City and is told that the Guatemalan catalog shows no telephone code for this village.

"I suppose you'll have to go in person, kid."

Ernesto calculates that the money he has is not going to be enough for travel to another country, much less for crossing a continent.

"I don't want to ask my parents for money for this," the boy confesses, as if seeking advice.

"Be patient, my friend. You don't need to do it all in one trip."

Ernesto agrees. He thanks Mr. Moreno for his time, for having opened his eyes to this new reality, and for his hospitality. Then he says goodbye.

"Good luck, my friend. It was a pleasure meeting you," says Mr. Moreno, extending one hand to Ernesto, while with the other hand he slips a 500 pesos banknote into Ernesto's shirt pocket.

"Oh, that's not necessary, sir."

"Come on, Ernesto. You be sure to call or write to me so I can find out about your life."

Ernesto feels a bit embarrassed. "Yes, I will. Adiós, Mr. Moreno, and thank you for everything.

"You're welcome, Son. May God be with you?"

IV

"Ernesto! Finally! Where are you?"

"In Esperanza, Mom. I met a Mr. Moreno."

"Really? Is he your relative?"

"No. He says there are a lot of people named Moreno, and that there are other towns named Esperanza, too."

"Other Esperanzas?"

"Yes, the closest one is in Guatemala. There's a direct bus there from here. I still have money."

"Guatemala? But your mother was from Mexico, Ernesto!"

"Is there any proof of that, Mom? Did she tell anyone that? Did the note say so?"

Ernesto's mother remains silent.

"Mom, are you there? Can you hear me?"

"What are you saying? What do you mean, she wasn't from Mexico?"

Isabel Ruiz's trembling voice cannot conceal a tone of indignation. It's not possible that suddenly someone would question what has been established as a fact for so many years, destroying something so obvious. She is a smart woman. How could she have been wrong about something so important?

"So where was she from?"

"That's exactly what I'm trying to find out, Mom. You and Dad should go back to the convent and make that nun clear things up. In any case, I'm heading for Guatemala."

"Ernesto, listen, don't be so stubborn. Your father doesn't want you to ..."

Now his father is on the phone.

"Ernesto. What's this about you going to Guatemala?"

"I need to go there, Dad."

"Your mother is very worried!"

Ernesto's mother is back on the phone:

"Be very careful, Ernesto! We love you very much. We'll see what we can figure out from here."

Back in the park, Ernesto sits on a bench and takes a notebook out of his backpack. He has promised himself to record all the details of his travels, but a few dull phrases are all he can think of.

Mexico, Esperanza, September 20th, 1995. Today I found the village of the circle in the map. There are a lot of Morenos here, but none of them are my Moreno. That circle turned out to be empty!

He closes the notebook, reaches into his pockets and pulls out a letter from Grandpa Ruiz that he received before leaving. He re-reads it:

Dear Ernesto
I want to wish you a wonderful journey. I hope you find what you're looking for, and if you don't this time, don't be discouraged! There are other roads to travel. After all, life is a journey and in this world we are all passengers and pilgrims.
Much love, Grandpa.

Shadows pile up in the park and engulf Ernesto's bench. He looks up and sees the yellow lights of the bus that will take him to the next station.

2. The Birthday-Girl

I

Don Pablo's business in Baeza has prospered in the last three years. In 1992 he had only one telephone line in his house. Then he began adding one more line per year, and now he has four. From his house people can make long-distance calls to other countries and also receive overseas calls. Many people in the village —not to mention the jungle communes— lack telephones, so don Pablo can count on a constant clientele.

"The more oil they pump, the more misery there is around here, the more people emigrate, and the more they need to talk on the phone. What can I say, my friend, long live Ecuadorian oil!"

Few understand don Pablo's wry joke. To his clients, the important thing is that he continues giving them good service.

In Rosa's house everyone knows that the first and third Saturdays of the month, at noon, Alba calls don Pablo's business from a farm or vegetable packing house in the United States. It has been six years now, and she has never failed to do it.

When don Pablo's messenger arrives at the farm early, Grandmother Umi is a little surprised, especially since today is Sunday. He informs her that Señora Alba Caento has called from the United States. She is not particularly alarmed, however. Yesterday was Rosa's 15th birthday and her mother probably wishes to greet her.

"Rosita, get up. Your mother is going to call in a couple of hours. She probably wants to talk to you about your birthday," Grandmother says as she puts the finishing touches on her long black and white braid.

Rosa is up in an instant, dressed, and her rubber boots are on. She is anxious to tell her mother about last night's birthday party.

Grandmother and granddaughter set off down the trail to the village. Old Umi walks with the same agile, quick step as Rosa, and with the same youthful energy of former years. She does not change her rhythm whether the trail winds upward out of a gully or downward into one. Nor does she hesitate as to where to put her foot to avoid the mud sucking a boot off her foot. Not for nothing has she lived so many years in the jungle, she declares. It's difficult to tell how many, exactly, but somewhere between 60 and 70.

A little before the agreed-upon hour, the two are seated in don Pablo's parlor waiting for the promised call.

Alba is punctual. The telephone rings and a man's voice says, "Here you are, Señora Alba." In an instant Rosa is inside the telephone booth.

With a quick stream of words the girl recounts the previous night's celebration to her mother:

"So many people came, Mom! The banquet was fantastic and we danced and set off firecrackers and rockets all night long , no one left until the roosters started to crow. My dress? Gorgeous! You'll see the pictures soon." Rosa pauses for a few seconds, "It's terrible you couldn't be here, Mom. I missed you so much last night. I missed you so, so, much."

The happy tone has changed. Now Rosa is describing the food, but her words have lost their initial excitement and no longer conceal the painful feeling in both their hearts.

And that's how it always is. Conversations between Alba and her daughter begin with loquacious joy and end in silent tears. These talks are like the delicious mature fruit of the jungle, Rosa thinks, which delight the tongue until finally the seed is split and eaten, and then a bitter taste bursts onto the tongue.

It is true that in the last two years Rosa has built a thin protection around her heart; and she begun curling her eyelashes, making her breasts (not nearly as abundant as those of her neighbor, Anita) look bigger with good bras, and caring for her thick, jet black hair. Despite that, 1995 was difficult for her from the beginning, when her mother announced in January that she would be unable to return for the long-anticipated birthday celebration.

Her mother's absence on so special a day has awakened the old anguish.

Rosa passes the telephone to her grandmother and goes out onto the patio so that no one sees her crying. She sits on a log bench and for a while watches the birds enviously. How she would like to be a bird woman, like the one from The Arabian

Nights that Mr. Romero read to the class, who dons a feather cloak and flies off to her heart's desire.

But grandmother is taking a long time on the phone. What could they be talking about for so long? This telephone call is going to cost Mom a lot of money!

"Thank you for the message, don Pablo," her grandmother says while paying for the service. "Here's a little tip for the boy."

"What's happening, doña Umi?" the man asks, using the honorific "doña" that the Huaorani find so funny. "You look concerned. Is there bad news from the North? Is your daughter well?"

"No, she's not very well, don Pablo. She's sick, and she doesn't know, or doesn't want to tell me, what it is".

Rosa, entering, hears these last words.

"My mom's sick? Why didn't she tell me, Grandma?"

"Because she wanted to talk to me about it first, Rosa."

"About what?"

"About you going to the United States to take care of her."

That afternoon, Rosa goes out to sit on the riverbank. According to Mr. Romero, this stream flows into the Quijos River, which flows into the Amazon. She observes it flowing through the valley, quickly, crystalline, and then entering the jungle again. She imagines its source in the mountains where they say it originates. She has never seen it, but she knows there are underground waters, and sometimes, when she lies down on the grass, she believes she can hear their hidden whispers. She'd like to know how to listen to the subterranean current within herself, which today is agitated, and which leads her who-knows-where.

A dragonfly with bright wings alights on her hand and wafts the reverie away.

"To me, honestly, it's not a good idea," says grandmother Umi. It doesn't matter if the coyote is or isn't trustworthy. Everyone is forgetting that my daughter Alba was 30 years old when she went away, but this child is 15. Only 15 years old!"

"But Alba insists, Umi," says Numpa's wife. "Didn't she tell you she needs someone from the family to take care of her? That she has no one there?"

"I'd prefer to go myself!" says the grandmother, sitting up in her chair.

"What an idea! Go to the North at our age? We don't even speak English!" replies Grandfather.

"Or Spanish, to be honest, Grandpa," Enrique adds.

"Don't butt in, this is for adults," his father scolds.

"Rosa's not an adult."

"But she's the daughter. And Alba wants her daughter to go, not her mother or her saint!"

"That's true. And the money is already in the bank here."

"Alba is set on this."

"I wanted to make her change her mind, but ..." Umi says.

The conversation, a mix of Huaorani and Spanish, stops when the girl enters the house.

"Rosa. Mr. Zabala is coming tomorrow," Uncle Numpa informs her. "You know who he is, right? He's the coyote who took your mother in '89, and she says he's trustworthy."

Rosa's grandparents remain silent.

"You need to keep quiet about this," Numpa continues. "And you kids, too. Don't go around telling anyone. There's a lot of money involved in this."

"I don't know..." says Umi. " I just don't feel good about this."

Grandfather mutters a few monosyllables in his maternal tongue, which nobody hears.

II

On a little table under a large tree in the patio, Rosa has emptied her backpack full of school things. She is deciding what to pack for her trip. A flock of parakeets, which just a few months ago were tiny chicks opening their beaks for worms, have now learned to fly, and they congregate in the highest branches.

"Rosa!" calls her grandmother from inside the house. "Open the door for Anita. She's come to say goodbye to you!"

The parakeets fling themselves into the air in a great flap and fly to another tree farther from the house, where they continue their chatter. Anita lives closed by. In twenty-four hours the entire valley has heard that Rosa Epayuma is going to the North.

41

"You're *so* lucky, Rosa! I'd love to go with you."

"It's not going to be so easy there, Anita. Our English teacher told me that people who go there are called '*undocumenteds*' and '*aliens*'."

"What does that mean?"

"'*Undocumented*' means no identification documents', I mean, nothing to show who you are. Horrible, don't you think? And *alien*, according to my dictionary, means 'extraterrestrial'."

Anita looks astonished.

"They also call them '*illegal immigrants*', Rosa continues," which just means 'illegal'. I don't know which is worse."

"Well, I think it's worse to be illegal than to be an extraterrestrial, if I had to choose. Just think of what The Company did, dumping poison in our rivers! Now that's *really* illegal. And evil. My dad says so, and he's a member of the Indigenous Commission."

"I know, but I can't do anything about it, Anita! Besides that, it's not the same. What's so evil about not having documents? It's just not the same!" Rosa declares, a little irritably. The comparison seemed unfair to her and mean.

For a few moments the girls remain pensively silent. One by one the parrots return to the tall tree. Anita looks at a heart carved into the tree trunk with two words in the middle: "Rosa and ..."

"Rosita, we're going to miss you so much," she says. Are you going to write? Are you going to remember us?"

"Of course I'm going to remember you. Oh, here comes Mr. Zabala! He's the coyote, coming to a get his money. Anita, I need to go in and tell my grandparents."

"Okay, I'll be going now. Goodbye, Rosita. Don't forget about me!"

"Of course not!"

Rosa notices that before opening the gate the man's fingers rummage in his shirt pocket. He pulls out something small and white, and puts it in his mouth.

"We have some cake from the party. Would you like a piece, Mr. Zabala? With a little guayusa tea?" Rosa's grandmother offers.

"No, thank you, doña Umi, that's very kind. I'm getting a belly," says the man, patting his stomach, "but I'd accept some tea."

Rosa conceals her interest, but observes the man sharply. She is trying to discern in his minutest facial expression some indication of the character within. His nails are very clean and polished, and this produces in the girl an ambivalent impression.

"Mr. Coyote, I mean, Mr. Zabala, excuse me, but when do you think I'm going to arrive in the United States?" Rosa asks.

"Well, the truth is, it takes a while, it's not like going in an airplane, you know. A lot depends on weather conditions during the ocean part of the journey. Also, it's not as easy as it was in '89, when I took your mother there, because now there's more border control and lots of patrols in Guatemala and Mexico and in the United States. If everything goes well you're going to arrive in two weeks or a little more. But, as I say, it could be more. There are always unforeseen events in this type of travel. But we're very well connected over the entire journey and we can solve issues that come up with no problem for our clients, except for a little delay. Do you understand, don Caento?", he says, turning to the elderly man. "That's all."

Grandfather, who understands Spanish quite well but refuses to speak it, defers to his son.

"Don Zabala, we know your family very well," says Numpa, "and we know we can trust you. But Rosa is very young."

"Don't worry. I'm going to be in Guatemala to receive the group and escort them to the Mexican border, and from there to the States. But during the ocean part of the trip, from Guayaquil to Guatemala, Rosa will also be in good hands."

The man speaks with ease, which gives him an air of authority and inspires confidence.

"Well, good. As we agreed, here are the $4,000 up front. Afterwards, my sister Alba is going to pay you the other $4,000 when you deliver Rosa, in Oregon," says Numpa.

The man moves his lips as he counts the pack of hundred dollar bills, then holds each one up against the sun, squinting at them until satisfied.

"Excuse all this, but you know how counterfeiters have proliferated in this country. You have to be extra careful nowadays. There's so much crime, it's a dirty shame. But these bills are all good. Thank you, don Caento, here's your receipt," says the man, signing and handing over a piece of paper.

The old man thanks him with a nod.

"Well! Tomorrow you need to be in the village very early, Rosa. We'll pick you up at the corner of the cemetery. The bus we rented will be there at 5 A.M. sharp. Also, Rosa, your mother probably told you to pack light. One backpack is enough for two changes of clothes. Also, take some baby powder and deodorant, because they'll cover up the lack of hygiene. Remember that being on a ship isn't like being at home! Also, a hat—very important!"

Caento and the coyote shake hands - one hand sculpted by the jungle and the other softened by the soft rub of banknotes. They say goodbye until the next day.

Once through the gate, the coyote extracts the fake tooth he put into his mouth upon arriving and drops it back into his shirt pocket.

III

The shaman is walking up the hill with his wife and daughters. The torrential rainfall of tropical afternoons has lasted longer than usual, and only ended at 3:30 AM. It has delayed the meeting.

"Caento, the trail is impassable, and a flash flood swept away the bridge," the shaman says to Grandfather. "From my house down there's no way to get to the village. Fording the stream is impossible; the water's too high."

The family did not expect the weather to ruin their plans.

"Rosa's going to miss the bus!"

"I'm going to miss the boat!"

"We should've spent the night in the village!"

"But this has never happened before!"

44

"Nothing is like it was before. Even the rains have changed!"

The adults are united in a litany of complaints against the weather and against the times, which are becoming more and more unpredictable.

Rosa anxiously glances at her grandparents. Her tears well up and are ready to fall when the old man announces, "While you all were sleeping like little monkeys in the branches, I got out the canoe and cleaned it up. It was full of branches and leaves and frogs. I cleaned out all the moss and dirt, and gave it a new baptism in the river. It's like a Christian, born again!" says the old man, with his parakeet laugh.

"The canoe! I'd forgotten about the canoe, father!" exclaims Numpa. "Of course we can get there on the river."

"Oooh! We're going in the canoe! Finally!" exclaim the children.

"Grandpa, you're a magician, a flesh and blood spirit of the jungle!" says Rosa, embracing him.

"The jaguar knows more because he's old than because he's a jaguar," says Umi, who had secretly hoped that the bad weather would stop them.

Now that the fright has passed, Umi prepares the yard for the ceremony, and the first thing to do is light the torches, because it's a dark night and there's no moon. "Not even the moon wants to see Rosa leave," Umi complains, throwing herbs onto the fire. Then she arranges wooden benches into a circle and the family sits down to wait.

First the moths appear and begin to dance around the torches. Soon, the shaman and his children emerge from inside the house with their cheeks painted and adorned with an abundance of seed and feather necklaces, ready for the ritual. A dance of short steps accompanies the rhythm of the simple percussion instruments and the elemental three-note melody that defines the jungle song.

Even though the family has already adopted some Christian beliefs within the Evangelical protectorate, more through osmosis than through conversion, they have not

45

completely abandoned Huaorani practice, and today's blessing from the shaman follows the tradition of his people.

In bidding her goodbye, the man gives Rosa a carved jaguar amulet to protect her on the round-trip journey. The girl thanks him and puts it in her pocket.

Rosa is unbothered by this mix of creeds in her family. After all, God is One, she reasons, and one is God, because from Him we come and to Him we will return. Doesn't the Bible say so? Or something like that? Or is it her teacher, Mr. Romero who says so, when he talks about the "One"?

The night is cold. While the adults drink *chicha* the youngsters vie for the place each wants to occupy in the canoe.

A few minutes later the entire family is on board, one behind the other. Uncle is sitting in the front, illuminating the water with his flashlight. The current is strong and many branches float in the river. Grandfather, who says he sees in the misty night through the jaguar's eyes, reassures them. With veteran movements he dips the oars into the water, to give direction to the canoe.

As the leafy darkness of the riverbank slips quickly by them, eyes glow in the dark and then go out in the foliage; and here and there a nocturnal shriek makes a counterpoint to the frogs' concert. Rosa, with her mouth open and nostrils dilated, foreseeing future nostalgia, tries to breathe in all the perfumes of the jungle.

From the low sky of Baeza soft rain falls. A cluster of multicolored umbrellas, like a mushroom colony, crowd around a bus with its motor running. Sheltered under the umbrellas, several family members bid goodbye to their travelers. Nobody seems particularly bothered by the exhaust coming out of the bus's tailpipe, which scares the birds.

Their hearts, full of sadness, worries, and in some cases, envy, are with those who are departing for the North._Even the director of the *Don Bosco School*, the Italian priest who taught the catechism to Rosa, comes with his chocolate-covered cassock floating in the chilly air.

"Hide your money well," the priest calls out as he nears the group. "But always leave a little in your pockets, just in case,

God forbid, anyone wants to rob you. You don't want to make the thieves angry. Always give to Caesar what is Caesar's and to God what is God's!"

Lifting his cassock as he hops over a mud puddle, he proceeds to bless the passengers, the chauffeur and even the bus.

Rosa is very serious as she listens to all the advice. Her aunt asks her in a whisper if she has hidden the five hundred dollars sent by her mother for emergencies. Rosa nods, touching her chest. Other family members ask her loudly:

"Tell me, child, have you memorized your mama's telephone number?"

"Rosita, take care! There are bad people out there! Keep your eyes open!"

"Be careful who you talk to!"

"Don't walk around alone!"

"Goodbye, dear. Come, give me a hug."

"Goodbye, Grandma and Grandpa. Goodbye, uncles. Take care of my colt, Gabriel."

At the last minute Mr. Romero appears. The teacher, who was in charge of Rosa's group from first to seventh grade and became the chemistry and literature teacher after the new high school opened, to continue educating many of his older students, runs up to the bus door and hands Rosa a copy of *The Junglenaut* together with a little package of white cards.

"A writer should always have something to write her impressions on, Rosa," he says, "take good care of yourself! Remember, you can accomplish anything!"

Rosa thanks him and wants to tell him something more, something to make him remember her always, but her uncle's voice interrupts.

"Get on, Rosa, the bus is leaving!"

The last passengers step up onto the bus and their families are left gazing upwards with sad faces under a leaden sky.

The 30 persons traveling to Guayaquil are a homogeneous group. There a few Amazon Quichua and Shuar, but the majority are the so-called "colonists", those who came to the region some years ago, when only the Amazonian tribes were living here. The only Huaorani is Rosa.

"Well! What a young little traveling companion!" says a lady seated beside Rosa. "Are you also going to the United States?"

"Yes, Ma'am."

"And why would you want to be so far from your family?"

"Because my mother is there. She's sick and I'm going to take care of her. Why are you going? To earn money?"

"Yes, life is hard for us here. I don't have a husband anymore, and there's no work, so I have to leave my children with their grandparents for a little while. Only for a year. I have a sister in Connecticut.

Rosa knows all too well about this interminable year her mother said she would have to wait for her return. It is a year that stretches on and on, that dies and is reborn every Christmas when her mother announces, yet again, that she is not coming this time, that she has not saved enough money, that it will be next year, that she is sending presents in shiny paper from the United States; the beautiful wrapping paper Rosa uses to cover her school books.

"You're going to Connecticut?" says a young man seated nearby. "I'm going there, too. I have friends in Connecticut."

"And are they going to find you a job?" the woman asks.

"They say they will. But I'm on a different mission myself. I want to speak to people there about the logging companies cutting our trees down. You know how they're destroying the jungle!"

"Illegal logging, I suppose."

"Of course! They build roads, they bring power sources, machinery, cables, trucks— everything illegal! And they leave us land that's not good for anything. I've seen those red patches in the forest from the missionary airplane, when they took my wife and me to the hospital in Coca. I swear they're like blood stains. Here, I have some pictures to show the world how they're ruining the Amazon."

The man passes the photos around among the passengers, who are sympathetic to his mission.

"Yes, I understand. It's a shame," says the woman, "but those of you who live in the jungle also share some of the blame, don't you think? I know a family that cuts down a tree anytime they need money. And they sell it for a low price to the first Colombian who appears. I'm right, aren't I?"

"Well," he replies, "I know they're cutting down a lot of trees around here without permission. But you can't compare the few trees that we cut down with an ax to the tons of trees stolen by the logging companies. You've got to understand that!"

The bus has reached a dry stretch of road, and the dust makes them quickly shut their windows.

"But it's you folks who should set the example!" the woman insists, cleaning the dust from her face.

"Yes, yes. But sometimes there's so much need," explains the young man. "It's not like before, when the forest supplied everything. Now we have to pay our children's school. Just one tree that we sell pays for the uniform, the books, you know, and nowadays everyone wants their children to be educated, don't you agree? because even though we are Shuar, or Quichua, or whatever, we also want to be something else."

"Something else?" thinks Rosa. "Wanting to go to school, is that wanting to be something else? Like a different race? Like the colonists? What am I, then, since I like school so much? Do I have the soul of a white person? Does the soul even have a race? No, that's not possible. But we are what we are because of where we come from, right?"

Rosa writes her meditations, rather profound for one who is barely an adolescent. But Mr. Romero always says, "Writing helps us explore our inner selves."

"It's true, we all want the best for our children," says the woman, "that's why I'm going to the North."

Someone interrupts from the back of the vehicle. "Why do you complain so much about the trees, but you don't say a word about the oil companies that have been poisoning us for the last 30 years? Why didn't you take pictures of the nine hundred open pools of oil where they've been dumping their poison, and take *those* to show the gringos?"

"Because The Company is taking care of that now, they're cleaning it up, didn't you hear? They made an agreement last year.

49

Everyone's seen the Oodworclay [2]cleaning trucks going back and forth from Lago Agrio to Coca. They say they're going to clean up all the pools. This was the CONFENIAE's triumph. "[3]

"What are you saying? They're not cleaning anything! All they're doing is covering the oil dumps with rocks, mud and plastic. You call that cleaning up? I'm telling you this because I'm from there. The oil is still polluting the rivers, and my children are covered with blotches. It's worse than frog piss. They're not cleaning crap. It's all a big lie, so you should shut your mouth!"

Frog piss? Rosa remembers that her grandfather used to say that under the earth is an enormous beast and when white people poke her, the beast begins to throw black bile up out of her entrails.

She feels again the twinge of that old sorrow that does not let her go. That tireless bird that flies over one's memory has stopped on her father's image. He spent two years working in those oil pools, she remembers, to pay for her Mom's hospital bills. He died one month after paying off the debt.

IV

It is 9PM when they arrive at the port city of Guayaquil, after having crossed the country diagonally, climbed and descended the Andes and the water divide, and arrived at the Pacific.

Rosa's eyes, that have never seen a metropolis, are like a pair of little windows glued to the glass. Dazzled by the modernity of the main street, shiny as the day, crowded with people going in and out of theaters and restaurants, it seems the apex of urban sophistication. Her neck is sore from staring up.

A little later, with the driver speaking on his cell phone, the passengers begin to feel real respect for the trip organizers.

"When I arrive in the United States," one of them says to a neighbor, "the first thing I'm going to buy when I get work is a cell phone. I've always wanted one."

---

[2] Woodward-Clyde

[3] CONFENIAE: Confederation of the Nationalities Indigenous to Ecuadorian Amazon (Confederation of Ecuadorian Amazon Indigenous Nations)

"Always? But they've just arrived in Ecuador!"

"I mean, always from the moment they arrived in Ecuador. But listen, listen, listen!"

The driver's tone of voice puts a stop to all conversations, and the passengers prick up their ears.

"What's that? Okay. Of course. So we'd better get out of here."

He then turns to the passengers:

"Ladies and gentlemen, we have a minor problem. They say the police are looking for groups of illegals, and they're camped out in front of our hotel."

The passengers look at one another in alarm, and some of them whisper a complaint.

"We haven't even left the country and already we're illegals?"

'It's because this is a private bus. Anyone can see it's not public transportation. It's a charter, as they call it."

"How do they know who we are? Couldn't we be tourists on a visit to Guayaquil?"

"If they catch us, they'll know that we aren't."

"So what? Why do the police care? Is it illegal to leave the country? We're not in Cuba!"

The bus drives onto a side street, passes a fire station, and continues on for another half hour. Then it goes up some dark streets. The dialogue continues by cell phone:

"Where did you say I should turn? I can't find that street. I'm in front of a junkyard."

"What? No, there's no post office here! There's nothing. It's empty!"

"I think the driver is lost," someone says. "Yes, we've already left the city. We're on Santa Ana Hill," observes a male passenger who seems to know the place.

"Hey, there are people in the middle of the street. They're blocking the street!"

"They have guns!"

"And they're masked!"

"Oh my God, they're bandits!"

"Holy Virgin!"

The driver swears. Putting his cell phone away, he stops the vehicle. Three men wearing ski masks that reveal only their eyes and mouths get on the bus. One of them puts a revolver to the driver's head.

"Get off the bus or I'll blow your head off! Open the baggage compartments and put everything on the ground! Move it!"

Another criminal, pointing his gun, shouts at the passengers:

"All of you! Quiet! I want all your money, watches, and jewelry inside this bag. I don't want to hurt anyone, so don't even think about hiding anything. Do you understand?"

For an instant the passengers are petrified. Then, silently, and with cautious gestures, they take off their rings and watches and empty their pockets and wallets. The thief threatens a woman with his revolver pressed to her breast. The woman lifts herself from the seat and takes out the purse she had been sitting on to hide. The bandit snatches it from her with a brusque gesture and a stream of obscenities. He goes from seat to seat collecting his loot until he arrives almost at the back of the coach and spots Rosa. She takes off her seed bracelet from the jungle, made by her aunt, and hands it to him.

"Why are you giving me this shit?" the man snarls, throwing Rosa's bracelet out the window.

A wave of rage rises in the girl's throat but stops there. It's the first time she has ever felt true hatred.

"Who is this girl traveling with?" asks the man.

"I'm alone," she responds in a defiant tone.

"All alone, huh? You're pretty young to be traveling alone. You're coming with me, girl, I need a wife. Now where's your money? Hurry up! Give me your earrings. And the necklace! They're gold, aren't they? I don't want any tin. What the hell is wrong with you? Give me that necklace!"

Rosa's hands are trembling and she is unable to open the clasp. The thief snatches at her throat and rips it off.

"Now you're coming with me. No crying! I hate it when women cry!"

3. The Pilgrim's Guide

I

It's that time in the afternoon when the mass of humanity pours out onto the streets and boulevards and the maw of the subway swallows and regurgitates an enormous parade of commuters. Thousands of vehicles exhale, spewing out their smoke and their smells, which millions of noses inhale, recycle and expel.

The agile taxi slips between two mammoths panting on either side, slams on the brakes, changes lanes, lurches forward, passes cars on the right, speeds up at a yellow light, and makes sure to block any vehicle threatening to squeeze by.

"There's no rush," says Ernesto, clutching the handle above the door. "I'm not in a hurry."

"The thing is, there are twenty-four million people in Mexico City, and hundreds of thousands of vehicles" explains the driver with some pride. "If I let them all pass us we'll never get to your hostel, kid."

"I've heard it's one of the biggest cities in the world."

"It *is* the biggest," the driver corrects him, "and it keeps growing because people from the villages come here to look for work. Here in the capital it's easier to get work or just odd jobs. It may pay badly but it's enough to put beans on the table," he explains.

After a few more kilometers of battling the traffic in the pointless race, the taxi stops in a narrow street.

"Here we are."

Ernesto steps out of the taxi and enters a cloud of dust raised by a woman in flip-flops vigorously sweeping the sidewalk. Emerging from the dust cloud, the boy finds himself standing in front of a crumbling building. Knowing he had to stretch every peso he asked a travel agent in Ciudad Obregón for the cheapest hostel. He climbs the worn marble steps to the third floor and turns on a light. A single naked bulb hung from the ceiling illuminates a small room, which he inspects. A bed with a thin hard mattress, a wooden armoire, and a sink are the only furnishings.

At one end of a hallway is a shared bath with tiled walls which would be beautiful if so many weren't missing. There is no tub, but the electric shower in the middle of the bathroom drains into a grating on the ceramic floor. The electrical tape wrapped around the wires coming out of the showerhead is loose in several places. He'd already been warned not to touch them because the electricity runs at 220 volts.

None of this bothers him much. Not even the cockroach he saw climb out of the shower grating. The thought of being in a foreign country for the first time without his parents' or grandparents' supervision thrills him.

A cacophony of voices and honking calls him to the balcony where he can watch the movement of the city.

He puts his wallet in his jacket pocket and takes a bus downtown. He sees a town square and, attracted by some mariachi music, he gets off the bus. He sees an old marquee or pavilion, like a gazebo, in the middle of the square, with hints of ancient elegance and two beautiful staircases. The steps are a bit wet so Ernesto sits on his jacket. His thoughts float lightly along, much like the soft breeze of the afternoon.

He notices a statue on the other side of the square and walks toward it. The foot of the statue reads: Giuseppe Garibaldi. It strikes him as a strange tribute in a strange place.

At that moment the streetlamps come on. The square is enrobed in a soft pink light, and during a pause in the mariachi music he hears the *coo coooo coo* of pigeons resting their round bellies in the cornices of surrounding buildings. The musicians prepare for another number and Ernesto sits on a bench to take in the show.

The story, though somber, is sung to strident upbeat music. Ernesto sees a few tourists leaving dollars in a sombrero and wants to contribute. Without raising his gaze from the musician's sumptuous costumes, he feels for his jacket pocket. But he's not wearing it.

"Shit! I left it on the stairs!" he remembers in sudden panic. He runs to the marquee and sees it on the same step where he left it. But the wallet is gone.

"My money!" he shouts.

Someone says there were a couple boys running across the square who may have taken it.

"There they are! They're leaving the square! Look! Catch them!"

Ernesto hesitates for a second. Running after them in the middle of downtown Mexico City doesn't seem like a good idea. Even if he caught them, what could he do alone? But he's stronger than them, he realizes – after all, they're just kids. Even if he grabs one of them, he has a fifty percent chance of getting his wallet back.

He takes off after them, weaving through the crowd, but the little bastards have already slipped away, disappearing into the side streets.

Ernesto is alone on the sidewalk, glued to the cement, trapped in an endless loop of thoughts: "Now what? I have to call Mom and Dad collect. But what am I going to tell them? That I let myself get robbed on the second day? That I can't take care of myself? That they should send me money? I can't!"

He starts to wander the streets, directionless, mulling over his loss, guilt meeting him at every corner. He tries imagining an alternative to the shameful phone call he has to make, his thoughts returning again and again like a boomerang to his stupidity. "Damn it! If I hadn't hesitated I could've caught those kids. What's so good about thinking before acting?"

That's exactly what he'd grown up hearing from his father. The thought of that fateful episode with Carlo when "destiny played its cards", as he often thinks, still floats like a perennial cloud in his head.

What just happened confirms what he's been suspecting: that his nature, his true character, has been curtailed for years by a paternal mandate which he now detests for causing more than one stupid moment of doubt.

If he could, he'd kick his own ass. He realizes he's always been way too docile.

The city lights reflect off a sky of gray, heavy clouds that mingle with the thick layer of smog blanketing the city. It smells like rain. Without even a few coins for the bus, Ernesto walks to the hostel. He arrives at night, exhausted, dripping with sweat, and with a metallic dryness in his mouth. He goes upstairs and into the bathroom. He's about to drink water from the tap when some remaining common sense stops him. He curses the bacteria and goes to the filter in the hall. Back in his room he hurls himself onto the bed. A couple of rosy and translucent little lizards eye him inertly from the ceiling. He eyes them back.

It starts to rain.

In the corner of the room a bead of water forms on the ceiling, becomes a little globe, then splashes into a puddle on the mosaic floor; and then another and another, in a progression of chronometric distress. The boy goes downstairs and tells the receptionist that it's raining in his room. The man gives him an aluminum bucket, returns his passport and adds that breakfast is not included in the price.

Back in his room, Ernesto puts the can under the drip.

Now the *toc-toc-toc* of the droplets sound like a rhythmic insult: "*dumb-dumb-dumb*". He undresses, climbs under the sheets, and shields his head with a pillow in case one of the lizards loses its footing.

II

A ray of sunshine streaming through the flowered curtain projects a colorful, undulating pattern on the wall. A clamor of shrill voices brings Ernesto to the verge of consciousness.

"Not that bird again!" he thinks. "I told Mom I don't want that canary near my window." Opening his eyes, Ernesto sees the unfamiliar curtain. Looking around, he sees the aluminum bucket full of water. Suddenly, the details of the previous day's events come rushing back in sharp relief. He gets up, walks to the balcony and peers down the street. It's a group of kids making all that racket.

Dejected and hungry, he gets dressed and goes for a walk. And once again he wanders aimlessly along streets where the houses comingle with stores, minimarts and street vendors. It looks to him like these neighborhoods grew up spontaneously and organically, in a kind of functional chaos.

A strong aroma of coffee and buttered bread assaults his already intensified sense of smell. He flees to the other side of the street and keeps walking.

"Maybe I should look for work" His mind's eye shows him kneading bread in a bakery.

On the sidewalk is a group of men of all ages sitting on plastic chairs, smoking and playing cards. They holler comments ranging from flirtatious to vulgar at every girl who happens to walk by.

"I guess maybe there aren't many jobs around here," he concludes.

At the end of the street he comes to a small town square. It's a quiet place amid narrow cobblestone streets. A few small trees across the way catch his eye and he walks over to them eagerly. They look like they're full of ripe fruit!

"They're oranges!" he hears himself say. He can almost taste the sweetness of them. Or maybe they're tangerines. He doesn't care if they're lemons; he's going to sink his teeth into them anyway. Anything to tide him over until he thinks of something.

As Ernesto nears the tree, dozens of round-bellied yellow birds take flight, leaving Ernesto salivating as his breakfast disappears into thin air.

Perching on another tree, the birds take up their noisy chatter. *Chirp! Chirp! Chirp!* Ernesto mocks them, amused and annoyed at the same time.

"They say birds are just singing, but it sounds like they're saying, 'Hey, I'm over here! Are you there? Where are you? I'm here!' They're just like us, always communicating. We're so obsessive! And if there's no one around, we email or call someone on the phone. Families are just like birds."

"What about my other family? My other parents and my other siblings? Maybe they're wondering where *I* am, just like I wonder about *them*. Could there be someone somewhere on this continent wondering about me, baby Ernesto Moreno who was left at a convent? María Moreno, are you wondering about me? Where are you? I'm here, I'm here! Are you there, mother? I'm over here!"

The boy knows he should quit these childish thoughts so the pain that's suddenly clenching his throat doesn't overwhelm him. A mangy dog comes over to sniff him, and then sits there waiting for something, like a beggar. Ernesto apologizes for not having a crumb to give him. The stray's withered face and his unnecessary docility snaps Ernesto out of his self-pity. "That's enough! I have to make a decision," he tells himself, "I'm going to call home."

But he still hasn't thought of what to say to his parents.

He returns to the hostel determined to write down the previous day's events and exorcise the damn regret he's feeling. He rummages in his backpack looking for a notebook and finds the other letter from Grandpa Ruiz that he never opened. His father handed it to him before he left, because it had arrived inside another envelope directed to Esteban Ruiz. The envelope reads:

For Ernesto
Pilgrim's Guide
(to be opened only in case of spiritual necessity)

"My necessity is more material than spiritual, Grandpa" thinks the boy. But he knows that any guidance at this point would be welcome. After all, his spirit also seems to be breaking.

When he opens the letter he finds a hundred dollar bill wrapped in a sheet of paper with the following note:

The material is merely a bridge to the immaterial, as the known is a bridge to the unknown.

Do not settle for the material alone!

If you remain in the safety of the familiar shore, you will never know what is on the other side of the river.

"Thank you, Grandpa", he says aloud, kissing the letter.

III

A couple is saying goodbye on the station platform. From inside the bus, Ernesto, sees their tears and imagines the wistful sighs.

"Separation is a sad thing," says a priest sitting beside him and also observing the scene outside the window.

"Yeah, it is," says Ernesto, "really sad".

But he reflects that there are other types of separation that aren't so easy to perceive. Like his own. Separation from something unknown that the soul fervently yearns for nevertheless. ¿Separation from our own people? From the place a person comes from? From one's origins? Or is it something else? The boy reads Grandpa Ruiz's goodbye letter again because he's the one person who seems to truly understand the magnitude and nature of his desire. Furthermore, his grandfather added a dimension to his desire that now seems to reach beyond his individual circumstance:

Remember, my boy: there is the external pilgrim who visits the tombs of dead saints, and the internal pilgrim who looks for his own sacred places. And the internal pilgrim is always after something from which he feels separated, or feels has been lost; and he will always be a pilgrim, until he finds it.

His grandfather had told him once about these sacred places. Places where the stubborn memory of some lost Golden Age resides as if life were just a prelude to Life. As if our reality were an exile from Reality, from latent possibility, from incompleteness. The old man believed, and still believes, religion is precisely this: a *re-linking of* the spirit with its mysterious cosmic origin.

Ernesto wonders if the search for his family, which is something tangible, might not be just a facade, an exterior manifestation of this other, more indefinable search.

Nevertheless, the desire to know and to find the Morenos is unyielding. There must be a reason for that.

The driver puts the bus in gear and the priest crosses himself.

"The city is amazing," Ernesto says.

"Is this your first visit to the capital?"

"Yes, I'm from California."

"And what do you think of it? Is it like the cities up there?"

Ernesto thinks about the pulsating energy that emanates from these streets —vibrant, fecund streets, his grandfather would say. Streets that feel more like a Middle Eastern bazaar than an American city.

"A little" he answers, "but here, life overflows onto the streets more."

For the next two hours, the bus meanders through broad avenues, lined with ostentatious buildings and manicured gardens; it passes through nice neighborhoods, not-so-nice neighborhoods, and then goes into the very poor areas that surround the city in concentric circles.

A particular scene is played out over and over: a garbage dump, families picking through the trash looking for anything of value, a bonfire consuming the rest, the smoke rising and obscuring the sky's sunset blush.

"This is so different from downtown! The farther we go, the poorer the suburbs get".

"That's how our poverty belts are, son. The 'new villages', as we called them. They bake the bread downtown, and people here just hope to catch some crumbs. It's just one example of the injustice in this valley of tears."

"And a physical example of entropy," Ernesto thinks, "because the farther out you get from the source of energy the more it dissipates." He mentions this to the priest who confesses that he's never heard of entropy, but thinks it's a magnificent metaphor for the soul that distances itself from God.

After a while, the priest can't contain his curiosity any longer.

"You look like a Chicano, but why do you have such a strong Iberian Spanish accent?"

"I lived in Spain from when I was two until I was ten because my parents are from there. But I'm adopted so I must be Indian, or mestizo, and from around here. I don't know yet. That's what I'm trying to find out on this trip."

"That's so interesting! So do you want to find your biological family or get to know your ethnic group?"

"Both, for sure. I think that by the year 2000 scientists will be able to analyze people's DNA, don't you think? They'll be able to tell a person's ethnicity. But I don't want to wait. I want to find out now."

"Of course. To me, you're *mestizo*, because your hair is a bit wavy."

"Yeah, I know," Ernesto thinks. "I'm a diluted Indian, or a brown white guy, depending on which side of the Atlantic I'm on. Basically I'm a hybrid, like one of Mendel's sweet peas, except I don't know my ancestors."

"What about you? Are you from San Cristóbal de las Casas?"

"I've been assigned to a parish in San Juan de Chamula. The Protestant missionaries are gaining too much ground in the villages, you know? They're taking advantage of people's poverty. They make them sing and play the guitar and all of that. Basically they entertain them and make all kinds of promises so they'll convert. We don't use these manipulative methods. That's why the Holy Church is in trouble in Latin America."

After a while Ernesto asks, "So do you think I'll be able to find work in San Cristóbal?"

"I don't know. Unemployment is high, and there are a lot of Guatemalan refugees who came in the last decade fleeing violence that haven't gone back yet. And there are immigrants from all over Central America who come to work as day-laborers, because the situation in their countries is even worse."

After a couple of hours crossing the immensity of Mexico City and its concentric rings of prosperity and poverty, the bus enters the highway heading south. Outside, thorny bushes disappear into the night of that hard, dry plain. Inside, the passengers' voices begin to quiet down, the lights go out, and Ernesto's thoughts are spiraling into sleep.

4. The *Guayaquileño*

I

The man has grabbed her by the arm and is pulling her through the aisle toward the bus door.

Rosa, wild-eyed, her body assaulted by panic, stumbles along behind him. From the window she sees lights from the city below, their colors running together through the prism of her tears. The streets and avenues, which look festooned like a Christmas tree, the noise of traffic and the vibrant bustle of nightlife, happy and indifferent while she is falling into a bottomless abyss, make her nauseous.

In the dim light, the passengers tremble and pray under the gaze of a revolver and a steady stream of insults. The bandits want to scare them and cut off any attempt to interfere in the girl's kidnapping.

"Look, it's not my business," the conductor says, "but you're familiar with the laws about kidnapping girls under 14, don't you? This girl's only 13 years old."

"Thirteen?" The man looks at Rosa, who nods, without looking him in the eye.

"That's what's written beside her name on the passenger list," the driver adds.

"Get back to your seat!" the robber shouts, insulting the driver's mother as well as the government.

Color returns to Rosa's cheeks. Sobbing, she stumbles back to her seat and, collapses into it, and tries to make herself invisible. Closing her eyes, she thanks God for whispering such a brilliant lie to the driver.

While one of the thieves points his gun at the passengers, the other two ransack their bags for anything valuable, leaving anything that doesn't interest them strewn over the pavement. They quickly load their loot onto a pickup and then disappear into the dark night that has descended on the hill.

Only when they have disappeared into the distance do the passengers unleash their emotions. Some lament what they have lost, others, not recovering from the fright, laugh hysterically. One man refers to the thieves with disdain:

"Common thieves, really inexperienced," he says, "they didn't even search our shoes or underclothes."

After they have calmed down, the majority confess that they have not lost anything but small change, bootleg watches and cheap jewelry.

"Thank God for the priest's advice, right?" another man says.

"That priest is trickier than the devil!"

"Don't tempt Satan now, or they might return", someone says.

After recovering and putting away the things that had been left in the street — some people embarrassed that they had been deemed unworthy of robbery—the bus roars down the street, and in a few minutes they are in the city once again. The chauffeur resumes his dialogue by cell phone and receives clearer instructions on how to get to the new hotel on the outskirts of Guayaquil. It is evident that there are many establishments that serve the clandestine operations.

In their new shelter they meet an administrator who is waiting for them with dinner. Someone proposes a prayer and everyone unites in an Our Father—the ones who know it, and those who pretend to know it, like Rosa, who only moves her lips, albeit with genuine fervor. After the brief prayer they eat with gusto. Someone asks the driver if his cell phone allows him to talk to God, and he says yes, except he doesn't have the number. The joke is received with peals of laughter. Afterwards, the cell phone circulates among the passengers and the driver shows them the battery and explains how it works. It is a great novelty in Ecuador.

A man appears in the dining room at the end of the dinner and addresses the group:

"Ladies and gentlemen, my name is José Bustamante and I want to welcome you. Tomorrow we embark. My colleagues and I will come by at three in the morning to take you to a place that only we will use. The authorities don't know the site and there's no surveillance. However, to eliminate any risk—because, you know, some people have a loose tongue—when we arrive, you should leave the vehicle as quickly as possible, follow the guide and run as fast as you can toward the beach. There'll be boats waiting to take you to the ship. And I'll be on the ship, your captain, ready to serve you! So now, it's best you go to bed. Get some rest! See you tomorrow, God willing."

That night Rosa finds her bed too soft. After having slept for 15 years on a mat on the ground or in a hammock, this city luxury seems uncomfortable and useless. She puts the mattress on the ground, lies down and goes over the day's events in her mind, writing a few lines with many exclamation points on one of the cards Romero gave her. Then, holding her jaguar talisman, she falls into a deep sleep.

II

It is still dark. A halo of milky urban light dims the starlight. As the bus travels south out of the city the skies become progressively darker and the stars grow ever brighter.

Arriving at the rendezvous, the bus stops beside the highway. Forewarned, the passengers have their backpacks on. Like a cat watching a mouse hole in absolute concentration, each passenger watches the door, expectant and ready to jump from the vehicle when the moment arrives. No one speaks. The only sound is that of nervous breathing.

Then the order rings out: "Now! Get off the bus and run!"

A little forest of dwarf palm trees and low bushes does not offer much concealment. The guide runs quickly and people make an effort to keep up. A woman trips. Rosa stops to help her.

"Keep going, girl, run! I'll help the lady," says the other guide who is following behind.

No one can clearly see where they are going, but they have been told that they should follow the lights blinking in the distance. The lights move up and down. Sometimes they move sideways. They join other lights that blink off and on like floating fireflies in the night air.

Rosa feels the scratch of thorny shrubs on her arm, but pays no attention to it. The sea, the salty air laden with the smell of seaweed, and the growing rumble of waves pounding on the coast is the only reality at this moment. To the girl who knows only the sound of rushing streams, the roar is inconceivable.

Minutes later, from the height of a dune, Rosa thinks she sees, from the light of a pallid moon hanging from a cloud, an amorphous and colorless body that moves and merges with the sky and the thick fog.

Soon, she arrives at the beach. The cold air electrifies her. The moon illuminates a serpent of foam forming itself along the edge of the beach. And she watches, hypnotized, as the waves rise, and scratch the sand, and retreat, one after the other, with their rake-like fingers, always different and always the same.

Someone asks where the ship is, but the wind carries his words away.

The group's guide calls them together and shouts:

"We can't embark! The wind is too strong and the tide is still high!"

"When does the tide go down?" someone shouts in his ear.

"Maybe in an hour," the guide answers.

"But won't the sun be up? They might see us!"

"Yes, the sun will be up at six. If we're lucky, the police won't be around that early. But just in case, we have a lookout on the road."

"And the fishermen?"

"What about the fishermen? Oh, yes, they do get up early, but we can arrange things with them easily!"

III

It is not yet light. The waning moon with its horns pointing downward, as she likes to show herself in the tropics, is moving toward the horizon, and the rosy tones and bright pink edges of the clouds announce that dawn is beginning to break.

The wind begins to die down and the sky begins to clear.

Now, for the first time, she sees it: the Pacific Ocean, the enormous, ominous, much-feared sea that swallows people and gives fish in return. Nevertheless, it is this same legendary ocean that carried her mother six years ago to the other side of the world. Why shouldn't it carry her also?

She sees a multitude on the beach, many more people than the original 30 members of the Baeza group. And more people are arriving. But where they're coming from is a mystery.

As day dawns, the misty vapor begins to dissipate and reveals various small boats, rising and falling on the crest of the waves, like riders breaking horses on the water. And on each boat there is a lamp.

"The dancing lights!" exclaims Rosa to herself. "I knew they weren't fireflies!"

"Get ready, everyone, I'm told we're about ready to embark. I want eight people in the first boat. Hurry!" the guide shouts.

A boat leaves with a first load of passengers, rowing away over the turbulent, grey sea until it dissolves in the mist.

Soon the mist swirling over the sea begins to dissipate like smoke blown by the wind, revealing, about 100 meters away, the fragmented silhouette of a fishing boat. There is a shout of joy, then surprise, and then disenchantment, when the fog disappears completely.

"Look, look, the ship!"

"Finally!"

"I thought it would be bigger."

"You mean to say that that little ship is going to carry all of us?"

"But, that's not a passenger ship. It's just a fishing boat!"

"So what? If it was a fishing boat, it's now a tourist ship," someone laughs, to mask the bitterness.

"Very funny, but this is serious."

The complaints continue:

"That boat isn't big enough for 50 people. And there must be at least 200 here."

"Two hundred? But we were only 30! Have we multiplied that much in such a short time?"

"Can't you see, there are people here from all over the place? I've heard all kinds of different accents: Peruvian, Colombian, even Brazilian!"

"Where the hell did they come from?"

"Didn't you see those other buses behind us?"

"Let's go, it's our turn," someone says to Rosa, who is trying to ignore the seriousness of the problem.

She loves canoeing in jungle streams, and she has never cared how fast the current flowed. But those are crystalline rivers, she thinks; at least they have two banks and you can grab a branch if worse comes to worst and the canoe turns over. But the ocean is a turbulent mass of water that seems to go nowhere except into its own depths; and it stirs in the same place like a formless, soulless monster that could swallow her up at any instant. She tries not to look at the water, concentrating instead on the ship they are approaching.

Now, through the mist, she can read a name painted in green letters: *El guayaquileño.*

It's difficult to get any closer, because of the waves beating against the rowboat and the fishing boat, sometimes in opposite directions. With each attempt to come closer, there is more danger of crashing against the hull of the fishing boat.

A turbulent, dark sea and a boat that can't be boarded ... Rosa digs her fingernails into side of the rowboat.

In what seems to be a moment of calm, the rowers approach the fishing boat and one of them catches a rope ladder thrown from above.

"Hold on tight and climb!" orders the man, pulling on the ladder.

Some with agility, some trembling with fear, everyone climbs up the three meters between them and the strong arms of the sailors waiting on top, pulling them on deck. Rosa, lithe as a vine and able to shinny up a coconut palm, boards the ship in a matter of seconds.

"Ramón, send everyone below deck," bellows an agitated José Bustamante, "no one can stay on top. Quick!"

As soon as they start boarding, Ramón sends the passengers down into the engine room. Confused and dismayed everyone nevertheless obeys and crowds down the staircase. Down below, a crew member hands each passenger a plastic bag and points out their places in the lines and circles already demarcated on the floor of the hold, where they can put their backpacks as well as their bottoms.

The room, absurdly small for such a large group, smells like old wood, fish and fuel.

"Don't go over your line," Ramón shouts as he continues to distribute plastic bags, "because more people are coming." Sure enough, the human wave continues to descend and find their allotted place on the wet and slippery floor. Back to back, there is only enough room to stretch their legs halfway."

"All right, chief. Two hundred and ten, not counting the crew."

"Okay. Ready to set sail," says Rubén, who is the second-in-command. "No one can go up now, is that understood? If you get seasick, use the plastic bags. There's a bathroom in the back."

The two hundred unhappy souls are so dismayed and indignant that they are momentarily dumbstruck. A few minutes go by before they begin to vent their fury:

"We were told we'd travel comfortably! We didn't pay thousands of dollars to be packed in like sardines!"

"Nobody told us that we'd be traveling in the hold!"

"Bastards!"

"Shitheads!"

After a few minutes, a man with a strangled voice shouts, "We're like Jonah in the whale's belly, brothers!"

"Hey, calm down," someone says—the image is gruesome for him. "We're stuck here and we can't do anything about it, so let's calm down."

"Yes. We're in God's hands now," a voice assents.

"I hope we are," Rosa tells herself, more frightened by the tumult than by the size of this so-called fishing boat.

Little by little the protests die down. The boat continues rocking in its violent cradle, and the passengers submerge themselves in the silent swinging of their own fears.

IV

The engine starts with a sudden roar, provoking startled yells followed by nervous laughter.

"Well, at least we don't have to row, man!" someone says.

Suddenly, the smell of diesel permeates the room. The passengers alternate between covering their noses with handkerchiefs, covering their ears, or retreating into themselves with their heads buried in their backpacks. Without windows to look through, only the sick feeling in their stomachs tells them that the boat is now moving. It is time now to recommend their souls to God, to a patron saint, or to kiss the crucifix that many carry around their neck; or perhaps to clutch the little locket with a portrait of the Virgin, or the first little tooth of a baby, or a lock of hair from one's beloved. Rosa, however, clutches her talisman.

The hours pass slowly, colorless. There is no place to lie down, not even a pillow on which to rest one's head. Soon, one or another person offers a shoulder to a neighbor, or a space to stretch a leg, to calm a tingling sensation or a cramp; and these kindly gestures create a current of affection and sympathy among these mortified travelers, and they soon fall into sleep.

But the peace is temporary. After some hours surfing the waves mouths begin to salivate and eyes glaze over. Getting to the latrine among this miserable crowd is a difficult task, and plastic bags are put to use. Rosa, who happens to be near an exit, goes up to the deck, not caring about the prohibition, throws up her breakfast near the stairs.

A sailor appears, carrying a box of sawdust for covering up any vomit that happens to escape the plastic bags.

"That's right, cover the filth, like the cats," says a bitter voice.

In a short time the rancid air of this gloomy place becomes unbearable. A modicum of hygiene is achieved with rags and old newspapers kept in the bathroom for that purpose. A strong pine smelling aerosol wielded by Ramón brings the stench down to a mere stinking level. Humiliated by their own vomit and smells, everyone withdraws into him or herself, swallowing the shame. Some even lament ever having embarked.

Not Rosa.

Between attacks of nausea, the girl passes the time remembering and writing down her memories.

"Memorizing the trail one has walked," her grandfather likes to say, "is the only way to know how to return home. That's the law of the jungle! "

A mystery can of food, some crackers, a banana, and potable water are served for lunch. The misfortune of some, prone to motion sickness and without appetite, means joy for the hungrier ones who thus receive a double ration. Rosa eats half her ration, hoping her nausea will also decrease by half, and gives the rest to her neighbor.

After lunch a slow pilgrimage to the bathroom begins. It is just a tiny wooden partition with a hole on a small pedestal at one end of the room. Since it is the only facility available, a line of 10 to 20 persons becomes permanent.

At sundown, which can be deduced by a slight rosiness to the little light filtering into the room, dinner is served: more cans of food, bread and oranges. Rosa eats just one orange and the neighbor lady is once more the beneficiary of the rest.

Someone turns on a radio. The reception is very poor.

A crew member, whom Rosa has already seen when she got on the boat, appears in the doorway and, with a discrete gesture, calls the girl to the stairway. She gets up and goes toward him, rather embarrassed, fearing a reprimand for the vomit. The man whispers something to her. She goes back to her place with a pleased expression and tells her neighbor, whose name is Mabel, that she will now be able to stretch out, using Rosa's space, because she is going up to the deck.

"He says that since I'm a minor, the captain's going to let me sleep alone in a cabin."

"Hmmm. If I were you I wouldn't," the woman responds. "Unless you don't mind paying for it with your services? Well, you'll know what to do. You're not a child. But remember that nothing's free on this trip."

This revelation hits Rosa like a slap on her face. So that's what he wants! She goes back to her assigned place and rests her head on her knees, angry at herself for her naïveté. How could she have forgotten so soon the advice she received before leaving? No need even to write it down, she thinks, because this is inexcusable and unforgettable stupidity. She has forgotten the advice! She has forgotten to remember!

The dim light that entered the room diminishes until everything becomes shadowy.

"Ladies and gentlemen, whoever had the radio on, please turn it off. We need to respect everyone's rest," says the captain over a battery-powered loudspeaker. "Good night."

Rosa leans closer to her neighbor.

"Do you mind if I take your arm, doña Mabel?"

"Of course not, dear. No one's going to take you away from here, don't worry."

Immobility, numbness in the legs and the maddening noise of the engines becomes a torment. Doubt and repentance keep some travelers awake for a long time. In others it causes terrible nightmares. Finally, with her extreme weariness and the movement of the ship, Rosa closes her eyes and falls asleep. But her dreams are of a turbulent and agitated sea. She wakens with a start. The heavy air of their chamber is full of sonorous snores, of *Ave Marías* murmured with each bead of a rosary, of startled cries elicited by confused and violent nightmares. Of prayers. Of curses. Time drags on, seems to stop, to go backward. Rosa feels like crying. But the plump, warm flesh of her neighbor's protective arm reminds her that things could be much worse. The gratitude she feels toward doña Mabel is as wide and extensive as the ocean itself. And this, well, she will never forget it.

V

The radio is playing a song about immigrants. It's not just a coincidence, nor divine intervention that has descended on the radio studios this morning, as some seem to think. Neither explanation is needed, because it's Mano Negra's hit song.

A crew member's voice is heard and the volume is turned down. He is speaking in an imposing voice.

"Good morning, ladies and gentlemen. It's my pleasure to inform you that we're on the high seas and outside Ecuadorian waters. We're now sailing in international waters and out of danger! Those of you who would like may now come to the upper deck and breathe fresh air."

Euphoria explodes like gunpowder in the engine room. Though the song has resumed, no one listens anymore. In a few minutes, the two hundred suffering bodies are on deck, squinting like nocturnal animals in the bright light, and dazzled by the immensity of the ocean on this sunny morning.

"Wow!" exclaims Rosa, overwhelmed by the majesty of it all.

"Oh my God, I never thought ... it's enormous!" a man says.

"You've never seen the ocean?" another man asks with a superior air.

"No, never."

"Well, you're going to get tired of seeing it. We're going to be sailing for eight or ten days, if everything goes well. I mean, if the Coast Guard doesn't arrest us. Or if the gringo patrols don't find us—they're out here looking for drug dealers disguised as fishermen. And if a storm doesn't shipwreck us and we wind up at the bottom of the sea sleeping with the mermaids."

This litany of bad omens dampens the mood. Mention of the ocean depths reminds Rosa of the ancient tales her teacher used to read to the class; they make a knot in her stomach. She has a vision of marine serpents wound around her legs, octopuses sucking her head, giant slugs sliming her body on a bed of algae, crustaceans stuck onto her eyes and face, like the ones she saw on the beach, stuck to rotten driftwood and eating it away.

"Don't be a spoil sport, man!" Someone reprimands the pessimist. Can't you say something positive?"

"God Gracious!"

Rosa reflects and then says: "None of this is going to happen. My mother also traveled in a boat like this one. Ships don't sink for no reason. Mom wouldn't have asked for me if it was so terrible."

"Well said, dear."

Hours later, Rosa goes down to look for her straw hat. The sun is at its zenith in the very blue center of the sky.

"Ladies and gentlemen," the captain announces, "we've just crossed the equator. Welcome to the Northern Hemisphere!"

"Do you see, Mr. Pessimist?" Rosa says, silently. "We're in the North. And in the North, nothing bad like that can happen."

5. Among Gods and Tombs

I

San Cristóbal de las Casas, a city rich in Mayan culture and colonial architecture, has become a magnet overnight for scholars, missionaries and all sorts of curios types. Armed soldiers watch suspiciously from every corner.

In one of those *vanguard* cafés where journalists, academics and tourists converge, Ernesto learns about the Zapatista attack last year.

Someone explains that the Army came from the capital and retaliated by bombarding the suburbs.   "The   rebels retreated into the Lacandon jungle but soon re-took some villages around here, so things are still pretty tense."

Ernesto feels an immediate affinity with the native inhabitants of Chiapas, who become brave warriors in his imagination. He likes the idea of having Mayan blood in his veins. Who knows!

He asks someone where to find a youth hostel to spend the night. He plans to leave for Guatemala the following day. He is sent to the University District. There he finds a bed in a room with another student. He pays a modest sum and leaves his backpack. On his way to the lobby, he stops to look at a bulletin board. A small drawing of a Mayan profile on a job announcement calls his attention. It says: "Seeking English and Spanish speaker for archaeological project."

He writes number on his hand and heads for a phone booth.

An hour later he is in the office of archaeologist Luis Guerrero.

Luis is a good looking young man with abundant black hair and brown eyes. And Ernesto notices that he's as pale as the walls.

"You would be the ideal person," says Luis, "but you're not Mexican and you don't have a work permit, right? These government contracts have a lot of red tape."

"So what's the project?" Ernesto asks just to buy time while he tries to think of something.

"An ancient Mayan cemetery has been discovered buried in Palenque, and the Museum of Anthropology and History hired me to lead the excavations. I'd love to have someone like you, who's not only bilingual but well-educated. You would classify and label the artifacts in both English and Spanish. But I'm afraid it won't be possible. I'm sorry."

Ernesto thanks him and asks him to call the hostel, if he comes up with a solution. He'd do anything to get the job.

They shake hands and Luis tells Ernesto to be sure to visit the ruins in any case.

Crestfallen, Ernesto leaves thinking that if he weren't so afraid of going to a Mexican prison it would be really easy to buy a fake ID. But that wouldn't work either since he already gave the archeologist his real name. Why didn't he think of that!

As he crosses the street he hears the archaeologist call his name.

"Listen, I just thought of something. Since our funding comes from Berkeley, they might be able to hire you directly. Then we'd just have to get you a work visa. I can't promise anything, but give me a little time."

The boy's heart leaps with hope. Actually, it seems about to burst. He wants to call and ask his father to call his friend at UC Berkeley, and have him call a colleague, who would ask another...

"In the meantime bring me your passport. I'm going to send a fax."

Ernesto thanks him and says good bye. Somewhere east of there, among the giant leaves of a prehistoric forest, a city of pyramids and cemeteries and secrets floats into his imagination. It would be awesome to work on this project! He sits down on a staircase. To quiet his mind, he takes out his travel journal and writes:

The Mayans wanted to learn about the universe, just like me. They built that city of pyramids to decipher the heavens. I wonder if there is a curiosity gene. I'd like to have some trace of the Mayans in my genes.

He reads his words and finds them silly. But he leaves them.

II

Ernesto's employment paperwork was relatively simple. A few e-mails between the two institutions and a few documents sent by fax. Plus the recommendation letters from Luis and the Berkeley professor helped cut through the red tape. During Ernesto's breakfast the archeologist brings him good news along with a stack of papers to sign. They're leaving today.

"I've had amazing luck," Ernesto reflects. "That day I almost killed Carlo his insults were torturing me. But actually that's what brought me to where I am now. I'm so close to that wonderful place, Palenque, and with such an important mission!"

In the afternoon Luis and his helpers come to pick him up in two pickups full of supplies for the expedition. Ernesto climbs into one of the vehicles and introduces himself to the group of six men.

In a few hours they arrive at the small town of Palenque. Not far from there, on the other side of a dense forest of mahogany, cedars and ceibas, the mythical city of temples rises at the edge of a plateau.

Among enormous step pyramids culminating in columned galleries, there are altars and superimposed towers. The gray and white stone stands out against the intense green of the jungle threatening to engulf it.

Ernesto climbs the oversize steps up the Temple of the Inscriptions. From above he has a view of the vast plains that stretch to the north, at the foot of the plateau.

For the first time in a long while he feels a wave of joy swelling in his chest.

In the abrupt transition typical of these latitudes, night falls in what seems like just a few instants. The team sets up camp by the glow of their lanterns. They have dinner and go to bed as the creatures of the forest are taking shelter for the night.

After breakfast, the team gathers their equipment and sets off following a local guide. Luis informs them that radar imaging shows chamber buried about 15 feet down.

After a short hike, the guide stops in front of a stone in the angle of a smaller pyramid. Luis checks his map and confirms that they are in the right place. It is a three-by-five foot monolith which serves as the door to the chamber. A ferocious face is carved on it.

Using shovels to dig a trench and strong boards for leverage, the boulder gives way to an opening where the team and equipment can descend. The guide shines a flashlight.

"Follow me, but watch your head. The ceiling is low."

In single file, the men climb into a cold damp tunnel, and the flashlight reflects a silvery light off the rock walls. A pack of bats takes flight and flutters in the darkness. Wherever Ernesto points his flashlight, little blind eyes shine back at him. The air is laced with the scent of animal urine.

They descend though another tunnel, even more constricted than the first. Crawling now, they make their way over a bed of mud and rock.

After an hour of slow progress encumbered by slippery terrain and a surprising number of quietly copulating toads, the tunnel rises and opens onto a large dry space. The men set down their flashlights. The yellow light reveals a square room with rock walls and a rock floor.

A feeling of awe and deference, and a mild fear of desecration, silences the voices for a few moments.

Someone pronounces a few Mayan words.

The walls are covered with intricate hieroglyphs. In the center of the room is a limestone boulder with a flat top and a magnificent, aquiline Mayan profile carved on its side.

"This is a sacrificial table," explains Luis. "Judging by the size, it might have been for children."

"I've always wondered why people would satiate their gods with the blood of their young. Why not sacrifice a cougar, or a man, or an elephant?" Ernesto ventures to ask.

"The Mayans sacrificed men more than children. But it's true that there was a preference for children, sheep and virgins."

Luis agrees. "We find this type of thing in societies that have never met so it couldn't have been copied behavior."

"So, is it just a coincidence?"

"Well, I don't think it's really a coincidence. It seems to be a human tendency to see the world as corrupt and the gods as perfect. And to please the gods they give them something that is still pure."

"That's why there are so few virgins!" Someone jokes.

The men laugh and then feel guilty. Mournfully, the walls echo the laughter, which now sounds sacrilegious.

"This echo is a bad omen", someone whispers.

"I don't like it, either," says another.

"Don't be superstitious," says Luis, "shine your lights over here".

He thinks that somewhere there must be a door leading to the chamber he's looking for, and he starts a thorough exploration of the place. He finds a pile of rubble and the men help clear it away. Beneath it is the stylized figure of a royal Mayan, carved on the floor.

They continue to inspect the walls in hopes of finding a door, perhaps camouflaged by carved designs, or a slit in the stone marking an entrance. As it turns out, however, the Mayan nobility have taken good care to conceal their secrets.

After a fruitless search, Luis concludes that there must be a mistake in his calculations and sends the men back into the tunnel to investigate its walls in case they missed a hidden door somewhere along the way. A full hour goes by in this inspection, and Ernesto asks permission to return to the room with the hieroglyphs.

He calls out to Luis from the semi-darkness. "Do you think this carved figure might be an indication of something? Underneath?"

Luis looks surprised and hurries over to Ernesto.

"You could be right!"

The sound of pickaxes and sledgehammers are amplified by the rock walls. Sweat gleams on every brow. What looked like a raw rock design, now takes the shape of a stone slab. When they finally remove it, their lanterns reveal a narrow staircase covered in pebbles and dirt. They clear it quickly and in less than 15 minutes they're climbing down it.

"It's here. It must be here!" says Luis, shining his flashlight around the room they've descended into.

As the team shines their lights around the room, an avalanche of rock and earth falls upon them. A rock strikes Ernesto's head and he hears confused yelling. He can't tell if the absolute darkness is because there is no light or because he's gone blind. He touches his head, feels the warm blood flowing from his wound and running down his face. He hears the groaning of his companions. Flashlights come on and begin to dart about the rocky chamber in vainly searching for an exit.

"Are you guys okay?"

The men's voices tell him that, although the collapse shut off the entrance, it didn't bury anyone. But if light can't come in, he thinks, air can't come in either. He asks Luis how much time he thinks the oxygen will last until there is only carbon dioxide left and everyone slowly dies. But Luis is busy trying to find his radio among the rubble and either can't hear or doesn't want to answer.

Someone with an unsteady voice says that they must be paying for the sin of having degraded a sacred site. Others pray. Some grumble about their aches and pains.

Luis tells them to keep quiet and save their energy. The air is already getting thin. He also tells them not to use their flashlights to save the batteries.

Ernesto's mouth is already dry and his throat hurts. He doesn't say anything, but feels like there are rocks in his head trying to break out through his skull. He listens to the loud drumming of his heart in his chest and the rush of blood coursing through his veins. "Jesus, I think my temples are going to burst."

"Luis, I'm hurt," he finally says." I'm bleeding."

Luis turns his flashlight on him, then takes off his shirt and wraps it tightly around Ernesto's head.

"Try to keep still, and lie down here."

Ernesto thinks about the strangeness of his destiny. Just yesterday he was remembering that afternoon at school five years ago, and Carlo, and the chain of events that brought him to Palenque. And he was happy. Now he remembers that same event again, which also led to this terrible situation in which his life depends on finding a radio lost in the rocky tomb. Yesterday's joy now feels like destiny's bad joke.

But did it really cause this? Who is to blame? Carlo, for giving him the idea? Luis, for being incompetent? María Moreno, for abandoning him? Or does a moment in life, including the instant of death, have a multitude of causes and effects that comingle and intersect in a convoluted plot that only God understands? Or maybe even God doesn't understand it?

Questions drift into his consciousness and drift out again, unanswered.

He thinks about his parents and about the parents he's never met. He thinks about his life and about the fabric of his story which he wanted to unravel, to understand its design, to find the key thread; that thread that's quickly slipping from his hands. He asks forgiveness for the times when he could have done good and didn't, and for the times when he was selfish or simply indifferent.

Lying on a bed of rocks, time becomes a tangle of broken memories. They shift and merge in the halls of his consciousness, stricken by the brutal reality.

His shirt is drenched.

He pictures his parents' grief as they take him home dead, and feels tears mingling with dirt and blood.

His thoughts become more confused and imprecise, evaporating when they have scarcely formed, and then Luis announces that he found the radio.

III

A small fishing boat with four crew members and 210 clandestine passengers navigates the calm waters of the Pacific Ocean, 100 nautical miles north of the equator.

It is the fourth day of the voyage and dawn has begun to stain the water red and gold. The travelers, most of them unaccustomed to the sea, still find themselves in an unnatural element, although a little less threatening. The noise of the engines has become less bothersome, mingled now with the pounding of the waves and the chattering of people on board; even the smell of diesel oil and fish has lost its intensity, combined with so many foul odors, human and non-human.

Furthermore, they are less cramped now that they are allowed to go up to the deck.

This is their new reality, and what was abhorrent has become a bearable routine.

But not for everyone.

The absence of a passenger has been noted. A taciturn man of some 50 years has not been seen since the previous day. His friends look for him and call his name with no effect. They imagine the worst: dizziness, a fainting spell near the rail, a moment of distraction.

"Or suicide," someone adds, staring at the shiny water with sad eyes.

Finally they find him, squeezed into a very tight space between engines, hiding his face with his hands.

"What's the matter? Can we help you?" they say, seeing his dejected expression.

"It's nothing, nothing, just that, I miss my family, my wife, my daughters, my little grandsons ... Why on earth did I come on this trip? It's all my fault."

He begins to weep like a baby.

"Look, all of us have left our families somewhere," someone says.

"And now, we're one big family," another person says.

"Come on, sit down here and talk it over with friends. Let's chase away that sadness."

And so, with empathy and friendly words, they coax him out of his corner.

This episode moves Rosa deeply. She has never seen a man crying. Men do not cry. Huaorani men, at least.

After a few moments, a woman says: "It's this enormous, endless ocean's fault; it makes our hearts shrink."

IV

A hot day dawned, the barometer reading low pressure over the Pacific Ocean. The sea is calm and the air dense and static without a hint of breeze. Rosa takes advantage of the calm to write, although she feels an unusual weakness. Yesterday she dreamed of the dolphin's songs she heard before going to bed. They were singing in front of the boat for quite some time and afterwards disappeared, leaving a note of melancholy within her.

A place in the Pacific Ocean. September 25, 1995.
Dear Mom: I'm writing this letter, hoping I can send it to you from Guatemala. Today is the fifth day on the boat. I wish you could see how calm it is today! Yesterday there were a ton of flying fish and dolphins swimming beside the boat, doing tricks. They were with us for hours. There was a small dolphin swimming with its mom and I think it was smiling. I was thinking that we were those dolphins and we were together. Then I heard them singing. They sang and then they left.

The sky has become an unsettled grey, and the skin of the sea, which had been like a wrinkled sheet, has begun to get rough. Rosa realizes that the serenity of the morning was untrustworthy, because the detestable churning in her stomach has started up again, and this time it is so revolting that she has to abandon her letter.

Recipes for curing seasickness spread from one passenger to the other. Some say they should fight evil with evil by drinking seawater; others say one should lie down in the middle of the boat to diminish the rocking sensation. This is the most acceptable cure for Rosa and she looks for an open space among the passengers who have followed the same advice. She lies down on the floor like a rag doll and dozes fitfully. Later, when she opens her eyes the sea is dark and somber. A cold west wind is blowing, taking away her drowsiness, and the sky, heavy with clouds, lets down fat raindrops that pound the deck.

In a few minutes, and without preamble, as if they had risen from the depths of the ocean, the waves begin to rise up in towers. Rosa watches with horror, how from one instant to the next a wall of water crashes onto the deck and almost pulls a man overboard. A sailor grabs him before he is swept to sea.

"Hang on tight!" Rubén shouts.

"Everyone below deck!"

A storm has crashed down on them without warning.

The ship oscillates violently from stern to bow. The captain turns the boat and now the rocking is lateral and no less terrifying. The screams of passengers fly into the wind and spread until the air is filled with anguished cries.

"Where are the life vests?" someone yells.

"In the hold. Pancho, pass out the life vests!"

Those who are still on deck hang onto a post, a companion, or a prayer; everyone implores God for protection. In the midst of the general pandemonium Rosa runs toward the engine room, not knowing what else to do, and someone on the staircase offers her a life vest.

"Put it on quick! There aren't enough for everyone—we're running out!"

She is about to put on the vest when, near the stairway, she stumbles onto a woman who is hugging a post, crying. Her face and hair remind Rosa of her mother.

"Take my vest!" Rosa cries, and climbs down the stairs.

Some days earlier, in a corner of the engine room, behind the bathroom, she had found a large wooden box that must have been used for storing fish on ice. It seems to be well sealed, and now it contains only some nets. Rosa discovered that she fit inside this box. She had cleaned it out as best she could, sprinkled powder on it to absorb the moisture and the smell of fish, and lined it with newspapers left over from the initial bout of vomiting. She spread the netting like a mattress and converted it into her little shelter. Since then, when she wanted to be alone in the midst of the multitude she would hide herself inside this box, cover herself from head to toe with newspapers and disappear from sight.

Now the girl thinks of the box as her salvation. No way is she going to put on the life vest, with her head out of water, and her legs hanging down, vulnerable to the nibbles of fishes that could bite her foot or carry away her toe. No, the box is better, because it is light and it will float. If there is a shipwreck, she will be safe and sound floating on the sea and safe from its creatures.

Some unlucky passengers are desperately looking for a life vest that might have been forgotten about in some corner. She sees the box behind the bathroom. The moment she settles herself inside, the lights go out. She covers herself with the nets and imagines that she is a pearl sheltered by an oyster in the ocean. The screams of the passengers mixed with the roar of the furious ocean are muffled in her ears, and the smell of collective vomit now seems filtered. Shrouded in nets and shadows, she snuggles into her maritime crib and goes deeper into her imaginary identity of the untouchable pearl.

A torrent of water roars down the stairs, flooding the engine room, and then another and another, as the boat pitches and rolls. In a few minutes the box begins to float up. Only now does it occur to Rosa that if the boat capsizes neither she nor anyone else in the engine room will be able to escape. They will go down with the boat, and will be forever interred at the bottom of the ocean. Or, if the water level continues to go up she will be trapped against the ceiling of the engine room and the box will be her coffin as well as her crib in the midst of the sea. On the other hand, going up to the deck would be suicide because a wave could sweep her away in an instant, like a feather.

"Itota, Jesus, Son of the Creator, help me!" Rosa prays, unsure of whether she should abandon her little craft.

The boat shudders and pitches under the blows of wind and wave.

"Haengongui, Father, god of the rivers and of the jungle waterfalls, remember your Huaorani daughter who has never harmed any of your creatures! Let me go back to your freshwater kingdom!" the girl implores, breaking out into sobs as she repeats the ancient Huaorani invocation.

The water level continues to rise, however, and Rosa has run out of gods to implore for mercy. Then she remembers that her grandmother used to say, "For health problems, child, pray to Huaengongui. If you need money, Jesus of the Evangelists always helps. But for love problems, Rosita, remember the Virgin Mary of the Catholics, because when the Father doesn't hear, the Mother comes to the rescue."

"Virgin Mary!" the girl implores, "It's for love that I'm asking you to save me—because I love you! You're the Virgin of the Sea, *the Stella Maris*, the Star of the Sea. María, Maris, Marina, Our Lady Queen of Ocean Waters!" she sobs, "please calm the waters, I'm begging you to calm the waters!"

6. Sailing North

I

The wind is dying down. The clouds are breaking up and moving away toward other horizons, and the boat is sailing steadily. Rosa thanks whoever has heard her prayers. She jumps out of her box and climb on deck, rubbing her eyes.

She joins the others, panic still painted on their yellow, sick features. In the midst of the mess she finds her letter glued to a post, the ink running.

On the horizon, the light has spread its colors into a dazzling rainbow. Some of the passengers are looking at it, crying. Others are thanking God for the rainbow, a sign of His mercy.

Hours later, after the passengers have been counted, food supplies and damages assessed, and once the crew has pumped the machine room clear of water, the captain calls them to the deck.

"The storm took us off course and we lost a day, which means that rations are low. We'll have to," he clears his throat, "to tighten our belts."

"Tighten our belts?" Someone says. "My belt doesn't' have any more holes to tighten!"

Neither this nor other complaints disturbs the joy of the moment. Nobody wants to appear ungrateful to Fate.

II

True to its name, though not its custom, the Pacific is calm today, the sixth day of the voyage. Squeezed into the hold, the passengers celebrate the news that a crew member has just announced: from now until they arrive in Guatemala, they can count on good weather.

The sea is sparkling and the sun breaks on the crest of the waves. Rosa discovers that if she concentrates on the blue-green of the far horizon her stomach settles down a little. Staring at the horizon, she notices a far point that begins to grow. It's got to be a ship or a giant fish, she figures. It must be a ship, because it's getting bigger and bigger. Or is it an optical illusion? She puts both hands around one eye, like a telescope, to see whether it's in the shape of an object or an animal. Looking so far into the distance is a strange experience for someone who grew up in the jungle.

Now it is obvious that it's a ship. And it's coming straight toward them.

As Rosa comes to this conclusion, somewhat distractedly, the captain's voice crackles over the loudspeakers: "Everyone below! Immediately! Get down below deck—Now!"

"Why is he so alarmed?" someone asks, "It's not the first time we've been passed another ship."

"The captain must have seen something through his binoculars!"

"He must think they're after us!"

Like rabbits pursued by hounds, the crowd of frightened immigrants thunders down stairs.

"It's so humiliating to be a fugitive! As if we were thieves or pirates!" a man complains as he heads reluctantly down the stairs.

"Let's pray they haven't seen us," another man says.

"What if they've spotted us?"

"If they have, we're done for!"

In a few minutes, an enormous steel-colored ship flying the stars and stripes of the United States of America approaches. It is three times taller than the *Guayaquileño*, which shrinks alongside this great, imperturbable mass.

Now it is parallel to the fishing boat. The two vessels salute one another like old friends: the smaller one emits a high, strident whistle, and the immense ship's horn responds with tuba-like solemnity.

The men on board salute the "fishermen," who pretend to be busy with an empty net.

After the cordial exchange of sounds, the ship departs, sailing along the sparkling, silvery, water. The waves produced by its enormous hull rock the small boat, with its illegal, silent cargo that trembles inside in its belly.

Half an hour passes before the ship is out of sight.

"You can get out!" orders the captain.

"That was so scary I nearly shit my pants."

"What happens if they figure out who we are and come back, or send a tug boat, or a helicopter, or ... ?"

"It was just a merchant ship, not the Navy," the captain replies.

"What if they're pimps and are now informing the Coast Guard?"

"What a bunch of wimps! We're passing the Panama Canal," the Captain explains. "There are ships from all over the world here. We're not the only foreigners who 'fish' around here."

However, the passengers continue scanning the horizon, apprehensively.

It is the seventh day and most of the food has run out. That is, it's run out for the passengers.

"Attention, please, the captain would like me to inform you that from now on there'll be strict food rationing," Ramón announces. "Passengers will receive a plate of rice and some fruit once a day."

He uses the impersonal "there will be" and "will receive" so as to not feel responsible for the new regulations.

A murmur of disapproval arises among the people.

"And also it'll be necessary to share one bottle of water a day, between three people," he adds.

"Hey, at least we won't have to get up in the middle of the night to use the bathroom!" someone says, who is called "the sloth" because he spends most of his time sleeping. "You have to look on the bright side!"

Not everybody finds this funny. Rumor has it that there is something fishy about this lack of food.

Night comes, with no dinner. To block out the outcry of complaints and insults that are muttered under their breath, Rosa goes to sleep hidden in her favorite spot: the wooden box. Covered with nets from head to toe, no one suspects she is there. And so she goes to sleep, her stomach empty and her mind full of ghosts. But after a while she wakes up from the itchiness in her head and skin, which has been bothering her since the previous day.

She hears furtive voices, very close by; people are whispering something full of curses. A shrill voice makes her jump.

"I saw Ramón with several boxes of food in the crew's cabin," she hears someone say.

"I told you! Those bastards are hiding the food for themselves"! Another says indignantly.

"We can't put up with this! We have to do something!"

"That's right! The only way to survive is to take command of the ship!"

"A mutiny!" Rosa whispers to herself. She perks up her ears, but the conspirators are now whispering more and more quietly. She gets only snippets of conversation: "Before six ... Where do they keep the weapons? ... Are they really armed? ...I'll tell ...They wake up at six ... The helmsman ... We'll have to take hostages!"

With her eyes open and ears alert to any suspicious movement or sound, Rosa cannot and does not want to go back to sleep. The specter of this disaster left her wide-eyed and completely alert, and with a heavy heart she takes on the responsibility that has fallen on her shoulders. What to do now? Denounce the group to save everyone from a potential disaster? Or keep quiet and avoid the miserable role of informer? Or should she try to talk them out of it and risk being gagged and nailed inside the box, forgotten about, and trapped forever? All three alternatives are unacceptable. She bites her fingernails. As much as she tries to remember, she finds nothing within the folds of her brain that leads her to a wise decision: no Huaorani tale, no Christian parable, no true story that might help her with a model of behavior.

The internal debate leaves her exhausted. Her owl's eyes are now closing and she sinks into the darkness of sleep.

After a sweaty and sleepless night, the group of mutineers begins their preparations and Rosa wakes up, scared. She looks at her watch: it's five in the morning. She hears hurried footsteps, men talking to men, and fragmented, angry words. She recognizes a voice that becomes clearer. It's the man who is making this trip for the second time.

"How are the boatmen going to know we've arrived so they can take us onto the beach?"

"We could swim to the beach."

"Swim? Are you kidding me? I'll bet some of these people could drown in their own piss!"

"We'll have to force the captain to radio them. He's just as illegal as we are—he won't dare do anything. He won't have the guts to turn us in."

"Very well. And you know how to navigate—you've been on this sea, right?"

"Yes, sir. I was a fisherman."

"So, you know how to use charts? Do you know how to determine our position and course and speed to get to where we need to go? Can you read coordinates?"

The fisherman looks at him like he's speaking a foreign language.

"Do you think it's just a matter of grabbing the rudder?" the man continues. "You're all crazy! You don't even know how to read a nautical chart! If you want to play mutineers, go right ahead! I won't stop you. But no one else is going to be crazy enough to join your side!"

The stench of the hold becomes unbearable, and Rosa goes up to the deck. "Like Granddad says, sometimes it's better to let things find their own natural course, like the river," remembers the girl. She watches the group of hungry rebels disperse, with deflated, guilty faces.

The eighth day of the voyage, which Rosa will register as "The Day of the Rat", begins badly.

By midmorning, in the overcrowded hold the thermometer marks 110 degrees and the air is stagnant. There's a little breeze on the deck, but the sun beats down mercilessly. The passengers use makeshift umbrellas to protect themselves from the sun, but this does not prevent heat stroke. Fever and delirium are widespread. Rosa does not take off her straw hat.

Whether from the sun, or some inherent predisposition, the man who was lonesome for his family is on the verge of madness. It's a harmless madness, but still disturbing. He sees a rat, one of those ravenous ship-hold rats that compete with men for a grain of rice, and he convinces the others that the illness and the itches they are enduring are not due to heat, but the bubonic plague that is spreading through the ship.

"Don't touch them! They have the plague!" says the poor man, referring to those who are ill.

"Are you crazy? What plague?" replies another, "They're just hungry rats. Look, I'll cook this one and eat it."

So saying, the man grabs a rat by the tail and heads for the kitchen. The others look at him and spit on the ground. The man is now having a fit of rage. He runs after the other man, hits him on the back and the two fall to the ground wrapped in a furious embrace. The man who had the rat is on top of his attacker, hands around his neck, when several other men intervene and separate them. The rat, safe and sound, darts through a hole in the planks and disappears.

"If you don't control yourself we'll have to tie you up," the captain warns the madman. "And stop talking nonsense. The only plague we have here is you!"

But some are unconvinced. The mere mention of a plague affects those who are most impressionable, and they think they see symptoms of a contagious disease in the welts on their skin.

In fact, many of them are covered from head to toe with rashes, and the itching is a constant torture. Some are scratching their arms until they bleed.

"Look at this. I've got spots all over my arm; maybe the man is right," someone says.

"And I've got in on my head!" a woman adds.

"Let me see," says Rosa, who remembers well her elementary school days. She examines the woman's hair and gives her the verdict. "These are just lice bites— harmless little lice," she says, and she begins to skillfully pick at the woman's hair. Then she shows the woman the crushed parasite, a red spot under her fingernail. "Let's get a bucket with water and drown them all."

"What about these?" a man asks, rolling up his sleeves. He's dressed as if he were going directly to a job interview upon leaving the ship.

"That's from fleas," Rosa says. "See how there's red swelling with a lighter spot in the middle?"

"And these fleas live on rats, because there are no dogs around here!"

"And rat fleas carry the bubonic plague!" says another. "Everybody knows that."

The captain gives them some rat poisoning, diluted so it will cover the whole area. Soon, death squads are formed to kill off the rodents that have become comatose from the diluted dosage.

Rosa and a few others dedicate themselves to the primitive and comforting activity of picking fleas.

On the ninth day at sundown the captain calls all passengers to deck. He tells them that, if there are no difficulties, they will arrive on the following day, God willing, but they should prepare themselves for any emergency.

"We're going to disembark in a frontier town, on the Guatemalan side, called Tecún Umán. You're going to stay in safe houses, with families that work with us, while we wait to cross the border. If anyone gets in trouble with the police, do not, under any circumstance, tell them where you're from, because they'll deport you to Ecuador or to your own country, whichever it is. In Guatemala you're Guatemalans. And in Mexico, Mexicans.

"What about once we're in the United States?" Someone asks.

"Well, there, you're all wetbacks!" says Ramón, using the English pejorative word.

The joke causes laughter among the crew, but it is ignored by most of the passengers. Rosa looks for the word in her dictionary and cannot find it. Like the others, she's embarrassed to ask.

From now on, each one of you has a new name. So you need to destroy your documents right now: your identity documents, your birth certificate, your driver's license—anything that shows your name and nationality.

The people look at him suspiciously. He continues:

"I can't force you to do this; I'm just making a suggestion, because if the police arrest you, you're not going to have time to shove those documents where the sun don't shine."

Nobody finds this is funny and people are still looking suspicious.

Little by little, those who tend to obey authority figures approach him with their documents and, with rather uncertain gestures, throw them into the charcoal, which is burning in an iron grate fastened to the deck. The others, who are doubtful, let out a sigh and hand over their individuality. Rosa also gives in.

The iron bin is getting full. A crew member throws some kerosene into the coal, tosses in a lighted match and ¡boom!! A flame goes up, about three feet high. The crowd jumps back with the flash and the blast of hot air, looking dumbstruck as their identities are twisted and scorched, consumed by the flame. A fine, silky smoke rises and then dissipates into the nocturnal sky. The light − which turns blue when the fire touches a laminated document − is reflected in the pupils of men and women, until finally, everything is reduced to ash.

"I have one last suggestion," says the captain. "You should memorize the phone numbers and addresses for your contacts in the United States, and destroy those, too. You don't want to compromise your family or friends in any way."

After a short time, the crew asks for another round of documents, and soon they also burn and writhe in the flame, until they disappear. They ask again and again, until the crackling fades, and the wind scatters the last ashes, as the last passenger sheds his identity.

"This is a night of the witches", someone mutters. "I can just see the demons dancing around the fire!"

"Like the Inquisition," says an angry man, already regretting having succumbed to peer pressure. "We've been wiped out! We're nobodies now!"

"So why did you do it? Nobody forced you!"

"I don't know, I guess nobody likes to stand out. It's always easier to do what everyone else is doing."

After serving a plate of dry rice with some fish that has been caught in the nets, a crew member passes around a list of common Guatemalan names for people to choose the one they want. Rosa chooses "Rigoberta Mam," because it sounds exotic, but also familiar. She feels comforted thinking that just one vowel separates her from her mom.

91

That night the passengers go to bed feeling strangely uneasy. With no papers to certify that they are who they think they are, they are left feeling perplexed and pensive.

III

On the blue afternoon of the tenth day, just before sundown, someone shouts that he sees whales lying motionless in the distance. The captain explains that those are small islands, and that the line they see to the East between the water and the sky is the coast of Guatemala. A spark of joy runs down the boat, and shouts of praise rise up in the splendor of the afternoon. Even the sea creatures seem to rejoice at the news. Flying-fish leap up and, with a bubbly splash, fall back flat onto the wrinkled sea. Traveling left and right, colorful schools of fish follow the boat in a coordinated martial show. As the coast becomes more visible, hundreds of seagulls, fly up from the crests, landing on the rails and on the roof of the cabin, with a chorus of salty shrieks. They shriek in vain, since the passengers don't have a crumb to share; today they are more famished than ever.

At the other edge of the sky, the sun spills mercurial red and in the evening light a few albatrosses can be seen plying the air towards the ship. An hour later, late at night, they reach their destination in the north of the country. Darkness reveals the gleam of coastal lights. The ship's engine falls silent and soon those who were sick of the sound begin to feel a strange sensation, like they are floating in a void.

As a precaution, the captain refrains from using the radio. Instead, he signals their arrival by flashing a lantern in the direction of watercraft lying in wait a certain distance from the shore. Soon, several of these motorboats are moving in the ship's direction.

The passengers are herded in groups of ten down the ladders and into boats. One by one, they speed toward the beach, and then return to pick up more passengers. After half an hour, almost all of the passengers are on shore. The last boat returns for its final human load, including Rosa, who, remembering the teachings of her family, waited until her elders disembarked.

The star-hung sky is more beautiful than ever. Where is her constellation? She, who was born in September and is a Libra, the sign of equilibrium according to the cosmology of the white people, knows that after all suffering better times always arrive.

However, after a few minutes the motor stops with a puff, puff, puff.

"This damn motor is giving me more trouble!" says the launch pilot.

He yanks repeatedly at the motor to no avail.

"Are we out of gas?"

"It's the spark plugs."

Something is in the water. Someone screams. In the moonlight an enormous shape rises from the water on the right side. Its form is difficult to make out, but the glacial reflection of an inhuman eye staring at them as it circles the launch is clearly visible.

"What was that?" somebody whispers.

"A shark," explains the pilot, hardly moving his lips.

The people's neck hairs stand up straight, but no one utters a sound. Shortly, a brilliant silver back with a pointy fin shines in the moonlight, rises, and submerges again under the dark surface on the other side of the boat.

"This place is infested with sharks!" a man exclaims, with a trembling voice.

"Don't exaggerate. There are only two of them, so you can calm down – anyway, sharks normally don't attack boats."

The pilot seems nonchalant. If he isn't, he puts on a convincing act.

"Normally? What do you mean by that?"

"There are extremely rare cases."

"How rare?"

"One in a hundred. In the whole world."

Something about this statistic does not reassure the passengers. And perhaps it doesn't even reassure the man who cites it.

"So, are we going to stay here forever? Can't you call for help?" insists the man. He cannot hide the terror in his voice.

"No, we can't use the radio."

"What about a cell phone?"

"We don't have those here. We're in Guatemala, not Ecuador."

He flashes his lantern at the other boats that are up ahead. But no one on the other boat seems to notice. Everyone is fixated on the coastline of Tecún Umán. Their lights move further and further away until they are just tiny points bobbing in the night.

"Do you have a weapon to defend us with?" says the same man, anxiously.

"Yes, but calm down. Nothing's going to happen," says the boatman. To appease him, he opens his jacket and reveals a revolver hanging from his belt.

"Use it, damn it!"

"I told you, it's not necessary. It could make things worse," replies the pilot, exasperated.

A few minutes pass in tense silence. Everyone is shocked when the man, who is having a panic attack, lunges at the boatman and grabs the revolver. As he aims at the shark's head, the other man yells:

"Don't shoot, don't shoot!"

But it's too late. The man has already discharged various bullets into the animal's head. The shark shakes and thrashes in his own bloody foam. The boatman tries to grab the weapon from the wild man. Others help, grabbing the man from behind. All this movement causes the boat to rock dangerously to one side.

"Sit down! Careful! Everybody sit down!"

Women scream. Men curse. The boatman recovers his revolver and punches the man's head, but he is still out of control. He only quiets down when someone threatens to throw him overboard with the shark. They tie him up by the hands and feet.

The animal has disappeared, but there is an enormous bloodstain on the surface. The shark's agonized movements agitate the water, and this is even more nerve-wracking than when the creature was alive. Between insults and obscenities, the boatman explains that the smell of blood and the unusual vibrations in the water will attract more sharks.

Sure enough, in a few minutes several more sharks circle the boat in a hunting frenzy. The flapping of fins and the animals' backs bump the boat and rock it, back and forth. They are under the boat, beside it, and all around it. They feel its presence.

"They'll wait patiently," someone says, staring into the sea wide-eyed, "until one of us falls into the water."

"No one's going to fall in," answers the boatman, "unless one of you is drunk."

"I've heard sharks can leap really high and land in a boat," someone says, choking with fear.

"Don't talk that way, man!"

"Have you seen their mouths? What if they bite off a piece of the boat?"

"Shut up! Sharks don't eat human flesh!"

"Maybe they don't eat it. But I think that tonight they're out for revenge," says another, almost crying. "Why would they be swimming in circles around us? Why won't they go away? What else would they want? We should just shoot every one of them."

"If we do that, more will come," says the pilot under his breath, while opening the chamber to count the bullets.

Rosa trusts her lucky star, but Libra is nowhere to be found in this sky, so far from hers.

7. Drop Houses

I

Camouflaged in vegetation near the beach, several pickups are already waiting for the contingent of undocumented immigrants that have just disembarked, to take them to their new residences. As is practical in these cases, the pickup cargo is concealed with canvas.

After having been packed together in the hold, the rolling firm land puts the travelers in a loquacious and optimistic mood.

"When I come back to Ecuador from the United States, I'm going to take an airplane, friends. First class!" Someone says, practically yelling the words.

"Is that right? Will you be able to?" says some incredulous voice.

"Of course we can. The damned visa is not necessary for leaving, didn't you know?"

"Yes," someone says, " Down the mountain, all the saints help."

One by one the pickups drive their human cargo to different houses, part of the coyote web already well-established for years on the periphery of the city. Zabala manages ten families, and each one can shelter some 20 illegals, divided by gender as possible.

Arriving at their respective houses, the elation is generalized, but no one delays very much in celebrations because there is a priority: telephone calls to the families. These calls are made collect. In minutes the air is saturated with emotion from the kisses and hugs sent at a distance.

When the man in charge delivers his last human cargo, the owner of the house complains:

"You said you were going to bring me twenty 'chickens'. Here there are only ten!"

Only then does the other man remember that he has not counted the boats as they disgorge their passengers on the beach, and as he has been ordered to do. He drives back to the landing location and finds it deserted. He scans the horizon. He signals

96

with his lantern in various directions, and at a distance a light responds, turning on and off intermittently.

After an hour of reproaches and negotiations, the man arranges a boatman who, for an exorbitant price, agrees to rescue the broken motorboat.

The livid faces of the passengers reveal the horror of the wait. Some of them are soaked from the whales slapping the water with their tails; others have wet themselves from fear; and all are suffering from some degree of hypothermia. Only the maniac who shot the shark is relaxed, on the floor of the motorboat, under the effects of the blows given by his companions. The sharks, tired of their frustrating hunt, have disappeared.

The man ties a rope to the boat, tows it to shore and leaves it beached beside a rotting whale. With legs still shaking, the ten rescued travelers pile into the van and release all the accumulated stress with prayers of thanks or grim jokes.

"The sharks in their home, and we in ours!" proclaims Rosa, clutching her wooden talisman with hands stiff from the cold.

She is assigned to a residence that has two small bedrooms, one for the travelers and the other for the owners. As they all are, this one is also humble and in the outskirts of the town, in one of those dark neighborhoods with vacant lots characteristic of poor cities. But, in contrast to the others, here is a small garden and a backyard with some animals, next to a stream. The house is surrounded by an adobe wall with a wire mesh gate at the entrance.

When Rosa arrives, a woman with muscular arms named Blanca identifies herself as the cook, and is already in the room with the women, wiping her hands on her colorful apron. She tells them that if they wish to bathe, the limit for each one is five minutes, because the water in the tank runs out quickly. No one is bothered by this. Five minutes will be sufficient to rid themselves of the deposit of white salty layers that have lodged themselves on their skin and in their ears, and rinse out their matted hair after so many salt water baths. She also announces the meal schedule and the responsibilities that, as a group, they must undertake, since they will be lodging there for several days. This includes cleaning house and attention to the garden and the animals. It seems there are chickens, a cow that provides milk for the visitors, and a horse.

During the dinner, which consists of eggs and corn tortillas that receive exaggerated praise, the women draw straws for the tasks each of them will get, and afterwards they negotiate exchanges amongst themselves, in accordance with each one's preferences. Rosa is assigned the bathroom.

"Rosa, you are a country girl. Wouldn't you prefer to take care of the animals, and I will do the bathroom?" a woman proposes. "I have never milked a cow in my life and I'm not interested in learning it now. Besides, there's a huge dog out there and I wouldn't even think of getting near it. But you are Shuar, yes? You raise dogs."

"I'm not Shuar, I am Huaorani," Rosa explains, suppressing her impatience. "People from the mountains think that all Amazonian natives are Shuar," she muses, with a certain indignation. "Well, it doesn't matter. We do raise dogs for hunting. I'm not afraid. It's a deal!"

The room has only one table and a small wooden closet, and they have to spread out their sleeping bags or blankets and covers on the tile floor.

"I'm going to grab this little place far from the window," says one of the women. "I don't want anyone to steal me during the night."

"¿Are you sure you don't want them to steal you?"

"That depends! It depends on who's doing the stealing!"

Laughter converts the harem into a noisy hen house, until Blanca's figure appears in the door, clapping her hands, blackened with soot.

"To bed now, ladies, it's two in the morning. What a noisy bunch you are!"

"Yes, yes, excuse us, doña Blanca."

"Shh, shh, be quiet now, ladies."

"Yah, be quiet now, parrots."

In this and in the other shelters where the 200 passengers rest during their clandestine pilgrimage to the North, a well-deserved peace reigns. Even though they are squeezed into small rooms, here no anxious yells are heard like those during the claustrophobic nights on the ship. Nor is there a rocking boat that makes them sick, nor a wind to frighten them. This night, sleep comes over them sweetly and peacefully, like a lullaby.

II

By 8 A.M. Rosa has already finished watering the garden and milking the cow—who began mooing very early—and the guests have dipped their biscuits in cups of warm milk. Anyone who wanted coffee and bread could deposit a quetzal into a jar, for the right to a teaspoon of instant coffee and a roll sprinkled with sugar. Hot water and milk are on the house.

The floors have been swept, the dishes washed and the bathroom scrubbed. Rosa scatters seeds for the chickens. Then she turns to the dog, humming quietly, and holding out a bowl that Blanca gave her. It is full of cheap meat and giblets.

The dog's name is *Conde*, and he is an enormous and fearsome- looking brute given to the homeowner by a Brazilian friend. It is a ferocious animal, they say, a mix of the most dangerous dogs, bred during colonial times in Brazil to pursue escaped slaves—and to keep them in line. This is why the breed is called *Cão de Fila*, meaning "dog of the line". People in the house have tried to pronounce this name with that unique Portuguese nasality, without much success. Instead of *cão de fila*, they call it *"con" de fila*. That's where the nickname, *Conde*, came from, and that is why the animal has a name, explained his owner, plus a noble title. [4] During the day, the terrible Conde is kept behind the house, penned up behind a bamboo fence. Each bamboo post is slightly apart from the next, allowing Conde to thrust his snout through the openings. At night however, he is let loose in the front yard, which is also fenced off. This is why the women don't dare to go out after sundown, although in reality they wouldn't have much reason to do so anyway. They have been warned that the presence of many strangers near the house might awaken suspicions. After all, it is illegal to give shelter to undocumented immigrants.

---

[4] *Translator's note: *Conde*, "Count" in English.

"Don't go near Conde, he'll bite your hand off," Blanca has warned Rosa. "Just slide the gourd in under the gate. I'll let him loose in the afternoon."

"His fleas would probably bite me first," Rosa thinks. She doesn't think any dog is untamable. Rosa knows about dogs. She sits down on the ground in front of the fence with the bowl of food in her lap and watches him. Conde's snout pokes out through the openings in the fence. He snarls, bares his teeth, backs up a ways and goes running into the fence. It wobbles with each thrust of his huge paws. He barks furiously, and with each bark, the flesh hanging on the sides of his mouth flutters like a red flag. At each snarl or bark, Rosa responds with soft words. She sings to him, taking care not to look him directly in the eyes. Then she pretends that she is eating. She whistles—a long, piercing whistle used by the Huaorani to call their hunting dogs in the jungle. Soon, she gives him his first hunk of food, which he snatches in a flash of teeth. She gives him another, and another. Before each bite of food, she whistles to him. Pretty soon, his canine mind understands that a whistle equals food—food from this new hand that is not big and gnarly, but soft and delicate. Conde begins licking his lips.

As soon as Rosa perceives that she's won the dog's trust, she opens the gate, puts the bowl under his huge head, and waits. When Conde finishes eating she brings him water. He laps it up noisily while she caresses his neck and scratches him under his chin. She feels his warm breath, and his cool, moist snout, sniffing her hands. A happy feeling wells up inside of her.

The intimacy of this encounter reminds Rosa that she needs to call her mom. She leaves the dog's pen, remembering to lock the gate. Rosa knows from experience that tomorrow she'll repeat this same ritual, and that on the third day, she will be able to open the pen and put the bowl under the dog's nose with no ceremony other than a whistle. It wouldn't be hard to teach him a few commands, she thinks. Conde seems intelligent.

As always, when she calls her mother, Rosa leaves a message and a call back number with somebody else. At the moment, her mother is probably in a field picking fruit or vegetables. An hour later, the telephone rings and an anxious voice asks for Rosa. The conversation is short, but comforting to

Alba. Rosa tells her mother about her trip and only briefly describes a stormy afternoon, and a night with "very large fish." Alba is also holding back, Rosa thinks, because when she asks about her health, her mother answers very briefly and the quickly changes the subject.

"I'm going to make you banana cake when you arrive, Rosita, the one you love. Do you remember it, darling?"

Rosa tries to remember, but no matter how hard she tries, she can't bring back the memory. Recovering some lost memory of her mother is always risky, because it makes her sad.

In the yard, beside a neglected rosebush, there is a hand pump that brings up water from the well. Rosa pumps and fills a bucket with water. What if her mother is really sick? What if she gets to the United States and it's too late? What kind of sickness does she have? And why is it taking don Zabala so long to organize the border crossing to Mexico for once and for all? She pours water over her head and shampoos her hair, wishing she could wash her worries away. She braids her long hair and tells her sorrows to get into the thick twists, where they'll be trapped, and won't be able to wiggle their way into her head again.

Yes, I had better leave this sadness for another day, Rosa tells herself, because there are still chores to do today. She still has to attend to the horse.

His name is Telegram. Blanca has warned Rosa that she must also be careful with him, because he's an ornery horse, who tends to kick and bite. Rosa's only responsibility is to be sure there is food and water in his stall. Rosa misses her horse. She wonders if Gabriel will remember to bathe her, clean her hooves, and brush out the twigs and thistles that get stuck in her tail and mane; and above all, not let the horseflies suck her blood.

She walks inside the paddock. Telegram is a gold and white palomino, his tail and mane a silvery white—a variety that Rosa has never seen. She falls for him instantly. He is little more than a colt, not very large, but very spirited, and soon Rosa is stroking his fine, lustrous face. The horse snorts and tosses his head back. His brown pupils, showing flashes of ancient eras, shine in the center of a white background. His eyes roll, then steadily glare at Rosa. Rosa gives him a little grain in the palm of her hand. She scratches him softly and gives him some more grain, feeling that a little friendship is forming between them.

The day's chores are done, and Rosa goes to the house to rewrite the letter lost in the storm.

Don Zabala arrives late, after dinner. As he promised Rosa's grandfather, at this point he and his partner are going to take charge of the border crossing.

After introducing his colleagues and greeting Rosa and a few other acquaintances and fellow Ecuadorians, he explains the plan. "The Mexican border is very close. It's just a matter of crossing a small stream, the Suchiate, and Ciudad Hidalgo is on the other side. From there we'll take you in pickups to another town, Tapachula, to catch the train. The train will take you all the way to the U.S. border.

"When are we going to cross this river Suchi ...?" a young woman asks.

"Suchiate."

"Yeah."

"We have to wait another three or four days. My partners in Huehuetan, on the other side, are really busy right now with another group and they aren't ready for us yet."

The women do not want to stay shut up any longer. They complain that they are not prisoners, and need to go out and shop for personal things.

"This is a dangerous place," the coyote replies, "it's full of drugs dealers, gun traffickers and prostitutes. There's even child prostitution. There are all kinds of gangsters and bad people around here. Believe me – you're much safer inside this house."

"But we don't even have soap!"

"And no phone cards for long-distance calls!"

"There's not even any toilet paper!"

"Okay," don Zabala replies, somewhat taken aback, "if you want to go out, be very, very careful. Don't go out all together; go out in groups of three or four, at most, and don't go out alone. And never, ever go out after dark! I'll be back to update you on our plans in a couple days."

While don Zabala is engaging in this exchange with the women, one of his assistants stares at Rosa. Rosa notices and tries to ignore it. Pretty soon, the men say good-bye and are off.

III

The following day, the women take turns going out, walking arm-in-arm in groups of three. Rosa prefers to stay behind to rest, she tells them, and asks Mabel to buy her a bar of soap and some chocolate. In reality, she has other plans.

Rosa's house is the last one on the block. In front of the house, ditches filled with putrid, standing water line the dirt streets, where dogs and pigs fight over leftover bits of edible matter. Directly behind the house, where the patio ends, and on the other side of the stream, a wooded area is visible through the window. It's been a long time since Rosa has breathed pure forest air, sitting under a tree, listening to the rustling leaves. She figures there is no danger there; danger, don Zabala said, is in the village.

Rosa doesn't *actually* believe in that plethora of nocturnal spirits moving through the jungle, sometimes crying, sometimes laughing, as her grandfather does. And yet, she doesn't know how to explain a call that pulsates within her, in those magic moments when she has crossed the threshold of sleep, a call that whispers: "Rosa, Rosita, we are here." Once, when she was a little girl, she heard this voice so clearly that she went out of the house just before dawn. Her mother found her in the front yard, only half dressed, her gaze lost in the dark trees rustling on the other side of the river.

And there it is again, an ancient voice, a surprising voice. She does not know where it comes from. She heard it this morning and it still resounds in her mind, with its wild Huaorani grammar.

The owners of the house are having a siesta and the cook is gone for the day. The sun is boiling hot. This is the quiet moment just after midday, when eyes droop with drowsiness, and animals hide in their haunts; the precise moment Rosa has been waiting for. She leaves the house and walks toward the horse. She finds him swishing flies away with his splendid tail. Rosa sits on a rock and watches him. She loves the smell of the horse mixed with the dry smell of the hot rock.

"We're going to go out today, Telegram."

Amazonian Indians are not horse people, and there is no equestrian tradition in Rosa's family. But on the farm, two horses are used as pack animals. Just the children and Uncle know how to ride them, and only bareback. The pack saddles are wooden constructions with sharp, uncomfortable angles, made to accommodate cargo, and far less accommodating than the bare back of one's horse.

Rosa finds some rope hanging from the barbed wire and does what she's done so many times with her own horse: a short loop goes around the nose, a longer one fits behind the ears, and the last, long one, connects with the first and makes a rein. She does this with gentle precision and without haste. At each step the horse resists, but she does not become intimidated.

"This guy just needs a little love," says Rosa, scratching and soothing him once more, and whispering to him sweetly. Telegram tosses his neck and looks at her with his brilliant, liquid eyes, almost humanly perceptive, and accepts her offer of affection.

"There we are" she thinks. "We're friends now." Grabbing his mane with both hands while holding the bow in her right hand, Rosa jumps, and in one clean movement, she is on his back. Telegram, not used to this sudden movement, without a saddle and cinch to prepare him, stirs up the dust, whinnies, rolls his eyes and flattens his ears against his neck. He rears, giving Rosa a hard jolt, hoping to send her flying. She clings to his mane and tries not to scream.

The colt continues bucking, throwing himself into the air and rearing up on his back legs, and the rebelliousness continues while she keeps a tight grip on his mane and tries to calm him down. But now the animal explodes, as if stung by a horde of yellow jackets. The gate is open and they shoot through in the direction of the stream, which is just a trickle. With pounding hooves spitting rocks, dirt and water in every direction, Rosa gallops down a trail that passes through corn rows and sugarcane, into the jungle.

The ground shakes under the hooves of the runaway horse. Rosa flies along, her heels buried in his sides and her head bent down low, dodging limbs, screaming and celebrating this joyful madness. Her strong arms and sinewy legs, strong from years of work on the farm, keep her from flying through the air. Only when the trail becomes extremely narrow does the horse slow down. Panting now, he whinnies and snorts, and begins to move forward at a fast walk. Rosa appreciates his soft, delicate gait as he moves through thickets of leaf, fern, vine and jungle flowers, reminding her of another jungle she knows very well.

The colt is tame now, and their bond has been formed from mutual shock. Rosa moves deeper and deeper into the forest, hardly noticing the time, until the afternoon, tangled in light and shadows, begins to wane. Turning the animal around and heading back down the trail, Rosa sees a man in the middle of the trail, whittling a piece of wood and making a pile of splinters.

"What are you doing here all alone?" asks the man.

Rosa is not sure, but she believes she is facing don Zabala's assistant; and the sense of alarm that she felt right down to her skin, the day of the assault in the bus, in Guayaquil, immediately springs up again. She smells danger. She does not answer him. Pulling mightily on the rein, she swings the horse back around, to see if there is another trail. She feels the man's eyes on her back. Yes, he is on foot and she is mounted, she realizes; but she did see a rifle slung across his back.

A shiver courses through her body, chilling her skin, like the water of a smooth lagoon that quickens under a breath of wind. Urging Telegram on, he goes down, and up again, effortless, in a wooden ravine; and then he runs away at a brisk trot.

When the evening air becomes colder and the sun more elusive, and when unfamiliar birds scream with unknown voices, Rosa realizes that the new trail she has taken is not taking her back to her residence.

She knows it from the slanted beam of light pouring through the coconut trees leaves, like a moving fan. She tries to retrace her steps, but she does not recognize the trail nor the multicolored bark on the trees she sees on either side. She doesn't see any hoof prints in the soil. Turning around again, Rosa and Telegram squeeze into a different, narrower trail, which in a short time, leads them right back to the same line of mottled trunks. She realizes that they are going around in circles and that they are lost. Her shock, displeasure and nervousness from that encounter made her forget the golden rule of the Huaorani: memorize the trail.

The light is disappearing from the forest. She lets go of the reins and lets the horse choose the way. A half-hour goes by and the beams of light have become so tenuous that at any moment they will disappear altogether, leaving Rosa with only a half-shadowy light. Telegram picks up the pace until finally, they find the familiar trail. Lurking in the shadows in front of them is the same man, still standing there.

Rosa panics, and terror constricts her throat for a moment. Then a shrill and penetrating warrior cry cuts through the air, provoking a fluttering of birds in the treetops above. She digs in her heels and flicks the rope over the horse's sides. Telegram shoots forward like an arrow, with the girl clinging to his neck, and the trail resounds with the tremendous rumbling of hoof beats. She gallops toward the man, who leaps aside just in time.

Flying hooves destroy his hat.

8. October 5th

I

The house sheltering Rosa has illustrious visitors.

The living room table is long and narrow. Actually, it's nothing more than three side-by-side planks pushed together on top of two sawhorses. A wooden bench on each side accommodates ten or so people. When all are seated around the table—the travelers, don Zabala and a Spanish priest—the coyote introduces his guest:

"Father Javier, who's come from Spain to work with the Catholic Alliance of Tecún Umán, has been very kind to come see you and give you a blessing, because tomorrow we depart."

The group welcomes this news with cries of joy.

"Calm down, ladies, this sounds like a chicken coop!" one woman says. "Let's let don Zabala talk, and Father Javier, too. Thank you for coming, Father Javier. You don't know how much we appreciate it."

"Yes, yes, thank you, Father," the others respond in chorus.

"Dear sisters, the Church is not against the immigration laws of any country. However, it also does not accuse those who, due to *force majeure,* are obliged to abandon their home countries to support the families they leave behind. The right—I don't say 'duty,' but 'right',"—the priest emphasizes, "to a good job is a human right. The Catholic Alliance of Tecún Umán understands your unquestionable desire to find work. For this reason I would like to bless your trip and to bless each one of you individually."

So saying, the priest sprinkles holy water on every head and invites them all to join him in prayer.

That night, the ladies go to sleep with a beatific smile on their faces.

"I think that blessings in Latin, like Father Javier's, are holier than blessings in Spanish, don't you think?" someone comments.

"I hope so!"

"God willing!"

October 5th is the anxiously-awaited day of departure, and this morning emotions are already running high. There's quite a stir among the women, as they anxiously pack up their meager belongings. The bells call them to Mass, and the women head out to the church in groups of three, its white silhouette appearing through the morning mist on top of a hill.

"I can't go right now," Rosa excuses herself, "I have to call my Mom because it's Sunday. Maybe you can pray for me?"

"That's getting off a little too easy! And how would you like your prayer, in Latin or Spanish?" the women joke, with mock seriousness.

"In Huaorani," Rosa responds, in the same tone.

The owners of the house tell her, as they leave, to padlock the gate from the inside.

Rosa goes to the living room and calls the United States. She has five precious minutes left on her calling card and she and her mother talk until the time is almost up.

"Be careful, darling!" Alba says, with tears in her voice.

"Don't worry, Mom, everything's going to be okay. I'll be there with you soon!"

Rosa hangs up, feeling a little anxious. She noticed her mother sounded tired and weak, unusual for this normally energetic and decisive woman. Rosa would love so much to be with her, taking care of her!

She goes to her room to begin packing.

It's still before eight in the morning, and a little cold. Remembering that her clothes are on the clothesline, she hurries out to get them. She ties her heavy, long hair at the back of her neck; then she begins folding her few pieces of clothing, placing them neatly into a basket. A shadow passes over the clothing. Rosa looks up at the sky and sees the sun. A passing cloud, she tells herself.

Again, the white laundry becomes shaded in the form of a body. Rosa turns around and her stomach churns. On the other side of the wire gate, standing against the sunlight, is the repulsive figure of the coyote's assistant, leering at her with an idiotic smile.

"Why don't you open up so we can have a little chat?" the man says.

"I'm not allowed to open the gate for anyone," Rosa responds.

"Too bad. Guess I'll have to hop the fence," the man says, climbing up the gate and jumping down onto the patio.

"Stop! You can't come in here! Get out! Out!" Rosa screams.

"Don't be silly. I just want to talk. You owe me an apology, remember? Your horse stomped on my best hat!" he says.

Rosa wants to run in house and lock herself inside, but the man grabs her by the wrist.

"I just want a little kiss. Be a nice girl, just one little kiss for the hat you ruined."

"No! Get your hands off me and get out of here!"

"You'll be sorry if you fight me, okay? It'll be worse, so be nice to me and don't piss me off."

The man's eyes dart around the premises. The walls are high. There'll be no witnesses. He jerks Rosa's hair, painfully, dragging her toward the shade of a tree. When she feels the man's arm grabbing her chest from behind, she pinches the inside of his arm, between his elbow and armpit.

"Agh! You bitch!" Screams the man, in pain. Now he is furious.

With one movement, he throws her to the ground and pins her down. His breath reeks of alcohol, leaving Rosa momentarily breathless. She defends herself, biting his hand furiously, but the man is heavy and strong. He tries to rip her blouse with one hand, covering her mouth with the other. Rosa grabs two of his fingers and bends them backwards. The man loosens his grip and curses her. She screams and jams a bony knee between his legs; he lets out a yell and slaps her across the face. She screams even louder.

"Scream all you want! There's not a soul in the house or in the whole neighborhood—everybody's at mass! See what happens when you don't go to mass?   No one's going to hear you, you stupid bitch!"

Rosa screams with all the strength left in her lungs. The man is on top of her and rips open her blouse, bursting the buttons. He does not notice a massive, hairy brown creature coming toward him like a cannonball from behind the house, until it lands on his back. The man lets out a shriek and turns onto his side. Rosa jumps up and sees blood pouring down the back of the man's shirt.

"Enough! Don't kill him!" she shouts.

The beast turns his enormous mouth toward her, dripping with drool and blood. She lets out a short, loud whistle, and says in a firm voice:

"Leave him alone, Conde!"

Conde gives his prisoner one more snap before letting him go, and then obediently throws himself down in front of Rosa. "Thank God!" She says, "he hasn't forgotten my whistle!"

The man gets up, dizzy. Hunched over with pain, he fumbles for his pistol. His trembling, bloody arm aims at the dog. Rosa jumps up to stop him, but he shoves her to the ground. For Conde, this is a sign to attack again and he leaps up onto him. The man aims his gun again at the dog, but Conde's teeth are already around his jugular. A bullet lands on the adobe wall.

"Let him go, Conde!" Rosa exclaims.

The man falls down, inert, in a puddle of blood, which the parched earth immediately absorbs. Rosa runs across the patio and disappears behind the house, with the dog galloping behind.

II

Channel 11 filmed the rescue as they were being pulled out of the excavation. Despite his psychological state of shock, he had had a moment of lucidity and asked Louis not to give his name to the reporters. That way if *Univisión* picked up the story there was no chance that some busybody from the Hispanic community would call his family and drop the bomb. The last thing he wanted was to worry his parents.

A few days later, with a well-earned 300 dollars in his pocket and stitches on his head hidden under his hat, Ernesto went to the bus station. There he exchanged 100 dollars for quetzals, bought a ticket and water canteen, and separated a bit of change from the rest of the quetzals that he hid in the bottom of his backpack. He put one 100 dollars bill in each of his tennis shoes. Before going back to the hotel he called his parents to tell them that tomorrow he would go to Guatemala. They tried to dissuade him, though without much conviction this time, because they knew it was a lost cause.

Riding a bus that struggles to climb the Cuchumatanes mountain range in northern Guatemala, Ernesto goes over in his mind the events of the past two days and is even more amazed by the unpredictability of his life.

He is just 120 kilometers from the border town where Rosa is staying.

The Pan-American Highway winds through rugged mountains interspersed with lush, cool valleys. From the highest part of the mountain the silhouette of a volcano can be seen in the distance.

The young country school teacher seated beside Ernesto explains that Cuchumatán means, "joining higher forces" in the Mam language.

"Is that your native language?" he asks.

"No, my native tongue is Quiché."

Nestled between the peaks, low-lying valleys bloom with hundreds of villages bordered by rivers, naturally isolated from each other by the undulating topography.

"The valleys are beautiful," says Ernesto.

He observes the natural symmetry in the way these isolated communities are scattered among the mountains.

"Yes, they really are beautiful. And now people can finally return to these villages," says the teacher. "I just came back six months ago."

"Back from where?"

"From exile."

Ernesto frowns, puzzled.

"From The Violence."

The teacher realizes that Ernesto doesn't know what that term means in Guatemala. Lowering his voice he begins to explain that, when he was very young, his family escaped the soldiers who invaded his village, burning and killing. They walked endless trails for days and nights in long lines, until they arrived at a refugee camp in Mexico. They lived in exile for almost ten years. With each phrase, the teacher pauses and raises vigilant eyes to see if he is being overheard by any suspicious eavesdroppers.

"Why did the soldiers attack the villages?" Ernesto asks, also lowering his voice.

"They said we were communists, enemies of the country, that we helped the guerrillas. But it wasn't true. Maybe some people did, I don't know. But to catch one guerrilla fighter or sympathizer they killed thousands of innocent people."

"Thousands?"

"Over 200,000 dead and disappeared since The Violence began in 1959.

"Why didn't I ever see this on the news in my country?"

"Who knows. I think governments protect each other. Who knows."

"What about now?"

"Now they say the villages are safe. They promised us peace. We'll see. I hope it's true. But what about you? You're from the north, so what are you doing here?"

"I'm looking for my family," Ernesto explains, "because I'm adopted. They might be from Esperanza, near Quetzaltenango."

It's hard for him to pronounce the names of these Mayan villages: Huehuetenango, Quetzaltenango, Chichicastenango, but he likes the way they sound. Quetzaltenango means "land of the quetzal," his traveling companion explains.

"The quetzal is a magnificent bird with a long, multicolored tail," he says, taking a coin from his pocket and showing Ernesto the bird that is stamped on it. "It's not easy to see one, but if you go into the high mountains at dawn and keep very quiet, you might see one. I often take tourists and ornithologists to a place near my village where some quetzals still make their nests."

After a few long moments, Ernesto exclaims, "I would love to see a quetzal!"

Ernesto adds seeing the Mayan's sacred bird to his wish list. After all, he's kind of multicolored himself.

"I'll take you if you want," the teacher offers. "But we should get off at Huehue and go east to Cobán. That's a bit of a detour for you."

"That's okay!" he says excitedly.

After getting off the highway, Ernesto and the teacher take another bus line. Several hours later they arrive at a crossroads called El Limón. The bus driver announces that passengers headed north to Chisec will not be able to continue because the road is closed.

That's not a problem for Ernesto and his new acquaintance. The other travelers are disappointed but don't complain. Only one person manages to ask why the road is closed.

"Orders from Lieutenant Cachán. Looks like there's a problem near Chisec."

In another few meters the bus stops. The road is blocked by a military vehicle and several armed soldiers.

"Everyone off!" one of them bellows.

The passengers file off the bus in silence.

"Turn around, facing the bus," another barks, "hands in the air!"

A third soldier, using the same arrogant tone, orders them to hold up their IDs in their right hand.

"What do they want?" Ernesto asks in a low voice as he takes his passport out of his pocket.

"I don't know, I guess they're looking for anything suspicious. But don't worry. You're a gringo so they'll be nice to you. They won't even pat you down when they see your passport."

The soldiers begin pat-downs looking for weapons, and examine their documents.

"Everything looks good. You can get back on the bus! But not you. Get over here!"

Ernesto feels the tip of a rifle on his back and turns around, thinking they'll realize their mistake.

"I'm talking to you!"

"To me?"

"Yes, you. Don't be a smart ass!" one of the soldiers snaps at him.

113

Ernesto feels a blow to the chest, but it's just his own heart. Sudden fear grips his belly. He has no idea what his crime might be.

They tie his hands behind his back and push them into a Jeep. The last thing he sees before being driven away is his new friend's face pressed to the window of the bus, his expression clouded with fear and impotence.

The military car turns toward Cobán.

Within minutes the boy is drenched in sweat. The blood coursing in his veins like a wild river leaves him trembling. His voice quivers in his throat when he tells them they've made a mistake, that he's a tourist.

The soldier in the passenger seat turns around and, pointing his pistol at Ernesto's forehead, threatens to blow his brains out if he doesn't shut up. The driver turns on the radio and blasts music, then lights a cigarette.

Ernesto has difficulty believing it's not a nightmare. His mind fills with scenes of torture: punches, cigarettes burns, chains, pain, all the horrifying scenarios that tend to inhabit the mind when least wanted.

He curls up into a ball to protect himself from them. He imagines the motives or non-motives they have for detaining him. Nothing makes sense. How can he defend against senselessness?

After 15 agonizing minutes the car stops in front of a building with a sign that reads: Military Zone 21. Two soldiers swing open the gates and the vehicle drives into a large courtyard. A flagpole in the middle holds a fluttering Guatemalan flag.

"I see we have we have news!" says the lieutenant when Ernesto is pulled from the Jeep and shoved into the main office.

"We think he has a fake passport, Lieutenant. He must have stolen it from some gringo and changed the photo. He's probably one of the rebels from Chisec. We brought him in so you could decide."

Suddenly relieved at finding out the reason for this madness, and hoping to be listened to, Ernesto blurts: "I did not steal it! It's mine! I'm North American!"

One of the soldiers gives him a backhanded slap.

"Search him and lock him up" the lieutenant orders. "I'll interrogate him tomorrow. And you," he says, glaring at Ernesto, "shut the hell up or you'll get another one!"

III

Less than 200 kilometers away, to the west, two women are walking up a hill. Another two join them on the trail.

"So, did you hear the news?"

"No. Tell us!"

"We can't go tonight. Don Zabala told us that the river crossing, this …Suchi …is closed".

"Closed? How can they close a river? I can't believe our bad luck!"

"It's not the river that's closed! It's the road that goes to the village, on the other shore, in Mexico. I guess someone told the patrol on the other side that a big clandestine group was planning to cross over. That's us, of course. And now there are tons of border policemen blocking our way. Zabala says that the state of Chiapas in Mexico is the first immigrant traffic checkpoint and there's no way he's going to fall into their trap."

"Why do the Mexicans care about us? We're not going to stay in Mexico!"

"Not us, but other people do, because there's more work in Mexico. Besides, the government has orders, apparently from the United States, not to let anyone pass through Mexico from Central America, or from any other countries, without a visa, because they know that all they want is to get into the States. That's why there are so many patrols guarding the border now."

"Why does Mexico have to obey the U.S.?"

"Seriously? Haven't you ever heard the saying that the big fish eats the smaller one?"

"Okay, I get it. So where does don Zabala say we're going to cross?"

"I'm not sure, I didn't really get it. Did you?" she asks the other woman who came with her.

"He mentioned something about a taking different route, and he said they were going to get other buses to take us to another crossing. I think it's about a day's trip from here. It's pretty far, but it's safer, he said. And also … Hey! Who the hell is that running towards us?"

"It's doña Blanca. What's the matter with her? She looks horrified!"

"Something terrible's happened!" Blanca says, waving her arms, panting and sweaty. "They took that guy, Zabala's helper. They found him in the front yard, almost dead. He's got bite marks all over his face and arms and hands. Dog bites and human bites!"

"What was he doing in the house? Where did they take him? Who took him?"

"I have no idea what he was doing there! They took him to the hospital, the owners did."

Some hours later, when the yard has been cleaned of all traces of blood and gunpowder, and when the dust has settled, the women notice that Rosa is missing and that Conde's fence is broken.

"We need to find her," the owner of the house says. "That girl must've gone to the woods. Our old neighbor, the one that's in a wheelchair, heard a shot and then saw her running across the stream with Conde right behind her."

Rosa and the dog are not very far. Crouched behind a rock, like scared rabbits, they've been hiding for hours, following the events in the house with four ears. It doesn't take long to find them.

They tie Conde to a tree, since his pen is wrecked, and take Rosa home to grill her with questions.

Between sobs, she tells everybody what happened.

"What an asshole! I could tell by his face that he was a total creep," one of the women says, handing Rosa a tissue.

"Nice job, Conde!" Says another, looking out the window at the dog.

"And here I was afraid he'd break out of his fence!" another woman says.

"What's going to happen to Rosa? If that jerk survives and starts talking, they're going to accuse her of trying to kill him!"

"And, if he doesn't survive, the police will accuse her anyway, because that man is from here, and Rosa isn't."

"Even if she were from here! Women always get the blame."

"If you go to jail in this country, you'll rot away in there."

Rosa's blood freezes in her veins.

And while the women continue talking this way, Rosa leaves the room. She knows what she has to do now.

The terrible simplicity of the solution attracts and terrifies her, but it seems right.

She goes to the bathroom, and finds a razor. She passes her finger over the gleaming edge. A thin trickle of blood stains her blouse. She looks at herself in the mirror, and a big tear wells up over her eyelash.

With one hand, she lifts up her hair, sticking to her neck with sweat, and with the other she holds the blade firmly, like her grandmother taught her to do when killing chickens with the kitchen knife—with no fuss and no mess. She can hardly see what she's doing through the tears that stream from her eyes, but she keeps going. One by one, she hacks off large clumps of her heavy black hair. She does it furiously and with determination, but neatly, until just one centimeter of hair is left on her head. No one's going to grab her from behind now! She gathers up the mat of hair that has fallen around her feet and stuffs it into the garbage can with both hands.

Behind the door, Rosa finds a man's work shirt, covered in patches, and a ragged farmer's hat.

She can tell by the dust that they haven't been worn in quite a while. She takes off her cotton blouse and cuts off the lower part with the blade. She makes a band, folds it, and ties it around her chest, flattening her breasts down. She puts the old shirt on, which hangs halfway down her thighs. Then she puts on the hat, covering her ears. She looks at herself in the mirror.

She is transformed into what she wanted to be: a slender boy.

The women pay little attention to the teenage boy who enters the room until, all at once, they recognize that little face and those puffy eyes, under the big hat—their young traveling companion.

"Rosa! What did you do!?" They shout, covering their mouths in surprise.

"From now on I'm not Rosa ... or Rigoberta,..." she announces, with a defiant expression, and wavering voice. "Rosa's gone!"

Her seriousness leaves them silent.

"The Christians called my dad Eugenio. He's dead now. From now on I'm Eugenio. Eugenio Caento."

Rosa's tiny figure and her grave tone of voice make the ladies feel terribly sorry for her. They'd like to sweep her up in a great, big maternal hug. But respect for her new persona stops them. Mabel simply says:

"Way to go, girl. I mean, boy."

IV

With his hands still tied behind his back, Ernesto is shoved into a dark cell. The door closes and the click of a padlock ensures there will be no escaping.

A little light peeks through a narrow window near the ceiling and Ernesto sees that he's not alone. The prisoner gets up and offers to untie Ernesto's hands.

"Thanks, buddy," says Ernesto.

His shoulders and his wrists are sore and his hands are shaking. Actually, his whole body is shaking. He simply cannot believe the horrible turn of events of the last couple hours. As his eyes adjust to the dim light, and he starts to recover from the vertigo that overtook his body, he sees that his cell mate is just a kid. He looks like he's 12 or 13 years old. Ernesto offers him water from the canteen hanging on his belt, and a chocolate bar he finds in his pocket. The boy scarfs down the chocolate and takes a sip of water.

"Thanks, man. Why did they arrest you?"

"They think I stole a passport, but it's *my* passport."

"They make stuff up just to screw you over if they don't like the look of you"

"What about you?"

The kid doesn't answer right away, but when the pounding of military boots on pavement fades, he starts to talk. His name is Miguel Coy. He tells Ernesto, in a whisper, how that same morning soldiers invaded his village and killed many people. His family got away, but he didn't.

"I thought the violence in the villages had stopped," says Ernesto.

"So did we. All of us who lived so many years in the Chiapas refugee camp had been celebrating. It was the first year anniversary of our return to our village, Xaman, near Chisec. It was a great party, with a soccer tournament and everything, but all of a sudden the soldiers showed up. We didn't have any weapons, we were just partying. But someone started to argue with them and whacked of one of the soldiers' rifles, yelling, 'go away!' Of course they got pissed, and that's when the killing started. They shot at us with real bullets! I saw an eight-year-old boy, Santiago, being chased by a soldier who shot him in the chest and head. I *saw* it! They also killed his little sister, Maurilia."

Miguel covers his eyes and starts to cry.

The cell is getting dark and the boy keeps telling stories about others who were shot. Some already down and bleeding. Ernesto listens in horror.

"My dad was able to gather us all and we ran. But I went back because I didn't want to leave my dog, and that's when they grabbed me and brought me here."

The night of October 5, 1995 is the second time that Ernesto feels that death is imminent. But this time it's the death of his faith. The delicate fabric of his faith in adults is ripped to shreds with the violent images of the massacre.

The cell's dirt floor is hard and cold like cement. He sees a blanket in a dark corner, but the boy warns him that it's infested with hellish insects that will burrow into his skin. They're ticks. Ernesto stretches out on the floor, as far as possible from the blanket, and closes his eyes. The silence is absolute. The almost compact smell of urine emanating from the floor and the walls seems to sharpen his mind. That night, with the clarity of an insomniac, he concocts a plan.

V

Morning light streaking through the little window casts the shadow of bars on the cell floor. A soldier jerks open the door and leads Ernesto into an office. The lieutenant smokes as he dictates to an assistant who is pounding the keys of a typewriter with both index fingers. Looking around the room, Ernesto sees his backpack in a corner.

"So where did you steal this, you bastard?" the lieutenant barks, waving the blue passport in Ernesto's face.

"I didn't steal it," Ernesto says, using the American accent he knows how to imitate so well.

"You are one fucking liar. Cut the bullshit before I skin you alive".

"No, Mr. ... I mean, señor," says Ernesto exaggerating his accent even more. "I didn't steal it from anybody. It's mine. Sorry, Mr. policeman. I'm from California, American, just like the passport says."

"California, huh? So why are you in Guatemala? To join the fucking Communists? Those god-dammed URNG?"*[5]

"No! I came to study the quetzal," Ernesto lies." I want to learn about tropical birds.

He says all this with long vowels and badly rolled R's to imitate an American accent. He doesn't mention looking for his family. He takes his high school ID out of his shirt pocket. Under the Eagle logo is written:

West Redwood High School:
Home of the Eagles
Ernesto Moreno Ruiz

"Like I said, mister, I'm an ornithologist."

"It's Lieutenant," a soldier corrects him.

"Yes, Lieutenant, I'm a bird specialist."

The lieutenant studies the card.

"You're really from California?" softening his tone. "I have a cousin there. His name is Reinaldo Lacán. Maybe you know him? He's a doorman in a big building, in ...I can't remember the name right now, but I know it's a famous place. I

[5] Translator's note: URNG stands *for **Unidad Revolucionaria Nacional Guatemalteca** (National Guatemalan Revolutionary Unit), a leftist organization from the late 20th century.

haven't heard from him recently though, so I'm not sure if he's still there."

Ernesto says he might know this cousin, because he goes to many government buildings running errands for his father. He explains that his father is a lawyer who works for an agency connected to the United Nations. This agency happens to search for missing people all over the world over, so he has many contacts. Among other convincing lies, he says he can help find the Lieutenant's cousin.

"Well, it looks like you were telling the truth after all. But go back to your country immediately!" he says, tossing Ernesto his passport and backpack. "This is no place for a kid like you. And when you get there, if you find my cousin, give him my greetings. Reinaldo Lacán. Now go!"

"But, sir," Ernesto says, "that kid in the cell doesn't even know why he's here. I need an assistant to help me find quetzals, and he could be my guide."

"Forget the quetzals! There's not a single one left! They've all been killed."

"Let him go. Look, I have a camera in my backpack," Ernesto says, as he pulls out the camera and hands it to the lieutenant. "Keep it and let the boy come with me. I promise I'll look for your cousin."

The lieutenant glances toward the cell, then scrutinizes the eagle card again (he's seen that bird somewhere!), then inspects the camera with interest.

"How am I going to take pictures if I don't have any film?"

"Oh, that's right! I forgot about the film! I have a roll. Here you go." He says, taking one out of his backpack.

The lieutenant looks at the film and then orders the soldiers: "take the other one out of the cell."

"But, Lieutenant," a soldier objects, "why are we letting him go? We were going to interrogate him today, remember?"

The man scowls and responds sternly, in a strange language. Ernesto doesn't understand, but sprinkled among the quiché he occasionally hears Spanish words. Things like, *American government, disappeared, United Nations*. Ernesto thinks his strategy is working. His father's fake government position and made-up profession are protecting him.

And, like a man taking off one mask and putting on another, the lieutenant softens his expression when he again addresses Ernesto:

"Take him with you, if you want. My soldiers brought him here for his own good; to keep him away from the guerrillas, that's all. But now that I know he's in good hands, he can go. Besides, I am a man of compassion, even though it may not seem like it. We have to look out for the youth!"

And, pointing a military finger at Ernesto, he adds:

"But don't forget that our mission here is to defend our Guatemalan patrimony from Communists; the enemies of the state!"

"Of course, Lieutenant."

The cell door is opened and the boy is told to come out and thank this good gringo for his freedom. Miguel emerges from the darkness of the cell squinting at the bright light, and smiling faintly.

"Just one more thing, Lieutenant," says Ernesto, feeling bold. "Could you give me something for safe passage? A note in your writing, and on your letterhead, saying I'm an ornithologist? Just so no one bothers me in the future."

"What do you think I am?" he says, exasperated, "a social worker? Get out before I change my mind."

"Sorry, sir. Thanks anyway. Oh, I think that camera has new batteries. All you have to do is put the film in".

Ernesto and Miguel are leaving, deliberately moving slowly when the man calls:

"Hang on! How do I put the damned film in?"

"Oh, I'll show you!" says Ernesto, turning back. "It's like this. See this button? Slide it sideways, open the compartment, and put the roll in until it clicks. Then you close the lid and that's it!"

"Why don't you check and see if you have any more film in there?" says the lieutenant, getting up and going into an adjacent office.

"I dumped out my backpack and found these other rolls," says Ernesto when the lieutenant returns with a stamp and ink pad in hand. "You can have them. What would I do with them without a camera anyway?"

"You could shove them up your ass!" one of the soldiers says, laughing.

Up yours, Ernesto thinks, and rolls his eyes.

"Here," says the lieutenant, giving him a piece of paper signed and stamped. "For safe passage. You'll need it, because this war isn't over yet."

The boys say goodbye to their captors once again and take off, this time a bit more quickly.

9. Crossroad

I

"Thanks, I thought I'd never get out of there," said Miguel, once they were outside the base.

Ernesto feels like hugging the kid but instead just puts an arm around his bony shoulders and gives him a light, reassuring squeeze.

"It's a miracle that they let us go, don't you think?" says Ernesto.

"I think that lieutenant is scared shitless. You didn't understand what he said to the soldiers," Miguel adds.

"No, I didn't," Ernesto admits, somewhat irritated by his ignorance of the Mayan dialect.

"He told them the war might end soon, and that in the capital they're talking about an … *arminice*? I didn't understand the word. Something about the URNG militants and the government. He said there were groups of … Humans? I think, something like that, that are coming after them because of what they did to us in Xamán yesterday. Of course he says he was just following his coronel's orders. And, since you're from the North, and your father does government work, he definitely doesn't want to get in trouble because of you. Do you get it? He wants to wash his hands of all of it, like Portion Pilate. He'll need a shitload of soap. They all will, to wash the blood off their hands!"

"Pontius Pilate, you mean. And how do you know that the lieutenant said all of t that?"

"Remember that little vent in the cell? You can hear everything! I understood everything they said in Quiché, except that stuff about an *armin*…something"

"Armistice. It means "peace treaty." I hope it's true!"

"Me too. Hey, check out what I found in the cell."

The boy pulls a military cap out of his pocket.

"I thought it might come in handy so I took it."

Miguel puts the hat on. It covers his eyes. Ernesto looks at him, amused, and says it might be good for carrying potatoes home from the market.

"Well, then you wear it," he says, hopping up and putting it on Ernesto's head. "Wow! You look just like a soldier!"

Ernesto scruffs up the boy's already messy hair and they keep walking, enjoying their freedom, along the road to Cobán.

On a sidewalk in the village, a mother and her little girl are cooking corn tortillas over a grill and selling them for a few cents. Ernesto buys several and shares them with Miguel. Both boys are famished.

"So where are you going now?" Miguel asks, a little downcast, when they get to the center of town.

"To Quetzaltenango. What about you?"

"I'm going to look for my family. I know the trail they took really well. It goes by my house and a lot of people use it to get around. People who ran away to Mexico and those who came back also use it. It's called The February 20th Victory Trail. I also know where they're probably hiding, if they think anyone is trying to follow them. Ernesto, could you give me a quetzal so I can take the bus to the village?" Miguel gets a childish look on his face when he asks for the money.

"Yeah, of course."

Ernesto leads him to a public bathroom in the town square where he takes some money out of his tennis shoe.

"Here you go. For the ride and to get something to eat during the trip. Good luck, buddy! Take care of yourself!"

Miguel thanks Ernesto and looks at him sadly.

"Why don't you come with me, Ernesto? You have that paper the lieutenant gave you."

"I can't, Miguel. I have to keep going."

"What are you going to do when you get there in Xela?" [6]

"I'm looking for some relatives in a village near there. It's called Esperanza. Have you heard of it?"

"No, I haven't. But if you come with me, after I find my family, I'll take you to a place where you can see tons of quetzals. I promise you! You said you wanted to see them, right? It's the best place in the world to see quetzals. I swear, Ernesto!"

---

[6] Note of the translator. *Xela = diminutive of Qetzaltenango*

"I really can't, buddy. You know how to go. You can go alone. You're very smart."

The boy says goodbye, gets on the bus and looks back at his friend. Ernesto leaves, carrying his backpack on his back and a weight in his heart. His young cell mate will have to figure things out on his own. God will look after him, Ernesto thinks as he crosses the street.

Perhaps it's the memory of the terror he felt the day he was trapped in the rubble, or maybe the memory of a memory – a time when he thought he would die and lamented missed opportunities to do the right thing – whatever it was, something strikes a nerve somewhere in his conscience, and makes him jump. He sprints back to the square. The bus is overflowing with people, luggage, chickens, crates of fruit and vegetables, bundles of firewood and even a bicycle. He watches it slowly maneuvering through the narrow street, backfiring and spewing black smoke from the exhaust pipe.

"Stop! Stop!" Ernesto shouts.

The driver's assistant is still adjusting bundles on the roof of the vehicle when he sees Ernesto running. He pounds on the roof several times until the driver also notices and slows down a little. Ernesto jumps onto the moving bus and thanks the driver. He sees Miguel's round face in the back of the bus, grinning eagerly and flapping his arms in his best impression of a quetzal.

"Where are you going?" the driver asks.

"To Chisec."

"We can't go there. It's closed off."

"What do you mean closed? Who closed it"

No one answers.

"All right, I'm going to wherever is closest to Chisec".

Ernesto wants to go to Miguel, but it's impossible to get through the solid mass of bodies clogging the aisle. The assistant who was on top of the bus slides in through the back window, like a baby born breech, and squeezes through the crowd to collect fares.

II

After less than an hour on the gravel road they arrive at the roadblock.

The villagers get out and catch their belongings as the man on the roof tosses them down. With their bags, animals, babies and bicycles, they disband among various trails. The bus returns to Cobán.

The village is just a small collection of houses, but the boys find a tiny country store that sells a little of everything. They buy a flashlight, water and food.

Miguel tells Ernesto that the group his parents are with can't be too far from there. He saw his father carrying a chicken and a bag of supplies as he was running with the family. Behind him were more families with children and old people. He remembers they were even carrying a wounded man on a makeshift stretcher.

"I don't think they could've walked very far, Ernesto. If we run, I'm sure we can catch up to them in half a day."

Ernesto checks his map but it's not very detailed and he can't tell for sure how far the little caravan might have traveled since the day before. He realizes it's not a very rational plan. Days and nights scrambling mountains and running through jungles all the way to Mexico sounds crazy. But he promised himself not to chicken out at every crossroad. How many times has he heard the expression "follow your destiny" and not really understood what it meant. Now he thinks it has something to do with listening to that inner voice that sometimes speaks loudly. What we call a "hunch". It's like a guiding light that helps us recognize and read subtle signs in the blink of an eye. "Why be so guarded?" His grandfather would say. "Of course, there are times for reflection, but sometimes you have to make a quick decision. You might miss the train if you spend too much time counting stations!"

The impression left by his grandfather's words is not only because they're so eloquent, but because they ring true. They have the mark of authenticity. He sometimes wonders if his father, who is such a planner and rational thinker, might not also be adopted. He's nothing like grandpa Rodrigo, whose life is so well guided by intuition and an inner compass.

Of course, sometimes these "signals from the heart", as he likes to call them, have led his grandfather to do some pretty strange things. His father told him about the time when he was a teenager and was, for the umpteenth time, watching a TV show that grandfather didn't approve of. He simply rose from his arm chair, unplugged the TV, carried the heavy set outside, and unceremoniously smashed it with a sledgehammer. He then returned inside, sat back down and picked up his book as if nothing unusual had happened. "Sometimes you have to take the bull by the horns," was all old Ruiz said, though he wasn't that old at the time

"Let's go, then" says Ernesto, "we have a lot of trail ahead of us, so we better take the bull by the horns."

"What? There are no bulls around here, Ernesto," Miguel says, puzzled.

"Even better!"

The trail passes very close to the mountain village of Xaman. When they get to an overlook Miguel points to the valley. "Look down there, Ernesto, that's my village. Or what used to be my village. Look at it now."

Smoke from the burnt thatched roofs still hangs in the air, and they can even see ash particles floating around. Two helicopters are hovering over the wreckage.

"Look at them. They look like vultures circling over carrion," he says, pointing.

A reporter in a Radio Guatemala van is talking to a soldier from inside the car. More soldiers are digging holes with picks and shovels just outside the village.

"Why are they digging ditches now?" Ernesto asks.

"Those aren't ditches, brother. They're holes for burying people. Thank God my mom isn't one of them!"

Miguel's chin trembles as he tries mightily not to cry. Ernesto pulls him away and they continue on the uphill trail. The younger boy runs, and the occasional rabbit or badger darts away before him. Ernesto, panting, is soon falling behind. When he's completely out of breath and unable to keep up, he asks if they can share the weight. They remove several items from his backpack and wrap them up in a sweatshirt that Miguel slings over his shoulder, like a bag.

They keep running. The trail now snakes around banana trees and cornstalks. It leads them around a cultivated field where they find a farmer harvesting ears of corn by hand. Ernesto takes off his hat, as he's seen others in this country do when speaking with an older person. Miguel asks the man if he's seen a group of people coming through the trail.

"Yes, yesterday there were two groups."

"My parents are going to be so surprised when they see me coming" says Miguel, looking forward to the reunion.

Ernesto adjusts his hat and they get back on the path, which now cuts through dense foliage.

At first, bright rays of sunlight infiltrate the leafy canopy and flicker over his eyelids like the flutter of butterfly wings. An hour later, when the forest grows impenetrably dense and the light wanes, Miguel stops abruptly. A 44 caliber gun jabs into Ernesto's chest.

"Stop or I'll shoot!" says the voice behind the gun.

Ernesto raises his hands. Miguel does the same. A second man, also armed, steps out of the shadows.

"Now, walk! Let's go!"

They're led down a side trail that looks freshly cut by machete. Soon they arrive at an open place where several people are sitting on the ground. One of their captors tells a man who seems to be the leader that they caught the two of them running in that direction.

"May I speak?" says Ernesto, trying to sound calm and polite.

"Speak!"

He's about to tell them that they can have his money if they let them go, because killing them on the trail won't get them anything. But, noticing his captor's anxiety, something else comes out instead: "Watch that trigger finger, man."

"Don't worry. I got it."

"We don't have guns," Ernesto continues.

The men pat the boys down to make sure. Finding no weapons, one of them asks: "What are you doing here? What do you want?"

"What do *we* want? What do *you* want?!"

After a moment of mutual surprise, Ernesto explains that they're looking for Miguel's parents, who are probably close by since they left their village yesterday to escape a massacre. He glances at the people seated beneath the trees, and guesses there are about 40 of them.

"Well, there are no refugees here!" says the man with the gun.

Miguel looks fearfully at the group of people.

The men dump out the boys' packs - dry tortillas, a book, maps, a notebook, dirty laundry - onto the ground. They've lowered their guns.

"Can I put my arms down now?" Ernesto asks.

"Yeah, sure. So you guys weren't chasing us?"

"Of course not!" says Ernesto. "I already told you we're trying to catch up to Miguel's parents."

"So what are you doing with the army hat?"

"I think of it as a gift from the soldiers who arrested us," Ernesto jokes.

"Well, you scared the shit out of us!" says the other man, sitting on a log with sigh.

"You're the ones who scared us!"

"Ernesto," says Miguel quietly, "these people aren't from my village."

"Of course we're not from your village, kid," scoffs the leader. "All right, well, no harm done. Now you two get out of here. Just remember: you haven't seen anyone. Do you understand that? You haven't seen absolutely ANYONE!"

Ernesto nods and promises not to say anything. He has no interest in whatever these people are doing here. It's obvious they're heading for the border, and he asks that they take Miguel with them.

The answer is "absolutely not".

"Look, by your accent I can tell you're not from here, and you don't know anything about anything. I can't take an extra person. I have a boss too, and he wouldn't like it."

"I'll pay you for your services and Miguel has his own food and flashlight."

"It's not up to me to decide. And we don't use flashlights around here."

"Just pretend he's not here," Ernesto insists, "and your boss doesn't need to find out."

They keep arguing, each trying to convince the other and both coming up with objections.

Ernesto notices the group is listening closely to their conversation, and he appeals to them, recounting the story of the boy's drama.

A young boy in the group, dressed in pants far too big for him and a baggy, frayed shirt, gets up and says: "Guys, this boy is looking for his mother! We have to let him come with us!" And after a couple seconds he adds: "I'll take care of him."

Ernesto looks at the boy with surprise. Judging by his voice and appearance, he can't be much older than Miguel himself. Everyone is looking at Miguel with much more sympathy now. Someone says "It's a good cause, boss. Let the boy tag along and stop arguing about it."

"Fine," the guide agrees, resigning himself to the general sentiment. "But, let's not waste any more time. Finish your food and grab your stuff. We need to leave right away."

"What? You're leaving now? Ernesto asks, surprised. "It'll get dark on you along the way."

"That's how we like it, kid. We're like bats. We walk by night and sleep by day – hanging off trees"

Everyone laughs except Ernesto. The thought of bats sends a shiver down his spine.

The group sets off. Miguel insists that Ernesto should stay with them until morning, because alone he'll most likely get lost. When the sun comes up, he says, they'll go find the quetzals. And then he'll show Ernesto how to get to a road to catch a bus.

Ernesto doesn't think it would be very hard to find his way back alone, since there's still some daylight left. But something tells him that he should accept this offer to see quetzals. The "ornithologist" safe conduct from the Lieutenant will be more useful if he has some experience to back it up. So now he asks permission to go with the group himself until morning. The guide shrugs, tired of arguing.

The boys hastily gather their things off the ground and join the caravan.

III

"I wanted to thank you for speaking up," Ernesto says to the boy who advocated for Miguel.

"We're all stressed here, but it doesn't cost anything to lend a hand when you can," the boy responds.

"That's true, and you were great. Good job."

"Thanks."

"When did you leave your home?"

"Almost three weeks ago."

"Three weeks? Where are you from?"

"Ecuador," says Rosa, removing her villager's hat and giving Ernesto a shy smile.

10. In the Land of the Quetzal

I

Quetzaltenango is a university town and the cultural center of the country. Ernesto has no trouble finding a youth hostel to sleep in. He's spent the previous afternoon, evening, and much of the night walking, and now – feeling a bit like a bat himself – he has the urge to shun the sunlight. It's nine in the morning.

The place is quiet and cozy. His room on the second floor has a window that opens onto a small internal courtyard. Stretching his arm out, he can touch the leaves of a palm tree laden with little golden coconuts. Someone in the room directly across opens the window and pours out a vase full of water. The wide, fan-shaped leaves flap with the weight of the water splashing on them.

Ernesto throws himself on the bed and closes his eyes, but the extreme weariness that seems to electrify his muscles keeps him awake and kicking at the air. As is the avalanche of mental images from the past few days. Over and over again the face of the Ecuadorian girl with a boy's haircut appears at the edge of his dreams. Tossing and turning, he sleeps with that image burned onto his retinas.

Many hours later, when he awakens from a long sleep full of dreams of water and wet palm trees, he takes up his notebook and writes:

Quetzaltenango, Guatemala, October 7, 1995
What caught my attention at first was the voice - soft, gentle but firm - and the ready smile. When I asked her name, she said she lost it on the boat. I said that sounds very poetic, but they must have given her a name when she was born. She said her name was Eugenio Caento. I didn't believe her. Finally she admitted her name was Rosa Epayuma. Of course. I should have guessed before she took off her hat that she was a girl. I joined her group and we walked together all night at the back of the line. At daybreak, the guide gave a signal and we followed him up a trail

to a place where the group could rest safely. But she and I followed Miguel, who remembered his promise.

He puts down his pen and recalls once again the early morning hike to see the quetzals. The three of them walked for an hour until they arrived at a high, cool clearing. White mist drifted over the trees forming a foggy, vaporous veil which gives Guatemalan mountains a bridal air. There they lay on the ground looking upward, waiting motionlessly and in absolute silence, until Miguel whistled like a quetzal.

Soon they saw the birds, with their brilliant tails, swooping among branches and calling to each other with their songs. The magic of the moment made Ernesto feel like he was also flying.

When morning had fully arrived, we got back on the trail. I had to keep going. I told them our friendship had been sealed that morning, and the quetzal would be our secret symbol. Rosa liked that. And I liked that she liked it.
It was really hard to leave her! Maybe I should have stayed. But I know I need to keep going. She gave me her mom's work number, I gave her mine. Although it won't do us much good if I'm going to be wandering around those southern roads and she hiding herself along the northern ones. She said she'd be thinking about me.
And I'm thinking about her.
When it was time for me to go, we walked away from the group and she kissed me on each cheek. I didn't want to let her go so I hugged her tightly and kissed her on the lips.

Ernesto closes his eyes and remembers her warmth, her heart beating next to his, the feel of her dark honey skin, soft as a peach, and then that short, heavenly kiss. And most of all, the light that radiates from within her.

Later, returning to the notebook, he writes:

She travels alone. She is very brave. She says it's a hallmark of her people. She even showed me the knife she carries on her belt. She said she's a Huaorani, a very independent people who live in the Ecuadorian Amazon and have never been conquered. But when the oil companies came in the 70s they were pushed out of their land and relocated to an Evangelical "protectorate". And that's where she was born. Her father went to work in the oil fields in the North, "North Sara", I think she said. He died of leukemia a couple years later. They think it was caused by the toxins from the open pits. Afterward, her family was able to get a title to a small piece of land near a place called Baeza.

Suddenly he feels as if his blood had stopped flowing and frozen in his veins. A vague memory arrests his mind. He drops the pen and runs out of the room. He needs to call his father. He wants him to confirm, or rather, deny, that he was involved in the construction of the Vía Auca 20 years ago; the one that Rosa told him was built by Texapetrol all the way from Coca to the South, splitting the Huaorani territory in two and opening a corridor of death through the jungle.

"It can't be! Texapetrol! Please tell me I'm mistaken!"

II

On the trail "The Victory of February 20th "

Dear Mom: I hope you're doing well. I'm taking advantage of the last hours of light to write you some news:

We couldn't cross the Suchiate River. There was a problem with the police and we had to sneak away at night. But that was okay, because Tecún Umán is really ugly, and it's much nicer where we are now, away from the coast. I just felt bad I had to say good-bye to this crazy horse and dog that became my good friends.

They put us in three little buses, and we got to this village named Xuctzul after half a day of traveling. I love the people here. The women and even the little girls wear long, tight skirts and colorful blouses, and they put flowers in their hair. Anyway, it took us a while to get there because we had to take all these detours. The military closed the road at one point. And then they took us down this trail called "The Victory of February 20th ". Did you know that the trails here have names?

Don Sabino, the new coyote, divided the group in two, with a hundred people in each and we walked and walked down

135

the trail. After a few hours we met this American boy and another boy from here. They're traveling to meet up with their moms – just like me!

Rosa puts her pen down and wonders if she should tell her mom about the magic she felt when Ernesto hugged her, or the way her heart skips a beat every time she remembers his kiss. How can she talk about these things with a mom she hasn't seen in six years? Would she judge her?

She continues:

Now we're marching single file like ants, like we do on the trails at home. But at night, and with no flashlight or anything, so no one can see us. They don't even let us light cooking fires. Luckily, they're saying the Mexican border is pretty close, like a few days away. I hope there's a post office at the end of this trail! Take care, Mom!

Love, Rosa

III

Torn between fear and the need to find out, Ernesto runs out to the street and into a phone booth. He knows it will be difficult to confront his father. Writing to him would be easier, but the internet is a luxury that hasn't arrived in Quetzaltenango yet, and mailing a letter isn't an option since he doesn't have a fixed address.

Esteban Ruiz is happy to hear his son's voice. At first they talk about the beauty of the quetzals and of the local people. He's careful not to mention his run-in with the Army. Then he decides to hint at what's on mind.

"I met someone from Ecuador. You've been there, right?"

"Yes, many years ago, when you were little."

"Were you in the Napo or Sucumbíos provinces at all?"

His father hesitates a moment before responding:

"I don't remember the names of the places. It's been such a long time!"

"I think I remember you mentioning a place that had a woman's name. Sara, or something like that?"

"Sacha".

"That's right. I've heard Sacha is close to the Vía Auca. Did you work on that road?"

"I'm a petroleum engineer, not a highway builder!." His father sounds slightly irritated. "I worked in the oil fields."

"Right. And you also worked on those pools where they put the waste oil. What are they called?"

"Just pools. But, what's up, Ernesto? Am I being interrogated?"

"I heard something about the contamination along that road that goes through the rain forest. I just wanted to know your opinion, Dad. That's why I'm asking. In case you know something about it."

Ernesto hears his father clear his throat before answering.

"I don't know anything about the mess down there, because I left before that. By the time they finished the Vía Auca, I was already gone."

"Oh, okay."

Ernesto contemplates his father's answer. It's obvious his questions made him uncomfortable. Feeling a little guilty for probing him by phone from 2,000 miles away, Ernesto changes the subject to diffuse the tension, and then they say goodbye.

He decides to believe in his father's innocence. But the issue keeps bothering him, lingering on his mind, like a grain of sand in his eye, stuck there no matter how much it weeps.

He walks across the bumpy cobblestone street and remembers the click on the other end of the line. For some reason at that moment he had the vision of a shaking hand hanging up the phone. He wonders if his father has something to hide, maybe an unpleasant memory that he wants to avoid. Little does he know that Esteban Ruiz's memory is a minefield he prefers to avoid.

Back at the hostel, Ernesto gets directions to Esperanza. He finds out that the name is *La* Esperanza, not just *Esperanza*, but he prefers not to dwell on this. In any case, the quickest way to get there is to take a pickup from the town square.

On the way there he stops at a sporting goods store. It's the type of business that has been flourishing since the peace treaty greatly increased the tourists in town.

137

Ernesto buys a sleeping bag. He doesn't know how long his money will last and how many nights he will have to sleep under the stars.

The pickup, a common alternative means of public transportation in Guatemala, soon arrives. Its bed is outfitted with a cage-like structure made of metal bars where passengers hang on like trapeze artists. Ernesto hands the driver 20 cents and climbs in the back.

Once outside the city, the driver puts the little truck into high gear and begins a mad zigzag up the mountains. Ernesto feels every curve might be his last. Every now and then he musters the courage to look down into the deep valley where a river runs among planted fields. In its waters, women bathe children, wash clothes or their own hair, which they comb and braid and adorn with flowers.

La Esperanza is the last stop on the pickup's route, and Ernesto goes straight to a store in the town square. It's not a small village but it's not a large one either. Ernesto assumes that the residents must all know each other.

"Excuse me, ma'am, do you know anyone by the name of Moreno?" Ernesto asks the first woman he sees in the store.

The woman smiles at him, but says nothing.

"She does not understand you," says an elderly man who is sitting on a sheepskin on the floor." The women around here don't understand much Spanish. They speak our native language – but maybe I can help you. I've lived here my whole life and know all the families."

"Thank you. I'm looking for a family called Moreno."

"The only Morenos here are the Moreno Xequijel. They live outside the city, down by the lake."

Ernesto's hearts skips a beat.

Could you tell me how to get there?"

"I'll take you there if you like. They're good people and I haven't seen them in a while."

They head out together. The walk takes them through various neighborhoods filled with homes made of adobe and bamboo. In all of them the same scenes are repeated: mothers and sisters carrying babies in colorful wraps tied up and slung over their backs; men doubled over with the weight of firewood or stones carried on their backs; women grinding corn in stone mortars.

Ernesto and his guide follow a path that cuts through the red earth, and soon take a narrow trail lined with the foliage of tall corn plants. Silky beards, red and orange, hang from the ears, signaling that it's harvest time.

They keep walking until they come to an adobe hut with a thatched roof. Beside it is a smaller brick structure which, Ernesto later learns, is a steam shower. He looks curiously at the round clay oven near the house.

A man in his early forties is cleaning some tools.

"Good afternoon, don Matías!" calls the old man.

"Good afternoon, don Lucas. Good to see you! What brings you by?" answers the householder as he shoos some pigs who are sneaking out to eat corn cobs.

"I brought this young man, who wants to visit the Morenos."

The man motions for them to sit on some crates as he sits on the stump of what was once a gigantic tree. Trying to quell his anxiety, Ernesto picks up some seeds from the ground tosses them to the turkeys that are pecking at the dirt nearby.

Then he begins his story. He talks of his mother, her name and her village.

The man watches him kindly and says:

"Well, son, my family is called Moreno on my father's side and Xequijel on my mother's. My father was the grandson of Spaniards on the paternal side, where the Moreno name comes from, and my mother was pure Mayan. I had four brothers, but no sisters. No, there wasn't any woman your mother's age by the name Moreno here, much less one who traveled to the United States. We're humble people. Much too poor to travel to the North. Imagine that, don Lucas! Relatives in the North! That would be nice!"

Ernesto realizes that this can't be his family. He is about to say goodbye, but there is something appealing about the place. It might be the refreshing highland air. He feels like staying.

The lady of the house comes out to the patio and offers Ernesto some fruit. Some children arrive, a little girl and two little boys. They spend the rest of the afternoon chatting. Don Matías Moreno interprets for his wife, who speaks Kakchiquel, as they talk to Ernesto about their life. The children are healthy and like school, the man tells him, but selling corn is no longer enough to support the family. The price is very low nowadays, and it seems that even in the city they are buying foreign corn from the United States, because it is cheaper.

"I hear the United States pays their farmers to grow corn. Anyone could sell their corn cheap that way! But that's probably just a rumor and I don't really believe it. What do you think, young man? You're from there. Could it be true that in your country they give farmers money to sell their corn more cheaply?"

Ernesto, who doesn't know a thing about agricultural subsidies in the U.S., says:

"I don't know, but if it's true, it would be a shame if they exported it here, to the land of corn!"

"That's right! We can't even get a single seed —of the good kind—to sow. The seeds we do have produce very little. We just harvest poverty!"

Don Matías explains that they supplement their meager income with his wife's weaving on the belt loom, but it's very slow work.

"What about that foot loom you had, don Matías? That was much faster wasn't it?" asks don Lucas.

"Yes, that's the family loom but it doesn't work anymore."

The children take Ernesto by either hand and guide him to the back of the little house to show him the broken loom. Some sticks, a pedal and two boards on the ground is all that remains of a loom that used to be a good source of family income.

"And you know something, don Lucas?" continues don Matías? The bank here in La Esperanza won't lend money to poor folks – not even to buy a loom! They say that because our house is adobe it can't serve as collateral, as they call it. And our land is no good either, because it's not registered, and we don't have an official property deed."

"Good Lord! That's terrible!"

"Yes, it really is. This little farm has been in our family since before my great grandfather! Since before the Spaniards! Since before Jesus himself!"

When the day turns to dusk, Ernesto asks if he might spend the night under a tree, in his sleeping bag.

"Of course, the land belongs to everyone!"

Night falls and the cold air settles early over the highlands. The lady invites them into the house with its recently-swept earthen floor. The children have lit a gas lantern and a fire is crackling in the open stove. A dinner of soup and tortillas is served. After eating, don Lucas bids goodbye and everyone goes to bed.

Ernesto finds a smooth spot on the grass, unrolls his sleeping bag and gets in. He can't stop thinking about the land problem. With more questions than answers rumbling about in his head, he spends a long time looking up at the night sky.

The transparent mountain air and dazzling stars also keep him awake. Infinity seems so close he feels he could touch it by just lifting an arm. Such splendor in such a simple place!

Flattened by the weight of the stars and hypnotized by the sound of the loud roiling stream, Ernesto eventually falls asleep.

IV

Darkness descends upon the "20 February Victory" trail, leading north through jungle country, and it is time to continue on. Some travelers are washing up in the river; others are listening to the radio. The moon, encircled in a red halo, glows through the foliage. Rosa shudders.

The guide gives the order to set off.

"Señor Sabino, I think there's going to be a downpour, don't you?" Rosa asks the guide.

"How do you know?"

"See the moon? And how nervous the animals are?" The girl points to a branch, already rustling in the wind. "I'll bet a storm is coming!"

The guide startles at the harsh cry of a bird.

"Have you heard anything about the weather on the radio, Manolo?" Sabino asks his assistant.

"They said there was a huge hurricane yesterday in the southern Gulf of Mexico and that today there's going to be wind and rain here. It's called 'Hurricane Opal'."

The other man doesn't hear these last words. The wind that rustled and swayed branches gracefully now blows an icy rain on the leaves, swallowing his words. First, large and well-spaced droplets fall, followed by a heavy rain, which becomes heavier by the minute. Pretty soon a downpour blasts from the side, pushed by a furious wind that carries off Rosa's hat forever.

In less than half an hour, when they are marching down the trail, lightning slashes through the sky, illuminating the gray clouds that pour water over the land. The thunder and wind terrify both animals and humans.

Suddenly, dry branches begin snapping off the trees in a crazed windstorm that comes from every direction, landing all around the travelers. Soaked to the bone, they try to protect themselves with their backpacks. Miguel takes Rosa's hand and doesn't let go. As they arrive at a stream that will be difficult to wade through, the long human line disintegrates into an amorphous group of frightened individuals.

"We need to find a clearing," Sabino yells to Manolo, "before these branches kill somebody. See if you can find somewhere safe down that side trail we just passed."

Manolo returns in ten minutes and leads the group to a small clearing in the forest, an abandoned coffee plantation, where they can put up plastic tarps for shelter. In the downpour, they tie the ends of the tarps to coffee plants and the trembling people huddle underneath. In a few minutes the sheets cave in under the weight of the water, leaving everyone soaked and exposed to the weather.

After some attempts to tilt and drain them, they secure somewhat firmer shelters.

They settle in, packed like chicks boxed up for the market, some sitting on their backpacks, others squatting, one body pressed up against another for warmth and comfort.

Water and cold tortillas are all they get for dinner on this blustery night.

Rosa puts on extra layers of clothes and wraps Miguel up in a sweater. She's sorry about the loss of her hat. She also misses her friend Mabel, who is in the other group. Most of all she misses Ernesto and the warmth she felt in his embrace.

This battered group of refugees spends a sleepless night with teeth-chattering from the cold, the relentless rain drumming on the canvas, praying they won't be carried away by a blast of wind.

V

Day is breaking when Ernesto opens his eyes and finds himself face-to-face with a burro munching grass beside his sleeping bag. He stretches out a hand to rub the warm muzzle. The donkey responds with a bray, turns slowly, and trots off toward the river. A pink glow rises behind a hill and the boy remembers his dream. Grandpa Ruiz had been showing him a book called *Tips for a Pilgrim*. He wonders if his dream was influenced by don Matías mentioning his great-grandfather, or a mysterious metempsychosis message transmitted in his sleep. The dream reminds him of a conversation they had years ago that had been forgotten until now.

Those of us who walked the Santiago de Compostela Trail didn't carry any money. We trusted Providence! Remember, Ernesto, if you ever want to undertake this pilgrimage your soul and your pocket should be empty.

"Why should my soul be empty, Granddad?"

"So it can be filled with goodness!"

Señora Moreno Xequijel lights the oven to cook breakfast. Don Matías makes a fire in the hearth with some fresh-smelling logs. The smell of smoke and tree sap quickly impregnates the air and Ernesto's clothing. The mother now forms tortillas from a ball of dough. She rolls a little ball between her palms, flattens it with firm pats, and then slaps the tortilla back and forth from hand to hand. When it reaches the right thickness and size, a precise toss delivers it into a waiting iron pot on a bed of coals. With a neat pile of tortillas made, she boils water and prepares a white corn beverage, and calls Ernesto to breakfast.

143

Later, when the children have gone off to school, he speaks with his hosts:

"You've been very kind to me. I'd like to give you something." He opens his hand to show them. "Here are 800 quetzals. It should be enough to buy a new loom. Please accept this as if we were family, and maybe we are. I think all of us Moreno's must be related, don't you think?"

After his initial surprise, don Mateo stammers, "Thank you, thank you, my boy. May God bless you, you and all your family."

The mother takes Ernesto's hands.

"Matiosh!" she says, along with other words in Kakchiquel, which don Matías translates as "May God return it to you in happiness."

Ernesto says goodbye and leaves quickly, feeling unworthy of thanks. He tells himself he's not a true Pilgrim, because pilgrims rely on Providence, not money. He gave them all the money he had in his backpack, but kept both hundred dollar bills concealed in each shoe.

11. Where there Is No Doctor

I

Dawn breaks over the northern jungle. The coyote is impatient.

"The pickups are going to be waiting for us on the other side tomorrow," he says, "and we lost one night of walking. So I think we need to keep going now even though it's daylight. I'm going to tell Manolo to go up front and warn us if there's any trouble. But I don't think there are patrols in this area. We'll just have to be extra careful when we get close to the river."

"Sabino, some people are sick," a woman says. "They spent the night soaking wet and now they've got a fever."

"There's a man with pneumonia, poor guy," another woman says. "He was trembling just a minute ago and now he's burning up with a fever."

The coyote calls his assistant:

"Take care of him, Manolo," he says in a low voice." He's got symptoms of paludism. Just what we needed!"

Rosa asks if *paludism* is a sickness that makes people pale.

"It's malaria, girl!" One of the women says, laughing.

Rosa hates looking ignorant. Mortified, she feels herself shrinking down, smaller than the mosquito she has just swatted.

"And some people have diarrhea," a young man says. "They have to go every five minutes."

"Dysentery," somebody corrects, as if offering up a medical term could make the situation more serious.

"It's because they drank from the streams," another one says.

"I told them not to do that"! The coyote replies, irritably.

"It wasn't the water; they were just hungry," says a third person. "They found some green mangoes that messed up their digestion and gave them diarrhea."

"What were we supposed to do? All we got to eat in the last 14 hours was one cold, stale tortilla!" the man with dysentery complains.

"You told us there'd be enough food!" says another. "And we are people, not walking machines!"

145

The coyote observes the emaciated faces. It is not worth going on with all these sick people, he thinks. It could get ugly."

"All right. Let's spend the day here. Whoever has mosquito repellent, put it on and share it with the others. This is malaria country."

"That's right. War on mosquitoes!", Manolo exclaims.

Night falls at last and the travelers are somewhat rested and with some food in their bellies, a little more energetic. The coyote reminds them the rules they have to obey, because the trail from here on, he says, gets more treacherous:

"Stay alert. Remember that walking in silence, in the dark, can be hypnotic. This trail is like a snake. If you get distracted, the snake will bite you!"

The group begins marching through the darkness, carrying the sick man on an improvised stretcher and following the coyote. The coyote, who does not carry a flashlight either, follows the footsteps of his dog, and the dog follows his own snuffling nose, leading everyone along through the darkness.

With the exception of two stops for rest and a snack, they spend the rest of the night walking along a swampy trail, through the ghostly trees and over bumpy roots and fallen branches.

They slip and fall, passing warnings about branches and other obstructions down the line. But the trail is the most dangerous when it's clear, because some of the exhausted travelers begin walking in a trance-like state. Afraid to wander off onto a side trail and get lost in the immense night of the jungle, they step on the heels of the person in front of them for reassurance.

Dawn finally emerges through the foliage. They hear voices up ahead and Sabino orders absolute silence. A calm, wide river is in front of them.

"Mexico is just a few kilometers away, across that river," he whispers in a voice audible only to those who are closest. "Manolo and I are going to cross first and let our people on the other side know we're here."

This message is passed backwards down the line.

"Tercilio, you're in charge. Get everyone into that ravine and hide there until we're back."

Tercilio signals for the group to follow him. After a few minutes of walking through a forest still smelling of charcoal from a recent fire, they reach the edge of a deep ravine. The people go down the steep, slippery slope, carefully and awkwardly. Rosa and Miguel go up and down helping those who need it. Raised in forested mountains, this is child's play for them.

When most of the group has reached the bottom of the canyon, a cry makes them jump.

"This woman's fallen! Help us!" a young man shouts.

"Oh, oh God, oh!, I twisted my ankle! I can't walk!"

In seconds the woman's ankle is swollen like a billiard ball and a huge, puffy bruise covers the whole foot. Several people offer up diagnoses:

"She fractured her ankle."

"It's just twisted, that's all."

"It's sprained."

"Whatever it is, it's bad! Her foot looks like a sausage."

"Tell her to stretch out and wrap her foot in a wet rag."

"She needs a cast."

"How can we get a cast in the middle of the jungle?"

Rosa knows. She runs up and out of the gully and finds what she's looking for on the ground: the stalk of a dried banana leaf blown off by the storm. She picks it up, and with the blade she bought in Tecún Umán and has been carrying in the waistband under her shirt, she cuts off pieces of varying sizes, just like her grandfather did on the day she twisted her ankle. Thank God for this memory woven into my mind, she thinks. She flies down the gully with her handful of stalks and explains to Tercilio that she is the granddaughter— grandson, that is—of shamans, and that she has made the needed splints. The curved shape of the banana stalk will fit her ankle perfectly, she tells him. Tercilio looks a bit skeptical at first, and then curious. He remembers that this little girl dressed like a boy predicted the storm.

Rosa experiments with her molds until she finds one that fits the woman's upper ankle. She wraps a rag around it, adjusts the vegetable boot and ties it up with some bandages provided by Tercilio.

"Good idea," he concedes. "This will immobilize her foot and help the bone heal if it's broken."

"Yes, and it's hurting a little less now. Thank you, my angel!" says her patient.

Rosa feels vindicated in the sight of the adults and recovers her self-esteem, so wounded with the linguistic misunderstanding of *paludism*.

Sabino whistles and the group sets off. Two men carry the woman with the injured ankle out of the canyon and then the stronger ones take turns carrying her over the difficult trail.

They come to the river. A man poles toward them on a raft made of huge tractor inner tubes with boards lashed on top.

"Get on. No one's going to get wet," Sabino says proudly, now that the whole group is together again. "So no one can call you wetbacks!"

Although it's still early, they have to be careful. While Manolo and Tercilio stand guard at different points, Sabino and the raft man ferry their passengers across in groups of five. Flocks of red, green and yellow parakeets sail through the air, oblivious to the clandestine passengers.

After walking several more kilometers someone announces that the immigrants are now treading on Mexican soil. Here, the frontier between the two countries is unclear and no one knows at what exact point they crossed the border. More than by a political line, the two countries are separated by degrees of misery in a malarial jungle they share.

It is October 10, 1995. Rosa, safe, sound, and dry, walks for the first time on Mexican soil.

II

At a crossroads in a thin forest Miguel recognizes the trail that goes to the Chajul refugee camp where he hopes to find his parents.

"This is my trail, Mr. Sabino, thanks for letting me walk with you," the boy says.

Rosa gives Miguel her carved Jaguar, a powerful Huaorani talisman, she explains. Since he is going to be alone, he'll need it more than she does. He gives her a picture of

Mashimón, telling her that Mashimón is a great Guatemalan saint who will protect her from every danger.

They bid each other goodbye and Rosa returns to the group.

The trail from there to the next little village is a short one. Sabino leads his exhausted flock to their new temporary residences.

The houses are even more modest than those of Tucán Umán, but the place is more remote and therefore less dangerous. Everyone is disappointed when they find out there's no telephone for calling family members.

"Why isn't this boy with the men?" asks the woman in charge of the women's residence.

"She's a girl, doña Celia. Her name is Rosa. Her grandfather is a friend of my boss, don Zabala," says Manolo. "She cut off her hair and sold it in the market," he jokes.

"No, doña Celia, I cut it because it was giving me problems," says Rosa, who has no desire to go into detail.

Once they are settled into their new homes, the next order of business is choosing new names. Each person must undergo yet another metamorphosis, trading in their old identities for new ones.

"Choose more Mexican names, you know, less exotic than the Mayan ones," says the coyote, handing out a list of recommended names.

Rosa keeps "Eugenio," but she changes her last name to Moreno, for good luck.

Doña Celia calls Rosa in to her room and gives her a piece of elastic band that she uses for her varicose veins. Rosa thanks her. The wide elastic, fixed with a safety pin, is safer than the cloth Rosa has been using to flatten her breasts.

"You're really young to be traveling alone. You've got to be extremely, extremely careful," the woman says.

"Do you usually only get adults?" Rosa says, just to say something.

"A lot of families come through with their kids. They used to come here from Guatemala, poor people. The government soldiers burned their villages and their fields to get rid of them. They had to stay away for years."

"Why would they do that?"

"They said they were communists. They called them subversives. You know what that means?" the woman asks.

"Yes, I know, because in my country, the Huaorani organized against the oil companies, and they also got called subversives, like my friend Ana's father. They put him in jail."

"That figures. That's what happens when you stir the waters. But, you know, these Guatemalans, they were just farmers. The Mexican government accepted them as refugees. And we opened our doors to them because they're our brothers and sisters too. I mean, we're also Mayans, just living on the other side of a border invented by God knows who. Yes. As I say, a lot of them died here."

"You mean even the kids died?"

"Yes, lots of them. They were already weak when they got here, poor people, all skin and bone. A lot of them had malaria. Lots of babies died. There weren't any doctors here, and there still aren't any doctors. I remember a sister from the Marista convent. She used to come every day in an airplane or by boat and take some of the sick children to a hospital in Altamirano, or in San Cristóbal de las Casas."

These memories bring tears to Celia's eyes. Rosa is thinking about Miguel and his village.

"That trail you walked is soaked with tears." Celia says.

This history weighs heavily on both of them and Rosa wants to put it out of her mind— not to forget it—but to think about something else for now.

"For me, it's the trail that goes to the North, closer and closer to my mom."

"Of course. Will you get there soon?"

"They said it's just one day to the U.S. border. They're going to take us by train."

"Really?" the lady asks, surprised.

"That's what they said."

"Are you going to go on the roof?"

"Of course not! No one travels on the roof of the train!" says Rosa, with a smile. "We'll travel inside just like everyone."

"I see ..."

Celia looks at her, with concern, and doesn't say anything else.

III

Time goes by peacefully in the house. The women wash clothes in the river, bathe, rest and write letters. Some of them sit in the sun and paint their fingernails and toenails, all chipped from their trek through the jungle. Just because they're undocumented doesn't mean they're unhygienic, is their motto.

After dinner, don Sabino, returns from his nightly rounds and summons everyone to give instructions and distribute food and water for the next stage of the journey.

"Tomorrow morning two big trucks are coming to take us to the city of Arriaga, where the train departs," he tells them. "I hope the trucks come on time, because the second group is going to be arriving. And if the two groups are together, well, get ready to be a little squeezed in for a few days."

"Don Sabino," someone musters the courage to ask, "why can't we just take those trucks right up to the U.S. border?"

"No way we can do that. There's over twenty police checkpoints in southern Mexico on the North-South roads. It's crawling with border patrols looking for immigrants from Central America. The train is definitely safer."

"Is it dangerous from here to the train?"

"No. We're going to take a straight line from east to west. There's no checkpoint until Arriaga, because no one takes the route that we're taking. We're pioneers!"

The truck shows up several days later, causing great excitement. The group has had to share their already-cramped quarters with the second contingent.

Until recently the trucks have been used to transport cattle to the slaughterhouse. A quick wash puts them in fair condition for taking the immigrants, although it's evident that here and there a little excrement resisted the brush.

"This stinks like a barn!" exclaim some of the city people. "Gross!"

Others love the smell.

"To me, this is the smell of wonderful, Mother Earth!"

City and country folk, they're all part of the same flock now, anxious to set out once again.

The journey takes longer than expected, since they're off the main highways, on dirt roads severely damaged by Hurricane Opal. Every now and then the passengers have to get out and push the trucks out of deep, muddy potholes.

At a certain point they cross a major highway and, following Sabino's instructions, the truck beds are covered with canvas to hide their human cargo.

"You're not missing anything," says Manolo, who is traveling with them. "This is just like any other road. State Highway 199. It goes North and passes the Palenque ruins."

None of them have heard of it, and they ignore the comment, but Rosa feels her heart stop for an instant. It's *not* just 'any other road'—it's where Ernesto almost died! She tells the others that Palenque is not just any place, but a very important site. No one contradicts her and nobody cares. Resigned to the indifference of the others, Rosa sits back and enjoys the delicious memories of her encounter with Ernesto a few days ago in the cloud forest.

Ernesto's name flutters through her heart like a butterfly.

12. The Beast

I

On the night of October 16, two cattle trucks with their human cargo arrive in Arriaga, not far from the West Coast of Mexico. A little before entering the city, the coyote tells his passengers to find a bathroom, that is, a private place in the bushes on the side of the road.

"I don't need to," a young boy says.

"Doesn't matter. Go!"

"That's good advice," someone comments. "Who knows how filthy the bathrooms will be at the station?"

One of the vehicles pulls into a gas station. The other, where Rosa is riding, continues on for some ten kilometers, goes over a railroad crossing, enters a street parallel to the train tracks, and stops behind an enormous warehouse.

Where is the grand train station, Rosa asks herself, with high ceilings and enormous English clocks, the well-dressed passengers hurrying when loudspeakers announce departures, and all the people waving goodbye when the train whistles? Where is everything she saw so many times on TV at her aunt's house in Baeza?

Once again, in small groups, the immigrants silently run in the dark, crouching along a somber freight train until they come to the last boxcar.

Sabino stealthily opens the sliding doors, and gives them their final instructions in a low voice.

"Remember: no flashlights on the train until you've left the city, and be sure to turn them off when you come to a town. You want to have some air circulation, so don't close the car door, but don't open it more than ten centimeters, or someone might see you. And don't drink any more water than you have to, so you won't have to go to the bathroom. At noon tomorrow the train's going to stop to switch locomotives before it gets to the station. My colleagues will be waiting for you there. We've gotten two other trucks that'll take you to the Texas border."

He is immediately bombarded with complaints:

"Why aren't you coming with us?"

"What if someone has to go to the bathroom?"

"What if someone opens the door and sees us?"

"What do we do if no one's there when we arrive?"

"Nothing bad's going to happen if you obey your instructions," says Sabino from the darkness, and with a hint of exasperation.

Rosa sees, far away, a well-illuminated train station and imagines the happiness of the families traveling on another train, seated in nice leather seats, with a courteous gentleman dressed in white jackets offering them food and drink.

"All aboard! *The Beast* is about to depart!"

"*Beast?* Why did he call it *The Beast*?" Rosa wonders. The coyote peremptorily informs them that there is no time for discussion or hesitation, and one by one they pile on to the train, quite unwillingly, but without saying a word. They have covered a huge amount of ground, survived countless dangers and invested their life savings into journey. They're not going to quit now. Everyone finds a place on the boxcar floor and invokes their favorite saint.

When all are aboard, the coyote closes the two doors of the boxcar, leaving only a small space between them. Then he places a short metal bar that fits tightly into the slot to prevent the doors from closing with the rattle of the train.

"Don't move this; it'll let the air flow in, but without anyone seeing you. Good night everyone," he says, "try to get some sleep."

They are startled by the metallic sound of a bell ringing three times. The train emits a shrill whistle and then lurches forward. The steady rocking relaxes them.

As the train roars off, leaving behind the city, the people turn on their flashlights and get out some food. There are 50 passengers.

One after another, the passengers begin exchanging jokes. Soon, perhaps because their repertoire has run dry or because the late hour has made them more introspective, the conversation turns to their hopes and desires, their fantasies about life in that Northern country.

"I just want to save enough dollars to put new a roof on my mother's house," says a young man in his twenties. "A real

154

one, I mean, no straw that blows away in the wind. It's going to be a nice cement roof."

"Well, be sure you make the walls brick or cement," says a certain know-it-all, "because if you leave the adobe, the ceiling will come crashing down on her head."

"I'll be happy if I can send a little money to my wife and kids," says another man, "so they don't have to worry about making it last until the end of the month. It's crazy how expensive things are these days!"

"Yeah, the cost of living is just too much, and with inflation, and no good jobs. It's terrible this year. The export of Ecuadorian oil was supposed to help us, but it's only helped the rich."

"Shhhhh! It's late," complain those who want to sleep.

Rosa appreciates this intervention because talk of oil only brings painful memories. Conversation continues in a whisper between some sleepless passengers. She wraps her head in a sweater to avoid hearing it.

Flashlights go off, whispers are hushed, and sleep finally silences all. The rhythmic clattering of the train mixes with the snores.

II

A long, thin rectangle of light streams through the gap between the metal doors, announcing a morning without birds. Several heads are crowded around the opening, competing for a chance to peek out at the legendary Mexico of *corridos* and Mariachis.

"What do you see?" Ask the others.

"Nothing. Just fields. I don't know why we have to hide like this, as if we were going to steal something! There's nothing to steal!"

"Do see you see anything else?"

"Well, the sun, orange, moving along with us."

"Let me take a peek."

The young men crowd around each other. Everybody wants to peek through the narrow space.– Some are on their bellies, others squatting, others perched on the shoulders of other men. They form a human tower with eyes eager for any little diversion.

"Why are you all so curious about a country that doesn't want us traveling through?" says a woman.

But Mexico is neighbor to that other country that has so captured their imaginations; it is worthy of a certain respect for that reason alone. And so they continue peeking through the gap and narrating.

"I think we're near a village! There's a cemetery surrounded by cypresses," says a man who is spying from the top of the tower. "Now there's a little cluster of houses."

"Hey! Hey! What's happening now?"

"Somebody's coming off the roof of the train!"

"Let me see—move over! Oh my god, he's right, there's people on top of the train!"

"What the hell?!"

"I guess they're traveling for free."

"Let me see! Let me see! Yeah, we're definitely in a village now. Everyone, be quiet. There is a sign there, it says 'Morelia'."

The tower of watchers crumbles and everyone quiets down. The train stops in what seems to be a station. They can't tell for sure, since they are in the last car, but they hear footsteps and fragments of conversation getting closer and closer.

No, it's not around here. That one over there, maybe? Yes, that's it. Who told you ...? ...they told me that ....

Inside the boxcar muffled whispers flutter like the wings of frightened birds.

"Shhhh ...Everybody, be quiet. I want to hear what they're saying. I think it's the cops, or maybe a railroad guard. Shhhh ..."

The air is dense under the weight of fear. The people hold their breath, put a hand over their mouths, stifling their gasps and the "oh's" drowning in their throats.

"They're coming here."

"They'll see us through the opening."

"Close the door."

"Don't close it!"

"Close it! They're going to see us if you don't!"

"What if we can't open it afterwards?"

156

"I can open any door!"

"Close it now! They're coming! Pull the bar out!"

"Careful, do it quietly!"

While one of the men pulls the metal bar out, two others try to close the boxcar door as quietly as possible. They only have to move it ten centimeters, and in a couple of seconds it closes with a smooth click.

Now there is no sound from outside. Flashlights are off. People begin to pray. Some repress a cough. No one moves from his place. Fear has laid siege to each body.

After a few minutes of agonized waiting, there is a great clank and then the wheels begin to screech over the rails. When the sideways shaking begins, everyone relaxes and smiles of relief and gratitude spread throughout the boxcar.

They are outside the town whose name no one recalls except Rosa. For her, Morelia sounds like a delicious fruit.

"Thank God those bastards didn't find us!"

"Jesus, that was scary. It's so good to be moving again!"

Now that the immediate danger has passed, people wipe the cold, nervous sweat off their faces.

"Hey, you guys should open the door. There's no danger now."

A couple of men position themselves on either side of the metallic doors and begin to tug.

"One, two, three, now! Okay, let's try again."

"Shit! My hands are so damn sweaty they're slipping. Hold on." He wipes his hands on his jeans.

"There's nowhere to grab onto this fucking door."

"How did Sabino open it so easily?"

"He opened it from the outside! There's two handles, so it was easy for him."

"Well, there's no handles inside this shithole. These cars are for boxes, not people. And boxes don't open doors."

"Let's try again. We need more people. Everybody, lean up against the door and when I say three, we pull. OK?"

"OK."

"One, two, three!"

"Shit!"

Nothing.

Ten minutes later, the passengers realize that it's impossible to open the boxcar doors from the inside. Whether by design or "as divine punishment," as someone says, the simple fact sinks in: when the doors close, they are locked, "like the doors of Heaven to the unrepentant sinner," adds another, in a moralistic tone.

"Jesus Christ, what did I tell you? You shouldn't have closed it!"

"Listen, Asshole, if I hadn't closed it we'd all be in jail right now. Or getting deported."

"We're in jail right now, you jerk. Worse than jail – no air is gonna get in."

"Well, then, why don't you shut your fat mouth and don't breathe."

"Will you guys please stop? It's going to be a lot worse if we start fighting," says an older man. "We'll be there soon. We need to stop talking and conserve the air."

Rosa is crouched down in a corner. She looks at the locked door and understands what could happen to them. She looks for comfort in the little card given to her by Miguel: "Whoever you are, Mashimón," she pleads, silently, "please make this door open!"

The first hour is bearable. It's early and the sun hasn't yet heated up the metal boxcar.

A low groan occasionally accentuates the silence.

Those not blessed with ignorance remember the group of immigrants who suffocated in a U.S.-bound train. Rosa is aware of a change in the air. It's getting hot.

In a couple of hours the temperature rises to what feels like around 120 degrees. The boxcar is a furnace. One by one, people empty their water bottles.

"I'm getting leg cramps," a man complains.

"Lack of water."

"I think …we could die in here."

"Don't say that, man. We've got to be getting close to the station. Someone will open the door for us!"

"I wish I'd never gotten it into my head to go to the North."

"Let's just try to stay calm," says a woman. "Panic is our worst enemy—it uses up oxygen. Think about something beautiful. Think about God."

A low sob is heard. The woman adds:

"Don't cry— it uses up water."

In the next hour, a middle-aged man loses consciousness.

One after another, the passengers hear a buzzing; they jerk, and they tremble, and then they, too, fall back and faint. The women and the younger men last longer. How much longer they don't know. Someone asks the time. Rosa looks at her watch and wants to respond, but realizes that her voice is stuck to her throat.

Disjointed, incoherent phrases and gasps are heard. And then, unbearable silence.

Tears don't come. Rosa's weeping is dry, more suffocation than release. Now she hears the sound of water running over a rock, or little pebbles falling into a well, and water flowing close to her ears but very far from her mouth. On the verge of hallucination, in the fleeting moment in which consciousness can contemplate death, she thinks of paradise. "If I die today, I'll float up to heaven like a bubble and wait for Mom there."

13. María Moreno

I

The flight from Guatemala to Ecuador was turbulent. October is hurricane season in the Gulf of Mexico. Ernesto's plane flew over the Pacific but a storm's electrified tentacles stretched to the other side of the continent. But when he arrived in the Ecuadorian capital, by nightfall, the weather was clear.

From the window in his little hostel at the top of a hill in Quito, Ernesto now watches the lights of a city that curls, like a brilliant reptile, along a narrow valley among the Andes.

The following day he takes a bus heading north. Traveling on the Pan-American highway, the same road he travelled through Mexico and Central America, is like finding an old friend. He arrives in Otavalo at 10 AM.

The canvas-covered stands of Otavalo's famous Inca market fill the city's central square and surrounding streets. The sun is at its zenith but fails to provide much warmth today. Ernesto buys a poncho and a hat to fend off the cold that descended the mountains overnight.

"It looks good on you," the saleslady tells him: "just like a real Quichua."

Ernesto heads to the corral where people are selling livestock and leans up against the fence. Someone waves three dollars in his face and says "pooedo photo seeñor?" in painfully bad Spanish. Ernesto smiles at the tall blonde man and replies in English. "Sure, but I think you have the wrong model. I'm from California and I'm just passing through this part of the world."

The tourist blushes and, in an accent marked by open diphthongs, begs pardon for the misunderstanding. He half-jokingly tells Ernesto that, in a way, everyone is just passing through this world.

"Yup," Ernesto agrees, "we're all just pilgrims. And where are you from, sir?"

"Australia. I'm with a mountaineer group. We're going to climb the Imbabura Volcano."

"Where is that?"

160

"Just north of here. We'll start the climb from a little village nearby, called Esperanza."

"That's a coincidence! I'm also going to Esperanza."

"Really? No one goes there unless they're climbing the volcano."

"Well, except people from there."

"Oh sure," says the Australian.

Something tells Ernesto that he may be from this part of the world. He suspects he'll find the Morenos in one of these sunny, cool valleys. "I'd like to be from here," he thinks. He enjoys this industrious town full of women with black skirts, embroidered blouses and strands of golden beads; and men with wide brimmed hats, ponchos and three-quarter pants. From what he can see, this is a town of shopkeepers and artisans, of musicians and *luthiers*, of affable and creative people. He truly hopes to find Morenos here, and find his place in the world.

The trip to Esperanza takes an hour, including all the stops to let shepherd girls and their flocks of sheep pass. "And why not?" thinks Ernesto. "After all, this rich land was theirs before the highway was built."

The bus stops at a corner in the small village, and a local teenager approaches the mountaineers.

"My name is José Luis, and I'm a climbing guide. If you want to climb Imbabura, I can take you tomorrow morning."

After some brief haggling over price, more to follow local custom than from necessity, they set a departure time for the following day.

"What about you?" the teen ask Ernesto. "Would you like to go? It's beautiful up there. You can see all the way to the Cayambé glacier."

"I have something to do here first. Would you happen to know a family named Moreno?"

"Moreno, Moreno …let's see …" the boy seems to think hard. "Yes, there is a little old lady by the name of Moreno up on the hill over there. She's a widow, and lives alone."

Ernesto is a little disappointed, and he wonders if she might have family in another village.

"Can you take me there?" he asks.

"Sure, I can take you. When do you want to go?"

"Right now."

"Ok, you can leave your backpack at my house if you want. It's not far."

José Luis explains that the rocky trail that goes up the hill is part of the Great Inca Trail network that crisscrosses this part of the continent from Ecuador all the way to the top of Chile and Argentina. It's obvious he's a very informed guide.

"Did you say you were related to this lady?" he asks.

Ernesto tells him a quick version of his story.

"I know lots of people who've gone to the United States. Especially musicians from Otavalo. Maybe your mom went north with a musical group."

Ernesto smiles to himself and thinks his grandfather would love the sound of "María Moreno, Quichua musician from Otavalo."

At a bend in the trail they come upon an oxcart loaded with a massive heap of yellow hay. Three kids are seated on top like little maharajas, each one cradling a baby llama in his arms. They exchange greetings.

A little ways further on, Jorge Luis stops and points to a spot on the other side of a gully.

"That's the house."

The adobe hut with its straw roof decorates the emerald hillside like a golden brooch.

Once on the other side, they find themselves in front of a fence made of rocks and prickly plants which surrounds the house delimiting the property. Inside the fenced yard, some laundry has been stretched over rocks to dry out. In the distance are several planted fields.

"This is where doña ...Moreno lives. I can't remember her first name."

From his cage hanging in a tree, a parrot squawks to announce the visitors: "*Cholito! Cholito*! *Brrr, brrr. Cholito*!"

An elderly face appears in the window. José Luis says something in Quichua and the woman responds in the same language. In a few seconds, having put on her hat, she is at the door.

162

II

She is a short, somewhat stooped woman. Or maybe the stoop just makes her seem short. Her name is Alcira. The black felt hat, like that of a 19th century English gentleman, gives her an air of dignity and elegance. The full, calf-length, blue wool skirt is trimmed with bright red piping at the hem. A thick white braid falls from the English hat down to her waist. The woman's skin is the same hue as Ernesto's, but the dry mountain wind and her advanced age have left its mark on her face in the form of a hundred thin lines.

The two Quichuas continue speaking in their language until the lady invites them to enter the house. When Ernesto's eyes adjust to the dim light, he sees that the house consists of just one room, no larger than his own bedroom in the States. The floor is of packed earth. Tools for working the fields stand in one corner, along with a loom. On the opposite side is a stick ladder leading to a small loft. This seems to be the woman's bedroom. Beneath the loft is a cubicle for the animals, where Ernesto immediately recognizes several furry critters from his childhood. Their endearing high-pitched squeaks remind him of when he used to give them baths in the sink, something his father warned him not to do:

They're going to die on you, Ernesto. You shouldn't bathe guinea pigs because they're from a dry climate. The Andes Mountains are cold and dry.

So why are they called "Guinea" pigs? Or "India" pigs in Spanish?

I have no idea. But I used to see them in all the Quichua houses when I worked in Ecuador.

Did you work in the Andes, Dad?

No, I worked in the jungle to the east because that's where the oil was. But there are Quichuas there too, Amazonian Quichuas, and they raise guinea pigs just like yours. And they keep them dry!

José Luis sees Ernesto watching the animals and explains that she raises them to sell in the market.

Ernesto picks one up and pets it while he talks to his guide, who is now his translator:

"Please tell her my story. I'm wondering if she might be my grandmother."

The boy speaks in Quichua for a few minutes and Ernesto holds his breath as doña Alcira watches him with interest. Then, clasping her callused hands over her lap, she speaks for a long time with José Luis. Then she takes Ernesto's hands in hers, looks him in the eyes and says something that Ernesto doesn't understand a word of.

According to José Luis, the woman says that she had a daughter who moved to Quito to find work. Her name was María. María Moreno.

Ernesto inhales sharply and feels a rush of excitement. Could that have been his mother?

"She says that one day she got news from her daughter that she was pregnant," the translation continues.

The two Quichuas look intently at Ernesto. For a moment, time seems to stop for him and the imagined baby dances in his mind like a little trembling flame.

"And soon after her daughter sent word that she was going to the United States with her baby."

Was that me? Oh my God! Was that me? Ernesto asks himself, but the narrative continues without pause:

For a while she received money from her daughter in the States, but then it stopped. And then one day a letter arrived.

A suffocating knot forms in his throat. His mother had him in Quito, without any friends or family? And then she went alone with him to the United States? What else? What happened then?

The story continues in Quichua. If this is his grandmother, Ernesto muses while the other two are talking, he is definitely going to help her. When he gets a job and has money, he will buy her a house in La Esperanza, one with no ladder, and with a little garden. He is going to…José Luis interrupts his thoughts:

"Doña Alcira is telling me that one day she received a letter informing her that her daughter had died and had left a baby. The letter came from the United States. It was written in Spanish, and a friend translated it into Quichua. She still has it."

164

Ernesto had already imagined the possibility that his mother may have died. But to hear it this way, from a real person, suddenly hits him very hard. He asks if he can see the letter. He is consumed by desire to learn about his mother and steels himself against the tragic ending. Doña Alcira perceives his nervousness and offers him some coca leaf tea. This will give him strength of spirit, she tells him, and he'll feel better.

He accepts, and as the fire has been kindled since morning, the water boils in just a few minutes. The grandmother puts in some of the magical leaves, steeps the tea, and pours it into three little aluminum cups. While the boys sip their tea—José Luis with gusto and Ernesto with almost religious solemnity—the woman retreats into a dark corner of the house.

Loose guinea pigs dart around; the parrot takes up his monologue "*cholito, cholito*" and the seconds pass slowly for Ernesto. Has grandmother misplaced the letter? Does she not remember where she put it? Or has she, in her dotage, imagined the entire story?

When the woman emerges from the shadows, she carries a little box in her hand. It is tied up with a ribbon that was pink in former times. Her arthritic fingers have trouble with every loop and Ernesto restrains himself from snatching it from her hands. The paper is a like parchment, and the ink of the letters typed on an old typewriter has faded somewhat, but the words are still legible. Ernesto reads aloud:

Mrs. Alcira Moreno Quipé:
We regret to inform you that your daughter, María Moreno, passed away on this day in the city of San Diego. The weeks-old child has been placed in the care of a convent of this city. If you wish to make arrangements for the extradition of the baby and/or your daughter's mortal remains, you must present this letter to the Embassy of the United States in Quito and cover all costs.Our sincere condolences and profound sympathy on the loss of your family member.
Wilson Freitas, M.D.
San Diego Medical Center

Tears fill Ernesto's eyes.

III

He returns the letter with trembling hands.

"María Moreno, the convent, San Diego. It all fits!" Ernesto gazes out a little window toward an immaculate Andean sky as he ponders these details. Even the vastness of his old dream can't contain his excitement.

"So this is really my grandma!" he thinks, "and I'm from here, from these mountains on the belly of the world, the land of the great Inca Empire! Who knows, maybe I'm the descendent of some Inca warrior who defended his people against the Spanish invaders. I have to find out more!"

"What about my birth date, and the date on the letter? Let's see, does it say?"

He looks at the letter again, and sees some faded numbers at the bottom of the page. He shows it to José Luis, then drinks the rest of his coca tea in one gulp.

"Oh, man!" exclaims José Luis, "It says 1960, so you should be 35 years old!"

Ernesto's inflated Inca fantasy falls to earth with a crash.

"How could it be such a coincidence?" he wonders after a long silence.

"Well, every other woman in the world is named María," José Luis points out. "As for Moreno, I don't know how common it is… But I know a lot of people end up in San Diego when they move to the United States. At least they start out there. It's like the front door."

Doña Alcira refills their tea cups and changes the subject to this year's potato harvest and the price of quinoa. Ernesto still feels moved and wants to give something to this ancient woman who lost a daughter—a daughter with the same name as his mother—and a grandson lost to her somewhere in the United States, who might at this very moment be wondering about the other María Moreno.

He asks if there is anything in particular that she needs.

"If someday you could send me a pair of glasses," says the woman through her translator, "that would help me to keep weaving on my loom. I would be so grateful. My old eyes can't see the threads anymore."

166

Ernesto promises to send her several pairs of eyeglasses of different strengths.

With a quick movement the woman catches a guinea pig and says something to José Luis, who translates for Ernesto:

"Doña Alcira says that if you like guinea pig, she'll cook one for dinner."

Ernesto looks dismayed.

"*Dinner?*"

"Yeah. You've never had guinea pig? It's our national dish. It's delicious and healthy!"

"Um, no, thank you. That's really nice but ... I'm a vegetarian! Well, not all the time, but ... I'm on a diet."

The woman's wrinkled face breaks into a toothless smile as she hears the translation about vegetarianism and diet—two unfathomable concepts—and the sadness in the room lightens a bit.

As they say goodbye she places a confection she has made from the tuna fruit into Ernesto's hand, and blesses him in Quichua. She tells him that she will always remember him as if he were the grandson she has never met.

The boys take the trail back to the village. The sound of the parrot 's words, *cholito-cholito*, fades into the distance as they walk.

14. Twin Souls

I

The train's stopping. The few who are still conscious hear the metallic screech.

Bang! Bang! Bang! Frantically, they beat their palms and fists against the walls and doors of the boxcar. For some, this is the last effort they make before losing consciousness.

Suddenly the door slides open with a roar. The blinding light makes some people believe it is the door to hell. But it is not, they realize, because in hell there is fire and here is the blessed air of heaven.

Those who can launch themselves through the doorway gasping like fish out of water. Rosa crawls dizzily to the exit and lets her head hang outside to the boxcar. She breathes deeply, filling her lungs. With a clearer head now, she jumps down.

They are in a desolate place, no station in sight; other boxcars stand darkly on tracks parallel to theirs. Three boys are looking at them.

After a few minutes, the stronger passengers go back into the wagon, drag out those who are lying inert and lay them down on the rocky ground beside the railroad bed. Risking being seen, others go out in three trips with empty bottles, bringing them back full of water. Little by little the dehydrated passengers come to life and those who lost consciousness regain color in their yellow faces.

This miracle of resurrection, as someone called it, has left them in a strange mental state; they almost do not register the presence of curious faces, upside down, observing them from the roof of the train. Fifteen minutes pass before they realize that the three boys who were standing there, and probably opened the boxcar door, are part of a group that has been traveling with them on top of the train, all this time.

The locomotive emits a whistle. A wave of panic gets their hearts pounding and they fall over one another to get back into the heart of The Beast, which clanks backwards and then lurches forward with the familiar sound of wheels in movement. This time, by unspoken agreement, the doors remain wide open.

Those who went for water run alongside and are hoisted up as the train begins to accelerate.

The three boys take advantage of the confusion and get into the car, as if it were public property.

"Sorry; it's too sunny up there."

"Who are you?" they are asked.

"We're the ones who opened the doors for you. You'd all be dead meat if we hadn't."

"What the hell were you doing on the top of the train?"

"Going to the States, just like you. That's where you're going, right? Hey, anyone got any food? We haven't eaten for a day and a half, me and my little brother."

The boy speaks with that heartrending tone acquired through misfortune. Astonished, the passengers give them some crackers. The boys eat hungrily and speak between mouthfuls.

"It feels great to travel inside! First-class ticket!"

"Did you hear us banging on the door?" a man asks.

"Yes, sir, that's why we opened it. We thought these boxcars were full of grain. They're not usually empty. That's why we thought the noises were strange. Hey, how did you get an empty boxcar?"

"We paid a coyote. He arranged everything," the man explains.

"Oh, you're rich people! You gotta have a lot of money to pay the *pollero*. I'm gonna be rich too, when I get to the States."

"No, son, nobody's rich here. I had to borrow money against my house to pay for this trip. What are you planning on doing in the North?"

"Look for my mom and dad. We haven't seen them in six years. They send us money and presents and we talk on the phone sometimes. They keep promising they're gonna come back, but they never do. Pretty soon they're gonna forget all about us. That's why me and my little brother decided to go there."

Rosa listens, stunned. "They're looking for their mom and dad! Just like me! Of course, it's different," she thinks, "my mom would never going to forget me. At least, I don't think she would."

A flurry of alarm brushes her like the wings of a nocturnal bird, and she tries to shoo the thought away.

"What are your names?" Rosa asks.

"Darío. This is my friend Sergio. And this, my little brother, Manucho. What's your name?"

"Rosa. I mean, Eugenio."

The boy smiles and keeps talking.

"Our parents don't know me and my brother are going up there. We're gonna surprise them. I mean, if we get there. This is our fifth try. They always grab us in Tapachula and send us back before we can get the train. But this time, we're gonna make it!"

"Where are you boys from?" a woman asks.

"Nicaragua. We're from Managua—the big city!"

"I'm from Guatemala," says the other boy.

"How did you get this far?"

"Freight trains. But not in the boxcar like y'all. Just on top."

"Don't the railroads police make you get off?"

"Nope. We jump off the train when it starts pulling into a station. And then we run on the side streets—we run faster than the train! The train always stops for a few minutes, so we jump right back on at the end of the town, when it's still going slow. Nobody sees us that way. And if they do, it's too late! Ha! They're not gonna catch us this time, ain't that right, Manucho?" he says to his little brother.

The other boy does not answer. He is already asleep, with his head on a woman's lap.

"These are our guardian angels," the woman comments. "God sent them to us."

"I'm glad he's sleeping," says the big brother. He's really tired because I don't let him sleep up there. It's too dangerous."

"Why?" Rosa asks.

"Cuz you can fall off if you're sleeping" Darío says. "On the tank cars, you can tie a belt to one of those rods up there. But on the boxcars like this one you don't have nothing to hang on to."

"Has anyone ever fallen?"

"Oh, yeah."

The boy's expression is like a sad, little old man, aged before his time. Everyone is quiet. A little later, the boy's friend recounts in a barely audible voice:

"My friend fell off. The train went over him and cut off one of his legs."

"People fall sometimes and they're okay. But sometimes they fall really bad, between the wheels," Darío explains.

The people continue listening in solemn silence. Sergio continues:

"Sometimes you have to jump from train to train while they're moving, to get on the right one, cuz not all the trains go to the border, you know? But the tracks are old. See how the train rocks from side to side? You know how sometimes one boxcar goes to the right and the one behind it goes to the left? They don't go together. That's why it's dangerous to jump, cuz even when you plan it just right, sometimes the wagons come together, and sometimes they go apart. They're pretty bad! And sometimes they jump right off the tracks."

"What happens to the people who get, ah … hurt by the train?" someone asks.

"I guess there's hospitals where they take the guys who get really mutilated. The Diocese of Tapachula, of Arriaga, or the Immigrant House on the other side, in Tecún Umán. They say the kids who go there are 'fallen angels'. Sometimes the adults don't want to go back home cuz they're ashamed of going back with only one leg, or sometimes with no legs at all."

"I saw a guy fall. The train was going really fast and it went through some trees, lots of branches. We crouched down just in time, but he didn't. A branch hit him in the chest and he went flying off. I don't know if he lived or died."

"No wonder don Sabino calls it *The Beast*," someone mutters.

"Yeah, or the Train of Death."

There is a fearful nodding of heads and a long silence. The fathers and mothers who are listening tremble, just thinking of their own children.

"What do you do when it rains?" Rosa asks.

"We have plastic sheets. But one night it hailed. It was like the sky was falling on top of us. Like God was throwing rocks on us."

A few hours later the boys say goodbye. They will soon arrive at the crossing where they will transfer to the train heading to Nogales.

"Thanks for the crackers. If I were you I'd close the door, but jam something in it so you can open it up again. But not much, so the hounds can't stick their noses in. The *migra* and the railroad cops have dogs, you know," Darío explains, "to see if they smell any 'chickens' in the cars."

II

The train slows down. Since the totem pole of observers has not announced their arrival at a village or station, the other passengers don't know what's happening. The observers move away from the opening. Nerves are raw.

"It's gotta be some check point," says a thin voice, choked by the thought of an imminent catastrophe.

Whatever it is, they all agree that the doors must not be completely shut. Despite the risk of being caught by the police or sniffed out by their diabolical dogs, the metal bar is untouchable.

A far-off bark makes their hair stand on end.

"Did you hear that?"

"What? Some stupid dog, that's all."

"Dogs that bark don't bite."

"But they betray!"

"Man, you're scared of everything, even your own shadow."

"I'm just saying, what if they're police dogs? German shepherds can smell you from really far away."

It is 12:20 P.M. and the train has stopped. Sweat breaks out on their palms and brows. Their lips tremble in silent prayers.

With no warning, the door opens with a metallic screech and a bang elicits an involuntary and shrill 'Oh!' from many a throat, like the shriek of a bird. They see a uniformed figure against the light.

"Everyone out!" The order is given in an imperious tone.

Immobilized by the fear running through their spines, or perhaps by a determination to not surrender like a flock of sheep, no one moves.

"What the hell's the matter with you all? Oh, my uniform. It's just a disguise. I'm don Sabino's partner. Let's go, people, everybody out! The bus's waiting for us on the road. Now get your asses up!"

Everyone is caught up in contagious laughter, because to survive a disaster always fills people with joy, even if it is a nervous feeling of joy.

A stream of impatient travelers spills out of the boxcar and runs in the indicated direction. They are in a semi-desert and the risk of being discovered makes them step lightly and quickly like a cloud of insects.

In no time they are on board a modern, brilliant blue bus. From the windows, 50 euphoric faces observe the change of locomotives that has brought them to this point and that is now going to move onto another track. Rosa waves at the young boys less fortunate than her. They are preparing to jump from one wagon to another and continue their journey on the roof of another *Beast*. Their destination is Nogales; afterwards, the North.

The vehicle takes off and is soon navigating suburban avenues of what seems to be a good-sized town. They stop at a hotel on a quiet street. The owners, like the owners of the private buses, are part of a large multinational network of complicit, corrupt, public officials and criminal organizations working in the business of people smuggling.

There they will pass many hours, before leaving for their final, golden destination.

The place is modest. The brick floors of the indoor courtyard, like the bathrooms, smell of creosote. The travelers exchange currency at the reception desk. Rosa buys a used baseball hat, a few packages of cookies, and a telephone card.

As always, she must call twice: the first call is to ask them to find her mother in the rows of vegetables; the second is when she calculates that Alba has had enough time to get to the telephone.

"Mom, I'm in Mexico!"

"Rosa, it's so nice to hear your voice! I've been worried, honey. When are you going to cross over?"

"Tonight. We're leaving for the border in a few hours."

"Be very careful, Rosita."

Rosa hears a stifled sob when her mother says her name.

173

"And do me a favor, Rosa, call your grandmother. I have to go back now. There's a lot of work today."

"I'll call her right away. Okay, Mom, I'm sending you a big, big hug."

III

At three o'clock in the afternoon they begin the last part of their journey through Mexico. They are stopped at various checkpoints along the way, but the police do not check their documents, meaning that the clandestine travelers have "friends" on this stretch of highway.

By the time they reach the Mexico-Texas border, they have already journeyed more than 4,000 miles from their far-off port of departure, Guayaquil.

"Look, there's the Rio Grande," says the guide, pointing," the river that separates the country of the fortunate from the country of the unfortunate. There it is!"

"God must've been angry when he marked this division," someone observes.

"Maybe that's why here they call it the *Río Bravo*," the driver jokes. [7]

They arrive at a makeshift camp used by immigrants, on the outskirts of town. It is still day, and at nightfall, they will be taken across the border in trucks, hidden under boxes of merchandize.

"You can get off the bus now if you need to use the bathroom. There's a latrine over there," the guide says. "But come back soon: this is no-man's land."

With no law enforcement, this place functions as a meeting point for the poorest of all the illegal immigrants from Latino America, who gather on the south shore of the Rio Grande, as well as for the more fortunate like Rosa's group, their coyotes and guides

It is also a focal point of drug traffickers and criminals. As the driver has said, a den of outlaws.

---

[7] "Bravo" in Spanish = *angry*

Rosa also gets off the bus. She is burning with curiosity to see the river.

With a few others, she walks across the perimeter of the camp, encircled by a ring of rust, burned cars, and mountains of junk. She stands on the river shore. The ugliness of the famous river surprises her. The innocent blue sky is not reflected in its water, as she had expected; instead of water flowers and branches with green moss and silver lichen, she sees plastic sacks and bottles floating in the current. Nor is it lined with lush vegetation, but just a few clumps of scraggly *álamo* trees and junk piles left by the legion of undocumented travelers who have camped on this bank for years and years.

"An old river," Rosa thinks, "nothing like our rivers. It's disgusting. What would Mr. Romero say if he saw it?" she asks herself, remembering *The Junglenaut*, the book of poems her teacher gave her before she set off on her journey.

She walks toward the camp, disappointed. On the way, some children ask for food. Dirty, in rags and some with wounded faces and legs, they arrived on *The Beast* a few days ago and are waiting for the right moment to make the crossing. Rosa takes a roll of crackers from her backpack and gives each of them a few.

"What happened to your eye?" she asks one of the boys.

"The *judicial* got me."

"What is that?"

"The *judicial?* The Mexican Federal Police. They made us get off the train and they took us out into the trees and beat us up and robbed us," he says, speaking with a full mouth. "I lost everything I had, but at least they didn't throw me in jail."

"Yeah, they go around with hoods on so nobody knows they're from the *judicial*. But I saw their license plate," explains another boy, extending his hand toward the rolls of crackers.

"How did you eat if you didn't have money?" asks Rosa, continuing her line of questioning.

"He didn't!" exclaims another boy, laughing.

"Look at his ribs!" says another, lifting up his friend's shirt.

"Get your fucking hands off me!!" he screams to the boy. "Yeah, I had to get off the train in each town and beg," he continues, "or steal fruit from the gardens near the tracks."

175

"Me, too," says another boy, "these guys went through my pockets when they got on the train and then they hit me because I had so too little." He lifts up his lip and shows Rosa the blood encrusted holes in his gums where teeth should have been. "They were *Salvatrucha* gang members. I could tell by their tattoos. Could I have another cookie?"

"They took one guy off the train because he didn't have anything for them to steal."

"Yes, it's fucking ugly up there when the *maras*[8] come." That's why you have to take sticks and rocks to defend yourself. Any more cookies?"

Rosa takes her second and last package from her backpack and encourages the boys to keep on talking. She wants to hear everything. Someday, she promises herself, the world is going to find out about this—she'll make sure of it. Rosa is surprised by her own emotion. She didn't know she had such a capacity for rage. She's going to write it all down in her journal that very evening.

"At least the Mexican *migra* didn't get us. They arrested some other guys," one of the boys adds, stretching out his hand toward the food source, silently claiming his reward for this information.

The cookies are gone now, and one of the boys licks the wrapper.

"It's cuz they were just kids and they stupidly told the truth—they said they were Hondurans or Salvadorans. If they'd just said they were Mexican, the *migra* would've let 'em go for sure."

"Do you think they'll be locked up for a long time?" Rosa asks.

"Just a little while probably. They usually put all the Central Americans on a bus and ship 'em back to their countries. They travel for like, 10 or 20 hours, I don't know. Everybody cries when they go. The ladies, the boys, even the men. Cuz they have to go back home with no money, or nothing, without having reached the North."

"Yeah, they're embarrassed."

---

[8] Maras = *gangs*

"And they have huge debts to pay back!"

"That's why they call it the 'Bus of Tears'."

Rosa wonders what would happen if they caught her, if they'd send her back to Ecuador, - underneath the line that divides the world into two halves.

"It's even worse for other people" one of the boys says quietly. "My friend got killed by the train. He slipped and the *Beast* ate him. He'll never see his mom in the United States."

A silent cloud of sadness passes a shadow over the boys' eyes, all of them somehow aged by the sheer force of misery and tribulations.

It's getting late and Rosa knows she needs to get back to her group. Submerged in her thoughts, she passes a line of rusty vehicles delimiting the camp and goes to the spot where she got off the bus on the road parallel to the camp. She sees other buses, but they don't belong to her group. Her bus is an unmistakable bright blue. She doesn't see it. She thinks, for a moment, that she's on the wrong road, but there's only one, she remembers. She walks up and down the road, but there's no sign of the bus.

She returns to her starting place. There is no sign of any of her traveling companions either. She sits down to wait beside the road, motionless like a dog waiting for its master.

Her eyes become fixed, undaunted, looking in the direction of the road where the bus should be coming from, since the other side of the road is a dead end.

As the minutes and hours stretch out she becomes more and more worried. She sees the day turning sunset, the sunset turning into night, and the night becoming desperation. A shadow of pain blankets her world as Rosa realizes the bus is not coming back; her group has disappeared, her bright blue bus has gone on without her and she has been left alone. The night around her becomes terrifying and her world falls to pieces.

A whiplash of the hysteria shakes her.

She is on the edge of a dark, infinite abyss, looking down into its center. She feels it sucking her down into a cold and desolate hell. She walks back to where she found the ragged boys, running and swallowing her sobs at each stride. The sobs become convulsive and she falls to her knees. She feels her bones melting; she is drowning, spinning through the air without oxygen; she thinks that she is going to die right then and there from lack of air, on her knees, in no-man's land.

15. The Shuar

I

Standing on the terrace of his hillside hostel in Quito, Ernesto watches an illuminated procession carrying the image of a saint from church to church. Another procession within him is carrying its own images, from one Esperanza to another. But unlike the candle-bearing parishioners below he doesn't know which path to follow. Should he keep wandering this enormous continent looking for a village and a name that perhaps only existed in the imagination of a creative nun?

Ernesto has arrived at one of those crossroads where two opposing voices echo within. A part of him wants to acknowledge the foolishness of this endeavor and abandon it altogether. Something else vehemently urges him on. Giving up now is something he'll regret as long as he lives.

The uncertainty is depressing. He had hoped the climb to Imbabura would clear his head but the beauty of the place just magnified his woes. Those striking, snow-covered peaks and the crystal clear air of the Andes provided no guidance. He was hoping for molten lava and fire to consume his melancholy, but Imbabura is a dormant volcano.

In the kitchen of the little hostel the cook tells him what's on the menu for dinner: "shredded beef and yucca."

"Yucca? What's that?"

"Well, it's a root, also called manioc. It's a native plant where I come from."

"Where are you from?"

"A village in the province of Morona Santiago, east of here, the region called 'The Oriente'; it's a staple of the Shuar."

"The Shuar? I've never heard of them."

"In the old days the Spanish called us *Jívaros*, but that's not a nice name.

"*Jívaros* ... I've heard the name. But I don't know anything about them. What's your village called?"

"Buena Esperanza."

Ernesto looks dumbstruck.

"Are you all right? I think you need to eat," says the man in surprise.

"Yes, yes, I haven't eaten since noon yesterday. Could you bring me the meat with yucca, please?"

Ernesto slowly chews the crisp yucca fries while his mind travels the vast universe of his memories:

"*You were born in Esperanza, Ernesto. That's what the nuns told us.*"

"*But remember, Esteban, we don't know if it's Esperanza or Buena Esperanza. Don't you remember there was some doubt about that?*" his mother said to his father.

"*Doubt? What doubt, Isabel? There's no doubt that it was Esperanza. The Mother Superior decided to add 'Buena' just to complicate things. And she never let us see that famous document. Besides, there is no Buena Esperanza in Mexico. The village is called Esperanza. I think it's a typical case of false memory. If I'm wrong about that then my name is not Esteban Ruiz.*"

"*According to your birth certificate your real name is Estebani! Remember?*"

Ernesto smiles at the memory. He doesn't remember how the conversation ended but he knows his father has always been very stubborn. He's one of those people who never second guess themselves. And his mother, well, she's very persistent. "Is it possible that the village was called Buena Esperanza?" He wonders. "I wish I could get my hands on that document, assuming it even exists!"

"Can I ask you a question?" says Ernesto to the Shuar cook as he returns his empty plate. "Do you know anyone named Moreno in your village?"

"Moreno? No. I left the village when I was a little boy and I don't remember all the families' names."

"Is it possible to call someone there?"

"There aren't any telephones in the village. Maybe you should go there. The *Oriente* is very beautiful. It's a jungle, part of the Ecuadorian Amazon. You would love it."

I know, Dad told me it was beautiful, Ernesto remembers. There must be a lot more that he didn't tell me though.

"It is a very far?"

"By bus it's 12 hours to Macas, the capital of the province. And another 45 minutes to the village."

Ernesto thanks the cook for the information, although he knows that the possibility of a Moreno having emigrated from such a remote place is another delusion. But something extraordinary obliges him pursue it, something that defies logic. He feels like he's reaching his hand into the darkness hoping someone will take it. The surge of mental energy he got from hearing about this other Esperanza grows as it traverses his body. In a few minutes he is busy packing up his belongings and requesting a four A.M. wake up call.

II

The bus is disproportionately large for the narrow road it's navigating. Enormous plantain and philodendron leaves brush the sides of the vehicle and even enter the open window, caressing Ernesto's cheeks with their sylvan touch.

The driver stops at the head of a trail that cuts through a green and yellow field of soaring *guadúa* cane, each over four inches thick. The Shuar community of Buena Esperanza is at the other end of the trail.

The village is a collection of huts in a clearing clustered around an unfinished *plaza*. Not feeling very optimistic, he looks around, waiting for some signal as to how and where to begin.

A round-faced man in his thirties with a long black ponytail comes out of a wooden house.

"Good afternoon. I am Daniel Iaui, the mayor of this town. "How can I help you?"

"Nice meeting you, sir. I heard about your community and came to see it."

"Welcome," says the man, extending his hand. "Where are you from?"

"The United States."

The mayor calls his wife and other members of the community, and soon some 15 Shuar are standing around him in a tight circle. Some of the women have lightly tattooed faces, consisting of two or three lines extending from the inner corner of each eye and across the cheek like a fan. This indigenous touch contrasts with their modern clothing. Most of the men are dressed in khaki pants or jeans and white shirts, and have several strands of red and dark brown seeds around their necks.

The Mayor's wife brings out a wooden bowl filled with a white liquid. Her husband takes a long drink, and it is passed around to everyone.

"Have some *chicha*," says the mayor when the bowl gets to Ernesto. "Ours is made of yucca so it'll taste different from what you've had in Quito. They make theirs with corn."

Ernesto takes a few ceremonious sips. The brew is thick and has an unfamiliar, sweet taste. "Who knows what's in this!" he thinks skeptically.

"So how do you make this?" he asks, just to say something.

"First the yucca is cooked and mashed. To that we add a pre-chewed sweet potato and water, and let the mixture rest overnight. By the next morning it's already fermented and ready to drink!"

Ernesto tries to hide his reaction but blurts out: "So you chew a sweet potato and spit it into the mix?"

"Yes, a sweet potato or some other sweet root. The women do it. It's the saliva that produces fermentation and alcohol."

Oh, yeah, bacteria. And the alcohol comes from the sugar in the potato, of course, Ernesto thinks. He remembers a chemistry class that at the time seemed irrelevant.

"It's excellent for your health. Have some more!"

He obliges with a few more sips. The *chicha* soon lowers his inhibitions, and he delves right into the reason for his visit.

"Mr. Iaui, I'm looking for a family that may live here in Buena Esperanza by the name of Moreno. Are there any Morenos in this village?"

"Moreno? No. That's not a Shuar name. It's a white colonizer's name. We're all Shuars here. My name is Iaui, this is my brother-in-law, Jempe, that family over there is Chiriap. No Morenos, I'm afraid."

"And there never were any?"

"No. Never."

The Shuars look at him with curiosity.

"And you came from the United States to look for a family with this name here?"

"Yes, I came a long way."

"Did you come with friends? Or with your parents?"

"No, I came alone. I heard about this place yesterday in Quito."

After a somewhat awkward silence, the mayor starts to tell him about his community:

"Well, since you have come all the way here, let me tell you about us. We, the indigenous Shuar, used to live off of the bounty of the jungle." We built our homes out of cane and leaves. And we healed our bodies and spirits with medicinal herbs and *ayahuasca*. But when the missionaries came they made us change our customs and forbade us from speaking our Shuar language. They told us we needed to have money to buy things, and that we should build houses with wood instead of *guadúa* canes."

Ernesto looks at the Shuar houses made from long wooden planks and roofed with sheets of corrugated metal, and asks himself if this really is architectural progress.

"Then came the logging companies," the mayor continues, "and they were greedy for our trees. That's when the deforestation began. Many of our communities have been pushed to the edge of the jungle.

Ernesto can't tell if there is sorrow or resentment in the man's voice.

"But here we have this little piece of virgin jungle that you see, and we mean to protect it. And above all, we want to maintain our identity and our traditions at any cost!"

The Shuar's discourse continues for some time and Ernesto supposes that each visitor must listen to this rather depressing story from the mayor.

It's getting late and Ernesto wants to return to Macas, but the mayor invites him to spend the night in the village. Ernesto is hesitant but the man earnestly insists explaining that a storm is coming and he should not be walking the muddy trail when it starts to rain. Ernesto isn't convinced. He knows there is a bus at eight that night. But the Mayor informs him that the bus doesn't drive on the dirt roads when it rains. "Resistance is futile," Ernesto thinks with resignation.

The Shuar gather under a thatched awning that serves as the community center where Ernesto is going to spend the night. An enormous bonfire crackles at the center of the space and the smoke makes him teary-eyed. The women prepare *ayampacos*. A couple of babies coo in braided palm-leaf swings, and now and then someone rocks them.

"Smoked babies," Ernesto thinks. "The smoke and the rocking must keep them drowsy".

More *chicha* is passed around. Not wishing to disappoint his hosts he accepts every time they offer him a sip, noticing that it has higher alcohol content than the afternoon *chicha*. A three-note song accompanies the dance of some girls whose bracelets and necklaces sound like muffled castanets. Ernesto, seated on the ground and leaning against the shed's central post, feels a little dazed and dizzy. He closes his eyes and nods off.

When he opens his eyes, the Shuars have disappeared, and empty *chicha* bowls are strewn about the floor. The fire has burned down to coals.

The place is just a simple structure covered with palm leaves supported by cross beams and several poles. Ernesto unrolls his sleeping bag on a platform built in a corner to protect the occasional guests from vermin; he stokes the fire, puts his flashlight next to his sleeping bag and, certain that every precaution has been taken, gives himself up to sleep.

III

A cold wind awakens him. He doesn't know what time it is but, judging by the few red embers glowing in the fire pit, he guesses he's been sleeping for several hours. The darkness is absolute and the embers look like the piercing eyes of nocturnal creatures. A constant sound, like glasses clinking, is coming from the roof.

Dogs are barking. An overdue thunderstorm, more typical of the Amazonian afternoons than nights, abruptly breaks out and brings torrential rain accompanied by lightning. Between one gust of wind and another, Ernesto hears to the ominous clinking overhead. Struck by an intuition, Ernesto puts his shoes on, grabs his flashlight, and shines it overhead.

A shrill cry bursts from his throat when he sees them: hanging from the rafters are several tiny heads, barely larger than a clenched fist. Swinging violently in the wind, they clash and intertwine around invisible necks. A tuft of dry hair protrudes from each temple. The hollowed eye sockets, protruding cheekbones and involuntary smiles on crudely stitched-together lips point to elaborate ritual.

Something stirs in Ernesto's memory. And then it hits him like an arrow: Holy shit! The Jívaros! The head hunters and their vicious *tzantzas*!

He hears a moan, then realizes that it's coming from his own throat. Primal fear seizes him. He is so paralyzed by it he cannot look away from the galaxy of shrunken heads dangling a short distance above his own.

The day's events jump randomly into his mind and take on a sinister quality that he hadn't noticed before. It becomes obvious to him that they've been lying to him. They drugged him with that awful drink so they could get revenge for what's happened to their people! Soon their poisoned spear-tips will finish him off as a scapegoat. Who better than he to be sacrificed on this propitious night, leaving no trace other than his scorched, shrunken head? He himself told them: '*I came alone, no one knows where I am*.' And no one will *ever* know. How very naïve of him! He has served his head on a platter. The singing and dancing that evening were nothing but a preliminary ritual.

"I have to get out of here!" he thinks, in a panic.

His head spins with each wave of fear that washes over him. He turns off the flashlight so as not to be betrayed by it, and cautiously tries to orient himself in the dark. He suspects watchmen have been placed around the enclosure to prevent his escape.

But it's already too late.

In a flash of lightening, he sees several figures dressed in white and seeming to float through the air. They're standing in a uniform line in front of the shed. Sheer, immeasurable terror grips his throat and cuts off his oxygen for several seconds.

Not taking his eyes off his executioners, the boy takes several steps backward to get away. But someone is already coming up behind him. He's surrounded.

The figure behind him comes closer and shines a flashlight in his face.

"Where are you going, man? Did you have a nightmare? I heard you screaming and came to see if you were okay".

It's the voice of one of Daniel's sons.

"Uh, yeah, I had a bad dream. I was going ...to the bathroom", Ernesto babbles.

"Well the latrine is over there," he says, pointing. "I see my mother forgot to take the clothes off the line, and my dad's shirts are getting wet." He rushes over to gather the hanging clothes from the line. "Good thing the wind didn't blow them away."

"No wonder granddad says that fear has its own eyes," Ernesto thinks as he slowly returns from the latrine.

He stands in the rain for a while trying to clear his foggy head and watches the other boy put the white shirts under the palm roof, and then rekindle the fire.

"The wind is ruining the *tzantzas*" says the young Shuar when he sees the heads all tangled together. He takes them down from the ceiling and places them in a large jar. "They're my dad's favorite hobby" he adds.

"Are they *real*? I mean, from people?"

"Of course not! They're monkeys'," the Shuar replies, surprised by Ernesto's question.

Neither of them sleeps the rest of the night. They dry out by the fire and talk until the rain stops and the frogs fill the air with their crisp croaks. The boy explains to Ernesto that his community is struggling to protect the forest, but they have few resources. Ernesto wants to know how to help, and they talk about possible projects.

A rooster perched on a thatched roof performs his daily wakeup call with a jarring cry. The mayor's family gathers at the community enclosure for breakfast. At Ernesto's request, the conversation centers on the practice of head shrinking. He says he saw some in the night and they left quite an impression on him. He doesn't mention that it was a night of unspeakable horror.

The grandfather speaks in a difficult-to-understand Spanish sprinkled with Shuar words translated by the grandchildren:

"When I was a boy in the fifties, I got to do it with my father. Whenever we captured a warrior from an enemy tribe, he was beheaded. We would extract the bones and everything else, and the head was boiled for many hours in a clay pot. Then we stuffed it with straw and sewed up the mouth so that the spirit of the dead enemy couldn't get out and haunt us. They were our war trophies."

"Do you still do that?" asks Ernesto, striving to give his words a tone of merely anthropological curiosity.

"Only to American *gringos*" someone responds gravely.

After a couple of seconds the silence is broken with peals of laughter, hands slapping thighs and people doubling over in hilarity.

"No, seriously" says the mayor's son. "When the Italian missionaries came here, they catechized all the Shuar, and taught us it wasn't nice to go around lopping off heads. After a while people adopted the new religion and way of life, and we became Catholic." That was more than 50 years ago. But my father still shrinks some monkey heads now and then, just to teach the young people about our heritage. We don't have authentic *tzantzas,* shrunken heads, around here anymore. They're all in museums in Europe and the United States."

IV

When the time comes to say goodbye to his hosts, Ernesto takes some cash from his wallet and puts it into the mayor's hand.

"For the kids," he says, "and in thanks for your hospitality."

He would like to be part of this race that was never conquered by anyone. As he is leaving, it occurs to him to ask, more out of habit than anything else:

"Is there any other Esperanza around here?"

The mayor, punning on the meaning of the word says, "We never lose hope!"

"Of course not", Ernesto smiles. "But I'm wondering if there might be another town named Esperanza in this area."

"No, not around here."

"There is a community called 'La Esperanza' in the province of Orellana," one of Daniel's nephews informs him. "I used to work there. If you have a map, I can show you where it is."

Ernesto takes a map from his backpack and opens it on the grass.

"Well, it's not marked. But it's right here." He draws a little circle on Ernesto's map.

Ernesto's heart flutters as he remembers the circle of his childhood on a map.

"It's just south of the Napo River and east of the Vía Auca."

"The Auca Road," Ernesto muses, "the famous and infamous Vía Auca!"

"This is what you do: first, go to San Sebastián del Coca. There, hitch a ride on a truck from any oil company going down the Vía Auca, and ask the driver to let you off at the turn-off to La Esperanza. There, sooner or later, some car will turn down the gravel road going east which leads to that community."

"But nobody can go down the Vía Auca unless they live there or work for The Company, or they are missionaries!" someone reminds them.

"And who stops people from using that road? Who's in charge there?" Ernesto asks, unable to suppress his indignation.

"The military. They obey The Company. They have several checkpoints, and it's full of soldiers at the crossroads coming from Coca. When I worked there, they arrested some foreigners from an environmental group who were trying to sneak in."

"My father probably traveled that route from end to end," Ernesto mutters to himself. "How ironic if they don't let me through!"

"Well, there is another way to go there," Daniel's nephew suddenly remembers. "From Coca you can go down the Napo

River until Descanso, and there you can hire a guide to take you overland. La Esperanza is directly south, and there is a trail."

"But he'll have to cross Auca territory!" someone else objects.

"Who are the Auca?" Ernesto asks.

"The Huaorani people. South of the Napo all the way to the Curaray River is all Huaorani land, except for a six kilometer stretch on each side of the Vía Auca. That's where the settlers and people working for The Company live."

"And what's so bad about the Huaorani, or Auca?" says Ernesto, suddenly curious.

"They're bad people! They live to kill," says Daniel, adding that the hairs on his neck stand up at the mere mention of the word Auca.

"They've speared many missionaries, not to mention settlers who move into their territory without permission. Including quite a few of our relatives."

"I didn't know that Shuar territory was next to Huaorani tribal land," says Ernesto, noting the complexity of the ethnic mosaic in the region.

"It didn't used to be but after The Company came in some twenty years ago, several Shuar families moved north to find work there. The Huao did everything to antagonize them."

He hears a lengthy description of crimes committed by the Huao—as they are often called.

"What if I try to get permission?" says Ernesto, with increasing agitation.

Not that Ernesto really believes it could be *his* Esperanza. But he feels compelled to investigate, if only as an excuse to meet these legendary warriors. His curiosity is heightened by the thought that these are Rosa's people! Could she really be heir to such a brutal culture? Or are the Shuar exaggerating due to a long-standing rivalry among neighbors?

"They might receive you well if you take gifts, since you are neither Shuar nor Quichua."

Ernesto thanks his friends and bids goodbye, solemnly promising to return one day. He leaves the verdant splendor of the Shuar's domain daydreaming of Rosa's ancestral land. Perhaps just saying her name will bring him luck.

16. The Border

I

A group of boys approaches Rosa.

"Are you okay?"

"They left me …," she responds in a barely audible voice. "They left me behind!"

Her eyes are wide open and she feels dizzy and about to faint. Someone puts a hand on her shoulder.

"Hey, it's alright! I bet the *migra* appeared and they had to get hell out. I'm sure they didn't mean to leave you," one of the boys consoles her.

"Or maybe they all got arrested," says another, "and they're getting deported right now!"

The warmth of the friendly hand comforts her. She takes a breath, then sits down on a rock.

"Yes, it's the only possible explanation," she thinks, her stomach still up in her throat. "My friends would never leave without me unless they had a really good reason. Never. There must have been some terrible, terrible problem."

This thought brings her back to the world of the living and, little by little, her depression begins to lift.

As she gathers up the pieces of her broken world and puts them back together, her breathing returns to normal, and she tells her new friends that she wants to go to the other side with them. How are they going to do it?

"We're swimming across tonight," they tell her. "There's no moon."

Rosa remembers what her family told her about her mother's trip to the United States six years ago, just one day after her first communion. They said she had entered through Tijuana; the coyote had hidden her and 22 other passengers in his van, by taking out the middle and back seats. She had to lie down on top of the others in two human layers, and then he covered them up with wooden planks. Her mother said it had been uncomfortable but safe, and everything went off smoothly.

When arranging Rosa's trip, her uncle asked don Zabala if he would be using the same route. Rosa still remembers the conversation:

Things have changed, Numpa, the coyote told him that day. *There's been a major increase in border security with the Gatekeeper Operation this past year. Now there's a huge cement wall in various places, plus machines that sense human warmth, human tracks, even breathing, I swear! And on top of that, the patrols use those lights that make it so they can see without being seen.*

The devil's things! Grandma mumbled.

No, it's science, doña Umi. Science invented by the gringos to screw us. That's why creative coyotes like me have to adapt and find alternative ways of getting in. And that's why we abandoned the Tijuana entrance year ago and perfected the one at Nuevo Laredo. Don't worry about your girl. She'll cross over in one of our vehicles on a bridge connecting Mexico with the United States. And from there we'll put her in a private bus.

At 10 PM, Rosa is ready to cross the river swimming. The boys select a spot where they think that there aren't many whirlpools and where the current is the slowest. They well know that many immigrants have been sucked under by the infamous force of these water funnels.

They put their clothes in a plastic bag and stand on the bank in their underwear. Then they seal the bag with a strong knot and tie it onto their backs, like a backpack. The river is dark and blanketed by mist, and it's impossible to calculate how far they'll have to swim. But at least if the bag is tightly closed, nothing will get wet.

When they are ready, they all look at Rosa humorously.

"Look, everyone knows you're a girl. You're not the first one to try to pass as a boy. Too bad you didn't learn how to talk and walk like a one. Come on, take off your clothes. If you don't, you're not gonna be able to swim, or you'll get there all wet like a real wetback."

After a moment of doubt, Rosa answers, "You guys go on ahead."

II

"Make me invisible! Just once, just one little time in my life!" Rosa asks, invoking an imaginary magician. "Help me cross on invisible wings," she prays, "and then appear in flesh and blood on the other side. Just like the wind, or like radio waves crossing borders and traveling in the sky!"

Lost in a foreign land, and thrust upon her own luck and terror, Rosa walks aimlessly among putrid piles of garbage and strange people. The encampment is dangerous for a young woman, especially at night. It is saturated with gang members, drug dealers and addicts, stray dogs, prostitutes of either gender, and smugglers—not to mention the throng of people desperate to cross, just like her; all are using this as their squatting place and operations center.

She passes a group of people sitting around a fire, and a man approaches her and offers her something: drugs, probably. She pretends not to understand and quickly walks away. Two teenagers sleep on the bare ground covered with cardboard. Others have chosen the shelter of a burnt-out car that only faintly resembles a refuge.

She returns to the bank of the Rio Grande where she feels safer because the sound of water and croaking of frogs is familiar to her. It smells of excrement. She is startled by pigs rooting among fetid waste and debris.

A few meters away she sees a small group of men and women gathered around a lantern covered with fluttering moths. A man is preparing a raft, similar to the one Rosa used to cross from Guatemala to Mexico: inner tubes tied together with boards on top. She approaches a woman and asks if she can join the group.

"Ask the guide, kid."

Rosa begs her to ask for her. The woman examines her face with her flashlight and gives her a half-humorous, half-tender smile.

"Well, all right. Hey, Cirilo, this kid wants to know if there's any room for him. He wants a good price since he's so skinny," she says.

In the dim light, Rosa sees the woman wink at her.

"Don't matter if he's skinny or fat – it's 300 dollars to cross. Full service to Los Angeles is a thousand."

Rosa has a little under 500—the original sum sent by her mother—plus a few Mexican pesos and several Ecuadorian sucres. [9]

The woman whispers something in her ear. Rosa leaves the group, separates three hundred dollars that she has hidden in her clothes, and then goes back to the group and hands it over to the *coyote*.

"Here's three hundred dollars. My Mom told me that she'll pay the rest to whoever takes me to Los Angeles where she's going to pick me up."

"Tell your Mom that if she doesn't come up with the money when my partner calls her from L.A., we're not responsible for whatever happens to you. Do you get what I'm saying? If this arrangement doesn't work for you, I'll leave you off on the other side of the river and you can find your own way to Mom. Alright?"

Rosa nods.

"Okay, now get ready, because we're leaving."

Everyone helps slide the raft down the bank and into the water. The group, some ten people, settles onto the floating boards. They all cross themselves. Rosa prays to the Virgin of Guadalupe, since she is in her territory, as she was informed upon entering Mexico.

The *coyote* sticks his long pole into the muddy riverbank and the raft slides away. He pushes it to the bottom, only six or seven feet deep in this stretch of river. And so they move, pole by pole, now from one side, now from the other, negotiating the current and the whirlpools. Later, he abandons the pole, grabs the paddles, and guides them through the swirling water.

The crossing takes no more than 20 minutes and the much-desired northern bank is almost within reach of their hands. His partner should be waiting for them on the American side, the coyote says; he's probably watching them arrive now.

---

[9]Ecuadorian money in 1995

A flash of harsh light illuminates the river. The coyote swears. The noise of a helicopter sounds like a machine gun and a Spanish-speaking voice crackles over the speaker from above and announces:

You are entering American territory. Go back! Repeat: entering American territory is prohibited: go back!

The powerful beam of light encircles the travelers, who bow their head and cover their faces with their hands.

We repeat: go back! Go back to your country! insists the voice of the steel god from the sky.

The raft swings around to return with its occupants, but three of them jump into the water where they believe they are outside the circle of light. Rosa takes off her hat, puts it under her shirt and jumps in the water. Her country is too far away for her to go back, she tells herself.

At this spot in the river the water is cold and oily, but quite shallow. She goes under, imagining the anaconda that she saw one moonlit night back home, in the river that passes in front of her house. She swims noiselessly underwater guided only by an unusual sense of direction. Perhaps it is the sacred Huaorani spirit of the serpent coming to her aid, she thinks. Like a reptile, she glides toward the prohibited bank. She sees a frog jumping in the shadows. Then she sees the other three people rise from the water.

The light from the helicopter is moving back toward the southern bank of the river, making sure the raft and its occupants are actually returning.

Rosa hardly feels her body, numb with cold. Her skin is slimy as a fish. She joins the other escapees and is overjoyed when she recognizes the woman who made contact with the coyote. Her name is Delia.

The four of them crawl through thorny brush and hide themselves among the foliage, leaning against each other for warmth. Only then does Rosa realize that she has left her backpack on the raft. She does not grieve long over this; her money is safe and sound in the plastic bag underneath the band

194

around her chest. She's only sorry to have lost *The Junglenaut*, her Mashimón card, and her travel notes.

Wet and shivering, time goes by slowly for the travelers, with no moon to mark its passage across the sky. The second coyote who was supposed to be waiting never appears.

"These thieves are smart. When the heat is on, they go up in smoke!"

Hugo whispers. He is Delia's friend.

"Does anyone know what time it is?" asks the other man in the group. "I didn't bring a watch. I didn't want it to get wet."

"Neither did I," Hugo answers.

Rosa scans the sky. So often it has told her the time, outside her house while she was reading by a lamp. But it is overcast here, and as she has noticed on other nights, the dislocated stars in these latitudes mean nothing to the Huaorani observer. She cannot even trust in the course of the stars in this sky, she laments.

With the first ray of daylight, the travelers give up on finding the promised coyote, and they begin walking down a trail which, according to Hugo, who has traveled this way before, leads to a road. Tall yellow grasses wind and tangle around their legs. Near a house without a fence, a dog barks furiously. The four transgressors stop, frozen in place, without knowing how to escape this new threat. In a few minutes, a patrol car appears from an adjacent road and arrests them.

Their world collapses again.

"Documents," the officer demands when all four are seated, heads bowed, in the immigration office.

Delia and the two men show their Mexican ID cards. Rosa says that she has no documents, but that her name is Eugenio Moreno, from Tapachula, the only Mexican village that she can recall at the moment. After registering their names, the real ones and the false one, they are placed aboard a police vehicle. In less than 15 minutes they have crossed the bridge to the Mexican side. The officer leaves them on a corner and goes back to the bridge.

Hugo, a veteran of many years' crossing during harvest time, knows the way back to the camp. They set off walking, their clothing—as their eyes—still wet, and shivering from the intense cold of the morning.

"Well, kid, we can still say we visited the United States, even if our visit was only for a few hours," Delia says to Rosa. "By the way, it's pretty obvious you're not from Mexico. I'm sure the *migra* knew it, too."

"Yeah, he was one of the nicer ones," Hugo agrees.

"But it's good you lied," Delia continues, "because anyone who's not Mexican gets thrown in jail and then deported."

"That's the fucked up reality for illegals like us," Hugo says, "living in a world of lies, one lie after another. We're just trying to survive—it's a life fit for a dog."

Rosa asks herself if God will judge her harshly for having broken such an important command. Because she, too, has been lying all along.

The face of her mother, or rather, Rosa's imperfect and hazy memory of her face, tells her to trust in God's mercy.

III

Crestfallen, still trembling under their clothes, the returned group looks for their *coyote* to get their money back or to attempt another crossing; but the man has turned into a wisp of smoke.

In the brown, oily waters of the Rio Grande not a soul can be seen, either swimming or rowing. Only the current flows on ceaselessly. A few early risers can be seen with plastic jars made from trashed gallon bottles, pouring the soapy, slimy water over their heads.

Delia and Hugo announce that they are going to make another attempt that very evening. They will swim. Rosa is not so sure after the ordeals of that morning. How long can she keep up the lies about her nationality, her gender, and her name, without batting an eye? And if she is identified as an Ecuadorian, she'll be lost. Instead of depositing her in Mexico again, they'll put her in prison. In her case, being that she is from so far away, they may even throw away the key.

She tells them she has to think about it.

She checks her hidden wallet and is relieved to see that the money is dry. Inside, she also has a map, worn away from all the times her eyes and fingers have gone over it while traveling north. The border of the two countries is enormous, overwhelming, she realizes, discouraged. It goes from sea to sea, curving in and out according to the bends in the river, and then traveling upward and east in a straight line. This turbulent river with the detestable *migra* and their floodlights is no longer an option. California, according to don Zabala, is protected by an impregnable wall.

Where would there be a breach in this immense border for her to slip in unnoticed?

She remembers the capybaras and other animals that her uncle and cousins sometimes trapped alive, to be fattened in a corral until butchering. They'd run desperately from one end of wire fence to the other, looking for an escape! And then there was that bird that flew into their house by mistake when everyone was out. It stayed in there for hours, fluttering like mad through the gaps in the bamboo wall, trying to get out. When they arrived, it was almost dead, from thirst or fear.

Rosa can feel the doors shutting. She turns away from the river and cries. But she can't even do that publicly, since boys aren't supposed to cry. She dries her tears, takes out a few coins, and goes back to the camp looking for anyone selling food. Perhaps this stabbing pain in her stomach is because she hasn't eaten for the past fifteen hours.

Sitting on a log, she hungrily munches on hot tortillas. A mangy stray dog that has been hidden among piles of empty cans and garbage advances gingerly toward her, licking its lips with the extreme humility of a street mutt that has learned from sticks and stones. Rosa shares her tortilla as her tears spill out again; this time, she cries for the two of them.

She looks up at the sky and figures it must be about eight in the morning. She approaches a circle of raggedy children who have congregated around a fire, and finds the boys who swam across on the previous night.

"So the *migra* got you?" she asks.

"Yeah. The fuckers."

"They got me, too."

"I wish I had some cash to cross over with a coyote!" says one of the boys. "One of them has a special price for kids, but you have to go to Nogales. It's far away."

"How does he cross? By raft?" Rosa wants to know.

"No. I heard he goes through a wastewater tunnel."

"What do you mean?"

"I mean sewage: pure shit. But I guess it's dry where he goes through. You have to crawl though. And there's rats. Lots of them. If they bite you you'll get cancer, so you have to wear a whole bunch of layers of clothes."

The idea of cancer gives Rosa a shiver and she abandons the sewer idea.

"Isn't there any other way? I heard that some coyotes just walk you right across the border where there's no river, no fence, no tunnel. Nothing."

"Oh, yeah, the wire cutters. Yeah, they walk across the desert. There's hardly any *migra* there."

"Where is the crossing?"

"Too fucking far."

"Where?"

"I'm telling you, it's a long ways away. And it's damn expensive."

"How much?"

"I heard they charge 400. But you have to be a really good walker, because if you can't keep up, the *pollero* leaves you behind in the desert to die! Of course a snake or scorpion could get you first. And then the heat melts your brain and dries up your flesh and you turn into a mummy."

This doesn't frighten Rosa. She likes the idea of fewer *migra* in the desert and not having to hide her nationality and fake a Mexican accent. She pictures just a simple wire fence dividing the border.

"It couldn't be that bad of a walk," she tells herself. "These boys are from the city; they've never hiked through the forest carrying a load of yucca or firewood on their backs. I bet they've never even seen a real snake in the wild." Rosa decides to investigate this new possibility.

A pot boils furiously over the fire. Rags, from the look of it. The pot emits a nauseating stink. The boys tell her they're cooking meat given them by a butcher in the camp.

They offer her some, and she tactfully declines. Only dogs eat tripe in her family, and the nasty smell rolling off the pot makes her stomach churn. All she's interested in is learning more about these wire cutters.

"Can you please tell me where this place is with the barbed wire fence?"

"Yeah, I'll tell you, if you give me one of those crackers you had yesterday."

"I'm out of crackers, but how about some tortillas?" Rosa says, handing over the bag in which she has her morning leftovers.

"You go to a town called Sonoyta and from there you find a place called El Papalote."

Rosa makes a mental note of these names.

"You have all that money?"

"No, I don't."

After her trip through the river, she only has one hundred ninety dollars and some Mexican and Ecuadorian money left. She could ask her mother to send another two hundred dollars through that Western Union she uses to send money to her family. They say that this bank is everywhere...But then she remembers that her ID is gone. It went up in smoke in the ship when they had to burn their documents. She'd have no way to identify herself at the bank to get the cash. She feels incredibly stupid for not having foreseen the need of her real ID. Maybe she could figure out how to buy a new ID...

Clinging to this glimmer of hope, she says good-bye to the boys. She pulls her baseball cap down over her eyes and practices walking like a gangly teenage boy. I can do this, she tells herself; I have to do this.

She leaves the camp and goes to town, and finds a bus full of other clandestine travelers, departing to Ciudad Juárez. She buys a ticket and commends herself to God. From there, she'll have to transfer to another one going to Sonoyta.

At the end of the afternoon, a bus painted brilliant blue returns to the camp and parks at the entrance. The frustrated driver searches for an hour. Finally, one of the ragged boys informs him

199

that the girl from Ecuador who dresses like a man has gone in search of the "wire cutters".

IV

"Who's getting off in El Papalote?" asks the driver in a strident voice.

A passenger shakes Rosa's shoulder and she wakes up with a start.

"Weren't you getting off here?"

"Yeah, thanks."

Rosa is surprised to see the sun once again at its zenith. This means her trip has taken one full day. Time seems to have become elastic, sometimes stretching out slowly, other times practically disappearing. Shortly after boarding the bus in Ciudad Juárez she fell into a deep sleep. In the nebulous world of her persistent nightmares, she had crossed the desert many times, and had already arrived at her destination. Her dreams were always the same, with the demonic insistence of recurrent nightmares: she crosses the border and tries to run to her mother who is standing with open arms. But Rosa's legs are stuck to the ground, as if she had taken root, or as if she were a marble statue trapped under the sun. Then, a faceless man picks her up, puts her in a truck, and returns her to the Mexican side.

The noon sun of the Altar desert bakes the plain. Its merciless brilliance dazzles Rosa as she steps off the vehicle. She adjusts her baseball cap and looks around.

She was expecting to see a village, but all she finds is northern Mexico's Route 2 truck stop, a gas station, and some earth-colored brick houses here and there.

The air is static with the torpor of siesta time. Only the crickets seem to be awake, singing their unalterable tune in the one and only tree in the area. The residents seem to have secluded themselves behind wooden doors and windows tightly shut. Rosa immediately realizes that there will be no Western Union here. Not even a public telephone. But there is a little store owing its existence to the lack of a fortified barrier between the two countries. This is where immigrants stock up on water and food before crossing over. To Rosa's joy, she sees that it is open.

She asks the woman who runs the place if she knows of any group that plans to cross today and the woman points to a man sitting on a bench outside, smoking.

"Ask the *pollero*. That's him, and he's waiting for clients."

Rosa approaches the man and asks him how much he would charge to take her to the other side. The *pollero* appears to be in his mid to late thirties, with narrow eyes and an angular face.

"Three hundred and seventy dollars."

Rosa goes back into the store and pretends to browse the merchandise. She is contemplating how to proceed.

A minute later, she goes back to the *pollero* and says, "I have a hundred and sixty. But I can cook for the group."

The man looks her over from top to bottom before answering: "We don't cook in the desert."

Rosa seats herself under the cricket tree. She fights back tears and waits for a miracle.

An hour passes, and the *pollero's* group has formed and is about ready to leave. The man calls Rosa:

"Alright. I'll take you for one-sixty. Your job's going to be sweeping the tracks."

"Great!" says Rosa, not exactly understanding the nature of this job.

She returns to the shop and takes out her money. She has enough pesos for a small backpack, some canned food, a gallon of water and a cheap blanket. The Devil's Road, the shopkeeper tells her, is an oven in the summer, but now, in October, the nights can be very cold.

She regrets having lost her flashcards and sacrifices her last few pesos on a little notebook and pencil.

Outside, the group is becoming impatient. Rosa pays the *pollero* and he describes the job. In places where the land is sandy or the dirt loose, one person always go behind everyone with a greasewood branch and use it as a broom. He demonstrates how to sweep from right to left, and then from left to right, but lightly, as if blowing on the land, to erase their footprints and elude the patrols.

Rosa understands that she will have to keep up with the group, while walking backwards or sideways, like a crab. She practices a little before they depart. The coyote realizes how lucky he was with this new traveler. Adults hardly ever adapt themselves to this unnatural way of walking, and he would've had to do the job himself if it weren't for this boy.

"We're going to be walking 80 miles to United States Interstate 8. I hope you can keep up."

Rosa doesn't know how many miles are in a kilometer, and she doesn't want to ask.

17. Welcome to Huaorani Territory

I

The Shuar had already told him: Coca is the epicenter of oil production, and in that city, everyone's boots are stained with crude. Ernesto, therefore, is not surprised to find a heterogeneous mixture of colonists, natives, laborers, and executives on the black, oil-soaked streets. What did surprise him was the very visible presence of soldiers, some in the uniform of the United States Army.

"What in the world are they doing here?" is the first question he asks the waiter in the canteen where he is having lunch.

"Oh, lots of North American companies have concessions here," the man responds. "You can tell that the gringos don't trust our own armed forces to protect their executives."

At a neighboring table several young men enthusiastically discuss the local soccer team's last game against its rival. Hoping to steer the conversation toward what interests him, Ernesto calibrates his voice to be heard when he asks the waiter about oil exploitation in Block 16, in the heart of Huaorani territory.

"What do people here in Coca think about that?" he asks, watching the adjacent table from the corner of his eye.

"No matter what they say," responds the proprietor of the place, as he serves the other table, "you can't stop progress. Our country needs to export! We need development!"

His words have their effect.

"Export? What for?" responds someone at the other table. "The more oil we sell, the more dollars we owe the gringos, don't you get it? They give us their stupid loans that we never asked for, just to make us buy all this technological crap to get the oil!"

"But the Huaorani signed a contract—they accepted this arrangement," the waiter retorts as he serves Ernesto a plate of fried yucca.

"That's because they bribed a Union leader! The majority of the Huaorani was against it."

"Don't you remember last April?" another man says. "A Huaorani mob slashed 140 Maxus car tires." He turns to Ernesto to make sure he got it.

"The gringos got the land, but what's under it belongs to us Ecuadorians," another man avers. "To all of us!"

"That's right. And to extract what's below, they pollute what's above! The oil industry is occupying *one third* of the Ecuadorian Amazon! And do you know how long the gas from Block 16 will last in the United States? Thirteen days! If you don't believe me, read the RAN [10]report. Their office is just around the corner."

This information produces bewilderment from around the table, and for some time no one says a word, not knowing how to refute or assimilate this information.

Breaking the silence, Ernesto remarks that tomorrow he's going to La Esperanza and he'll have to go through Huaorani territory, and what do they think about that? Will he be welcomed?

"Welcomed in Auca territory? Yes, as long as you give them presents. Anyway, they'll see that you're just a *pelao*."

"A what?"

"A young person. You won't be a threat to them."

Ernesto calculates how much money he can spend. His resources are quite slim, he tells them, and he still has to find a cheap hotel. The canteen owner offers to let him spend the night in a half-finished room above the business for only three dollars. Ernesto accepts.

Although the walls are not yet plastered, the floor is smooth cement and Ernesto rolls out his sleeping bag. Before showing him to his room, the proprietor has given him an anti-mosquito spiral. He places it on the floor, strikes a match, and sets it aglow. Then he covers his body with repellent. He has read that Coca is a malarial zone.

At two in the morning a pack of snarling, barking dogs wakes him up. They have decided to fight just below his window, which consists of a square hole covered with a sheet. For an hour

---

[10] RAN = Rainforest Action Network

the boy tosses about on the floor, imagining different ways to get rid of them. Finally he gets up and fills a basin with water in the bathroom. He goes to the window and dumps it onto the dogs, putting an end to their meeting.

II

Ernesto quickly finishes his breakfast and goes out to look for a store. At the end of a few blocks replete with bars, restaurants, and houses of prostitution there is one that has what he needs. He buys some presents: aluminum pans and matches, and for himself, flashlight batteries, a pair of rubber boots and a mosquito net. All of this involves bargaining, and feeling slightly guilty when he gets things too cheaply.

The sun is already high when he sets off for the port of Francisco de Orellana with his load of presents swaying on top of his backpack. He gets on the first boat going down the Napo River. Four long years this fluvial port has been the launching place for travelers and missionaries who dare to enter *terra incognita*.

After several hours the boat ties up at a riverside village called Descanso and various guides present themselves to the passengers. Ernesto asks if someone can take him to La Esperanza.

"Let me find a bilingual guide for you" one of them says, "because you'll be going through a Huaorani community."

When the bilingual guide arrives, he negotiates the price with Ernesto who, following advice given him in the canteen, offers to pay half immediately and the other half upon their return. The guide accepts and brings along a helper. The three cross the river. Ernesto and the guide disembark on the opposite shore, to the south, and the helper returns with the boat to the Descanso.

Not far from the dock a narrow trail begins, plunging into the jungle in the direction of the mysterious Huao territory.

As in the Shuar jungle, vines and moss hang from branches in a tangle of prehistoric vegetation with gigantic, blooming bromeliads. The silence is cut at intervals by the sound of a bird or a squirrel monkey. But in contrast to the jungle in Buena Esperanza, which is a thousand feet above sea level, this one is hot, humid and plagued by voracious insects that lacerate the skin and open up wounds in which they lay their microscopic larva. Through the thick cloud of mosquitoes, Ernesto keeps an eye out for passing snakes.

Dodging roots and avoiding poison-tipped thorns, they march along for nearly two kilometers until the green-walled trail ends at a stream with deep banks. The humid, heavy air condenses on Ernesto's skin and perspiration has already soaked his shirt and begun to pour down his chest in little rivulets.

There is no bridge, but there is a *talabita*, a square basket that hangs from a steel cable that is tied to trees on either side of the river.

"This moves only by human power, my friend," explains the guide.

Four hands pull the cord to make it run through the pulleys; and, with no other motor than their own muscles, they begin moving over the stream in their little roofless box.

They resume walking the trail on the other side. The giant tree canopies, covered in ivy, are thick enough to hide the sun, but not to keep the rain out: and as it does every afternoon, the rain begins suddenly. The sky seems to release all the water in the universe and the land bursts under the colossal torrent. The temperature plunges in a matter of minutes. Inside a hollow tree trunk where they have found shelter, Ernesto trembles with cold. The guide looks at him smiling, his teeth also chattering. A second later, this smile turns into a grimace. A hairy brown and orange tarantula five inches wide is climbing his right boot. He takes off his T-shirt, traps the tarantula and tosses it a distance away. He does not kill it.

The downpour stops and the frogs begin a shrill chorus. The birds resume their chants and the men their walking. They come to another stream. This one has a long tree trunk for a bridge which poses a more formidable challenge. Beneath them, a roaring current rushes, throwing up a crown of white foam. The guide carries Ernesto's backpack and the boy goes across without looking down.

The trail continues for another kilometer and ends at a gate with a horizontal plank crossing it on which it is written, in Spanish:

The guide shouts something from the gate, and a few moments later, a Huaorani appears.

"This boy has come from afar to bring you some gifts and to visit you for a day. And tomorrow he wishes to go to La Esperanza," the guide announces.

In spite of having spoken in slow and deliberate Spanish, the man repeats the message in the Huaorani language. Some of the Huaorani speak better Spanish than others, the guide explains to Ernesto, and his interlocutor is not particularly well-versed in the language. The young people are more fluent, since they learn Spanish in school these days.

The Huaorani inspects the presents, accepts them and opens the gate.

"*Cowode* [11] staying two days," he says in halting Spanish.

"All right, I'll be going now," says the guide.

"What? You're leaving me here?" Ernesto says, looking at the guide with a stupefied expression. "We agreed that you were taking me to La Esperanza."

"I'm not really welcome here," the guide whispers. "Family issues, I'm a relative, but you'll be fine. They'll take you to the village and will treat you real well so you'll come back with more presents. I'll come get you the day after tomorrow, same time, same place, okay?"

"How do I know you'll actually come back? This is not what I had in mind when I hired you!"

"Hey, you owe me half of what we agreed on, remember? This is my business! And if I can't make it, my assistant will come instead."

Ernesto doesn't know what to do. He wonders for a second if it's all a joke. The person standing at the other side of the gate is short and stocky, with a wide and a muscular back. His skin is lighter than that of the Shuar. His only garment is a loincloth. The spear he holds in one hand and the animal tooth necklace adorning his naked chest is not part of a costume.

---

[11] White man or foreigner in Huaorani language

Everything is very real. Ernesto's choice is to be a chicken and go back with the guide, or to be a man and show his mettle.

"Boy, you seem indecisive," says his guide. "You've got nothing to worry about. I've brought a lot of people here—tourists, tradesmen, anthropologists. They may look different, but these people are merchants. If you don't believe me, look at those logs floating down the river. They sell them to the middleman I bring here who sells them to the Colombians. They aren't savages, like people think. They're just loggers. You have nothing to worry about."

This speech is delivered hastily, in a low voice, and while the Huaorani observes them with astute eyes, it is obvious that he does not understand the Spanish.

"Just keep your boots next to you when you go to sleep," he continues, "and before you put them on in the morning, be sure a centipede hasn't crawled inside."

"A centipede?"

"Or a scorpion."

Under different circumstances this would sound like just a joke, but the truth is that Ernesto is in unknown territory, and anything is possible. His brushes with death flash through his mind, as does his promise to follow his destiny without hesitation. He accepts the challenge, and enters the world of the Huaorani like a Greek hero descending into the Underworld.

III

Ernesto is received with all due ceremony. First, he is introduced to the hunting dogs (a custom the Huaorani learned from the Shuar, he has been told in Buena Esperanza), who sniff him and register his identity. The community then gathers in a central area clear of trees and brush, surrounded by A-frame cabins with roofs reaching to the ground. Then food appears: yucca and freshly-killed monkey meat, he is informed.

Some women are dressed like peasant villagers; others are clothed from the waist down only. Ernesto tries not to observe their naked breasts too obviously and makes an effort to concentrate his gaze on some monkeys tied to a nearby tree.

After eating, the young people show Ernesto how to use a blowpipe, the quintessential hunting weapon. The cotton they place on the end of a thin cane dart is from the fruit of a tree and is soaked in curare, an herb mixture that paralyzes its victim.

Ernesto tests his aim. If he blows too lightly, the dart falls out in front of him. If he blows too hard, it curves away from the target. "Like me," Ernesto thinks, "sometimes too slow, other times too hasty."

The dwellings consist of a single long, spacious room. In the middle there are two pyres where the fire is always burning, he is told. The smoke helps cure the monkey meat hanging over it, while rendering the roof impermeable.

"Who is the chief of this community?" Ernesto asks the youngest youth, who speaks perfect Spanish.

"Chief? Well that depends on the circumstances. We don't really have chiefs here like you have among the whites. People just do what they want. Unless there's some outside threat, then an assembly is called and the older people decide what to do about it."

The idea of a community without a chief or with a nebulous hierarchy strikes Ernesto as unusual. Someone speaks up and clarifies: "the chief of the Huaorani is the Jaguar. He's our invisible father."

The luminous green fringes of the forest canopy soon dissolve and, like the rain, the night also arrives suddenly.

The women light the tree-sap torches around the central area, lending an attractively phantasmagorical ambience. Faces and naked torsos become redder, shadows dancing behind them. Ernesto plays soccer with the children, but they are soon called inside by the adults.

They tell Ernesto that a smaller house reserved for guests has been assigned to him, and he asks permission to retire to his room. He hangs his mosquito net from the roof poles above his hammock, taking care not to leave openings. The malaria pills he bought in Quito made him nauseated and in disgust he tossed them into the brush.

After an hour or so of sleep, the deep sound of drumming booms into the air. Ernesto jumps up from his hammock and peeks out through a crack in the door. He sees something boiling in a pot in front of the shaman's cabin. People stand in line waiting their turn for a drink of the potion, while others sing and dance. Then, one by one, everyone disappears behind the houses into the darkness of the jungle until the central area is deserted. Ernesto goes back to the hammock without understanding the meaning of this ritual.

A little later, the sound of pebbles pelting his door wakens him. He pays no attention. But whoever is trying to get his attention is insistent. Finally, he jumps out of the hammock, cracks the door open, and peeks out. In the moonlight he sees a 13or 14 year old girl. She says, in a commanding, barely audible voice, while pushing the door open:

"Let me in."

"What do you want?"

"Do you have a flashlight?"

"Yes, but what do you want it for?"

"I want you to take me home. I'm not from here. They stole me!"

"They stole you?"

"Yes. I am Quichua. Please take me now!"

"I can't do that. I'm their guest. It would be a betrayal!"

"Please, please!" cries the girl, still in a whisper, as she slips through the door.

The light from the torch inside the hut dances through the darkness and illuminates the visitor. She is dressed as a colonist.

"They came into my village a few days ago," she says, kneeling in the position of a supplicant, "and they took me away while I was washing clothes in the river. It was revenge."

She is speaking in quick, fluid Spanish.

"Look, they could kill both of us!" Ernesto responds.

"No. Not tonight. They've taken *ayahuasca* and now they're behind their houses shitting and vomiting. Do you know about *ayahuasca*? And now that they've relieved themselves they're all sound asleep dreaming about the snake and the jaguar, and their ancestors, and the universe and all of that. No one's up.

Not even the shaman, I swear. They're all flying in another world!"

The girl weeps and leans her head on Ernesto's bare feet. He feels her thick hair brushing up against him, like a little bird with a broken wing. He, who has one family and is looking for another. And she, who's been torn away from the only one she has.

"You're the angel I dreamed was coming to help me. I knew it the moment I saw you come this afternoon," says the girl, with indescribable sweetness, letting her tears fall on Ernesto's feet while, from the corner of her eye, she discovers Ernesto's flashlight beside his backpack.

Once more the old uncertainty seizes Ernesto and wreaks havoc on his nerves. Should he put his life at the edge of a precipice, or ignore this girl and preserve his own skin? His father's faint voice counseling prudence comes from the background, but this girl's desperate voice, in the here and now, and that of his own conscience shake him into action. I'm not going to chicken out, he decides.

"Come on! Come with me!" the Quichua girl urges. "Grab your boots and the flashlight!"

They tiptoe out of the house. With furtive steps they come near the dogs, whose ears are pricked up. The girl approaches them confidently, caressing them one by one. Then they escape down the trail to the gate.

Twigs crunch beneath their feet.

Up to this point, the light of the moon and the torches hanging on trees has helped them. But passing the gate, the darkness of the thick jungle falls heavily over the two.

"Put your boots on now. I know that you people can't run barefoot. Hurry!" the girl urges.

Ernesto shakes out his boots. Something falls out of one of them, but he doesn't stop to investigate, slipping his feet in quickly. He shoves his hands in his pockets. He has his money and his passport. Good. If his hosts find his backpack and the sleeping bag and net, they'll think he has just gone out for a walk. And the girl? When they realize that both of them are gone, they'll go after them. With spears and blowpipes armed with poison darts, they will hunt them down. A surge of panic fills him with dread.

18. The Devil's Road

I

At five in the afternoon, Rosa and 19 other traveling souls are zigzagging through the wild frontier, on a path around flat shrubs.

"Listen," begins the coyote. "Since you're new to this business of crossing to the North, I'll tell you the golden rule: if by some mishap the *migra* gets us, do *not* tell them you're traveling with a coyote! I'm just one of the group. Remember that, it's for your own good!" he emphasizes. "And for the sake of your families," he adds, in a tone of veiled threat.

They nod, but their expressions denote some resentment.

Soon, the people devote themselves to the brief ritual of praying to their favorite saints. Rosa has heard the name of many He and She saints since leaving the farm. She doesn't want to take any risks, and she would hate to abuse the Virgin Mary with too many requests. Besides, she has lately become more and more convinced that above and beyond the populous Catholic pantheon, and the more humble Huaorani one, there must be a unifying entity; and to that entity she now directs her prayers, without intermediaries.

The border between the two countries is nothing more than a rusty barbed wire fence cutting through no man's land. A sign reads: "USA. Do Not Enter."

The *pollero* steps on the barbed wire, pulls the strand above, and with a theatrical sweep of the hand invites his "chickens" to cross into the forbidden zone.

It is October 20 when Rosa steps into the other side for the second time. "Hopefully, I'll stay a little longer this time," she thinks, feeling some trepidation.

She looks forward, then back. There's no difference. The northern desert is simply a continuation of the southern desert, and vice versa. The same semi-arid land dotted with cactus and coarse grasses, greasewood bushes with a strong smell of creosote, and thorny plants. Identical buzzards circle the same flawless blue sky under the same sun that beats down on both sides of the plain.

The coyote arms Rosa with a broom torn from the fragrant bush and tells her to get to work. She enters the land of opportunity walking backwards.

Everyone soon realizes that the guide is indispensable because *The Devil's Road* is actually an intricate set of trails, some clear-cut, some diffuse, all of them meandering between rocks and up and down slopes; they form a colorless and deceptive maze. We'd end up lost in some lonely moorland, they think, if it weren't for the coyote!

Here and there clouds of tiny flies float in the air and into their noses and ears. Rosa pays no attention. The terrain ranges from sandy to rocky, and where it's rocky there's no need to sweep or walk backwards. This allows her to rest and to scrutinize the amazing surroundings: Saguaros as high as three or four men; single-stemmed cactuses, like lonely sentinels armed with spikes; bleached bones; a dry nest here and there; a feather, slowly waving in the dense afternoon air.

"We're going to walk until dark," announces the coyote, "and then we'll start off again just before dawn."

The coyote calls himself Honorio, but his nickname is Twisty. Rosa, who thinks any man above 30 is old, addresses him as Mr. Honorio.

Their shadows are slowly lengthening. The afternoon stretches and bends westward as the sun slowly curves toward its hiding place beyond the yellow hills. The sluggish, waning sunset is new to Rosa, as she is used to a more abrupt solar rhythm. In Ecuador, the sun does not sink down little by little. It falls down all at once below the horizon, and night hits the earth as if God had turned the light switch off.

Autumn is almost over. The reddish brown dry grasses and the red and purple sky melt into one another in a continuum without boundaries. Now Rosa conceives of the distance between herself and her mother as one long stretch of golden earth. The air cools. The sun is on the other side of the world, and its glow lights up the hills.

The guide looks for somewhere to camp for the night.

"We can't light any fires or use flashlights," Twisty says. "The *migra* has got powerful light detectors."

214

The walkers eat their canned food and crackers in silence. Under a prickly tree, or behind a large rock, or in a small cave in a rock, everyone arms him or herself against the cold night and settles down to sleep. Rosa has chosen a flat, smooth area away from trees, bushes and boulders, in order to avoid snakes. If the snakes here are anything like those on her farm, they hate the open ground. She marks her territory with a stone circle and spreads out her bedding in the middle.

Taking advantage of what little light remains, she sits down with her journal. She is pleased that she bought the notebook. She writes nothing personal, but tries to reconstruct her journey since leaving that afternoon, taking notes of a saguaro standing out among others, or a stone of a peculiar shape. She is following the ancient custom of her people that still persists – to memorize the trail when they go hunting in order to find their way back. Rosa strengthens her memory by writing things down. Once her mapping is done, she puts the notebook away and lies down.

The night, which simplifies shapes and increases the size of the shadows, brings drowsiness. Her eyes close, and in seconds she is asleep.

II

The air is cold and stars are shining in a limpid, immense sky. It is four in the morning of the second day when the guide awakens the group. After a short breakfast, the march begins.

The group moves forward and a crescent moon floating above the low hills keeps them company. Here and there some animal's skeleton glows under the tenuous light.

As shadows rise, the birds wake up—parakeets, crows, sparrows and mockingbirds shake their branches and fill the air with warbling and cawing. Rosa's soul is filled with nostalgia.

The coyote is talking into his cell phone:

"What's going on over there, Raúl? Really? Okay, we'll take a shortcut. Let me know if there's any more news!" Addressing the group he says, "Looks like the Yuma patrol is behind this hill, ready to ambush us. Don't worry—we're not going to let that happen! I'll take you another way that they don't know about."

215

The group is relieved to have such an expert to rely on. Their money has been well spent, and they decide to forgive him for his veiled threats on that first day.

The sun is coming up and the red rays of early dawn have given way to clear sky.

Toward noon, when the sun is most intense and the travelers are nearly falling over with sleepiness, the coyote announces an hour of rest. Everyone tries to find a tree or rock that offers some semblance of shade.

There, under a mesquite, someone discovers the first hideous remains.

It has a human shape and it is leathery. The arms are raised rigidly, fists clubbed, giving the impression of death having surprised whoever this was in the middle of a fight for life. Those who dare draw near cross themselves, and after a brief prayer through clenched teeth, they quicken their pace over this desert whose toll is life.

"It's been mummified," says Twisty. "You're going to find more of them. That's the price they pay for crossing in the summer and getting lost. The temperature gets up to 130 degrees".

"Why don't they travel by night?"

"Some people do, but the problem is that you can't see where you're going in the dark. You could walk right into a snake, coming out of its hole, or crash into a cactus. It's hell. People die here all the time. Last summer the *migra* picked up more than 100 bodies."

"Why would anyone travel in the summer, knowing full well that it's an oven out here?" asks a man who is obviously not Mexican.

"They come for the harvests, that's why. They're seasonal workers."

In the afternoon the *pollero* has another cell phone conversation and receives more bad news: the patrol is following them. The travelers make a detour into a more tortuous trail to elude the officers. Frightened, they obsessively scan the yellow hills. Rosa works even harder at erasing their tracks.

"At least our coyote has connections," someone mutters. "The US patrol has been infiltrated by spies!"

By the end of the second day they've walked 40 miles. They have found more human bodies, darkened and shriveled under the bushes. Their initial shock and horror has been drained, and the bodies are ignored.

The twilight is already softening the edges of stones and the faces of men. Some women untie their hair and begin to comb it. A few strands stand up from static electricity. As Rosa wraps herself up in her blanket, Twisty steps into her circle.

"So what's the deal, Eugenio or Eugenia? Are you a boy or a girl?"

This takes her by surprise. The man's tone repels her. Avoiding his gaze, she says in a harsh voice.

"I am Huaorani."

"Well, I already know you're a girl, so why don't you just tell me the truth?"

His creepy voice gives her goose bumps.

"You should be glad I know you're a girl, because you're going to need my protection. It's rough out here, you know!" He draws nearer to Rosa with a stupid smile.

He reaches for her hand. Rosa jumps backward, as if on springs, and the sleeping jaguar within her wakes up and bears its fangs. She whips out her knife.

"Back off!" she shouts in a voice loud enough for all to hear.

The knife flashes with a coppery glow in the sunset, and the man leaps backwards, astonished.

"What the hell do you think you're doing?! I only wanted to help you, you savage little bitch! What are you all staring at?!" He roars at the people who have gathered around. "Don't mess with me, for your fucking own good!!"

The others look at their enraged guide, shocked. Their silence is even more disturbing in the utter stillness of the desert.

"If anything happens to me, everybody dies, because none of you idiots knows the way!"

"But I know how to go back," Rosa thinks, while glaring with her lynx eyes at the coyote, her blade pointing forward with an imperceptible tremble. The man turns around and, bristling with hatred, barks at those who are watching him again:

217

"Don't fuck with me! And go the hell to sleep! We're walking 16 hours tomorrow!"

He gives Rosa a final look as if to say, "Wait till I get my hands on you." A nervous tic twitches erratically over his face and he stomps away from the group.

Rosa wraps herself up and keeps her knife at hand.

The confrontation has made her jumpy and awake, and her almond eyes remain vigilant. Nearby, something shines on the dry ground, like a mirror with silver outlines. There is more than one. Twilight has given way to darkness, and everyone is asleep. Rosa silently leaves her bed.

She sees that these intriguing objects are nothing more than sardine cans the people have left strewn about the sand. It occurs to her that she should bury these telltale objects as a precaution, but her glance is attracted by the dull shine of something else lying nearby. This object, black and smooth, is interesting indeed.

"Well, look at that! Mr. Coyote has lost his cell phone in my territory! It must've dropped out of his pocket when he jumped backwards!"

She picks it up and puts it away.

Now the moon is up, casting its funerary light over the desert. Rosa slips away from the group.

"This is great! I'm going to call Mom. Or at least leave a message at her boss's office."

Rosa presses the button to turn on the phone, as she was taught by the bus driver in Guayaquil. The phone must be off to save the battery. She presses the button again, but the phone does not turn on.

"Why won't it go on?" she wonders. Thinking she should check the batteries, she opens the back cover and finds an empty hole.

"It's just a useless hunk of plastic! That idiot has been strutting around, pretending to talk with his "colleagues," just to show off to us! I can't believe it—what a pig! All that talk about the *migra* waiting for us was just a big lie!"

Rosa can't wait to share this with her companions. But then something tells her that she should hide this information, and save it for when she might need it. She leaves the phone where she found it. With relief, she loosens her elastic chest band, lies down, and covers herself up. Finally, she falls asleep, like a dolphin, with one eye half open.

III

On the third day, the temperature unexpectedly shoots up. Someone has a radio and hears that today's temperature will rise to 94 degrees. They begin drinking more and more water. At 10 A.M. the group crosses an area of cracked earth, broiled by the sun and as crinkled as elephant skin. By noon the sun shines blindingly off the sand; the heat is overwhelming.

The only shade to relieve the travelers comes off their wide-brimmed hats.

As a distraction, or from pure frustration, a boy kicks the ribs of an intact, sun-bleached skeleton, which collapses with the crisp rattle of castanets.

They walk for hours and the sun accompanies them with its beams of fire. Rosa feels intense discomfort where the elastic squeezes her chest. She could take it off, she thinks, since everyone now knows she's a girl. And she doesn't have to pretend to be a boy anymore, which was painful and tiring. But she decides against it. One never knows what might happen from one moment to the next.

The coyote orders a halt to eat and rest, and the people take refuge from the hot air in the long shadow of a mesquite, or the even shade of a saguaro.

A green fly circles around the food with an irritating buzz.

"Damn fly is driving me crazy," someone says, taking a swipe at it. At that instant, they hear the distant but unmistakable sound of a motor, and the throb of rotors cutting through the air.

"Run! Run! Hide!" the coyote shouts. In an instant water bottles and crackers scatter as the people run off like stampeding animals, but in different directions. They try to hide themselves under bushes. The helicopter comes closer, and then, suddenly, goes off in another direction. Perhaps another hunting area, they assume.

"Come back, *pollos*, don't be chicken," the coyote jokes when he sees that the danger is past. "Those sons of bitches won't come back today!"

With lips as dry and cracked as the terrain around them, they begin walking again. They are running out of water. Evening arrives with its blessed fresh air, and then night, with its cruel cold. Huddled against boulders that still emanate heat, the travelers stare at animal bones which give off a luminous, electrical glow.

"That's the bad light, the glow of tortured souls," some say.

"It's the natural phosphorescence of bones, which contain phosphorus," Rosa is moved to remark, by way of correction.

"Yes, the phosphorescent bones of tortured souls," comes the reply.

"Ignoramuses," she thinks, rolling her eyes.

IV

Toward the end of the fourth day, when the horizon is bleaker than ever, the silhouette of a squalid house beside the trail stands in relief against a sky streaked with fine, long clouds. It seems to be abandoned.

It's a windy afternoon. October gold has stained the leaves falling from three naked trees rustling at the doorway. Rosa has never seen a whirlwind of ochre leaves. She picks one up and puts it in her pocket.

The coyote tells them to change their clothes inside the house so they are more presentable when they arrive at the highway. Every face lights up with happiness; they are finally leaving the Camino del Diablo. They walk toward the house.

"I'm leaving now," says the coyote, when all are inside. "The highway is right over there."

"What? You said that your partner was going to pick us up in Sentinel! That was supposed to be included!" the travelers complain.

"He can't come. His van broke down. Says he needs another thousand to get another one. Sorry, that's what he said."

220

This causes great distress. No one has money. They look at the coyote and then at the floor. It's full and cigarette butts and scorpions hiding in the corners.

"Okay, everybody empty your pockets, and let's see how much we can all come up with. I'll see what I can do to help you out", the coyote says. "Eugenio, go behind that hill and watch for patrols. If you see any, whistle at us."

Rosa obeys, although she knows full well that the so-called telephone call is a farce. She needs to think up a plan to let her companions know that the coyote is lying, without him finding out that they're onto him. The coyote sits down on the porch, pulls out a bottle of liquor, and takes a few swigs.

When Twisty finishes his cigarette, he gives them a cold glance and says, "I'll give you guys ten minutes to see how much you can come up with. If you've got the cash, and my partner agrees, we'll take you to the highway. If not, you can find your own way out of Sentinel."

"You're blackmailing us!"

"The situation has changed. It's not my fault. Don't leave until I come back. Someone might see you."

The coyote gets up and walks up the hill. He sees Rosa sitting on a rock on the other side, gazing over a ravine. He sneaks up behind her. With blustery wind, she doesn't hear him until the last second. He grabs her by the shirt.

"I've got a bone to pick with you!" he snarls, smacking her on the side of the head.

Rosa staggers, but he's holding on tight, and he lifts her up. Although the sun is high, a glacial chill settles into her bones.

"That's for tricking me with your boy costume. And don't take your knife out because I have one, too!"

A gust of torrid, dusty air stirs the creosote foliage.

Rosa struggles, but he squeezes her arm tighter and punches her in the face. Her nose spurts blood.

"That's for humiliating me in front of everyone!"

The wind carries his words and drops them silently into the ravine.

Rosa screams and tries to thrash her way out of his grip, but she realizes, despairing, that this time there's no faithful friend to come to her rescue, no fierce *Conde* to sink his fangs into the man's neck.

"Game over, bitch!" screams the coyote, hurling her to the ground. The blood flowing from her nose stains the sand. Wind roars in her ears.

Twisty throws himself on top of her and a most unequal battle begins. With one hand on her face he presses her head into the sandy ground and with the other pulls down her pants. Rosa sees the veins of his neck swell and feels his sweat drop onto her belly. She's scratches at his face and he squeezes her throat.

"I'll kill you if you scratch me!"

His grinds his teeth and tears off her underwear. Rosa's squeezes her legs together so hard that they tingle. He tries to pry open her legs with his hands and she bites him as hard as she can. He punches her in the head again. When he's finally got her down, the wind carries the sound of a dog's bark. Frantic with rage, he kicks Rosa hard, and she rolls down the ravine.

19. Through the Amazon Basin

I

"My name is Leticia," says the Quichua girl as Ernesto is putting on his boots. "I know the way, so I should carry the flashlight. Here, take the machete. I took it from the hut."

Their escape begins. Leticia shines the flashlight over the trail as she runs, and Ernesto races behind, tripping over roots and nearly crashing into a tree. The intense cold of the jungle surprises him, since they are practically on the equator. After covering some ground, Leticia abruptly stops.

"Careful, there's a river. We have to walk over this tree trunk."

Ernesto remembers it well from the day before. The river flows noisily below, but cannot be seen in the darkness.

"Look at my feet and put yours where I put mine," she tells him, picking up the acrid scent of fear in his cold sweat.

Ernesto trusts in the magic of his instincts; in a moment of danger, his senses become razor-sharp. He crosses the narrow trunk breathlessly, following in the girl's footsteps. Once across, they pick up the pace. Ernesto remembers his trek through the Guatemalan jungle with Miguel, who was so agile, while he was so clumsy. But now it's worse because his arms are already lacerated by thorny vines.

He finally asks Leticia for a moment to catch his breath. He sits down on a tree trunk and asks her why the Huaorani wanted revenge. She takes a moment, then answers:

"Because of illegal logging. We don't want them to cut the trees, because we all live in the same jungle. That's why in my village we didn't allow the Colombians to come through. They were coming to buy logs from the Auca."

Ernesto hears nocturnal birds calling one another with languid songs. In the intervals between songs, the grunt of an animal makes him jump like a spring.

They continue their escape. Eventually they arrive at a place where the trail divides, and Leticia says:

"My house is that way."

Ernesto has no idea how long they've been running.

"Look, It's getting light!" she exclaims.

A quarter of an hour later, she enters her village with Ernesto close behind. People rush out of their adobe huts and surround them. Her parents embrace her. Ernesto collapses to the ground, panting for breath. He is trembling, soaked in sweat, muddy, and bleeding from the thorny vines along the trail. Leticia is impeccable, as fresh and vivacious as when they left. She relates story of her kidnapping and rescue, and the adults immediately begin to organize their defense against a possible Auca attack.

"You have to leave," they tell Ernesto. "They'll want to get revenge on you for what you did."

Two boys are assigned the task of taking Ernesto by canoe down a nearby tributary to the Tiputini. Once there they can wait for a motorized canoe to give him a ride up the Tiputini, all the way to the Vía Auca bridge and safety."

Meanwhile, the community girds itself for battle.

"They won't take us by surprise like they did when they got Leticia," they tell Ernesto. "We're going to post sentinels day and night. Let them come—we'll drive them away with bullets. Everyone here has plenty of lead!"

Ancient war cries between both tribes still reverberate in their memories, when they look at the hillsides, inciting warriors to battle. The men bring out weapons that they keep hidden in their thatched roofs. They sharpen their knives and women carry their children to hiding places.

II

The older members of the tribe hold a meeting. Since they are low on ammunition, they decide to radio the military base in Sebastián del Coca to alert the officer there of a possible altercation with the Huaorani. Even if they send only one helicopter, it'll make those Auca run home with their tails between their legs.

In reality, it's been decades since the Amazonian Quichua have made war with their traditional Huaorani enemies; and they are ill-prepared for one. After the armed conflict between Ecuador and Peru last March, the government confiscated most of their weapons to give to their soldiers, leaving only a few rusty rifles, including a pair of turn-of-the-century Winchesters, and some pitiful looking shotguns.

What's more, no one feels like firing the first shot: they remember too well the brutal cycle of vendettas and violence with those savages Auca, as they call the Huaorani.

The women pack a small, light aluminum canoe with a few bags of tapir meat and other snacks. Ernesto says goodbye and without further ado, they shove off. In a moment, they are gliding downriver through a tunnel of green foliage and between *guadúa* cane and huge trees. The brilliant red and yellow sun warms them as they float swiftly southward.

The Quichua boys are Chuqui and Suyana, who is Leticia's brother, Ernesto finds out.

They lament the fact that they weren't given guns; these are needed more urgently in the village.

The rivers running through this area originate in the Andean foothills, separating civilization from Amazonia. At the end of a long circuit through the Ecuadorian basin they flow into other tributaries which ultimately flow into the Amazon.

The river is swollen from recent rains and the canoe is swept along by the current. Islands made of trunks covered with brush and branches accompany them and sometimes collide with the canoe. In the quieter stretches of the river, they must row. For some time the only noise is the slow, deliberate plunging of oars in and out of the water.

They have navigated less than two hours when in the distance an enormous wooden canoe appears behind them. Six Hauorani men shout furiously, stabbing the air with their red-painted spears.

"They're after us!" exclaims Chuqui.

A rush of adrenaline courses through Ernesto as if by grenade explosion. In the back of the canoe, he is the easiest target. He musters his courage and looks at the row of hard Huao faces. They are still brandishing their spears. A devastating fear washes over Ernesto, and he crouches down in the canoe. His flaring nostrils take in the sharp odor of his own sweat.

"Don't worry, Ernesto," Suyana says, "the Auca never attack from behind. It's one of their superstitions."

At this point a Huao man signals his companions to stop rowing. He stands up, legs apart, and shouts at them in Quichua:

"Where is Leticia? Where are you taking this traitorous *cowode?*"

Suyana and Chuqui look at Ernesto. He did not understand the words, but is getting pale under his dark skin.

"Leticia is home! She asked him for help because she said you took her by force!" replies the Quichua boy.

"That's a lie! You know very well that your sister came with me because she wanted to. No one kidnapped her!"

In the quiet of the jungle river, the acoustics allow his words to arrive intact.

"Give me the *cowode*!"

The Quichua begin to row away. In front of them, an enormous tree trunk floats across the river. Turning parallel to it, they come to the opposite bank of the river. A narrow space allows their canoe to slip through. The Huaorani try to do the same, but their boat, which is actually longer than the river is wide at this point, cannot maneuver through it. The Huaorani canoe advances and retreats several times, but disadvantaged by its own size, it is stuck.

For a long minute the occupants of both boats wait in expectant silence. From one side to the other, Quichua and Huaorani glare at each other. Then Chuqui yells through the vegetal barrier:

"Why did Leticia come back, Awañetae, if she loved you so much? Does she love you or not?"

The other man pauses before answering:

"Ask her!" he says, telling his companions to lower their spears and row away.

Ernesto sees them turning upstream and he wipes his sweat on the back of his hand. The Quichua also begin to row downstream without another word.

Later, when the Huaorani are out of sight, Ernesto asks Suyana what they were saying.

"They were saying that Leticia went with Awañetae of her own free will."

"Is it true?" asks Ernesto.

Suyana takes his time answering, then says:

"Ask her!"

III

The waxing moon spreads a silver sheen over the Tiputini when Ernesto and the Quichua catch up to it. They decide to spend the night in an abandoned cabin on the riverbank. The sky's blazing starlight invites them to lie down on the sandy beach and talk about the infinite. A light flashes tremulously in the sky and goes out in an instant.

While they recall the events of the day, the Quichua boys don't know which was funnier: Ernesto's expression when he saw the Auca, or Añawate's when he saw they were blocked by the log in the river.

The water joins in their laughter with its rippling. Suyana explains to Ernesto the real cause of the rivalry between the two communities. A Huaorani baby died after a visit from a member of the Quichua village, who had gone to speak with them about cutting trees. The Huaorani took it into their heads that the Quichua had cursed the baby.

"I'm not surprised Leticia ran off with him, but something must've had her change her mind." Ernesto asks them if the Huaorani would've really killed him if they'd caught up, or if it they were just trying to scare him. The boys shrug.

"With the Auca, you never know..."

At daybreak, the familiar sound of a motorboat wakens them and, in an instant, they're on the bank signaling that they'd like a ride upstream. With a rope, they secure the canoe to the motorboat, and in less than half an hour they're tying up under the Vía Auca bridge. The Quichua boys thank the motorboat driver, and Ernesto offers some money for the gas.

"Don't worry about it, kid," comes the reply. "The Company pays for it."

Only then does he realize that the motorboat bears the name Texapetrol-Gulf, painted on its side.

Hours later, Ernesto is following his companions, who carry the canoe on their heads, like a pirate hat for two, over a trail that borders the river north of the bridge. The Quichua boys plan to wait on the Vía Auca for a trucker willing to take them to the Napo crossing. From there they can easily return to their village downriver.

"Do you mind if we stop by a friend's house, here in Dayuma?"

"No problem," Ernesto replies.

"Did you know that my name in Quichua means hope?" Suyana suddenly says.

At other times, the boy would've taken this as a signal that the stars were lining up in his favor. But his belief in his search has diminished of late, and now the whole thing seems utterly pointless.

The canoe moving along on four legs continues with Ernesto behind, and soon they arrive at a clearing where a man is stoking a fire on the ground in front of a cabin.

"He's a Huaorani, one of the members of the ONHAE,[12]" explains Suyana. "It's the National Organization of the Ecuadorian Huaorani."

Ernesto's jaw drops in surprise.

"They're good people, don't worry. The Huaorani aren't all the same. Some are civilized; this one is also an environmentalist, against cutting down the forest."

The man receives them with handshakes.

"Welcome, friends. You've come at an auspicious moment!"

He is a sturdy young man, his long, flowing hair parted down the middle and with carefully trimmed bangs over his forehead. He is wearing jeans and a white T-shirt with the ONHAE logo printed on it.

An iguana split down the middle is roasting on a grill, the embers glowing beneath.

---

[12] ONHAE = *Organización de Nacionalidad Huaorani de la Amazonía Ecuatoriana* (Organization of Huaorani Nationality of the Ecuadorian Amazon)

The boys sit down on a log bench. Lunch lasts an hour until the last, tiniest bone of the animal is gnawed and licked clean. But besides the good food—priority number one if you are an Auca, the Quichua tell Ernesto—their host shows great interest in speaking with the foreigner when he finds out that Ernesto is from the North.

The Huaorani's name is Mateo, and he was born in the protectorate of the American evangelist Rachel Saint, where his clan has been relocated. For a time he believed that living like a savage was evil and felt ashamed of his parents. One fine day, however, when his father had been prohibited from singing traditional Huaorani songs, he had had a "reverse conversion", so he says, and "saw the light". He abandoned the Evangelists and went to Coca. There he met members of the ONHAE and they invited him to the city of Shell, where they have their headquarters."

"The *city of* Shell?" ask Ernesto.

"Yes, it is a small city, founded by the oil company when they first came to exploit oil here. As I said, he joined the Huaorani cause, and from then on called himself Moipa, in honor of his great warrior uncle who attacked six Shell employees in the fifties when they entered his territory to perform seismic tests. Since Moipa joined the "enemy," the evangelists put him on their black list under the label "communist."

When the Vía Auca first came through here," he explains, "the colonists started coming. Their houses popped up from one day to the next, like mushrooms after a good rain. They came with their power saws to cut down the trees, and with their cows and pigs that trampled and ruined the jungle. And with their diseases."

With only a few years of high-school education, Moipa's acquired his learning through the Indian Nations organizations.

"We need to protect what's left of our land," he continues," and that's why we're fighting against illegal logging. The problem is that some Huao won't collaborate, like the ones you met. They'll sell no matter how low the price is. In Tigüino, the settlement at the end of the Vía Auca, they're selling their wood to the Colombians for a dollar a plank. One dollar!" Moipa emphasizes the number by stretching out his longest finger, a gesture learned in the bars of Coca.

At this point another young Huaorani comes from the trail and Moipa introduces him as his brother. His name is Kimo.

The large, elongated holes in his earlobes, filled with painted wooden discs attract Ernesto's attention. Kimo was not born in the evangelist protectorate, they explain. His long hair, hanging loosely behind him, and his well-trimmed bangs, are identical to his brother's. He wears leather sandals, and Ernesto notices that his toes spread out like a fan, and that the big toe is spaced even farther from the rest. These are feet well suited to gripping a branch high up in a tree, the kind that conceals bees nests or a juicy prey.

"With the colonists' logging, the clear cuts, and the Company's pollution, in 10 or 20 or 50 years there'll be no more jungle. Unless we stop them," Kimo ads.

"Are there major oil spill problems in the Huaorani territory?" asks Ernesto.

"Oh, yes. The oil spills here in Napo Province are routine".

"And the oil wells explode sometimes," Kimo ads. "One of the Cononaco wells burst into fire one time. The flame was as high as the buildings in Puyo and it went on smoking for weeks".

"But the majority of the 'affected', says Suyana, using an expression that has become common in the area, "are the people living up north in the Sucumbío province, in the wells of Shushufindi-Aguarico, Sacha, Libertador, to mention a few. Those spills started 30 years ago and they're still there. They affected 150,000 people, natives and settlers, with sicknesses. Thousands died. They wiped out the Cofán and Sequoia tribes."

"It's not going to happen here," says Kimo, grasping his weapon. "If they open up Block 16 to oil production, our friends are going to cut *chonta* cane and sharpened their spears."

Kimo's spear cuts through the air and plunges into a tree, trembling.

"Wait a minute," Ernesto interrupts. "What wells did you say, Suyana, the ones up north?"

"Shushufindi, Aguarico, and Sacha were the worst."

The names resound in Ernesto's mouth and one clings to his throat.

"Sacha"?

20. On the Other Side

I

"Freeze!"

The voice resounds over the desert slopes of Sonora and the echo reverberates: *eeze!,eeze!, eeze!* "Hands up! *up! up! up!*"

Livid, Twisty raises his hands. The owner of the voice points his gun at his chest. The German shepherd he has on a tight leash is ready to throw himself on the coyote. In a minute, a pick-up is parked in front of the house, and a second one soon appears. Another man approaches carrying Rosa in his arms. He carefully puts her in the back of the second vehicle and covers her legs with a jacket. Twisty babbles in Spanish, but the other man says:

"We don't speak Spanish! Get moving!"

The coyote turns his contorted face toward Rosa, while being walked to the first car.

"Hey," Twisty says in a shaky voice, "You know I was just joking around... We're still friends, right? Tell them you're my girlfriend and we got in a little argument. Tell them I'm an immigrant like you, because you and I are both Indians, you and I, poor Indians, that's what we are ... fucking Indians... tell them I'm your brother!" he mutters under his breath.

"My brother? It wasn't my mother who gave birth to you!" Rosa murmurs scornfully, with her puffy, blood-soaked lips.

The coyote pleads pathetically while the man shoves him into the first car, which has painted on its side the words:

Yuma Border Patrol.

The sun is already setting.

II

The vehicle stops in front of the clinic as the sun disappears from the Yuma sky. A stretcher is brought out and Rosa is rolled inside. She is in a state of shock. She resists the removal of the jacket that covers her nudity and is restrained by three nurses, who inject her with a sedative.

After a general examination, one of them calls through the intercom:

231

"We've got a different case here, Mr. Gordon," says the woman in English. "She doesn't have any ID on her, but we found some sucres. That's Ecuadorian money, right? ...Yeah, she's doing okay. She took a real beating, but there are no fractures ...Yeah, okay," she continues in Spanish, "that's fine. You can talk to her in an hour."

Rosa has understood the words "Ecuadorian" and "sucres", and her hopes shatter into pieces like a sailing ship falling apart plank by plank on a reef. She can't believe she didn't realize that those dirty sucres would identify her! What sort of dirty lie will she have to come up with now to wipe out her true identity? How can she avoid being sent back to Ecuador? How would they do it? Would they lock her up in jail? She wants to get up and make a run for it, but she can barely move.

The nurse helps her walk to the bathroom and to get into the shower. She begins to give Rosa a sponge bath, but Rosa tells the woman that she doesn't need help.

"You can wear these clothes when you get out," she says, leaving Rosa alone.

Sitting on the shower floor with water pouring over her shoulders, Rosa weeps. She cries for her mother's sacrifice, for her own downfall, for the reflection she sees in the mirror: her face the color of chocolate, a yellow and purple circle around her left eye, swollen lips and a disfigured nose, and the black and blue bruises that cover her body.

The woman knocks on the door, cracks it open, and tells her she shouldn't cry—that in this very place she has seen many young girls who have been raped—or worse—and that Rosa must have been born under a lucky star. But what good is a lucky star if it doesn't lead her to her mother? If it abandons her at the doors to paradise but doesn't let her enter?

The water, her clean skin, and her crying spell have made her feel better. She dries herself off, feels her cracked heels, which remind her of the rough, straw-colored desert, and puts on her clothes. The fresh, fragrant clothing give her some comfort on this fateful day. But a glance at the mirror brings her fearful condition to the forefront once more, and she returns to the emergency room trying stoically to hold back the tears welling up in her eyes.

The nurse conducts her to the policeman's office and he, the same man who arrested the coyote, addresses her in Spanish:

"What's your name?"

"Rosa."

"Rosa what?"

"Rosa Moreno."

The officer types the name into his computer and then takes her fingerprints, which instantly appear on the screen. Her crime is entered into the computer, and the discrepancy between the name she gave and the owner of the ten perfect fingerprints is now forever recorded in the electronic circuit of that ominous government machinery. As to what punishment her offence will bring, and when it will begin, Rosa has no idea, but she knows that at some point they will find about her false identity and she will not be able to deny her fraud, because it is now irreparably registered.

"Where did you meet that man?"

"In El Papalote, on the other side."

"Is he an illegal immigrant, like you?"

"No, he's not like me. He's the coyote."

"Do you know his name?"

"Honorio, but they call him Twisty."

"He was trying to sexually assault you, is that correct?"

"Yes, twice. But I didn't let him."

"I see. And do you know what happens to young people like you who come from far away?"

"No, sir. But I'm from Mexico," she says, trying to muster a convincing tone.

Should she lie again and say that she found the sucres on the street? Or that someone gave them to her?

"Don't waste your time lying to me, Rosa, or whatever your name is. You're about as Mexican as I am, and I'm from Minnesota. Look, there are no funds to send you back to Ecuador by plane. You're going to be taken to the Juvenile Detention Center until a family member comes to get you, or until a judge decides what to do with you. Do you have any family in the States?"

This question strikes her like a thunderbolt. If she says she has her mother, they'll both go to jail, because her mother does not

233

have that mighty green plastic card that opens all doors. She shakes her head.

"I know you're lying, but it's up to you," says the man. You can either call one of your parents or relatives, or you're going to the Juvenile Detention Center.

"I understand, sir."

Rosa lowers her head and buries her chin one her chest. "It's in God's hands now," she says to herself, with total resolve.

III

On a dreary, cloud-covered morning a few days later, the girl arrives at the Juvenile Detention Center. All her belongings have been confiscated in Yuma: clothing, backpack, and the telltale money.

Two boys who traveled with her from Yuma arrive in handcuffs. For some reason, Rosa has been spared this humiliation. But not this other one: after passing through eight metal doors, she is deprived of the clothing given her in Yuma. She is stripped naked, asked if she is carrying drugs, and to make sure she is telling the truth, she is made to get down on all fours like an animal. A rubber-gloved woman brusquely sticks her fingers into Rosa's private parts to see if any containers are hidden there.

Mortified, Rosa signs the documents that are thrust at her without reading what is written on them; she only notices the letterhead:

Correction Corporation of America

Correction of what? Of being a daughter?

She is led to her cell and as she passes through the door, she spits on the floor.

Once more she is forced down on the floor, made to lick up the spittle, then roughly shoved inside.

The room is long and narrow, with two double bunk beds, a chair, and a skylight near the ceiling. She sees two other girls in this cloister. She asks them what city they are in. One is hidden under a blanket and does not respond. The other does not know.

She says she doesn't care because they're going to deport her. She is from El Salvador.

Rosa lies down in the bed assigned her and pulls the covers over her head.

In the afternoon the girls are let out onto the patio for a couple of hours. The patio is enclosed by walls, four meters high, topped by several rows of barbed wire. The inmates, 12 to 16 years old, wander around aimlessly. In a far corner are those who broke the immigration law, that is, illegals like her, who speak her language. Some are sullen, others apathetic—the remains of their shattered dreams are painted on their faces. They have segregated themselves from the American prisoners and are united by a common goal and anguish. There are those who rode on top of *The Beast*, slipping past the terrifying gangsters and police. There are also those who swam across the infamous Rio Grande, and others who crawled their way north through the rat-infested tunnel. All were impelled by the desire to see their mothers and fathers who immigrated before them; all urgently cling to their parents' memory before time wreaks havoc on their recollections; before their own faces begin to dim in their parents' minds and hearts. Or, worst of all, before their love takes on the misty, imaginary quality of a daydream. *You had a child in Nicaragua? Yes, I had a child, but ...she was raised by her grandmother.*

This is the fear of the jailed minors: that their parents will forget them forever.

The bathroom is a row of toilets and showerheads without walls. Rosa detests the lack of privacy. She lies in bed and weeps. The skylight admits a beam of dust-speckled light streaming toward the floor.

The following day, after a restless night, Rosa awakens early; too early for someone who has nothing to do. Her eyes have been open much of the night. She has lain in quiet confusion, listening to church bells tolling their way into her cell.

The violet mantle of fluorescent light only enhances her distress. She climbs to the top bunk to look out the skylight. Perhaps she will see the church tower. Perhaps she will see something beyond herself, to which she can direct her silent prayers. It is not to be. The little patch of sky contains nothing more than the grim gray of five o'clock in the morning. She hears the intermittent noise of a street.

"It's boring staring out that window," says the Salvadoran girl.

Her name is María Estela and they are about the same age. Rosa climbs down from the bunk.

María Estela, who is more loquacious today, tells Rosa that she crossed the border through a tunnel.

"Where there are rats?" asks Rosa.

"No," says the other girl, "maybe they drowned, because the water came up to my neck. We had to hold onto a rope, in case there was a hole. And we had to keep our heads up and try not to swallow any water."

"So, it wasn't sewer water?"

"What do you mean…?"

"You know, where all the piss and stuff goes."

"No, yuck! It's runoff from Nogales. There are two Nogales, you know?"

"Yeah, the Mexican Nogales and the one in Arizona. I saw them on a map."

"Yeah, but that's not what I meant. There's the Nogales you see and one that you don't see—the one on top, where people walk on the streets, and the one below, where people walk through the tunnels. The tunnels fill up with water when it rains, because, like I said, it's the city drain."

"Why didn't you just cross when it wasn't raining?"

"Because the coyote said that when it's dry the street kids take over down there. They're bad. They attack the immigrants and rob them. And there's a lot of them! Plus there's patrols and police from both countries looking for illegals, and all kinds of dangerous people. So you can't cross during the dry season."

Rosa shudders at the image of a subterranean labyrinth strewn with swollen rat cadavers and motherless children. The only tunnel she knows is the fresh and green dome of vines and orchids arching over the Amazonian streams.

"We were so excited when we finally reached this side," continues the Salvadoran girl, "and right then, we ran right into the *migra*. I hate them. I didn't come to steal anything. I just want to get to St. Louis to see my parents."

The two girls sit in silence. The sudden memory of jungle rivers fills Rosa's soul with fragrances and sadness.

"This is the second time I've tried to cross over," María Estela continues. "The first time the ranchers spotted me when I was walking through a field full of cactuses. They have their own vigilantes, you know? They've got rifles and I've heard that they'll shoot to kill."

"Did they shoot at you?"

"No. They shot into the air and we all ran away. I got all scratched up by those horrible cactuses. Then the patrols got there and rounded us up."

"Why do the ranchers care so much about people crossing? It's not like we're trying to steal their cattle!"

"Who knows? They hate us. They say we're trespassing on private property. But the truth is, they just hate us. I mean, obviously some gringos are nice, and some of them even leave water so the illegals don't die of thirst in the desert."

"Strange country. They shoot at you, they give you water." Rosa's voice trails off.

"I guess it's like that everywhere—good people, bad people. You run into everything when you leave home."

Rosa agrees.

The other girl sharing the cell is somewhat older than Rosa and María Estela. She is sitting on the bed. Her hair is long and greasy, her face expressionless and her gaze lost in contemplation of the wall. Rosa leans forward to talk to her, and sees that one of her eyes is bruised, her nose is disfigured and her arms black and blue. The girl answers in a mixture of groans and sorrowful sighs before retreating beneath the covers.

"She's all beat up," whispers María Estela in Rosa's ear. "She came the same day I did. I tried to talk to her but she won't open her mouth."

"Do you know what happened to her?"

"The nurse told me she was raped. She came on the train, you know, right on top. I guess the gangsters climbed up and grabbed her. They passed her around and then left her for dead. It was dark. Someone found her next to the tracks, all bloody. They called Borstar, do you know them? They took her to a clinic."

Rosa is shocked and remains silent. The horror of the image makes her mouth suddenly taste bitter and she keeps it tightly shut.

"It's a group that rescues immigrants. She spent a few days in a clinic and now they're going to ship her home, back to Honduras. Honestly, I think with everything that's happened to her, she's gone a little crazy."

Rosa wants to ask her who did it, but she can't get the words out. What does it matter anyway? She thinks of them as beasts who have lost their souls, or perhaps God never gave them one. Or maybe He gave them a soul so horrible that none of the world's goodness got into them, and they are just wells of evil. Rosa turns her gaze once more to the violated girl and asks God that to cure her wounds and restore her sanity. If the Divine Creator can't do it, or doesn't want to, then His works have nothing to do with human beings and it's better to forget Him. This last thought seems extremely sinful to Rosa; but whatever rebellious corner of her mind it has come from, it is powerful, and she is unable to retract her heresy. Why should God save some people and not others? Without knowing it, at that instant, she gets rid of God and his saints and stoically faces her new agnostic state.

She doesn't know if this is a sign of madness or sanity. But she is conscious that to her everyday fears of the world, another has been added: fear of the Divine Injustice.

Foreign teenagers are kept for a few days and then sent back to their countries: Mexico, Guatemala, El Salvador, Honduras, Nicaragua, whatever. All are sent home, even if this means the home of a relative who is reluctant to accept them, or home to a church doorway. The next day, María Estela says goodbye. She is leaving on the "Bus of Tears".

"We're like migrating birds," says the girl.

"Not even that," Rosa thinks, "at least birds come and go as they wish. We're birds with broken wings, lost in the wind."

The days go by with no news for Rosa and the hours go by without meaning. She tries to find something to do other than biting her fingernails. She has seen a girl pulling out the hairs from her arm one by one.

She lays on the bed and stares out through the skylight. The afternoon shows her a red sky, like an open wound.

At the end of one week, she is alone in her cell. The Honduran girl, with her wounds and her madness, has been taken away. New prisoners come and go, saying little, and disappearing on the following day. And in this tedious place, where light from the long, naked florescent tubes pitilessly invades every corner, there is nothing to kill the time. Since seeing the face of Injustice, she is no longer able even to pray. She misses her farm, the twittering of the birds, and most of all, her family. She is in agony for her mother. If only there were a book, a notebook and pencil, a window to look onto a tree. But no, there is only the sick tedium and a solitude that is wider than the desert. Even though she is under a roof, she is unsheltered.

Loneliness bordering desperation sticks its sharp thorns into her chest. She feels sick.

IV

During the day no sound reaches her ears, but the sad dong of the church bells. This makes her think that today is Sunday. The dusty beam of light coming through the skylight has moved a little to the right.

A female guard is turning out the lights in the corridor when she hears a wailing from the cell. It is the Ecuadorian girl. She is suffering intense pain on one side of her body. She groans, twists and turns in bed, and holds her stomach with both hands. Her weeping eyes beg the woman to call a nurse.

"It hurts, it hurts so much!" Rosa cries, "Mommy, it hurts so much!"

A nurse hurries in and quickly comprehends how serious the situation is. She calls the paramedics. They say it appears to be appendicitis, because the pain is localized, and intense. They must act quickly.

The ambulance arrives promptly, and is already waiting at the front entrance. Rosa continues to cry out in pain. They put her in the vehicle. With the flashing lights and siren at full wail, they arrive at the hospital in under ten minutes.

Two paramedics are carefully lowering the stretcher, while the lights still flash, when Rosa jumps off like a mountain lion. And in the blink of an eye she is running toward the street. *Run, Rosa, run!* She hears her grandmother exhorting her from somewhere, *Don't let them catch you! Quick, the light's turning red! Watch out for cars! Don't run into that old man! There you go! Don't look back, Rosita! Run, my dear! Don't let them catch you!*

The paramedics are still in a state of dumb shock when the police arrive. A cop takes off running and follows Rosa for a few blocks before losing sight of her. He is incapable of following the mad dash of the Huaorani. He stops and wipes his brow. The Ecuadorian girl, he admits, has gone with the wind.

A group of people are leaving a church. It's a wedding party. Rosa runs into the church through a side street. In the very back of the building she sees a door, and on impulse, she opens it and finds a small room. She will, at least, be able to hide there until nightfall. No one is around except for three faded saints statues, who stand in a corner. It occurs to her to hide behind them, but there is a crucifix on the wall and it is looking straight at her. After the bad thoughts that she has nurtured over the past two days with regard to the Creator and his truly awful distribution of justice, she decides that she had better have nothing to do with the saintly and the sacred. But right there is another door. She puts her ear up against it. There seems to be no one on the other side. She opens the door cautiously. It's small room where cleaning products are stored. Luckily, there are rags, brooms, a rolled up carpet, clothes, dusters; in other words, it is full of things to hide behind, if she should hear any noises.

Soon she discovers a little closet, which she enters. There is a light. She turns it on and closes the door.

With her heart beating wildly after her run, and her hands trembling, she would like to pray. Faith, however, has abandoned her, and the words refuse to rise from her chest. She thinks of Huaengongui, father God of the jungle, but no prayer comes for him. Suddenly, a new state of consciousness is born within her, a revelation that her mind, freshly oxygenated and alert, celebrates. No more asking saints for favors like a Huao beggar. If she is able to escape, she tells herself, she will give thanks to her intelligence and determination. And she will give thanks to her memory. After all, it was the memory of the jungle that gave her idea to fake appendicitis. She and her cousins had more than once come upon animals playing dead, only to have them escape when the children were distracted. How great that she remembered this today!

Amazed by the sudden force of this thought, she knows what she must do. There are work clothes. She takes off the detestable prisoner's uniform and puts it into a plastic bag. She puts on a pair of jeans that she has to hold up with a belt, turns up the cuffs and puts on a shirt, which she leaves hanging outside her pants.

Then she turns off the light and stays in the closet for a few minutes until her racing pulse is semi-normal. It occurs to her that this is the first time in her life that she has stolen anything. But this is not theft, she tells herself, it is momentary expropriation dictated by circumstances. If she gets through this, she promises herself that she will return everything.

Satisfied with her self-absolution, and wrapped in the velvet darkness of her hiding place, Rosa closes her eyes and rests. She thinks about everything that has happened up until this moment and vows not to forget it. She thinks about her mother. She thinks about other children looking for their parents. And about Ernesto.

The tolling of the bells startles her. The priest is busy now, pulling on the rope. No time to lose; now is her chance to get out!

She slips out into the same street she entered, but this time she goes carefully. She finds a trash can and drops the plastic bag with the prison uniform inside. The clang of the last 8 P.M. bell vibrates in the air for a few seconds. She walks away quickly, following the sound of downtown traffic.

Night has fallen when Rosa arrives at a bustling avenue. The city is intimidating and she's afraid of being noticed. If she had the tail of a *saimirí* squirrel monkey, it would be between her legs. She keeps walking, staying close to the buildings. She sees her reflection in a shop window, and it doesn't look too bad. But the feeling of well-being and freedom doesn't last long, because the reflection also shows uniformed officers behind her. Now she really is a surly monkey cornered by hounds, with no tree to leap into. Without turning around, practically glued to the glass and with her head down, she darts inside the shop door. For some time, from behind a mannequin, she keeps watch on the street outside. When she thinks the hounds have gone, she slips out onto the sidewalk again and sees the tail lights of a police car driving off.

She comes to a corner where she hears a group of women speaking Spanish and asks them if they can help her. She has lost her money, she says, and needs a phone card to make a call, because where her mother is they do not accept collect calls. No one has a calling card. One of the women offers her a little money. Rosa asks if it's enough to get to a bus station. They tell her it is, but that it's not a safe place for a young girl to go to at night.

"We're going that way. You can come with us."

Eager for the protection and the company, Rosa gratefully accepts. And so she becomes part of a group, like a bee stuck fast to a honeycomb.

The women get on a bus with Rosa.

"Where is your mom?" one of the women asks her, sensing drama in the life of this girl.

"In Oregon, on a farm."

The others immediately understand the situation and ask for no further explanation.

In a few minutes they arrive at the terminal. One of the women accompanies Rosa to the telephone booth and when she dials the number that she has so well memorized it does not seem to be that of her mother. The person on the line says there's no one there by the name of "Alba" and hangs up on her. Rosa's face melts into tears.

"No use crying, sweetie. You can come with us if you want. We work in a hotel a couple hours from here and today is our day off," says the woman who seems to be the oldest. "I think they're looking for a new cleaning person."

Rosa dries her tears and accepts the offer, smiling. She sheds a few more tears and thanks them again.

The women pay her bus fare, and she sets off with them.

"What's your name?" asks a twenty year old woman.

"María…ah… Estela. María Estela."

"Look, you don't have to hide your name or your story from us."

"OK. My name is Rosa Epayuma. That's my real name. I'm from Ecuador."

Well, Rosa, nice name. Let me fix you up a little. I'll lend you my earrings. These big ones are going to look good on you. And let me put a little lipstick on you. Just a little. You're a pretty girl, no need to put on a lot of makeup. Just a little blush now. Oh, that's nice! So *cool!*" says the woman, using the English expression. She holds a mirror up to Rosa's thin face.

"I like it!" says Rosa.

"Good. Just give the boss a smile and everything's going to be fine, okay?"

Rosa tries out a smile, showing an impeccable row of small, white teeth, which elicit unanimous approbation. Her eyes sparkle.

The hotel manager is a middle-aged man, with a beard, black hair and more polished manners than the other Mexicans Rosa met in the desert. He begins the interview immediately, finding her different accent and delicate manners very agreeable.

"How old are you?"

In the past, subtracting years helped her. But at this moment, she realizes that being a minor could be a hindrance. On the other hand, if she adds a few years, he might not believe her. She may as well tell him the truth.

"I'm turning 16."

"I see. When are you turning 16?"

Rosa thinks for an instant.

"In 11 months and 12 days."

"So you're a smart one, but do you know how to clean a bathroom?"

She has to think a little more this time.

"I'll learn anything you teach me really fast, sir."

"Yeah, I believe it. But what would you do if the *migra* came here?"

"I'd hide in a closet," she replies immediately.

"What if you came face-to-face with one of them?"

"I could tell them I was your daughter, sir, if that's okay with you," she says, surprised at the audacity of her answer.

The man bursts out laughing.

"I wish I had a daughter like you instead of the three good-for-nothing boys I have, who only know how to get into trouble! Alright. The girls will give you a uniform and get you started. Your salary is fifty dollars a week. Good luck."

V

Rosa's co-workers give her a uniform. They also found some clothing her size.

The work is simple and she learns to fly through it; and between making beds and scrubbing bathrooms, she runs to the telephone. No matter how many times she tries the number, and at whatever hour, the answer is always the same: Nobody here by the name of Alba.

Rosa understands the English word *nobody*, but she still cannot believe it. She asks her co-workers to listen to the message, and the women confirm it.

"Are you sure that this is your mom's telephone number?"

"Yeah, it's definitely hers! I've called her so many times with this number!"

She begins to doubt. Was it 503 or 530? Was it 981 or 891? She tries alternate numbers. Either her memory melted away with the heat of the desert, or something happened to her mom. She borrows money, buys a telephone card and calls don Pablo in Baeza. She greets him briefly and gives him the hotel number where she can be reached. She knows that her grandmother will rush to the village the moment she gets the message. Sure enough, Rosa receives a call that very day.

"I don't know what happened, Rosita," says her grandmother, her heart half sad and half happy. "That's your mother's number for sure, but she hasn't called us in two weeks, and the farm isn't returning our calls, either."

There's only one way to find out what's happened, she concludes: save up enough money to go where she is.

On the seventh day of Rosa's new job she receives her pay. She cleans the bathrooms with quick efficiency, fixes herself up with greater care than usual, puts the money in a purse given to her by one of the women, and races to the bus station. She looks at the schedules and prices, choosing a ticket booth with a *Se habla español* sign on the glass.

"One ticket for Eugene, please."

"When would you like to leave?"

"Tonight."

"Your ID, please."

Rosa is thunderstruck.

"Just a minute. Let me get it," she lies, in order to say something.

Returning to the hotel, she shuts herself up in the bathroom. The image of her face with tears-streaked makeup startles her. She wipes herself with the back of her hand, smearing the makeup even more. With the eyeliner in great black circles around her eyes, she looks even more like a scared, lost little *saimirí*.

Suddenly the *saimirí* stares directly at her from beyond the reflection, and a lights turns on inside her mind. She retrieves from her memory one more number, rushes to the phone, and dials.

"Hello?" answers a woman's voice in English.

"Is this the Ruiz family?" she asks in Spanish.

"Yes, who is this?" the voice answers in Spanish.

"My name is Rosa. Ernesto and I are friends."

21. Sacha's Towers

I

"Did you say, Sacha?" Ernesto interrupts the Quichua man.

He wants to be sure he heard correctly and it's not some erratic thought mingling memories with reality.

"Yes, in Sacha there are four oil platforms. They're not far, just across the Napo River," Suyana adds, "about an hour from here."

"Do you want to go?" Moipa asks. "If you want to see what The Company did, that's a good place to look. Then you'll see why we don't want any drilling on our land. More than 30,000 people, natives and settlers from the province sued Texapetrol two years ago, and they're still in court over it. And you know, even though Texapetrol doesn't work there anymore, our health problems are as bad as ever and they keep getting worse. It's because the pipes they left are rusting out and leaking crude oil."

As Ernesto listens to the words a sea of images floods his mind: cancer, tumors, open sores, children with fused fingers, animal carcasses, stomach diseases and brain diseases, all the while the word "Sacha", "Sacha", is repeating itself in his mind like a mantra. Yes, he is sure, certain actually, that he's heard that name from his father. And he confirmed it just the other day on the phone.

"Yeah, I want to see it," he says, when the other Quichua runs out of calamities.

Finally, he asks about the village called Esperanza that he's been looking for. When he hears it's a relatively new community, the product of recent colonization, he loses interest in visiting it. His inner compass is explicitly pointing due north, toward the nefarious oil platforms.

"Then we'll take you because on your own you won't find what we want to show you."

Moipa never loses an opportunity to show outsiders the social and ecological mutilation of the jungle. "Moipa is a true activist, and smart too," Ernesto thinks in admiration.

The Vía Auca is not far. In fact, the smell reaches Moipa's house and Ernesto can almost taste the crude oil in his mouth.

A Company truck that dropped off a load of day workers and is now heading back to Lago Agrio soon stops for them. Ernesto and his four companions get on with the canoe.

"Nobody asked for my entry permit," Ernesto notices, remembering that the Vía Auca is off-limits.

"The permit is just to get in. Nobody ask for it when you leave."

The Vía Auca is an oil-soaked lane cutting through the rain forest over undulating terrain, against a horizon crowned by volcanoes. That's where the Andes descend and scatter their rivers throughout the vast Amazonian basin; and where distinct microclimates compose a fantastically beautiful and biologically diverse corridor.

"This is a scar on the delicate Huaorani skin", says Moipa.

Three oil pipes are a constant feature along the sludgy lane. Often rusty, they are suspended just high enough for the local kids to use as monkey bars, though they run at ground in several places, according to the undulations of the terrain. The road is also flanked by the humble dwellings of the thousands of settlers who established themselves there as they roads were being built—and their inseparable oil pipelines.

Moipa points out a child drinking water from a red barrel stamped with the name of its previous owner: TEXAPETROL. "People use the barrels to collect rainwater," Moipa explains. "It's cleaner than the river water."

Every now and then the pipeline passes through separation stations where enormous flames burn gas and cast a constant red glow on the houses, trees, and even the clouds, day and night. The roar of the fire is deafening.

"There are a lot of oil spills on this road. Either by accident or negligence, there is always crude oil leaking out of some place," Moipa explains, "or it spills off the trucks and winds up in the rivers. That's why the fish taste like diesel."

"So whose fault is it? Who's responsible for all that?" Ernesto asks with concern.

"Texapetrol was first. They set the standard for the rest of them. The others copied everything: Petroecuador, Maxus, Occidental, Conoco, who else, Kimo?"

"Arco, Oxy, Elf, Mobil; new flies, same old shit!" says Kimo, eloquently. "Look, a few months ago ONHAE protested against Maxus for the spills and a hundred Huao occupied the platforms. The Company called in the army and that was the end of the protest."

"That's right. The army and The Company are like two peas in a pod," the others agree. It's been that way since Shell discovered the oil in the jungle."

In less than an hour the truck arrives at the Napo River bridge and the driver parks before crossing. The Quichua say goodbye and glide away over the muddy waters, letting the current sweep the canoe downstream toward their village.

II

They are watching the afternoon news when the phone rings. They haven't heard from Ernesto for days, since he called from Quito, and the ring makes both of them jump up from the couch.

"You're Ernesto's friend? Do you have any news from him?"

"Yeah, we met in Guatemala," says Rosa, nervously.

"How is he? Is he still in Ecuador? Did he tell you where he is? When is he coming home?"

The avalanche of questions from them, each from a different phone, overwhelms Rosa.

"He told me he was going to the very tip of South America, something like that."

This stops the Ruiz's in their tracks.

"He said I should call you if I had any problems when I got to the US. That's why he gave me your number. Sorry, if this isn't a good time?"

"No, no, that's fine. Where are you, Rosa? At the airport?"

"No. I'm in a hotel."

"Do you need a ride somewhere? Do you want us to pick you up?"

"If it's not too much trouble …."

"Okay, tell us where you are, your address and room number."

Rosa gives them her address and tells them to ask for her in the lobby.

The hotel is about two hours east of San Diego, but without a moment's hesitation the Ruizes jump in the car and speed down the freeway.

Anxious to meet someone with fresh news of their son, they wonder what kind of trouble this girl is in. Isabel suddenly remembers Ernesto mentioning an Ecuadorian girl who was traveling with a group of immigrants, to join her mother in the U.S.

"It must be her, Esteban! The teenage girl Ernesto told us about!"

The car is now parked in front of the hotel and Rosa is waiting in the doorway.

"Rosita, don't forget about us, just because you're going off with gringos!" her friends say by way of goodbye.

"They're not gringos. They're from Spain, the mother country!"

She bids her colleagues farewell with hugs and kisses, then turns and extends her hand to Mr. and Mrs. Ruiz. Esteban Ruiz asks for her luggage and she shows him the small bag in which she keeps a change of clothes, her lipstick, and a notebook. She thanks them for their kindness and settles into the back seat.

Driving down Route 8, Esteban Ruiz looks at Rosa through the mirror. He is in a silent, almost mute state, uncharacteristic of himself. Isabel is aware that this little teenager with skin the color of almonds, dark eyes and delicate features has reminded her husband of something. The sweetly accented Amazonian Spanish, the cadence of her voice and her open, genuine smile have captivated Isabel Ruiz from the first instant.

"So, Rosa, are you from the mountains or from eastern Ecuador?" Esteban Ruiz asks, breaking his silence.

"From the East, sir. I am Huaorani."

"I thought the Guaraní lived in Paraguay." Isabel interjects.

"Not Guaraní, ma'am; Huaorani, with an 'H' and no accent," Rosa explains.

"It's funny how similar the names are," Isabel observes. "Maybe in the remote past they were the same people, don't you think, Esteban?"

"Hard to say," responds her husband absentmindedly. It is evident that his thoughts have gone somewhere far away.

"Well, Rosa, tell us about yourself. And tell us about Ernesto," says Isabel.

"Well, I met Ernesto the day he got out of jail in Guatemala."

The instant this statement slips from Rosa's lips she regrets it. But it's too late. Esteban Ruiz's foot hits the accelerator and they lurch toward the fender of a truck just ahead of them. He slams on the brakes in the nick of time, and wherever his mind has been wondering, the shock brings him to the present.

Isabel suggests they stop for a bite of food to wait out the traffic, and to relax for a bit and hear what Rosa has to say. Esteban pulls into a diner parking lot.

Hearing Rosa speak confirms for the Ruizes that she is the same girl Ernesto told them about. Isabel asks her to tell them all the details about Ernesto, and Rosa relates the story as Ernesto told it to her. She doesn't want to shock them again, and makes sure not to let slip any hint of his near-fatal accident in Palenque.

"Well, you've got to admit it: the boy has guts!" says Esteban with a proud smile, "and he's pretty clever, too. Can you believe it? He made that man believe he was an ornithologist! Ha! And he even got little Miguel released!"

"Yeah, sure, but I'd rather have him home than wandering the world righting wrongs!" says his wife.

Night has fallen by the time the Ruizes arrive home. Rosa thinks she has arrived in a palace. They set her up in their guest bedroom, the nicest she has ever seen. It's even more beautiful than her aunt's place in Baeza, because there are carpets, not linoleum.

She gets in bed and falls fast asleep, stroking the dog lying at her bedside, dreaming of interminable embraces.

III

The truck continues its trajectory north, and after some time they see the enormous columns of fire under a violet sky coming from the famous oil drilling station. Pretty soon an industrial camp appears, packed with towers, a labyrinth of tubes, cables, electrical posts, buildings and tanks, all surrounded by an extremely high electric fence. The only thing that escapes the premises is the constant noise of the pumps, the dull roar of fire consuming air molecules, and the smoke; a thick smoke polluting the air and floating into clouds that turn the sun into a faded, yellowish disk.

A helicopter slides off to the left hammering the afternoon with its chop-chop-chop as it descends into the center of the industrial park.

The vehicle goes by the compound, and Kimo bangs on the roof for the truck driver to stop. They thank him for the ride and disappear in a place with no sign of demarcation.

Moipa takes the lead. As they walk down the trail leading away from the highway and following a secondary branch of the oil pipe, the gigantic jungle leaves lose their natural luster under an oily film and the land becomes progressively more hostile to vegetation. Suddenly they come to a swamp full of black mud. In this section a rusty pipe with a broken joint releases a gooey liquid, drop by drop, forming a puddle beneath, from which a rivulet of mucky oil extends to a nearby stream. On its banks, ferns hang languidly in the stinking air and an anorexic ceiba struggles in vain to produce a flower.

Enesto observes this tainted landscape with shock and rage.

"This is where a section on the tube broke," Moipa points out. "Look at how they repaired it: with a rag!"

"The Company spilled millions of gallons of crude, contaminated water into the rivers and estuaries and excavated nine hundred pools without bothering to line them. They're still soaking their toxins into the soil," explains Moipa; "they say they're doing a cleanup now," he adds with a gap-toothed smile. Want to see?"

The trail leads to a barbed wire fence with a sign saying:

IV

Today is Saturday and breakfast is served late in the Ruiz household.

Isabel encourages Rosa to tell them about her own travels. Rosa girl elaborates on some episodes, abbreviates others and neglects to mention a few. Isabel, moved, listens intently.

"How did you manage to jump out of the stretcher? Weren't you buckled down?"

"I was, but on the way over I asked one of the Spanish-speaking paramedics to loosen the belt. I said it was squeezing me and it hurt. He must've felt really sorry for me because he loosened it all the way, and I slipped out under the blanket."

"You're a brave girl!" Isabel remarks.

"Not surprising," her husband says rather dryly, "she's a Huaorani, after all."

"So, you know my people?" Rosa asks with a hint of pride.

"A little. I know they don't shy away from conflict. If they don't like something they don't waste any time."

"Is that right, Rosa?" Mrs. Ruiz asks.

"Yes it is, ma'am."

"The Auca were the ones who killed the four American missionaries in 1956, Isabel," says Mr. Ruiz. "The world found out about it when it was reported in Life Magazine. Do you remember? There were lots of photographs."

Rosa feels a rush of shame on hearing the term 'Auca'.

"I remember hearing something about it. Weren't those the missionaries who made first contact with the ...ah ...inhabitants of the Ecuadorian jungle?"

"Yes, and not long ago their airplane was found on a river beach," the man adds. "They also killed a priest—I don't remember his name—and a Colombian nun who was with him. The people who found him said they stuck him so many times he looked like sea urchin.

"Do you know the Auca, Rosa?" asks Mrs. Ruiz in a tone of surprise.

"The Auca and the Huaorani are the same people," Rosa explains candidly. "Yes, the Huaorani killed Nathan Saint and his companions. That was in my grandpa's day. My clan wasn't involved. But Bishop Labaka and sister Inés were killed by the Tagaeri, who are not Huaorani; well, they're a distant branch, a very distant branch."

After a somewhat embarrassed silence, Rosa adds: "We don't like the term 'Auca'. It's an ugly word meaning 'savage'. The Quichua call us that."

"Aren't they savages? I mean, they walk around in loin cloths and feathers on their heads," Esteban Ruiz insists. He is a man who considers tactfulness a waste of time, especially with a Huaorani.

"Some are," Rosa agrees. "The ones who were afraid of what the oil companies were doing retreated deep into the jungle, and yes, they want to preserve their customs, like the Tagaeri and others. But other Huao, like my family, have been catechized, or evangelized, and civilized, for years now."

"So, your family doesn't live in the jungle?" asks Isabel.

"More or less. We don't live in the city or towns with the settlers, but we also don't live in the interior, like before. We're border people, my family, I mean, we live on the edge of the jungle near a small town where there are schools and cars and stores. We have bamboo and thatch roof houses, but it's because we like it that way. Corrugated metal roofs are awful, they get so hot you can't stand it."

Isabel nods. Esteban is staring intensely at Rosa. To reinforce her 'civilized' status, Rosa adds: "My mom finished elementary school. I'm in high school and I'm going to go to the University in Quito. I have a cousin studying there who's going to be a doctor."

The Ruizes exchange a glance. Rosa's manner of speaking leaves no doubt that she has leapt an important cultural barrier. Rosa, however, feels somewhat uncomfortable by the Auca matter, and she wants to clarify a thing or two.

"My grandfather was a hunter and a warrior, but he hasn't hunted since he was expelled from his land."

"Why was he expelled?" asks Esteban Ruiz, who in the next instant deplores having asked the question.

"The Company did it. The oil companies, you know? They relocated everyone to a missionary protectorate. But even before that, the fish started coming down the rivers dead. They died of the same thing my dad died of. Now the place is called Block 16."

"How did that happen?" Isabel asks, disturbed by the turn of the conversation.

"It was in Texapetrol's time," Rosa continues. "My dad worked for them because my mom got sick and they had to pay hospital bills. Then, one day he came home all covered in oil. Then he started feeling bad. They say it was because he drank the river water; other people say it was because of the vapor coming off the oil pools he was working in, where they store the waste, the stuff they can't use. I don't know what it was. But he got leukemia and a little later he died."

"Where was this?" Ruiz asks. A slight feeling of nausea goes up to his mouth.

"Sacha Station." Rosa squeezes her lips together to stifle a sob.

Ruiz makes up an excuse and goes up to his office on the second floor.

Rosa feels more comfortable with Mrs. Ruiz, and she takes the opportunity to talk about the anguish over her mother that's tormenting her.

"No one answers the phone. That's why I'm really, really worried. I don't know what's happened to her. I have the money to go there, but they won't sell me a ticket without proper ID."

Isabel puts a plate of cherries on the table and tells Rosa to help herself. Rosa thinks these cherries could very well have been harvested by her mother's hand.

"Don't you worry, Rosa, we'll find a way," says Isabel. "We know people in Oregon and I'm going to call them today to see if they can help find your mother."

Mrs. Ruiz gives Rosa a kiss on the forehead, and this small gesture makes the girl feel her mother's absence so acutely that a torrent of suppressed sobs bursts forth. Isabel puts her arms around her. Rosa wipes her nose with a paper napkin, thanks her hostess, and eats a few cherries between hiccups and barely contained sobs.

V

It is past noon, and Esteban Ruiz is still in his office. His wife finds him sunk into an easy chair surrounded by papers and photographs faded by the years: Engineer Ruiz with Texapetrol workers; handing a treat to a monkey; posing on a platform beside a recently-inaugurated pump; leaning against a tree. How young he looks! How satisfied he seems!

"What an idiot!" he thinks as each place and each occasion runs through his mind.

"You didn't eat, Esteban," says his wife, putting a plate down on a tray beside him. "Eat this sandwich at least. Whiskey on an empty stomach? You'll regret it. In any case, it's too early for a drink!"

"Look at this, Isabel - they all look like Rosa," says Ruiz in a low voice, showing her a photo in which a laughing Huaorani family surrounds him as they place a toucan-feather crown on his head. "This was taken in Sacha, not far from Limoncocha, where the missionaries took the Huaorani. A lot of them worked for me."

"I know it's bothering you, Esteban. Why do you keep beating yourself up? You did what you had to do, what they sent you to do. You didn't know what the consequences were, and neither did they."

"Of course they knew! The methods used in Ecuador would never have been approved in the U.S."

He looks at his wife with desperately sad eyes.

"Isabel, the contamination was the result of a conscious financial decision on the part of Texapetrol. There's no doubt about that," he says, with his usual certainty. "All to save three measly dollars for each barrel of crude oil!"

"But you didn't know."

"But I should've known, or should've suspected," continues Ruiz, his tone oscillating between anger and bitterness. "I only figured it out when the natives started getting sick. The cofán and the secoya tribes, haven't I told you? We decimated them!"

He pauses, searching his intricate interior landscape for answers. Where and why did his intelligence and his conscience fail him? He finds only tumultuous reproaches.

"What astounds me the most is that I didn't immediately resign. When I found out what was happening and went to complain, nobody listened. But I didn't resign. Why did I remain complicit? I even agreed to return later to conduct seismic tests in Huaorani territory! Even though my conscience was eating at me. That was in the Yasuní reservation, in Block 16, the same place where this girl's family lived, dammit!"

Isabel goes to the kitchen and returns with a cup of tea.

"Esteban, you've already paid for what you did and didn't do after all these years carrying around the specters and this *mea culpa*. Don't think I don't know."

It never occurred to him that his guilty conscience might have overflowed from his own personal abyss. And Esteban Ruiz, who never seemed to doubt anything, hides his face in his hands.

"And this son of ours who doesn't come back, Isabel! I'm worried about him. You know, he means everything to me! And I owe him an explanation. Remember when he confronted me on the telephone? About whether I worked in the jungle, if I was involved in the construction of the Vía Auca, that kind of things."

The sweet fragrance of a gardenia wafts into the room through the open window and the afternoon sun streaming through the blinds projects bars of light and darkness over the photographs. Esteban speaks at length about his four years in the Ecuadorian East. Isabel is familiar with the story; she has always heard a litany of complaints and accusations against the firm that exploited him for monetary gain. Today, however, she hears a confessional running through Esteban's narration. Returning to this undesirable place in his memory is distressing, but, she understands, it is necessary. His story is cathartic.

They speak of Rosa and of the difficult world of the border. Not the one she crossed, evading the blind and deaf law, but the other border from which she comes: the border dividing the Stone Age world of the Amazonian natives from a modern world advancing brutally, invincibly, over them.

"I just want Ernesto to come home, Isabel "says Ruiz in a contrite voice. "I'll tell him everything that happened in those years, and I want him to forgive me, because I love him and because it was my mistake, and he should learn from his father's mistakes, so he doesn't repeat them."

Esteban remains silent for a few moments.

"And above all, Isabel, I hope he never, ever, goes into that insane jungle and sees the damage that his father helped to create".

VI

The sign, black letters on yellow, is clear:

Cleanup Operation Texapetrol-Golf. No Trespassing

The Huaorani don't pay attention. Moipa lifts up the barbed wire and Ernesto and Kimo slip through. Every time they lift their boots out of the spongy ground, oily, black liquid oozes into their tracks.

In a short time they come to a pool some twenty meters across with a black, shiny surface, almost plastic-like, broken only by the carcass of a large animal floating near the edge. From the center of the pool rises a pyramid of fire, now red, now yellow. A swirl of smoke like a whirlpool or an enormous spiraling worm shifts with the wind.

"This is one of the 960 open pools dug by Texapetrol. They put them on elevated ground," explains Moipa, "to facilitate drainage. When they flood, the waste runs into the rivers. At other sites they took advantage of natural ponds where animals would go to drink. Those became cemeteries."

Once again Ernesto has that feeling of anarchy and chaos, and anguish overtakes him. The noxious air assaults his windpipe and makes his eyes water. "What was my dad thinking when he came here? Why didn't he ever tell me about these fires and smoke? He only talked about beautiful wild birds and flowing rivers."

They come to another pool that the cleaning operations have not touched.

"This one provided water to the residents of this area. Before The Company came, of course," says Kimo, pointing to some nearby dwellings.

The vegetation surrounding the pool is thin: a few stunted palm trees and dirty ferns on black soil. Near the shore, a dying duck flaps a sad, muddy dance of death.

"This is what we're fighting for," says Kimo as he picks his way with carefully-placed feet back toward the bank. "We don't want Huaorani territory to be another Chernobyl. They can offer us all the hospitals and schools they want, but that won't save the jungle or our livelihoods!"

They see a squalid dog crossing with trembling feet over some planks that have been laid in oily mud.

Soon they come upon a cleanup team at work: a band of men in shorts and naked torsos moving through the sludge. With bare hands they are gather up clumps of muddy oil, branches, dead and half-dead birds and frogs, and put it all into plastic bags. Full bags are thrown into a freshly-dug pit.

"Why are you putting the bags in there?" Ernesto asks the men.

"When one of these pits gets full we cover it up with soil and, pronto," says one of the workers, a man with sickly, pale skin, making the universal gesture of cleansing his hands.

Ernesto notices his skin is mottled and sore-looking.

"These people are very poor," Kimo whispers. "They're the landless of this country who come to the jungle looking for work."

"And their work is useless, because when the plastic degrades the oil seeps out and continues to contaminate the ground," Moipa says in an exasperated tone.

"They didn't even bother to dig further from the rivers! Why the hell didn't they at least choose a more remote site?" his brother says.

"None of this is our fault," says one of the workers, with welts covering his face. "And it's none of our business. All we care about is getting paid for mucking around in this shit."

"Some of them faint from breathing this air day in and day out," says Kimo, between gritted teeth.

"Do they get medical treatment?" Ernesto asks.

258

"The Company fetches them with a pickup and drops them off at home or in the camp. Those days they don't get paid."

Overwhelmed with compassion and pity for these men, Ernesto wants to shout at them to drop everything, to tell them that they are selling their lives very cheaply, that these pollutants cause cancer, that there's arsenic in there, lead, mercury, cadmium … Don't they know this?

"Why don't you use plastic gloves?" he asks.

"Do you see any around here?" one of the men says, with muffled anger.

The last rays of the sun, beaming through the foliage, form tiny rainbows in the mist rising from the soggy earth, giving the workers' skin a shimmering, iridescent hue. Sitting on the earth or on tree trunks, each one proceeds to clean himself meticulously of the black goo.

"The Company gives each of them a rag and a can of benzene per day. They can't go back to the camp covered with all that oil," Kimo comments. "Their wives wouldn't want them like that!"

"Prostitutes, that is. In those camps there really aren't any wives," Moipa corrects him. "Just bodies for rent."

"That's right. The only thing The Company brought was pollution, alcoholism, and prostitution," his brother agrees.

A Company all-terrain vehicle pulls into the cleaning area. Its driver gets out, followed by armed bodyguards. The man, who appears to be the foreman in charge of this cleaning sector, doesn't stand on ceremony when he sees the visitors. He tells them in an aggressive tone that they are trespassing, that they must've seen the sign, or can't they read? And that they should go to the company office if they're looking for work.

"No, thank you. If I wanted to commit suicide I'd choose a faster way," Ernesto tells him without hiding either his indignation or his accent.

"So what the hell are you doing here, then?" the man demands, raising his voice. "People come here to work, not to gawk! Now get out of here!"

The bodyguards gesture toward the road with their guns.

"I only came here to see what my father did, Engineer Ruiz, I mean. He's the one who ordered these shitholes to be dug in the first place," says Ernesto in an erratic, pained confession that he blurts out in spite of himself. The Huaorani, surprised, spring into an attack posture with arms up as if balancing their spears him.

"Your father worked for Texapetrol?" the foreman asks.

"Well, not my real father. The man who raised me," says Ernesto, in an attempt to put distance between himself and the man responsible.

His declaration burst out of him like an arrow and he would like to retract it. But this further information doesn't improve his situation in the least. On the contrary, he is sinking deeper and deeper into the mud—both metaphorically and literally—as the Hauorani stare at him with alarm and as his boots sink further into the oily mud.

He drops his gaze to the oil-covered mud holes. The surface is strewn with the corpses of butterflies that were caught in the oil. His brain is a mental cesspool. He babbles incoherently, asks for forgiveness without knowing for what, exactly, and bows his head, gritting his teeth with shame and anger.

"Well, there are many oil stations around here", someone interjects after a silence, "so you have several days to check it out if you want to find out what your papa accomplished."

Ernesto's agitation is evident to everyone. Whether out of respect for his father's rank, or in commiseration with the boy's emotional state, the foreman extends a hand and helps Ernesto extricate himself from the gelatinous pool he has been sucked into.

Moipa, remorseful about his hostile reaction, offers Ernesto a cigarette, which he does not accept. But he insists, lights it, and thrusts it at him.

"Here. Relax."

When the tobacco smoke mixed with the effluvia from the pool hits his stomach, Ernesto doubles over, vomiting the undigested iguana lunch at the foreman's feet. The hurling sound startles a nearby buzzard.

22. Cortesy of Texapetrol

I

The enormous torch covering the western sky goes out just as the tuck drops Ernesto off in Lago Agrio. It is 7 P.M. and the Huaorani return to Dayuma on the last vehicle driving on the Vía Auca.

Ernesto is familiar with border cities and he knows that they are the cauldron of marginalized populations. Lago Agrio, just 20 kilometers from Colombia and verging on the jungle lowlands is no exception, with the caveat that here one smells, breathes, and walks on oil. A belt of misery larger than the original town itself surrounds it and has been expanding since the arrival of Texapetrol in the sixties.

"The slums around the original village grew like mange on a dog," they told him in Coca. "The only things that prosper there are prostitution, drug traffic and filth. Aside from the oil companies, of course."

Ernesto walks down the main street where the heat and the humidity become even more intense due to the chaos of traffic and the presence of hundreds of transients: settlers, opportunistic Colombians, overwhelmed natives, and hundreds of street vendors. And, of course, foreigners connected to The Company. Heavy trucks rumbling through the potholed streets splatter black mud on people and animals indiscriminately. "It's democratic, at least—like the rain," Ernesto muses.

What he most wants is to find the best hotel in town and immerse himself in sleep therapy. He has already decided to swallow his pride, call his parents, and ask them to pay for the hotel with their credit card. His sparse resources are only enough, in the best of circumstances, to pay for a dorm bed in a room with 20 other men in a hostel maintained by the diocese. Assuming they have room, that is.

He sees an agreeable-looking hotel at the end of a street. "I'm sure they accept plastic," he thinks.

He walks toward the reception desk, his boots leaving marks of oily mud on the polished wooden floor.

"No, no! You can't come in here!" comes the horrified voice of the receptionist.

Ernesto looks at the man in surprise, but does not retreat. The man makes an impatient gesture to the doorman to kick this Indian out of the vestibule immediately. Ernesto is too tired and confused to realize what's happening. When the doorman grabs his arm Ernesto twists around and pushes him. In seconds, two thugs are half dragging, half carrying him toward the street. They shove him out and threaten to call the police.

Ernesto is beside himself, his arms and jaws clenched, blood vessels about to burst in his neck, and he has an overwhelming desire to hurl a rock through the hotel's window, which looks out onto the street. But then he sees himself in the reflection. His shirt is ripped, his pants muddy, his hair wild and his cheeks scratched and smeared. He sees himself as others are seeing him: a poor Indian, almost certainly drunk or crazy.

As his eyes focus beyond his reflection in the window he sees the figure of a man, glass in hand, who is looking back at him. He looks like an American— a businessman, perhaps connected to the oil companies.

He fumbles for his passport, opens it, and presses it against the glass for the man to see. Then he writes down on a piece of paper, which he also presses to the window: *Tell that asshole that I'm going to smash the window and complain to the American consulate if they don't let me in. Please.*

Ah, the language that opens doors in these small circles of the Third World where the elites spin! And the document that, like a flag, legitimizes his presence in so elegant a place! The man comes out to speak with Ernesto, who introduces himself. He tells him that he's from San Diego and explains that he's been in the jungle. The man reenters the hotel, says a few words to the manager, and in five minutes the boy is in the bar, boots under his arm, and in respectable company.

"I'm Andrew Erikson," says the man, extending his hand to Ernesto. Here, they call me Andrés.

Soon an enormous plate of banana empanadas and a soda appears before Ernesto, who digs in hungrily. The man's blue eyes, which don't quite match his deeply tanned face, look at him with interest. He listens to the story of the boy's incursion into Auca territory, and nods his head. He is aware of the rivalry between Quichua and Huaorani, of the illegal timber sale and the voracity of the Colombian wood merchants, and of the anger on the part of Huaorani environmentalists.

"I'm a consultant for Texapetrol. The natives are suing, and I'm basically a mediator. There's a lot of animosity on both sides. Just yesterday a Huaorani wounded a Colombian with his spear. It was in the Texapetrol camp on the Cononaco River during one of our meetings. The soldiers took off when they saw the spears and the blood; A few of us were evacuated by some brave men and the meeting ended in chaos. The truth is, these Huao are pretty aggressive."

"Why was the man attacked?"

"From what I hear the Colombian man had been sent by an oil company, I'm not sure which one, to burn down the Huaorani's house, because he didn't let the company trucks use the road next to his house. They offered him money and everything, but he refused."

Ernesto is intrigued by this man's ambiguous position; it's as if he doesn't know which side he's on.

"He must have his reasons to refuse," Ernesto says.

"He's got his reasons for sure, and he has balls, as they say around here. These people saw the ruin of the Cofán and Secoya tribes. There's probably fewer than a hundred of them left, and the Huaorani don't want the same thing to happen to them. The Tagaeri had enough when a seismic test team in 1984 killed their leader, a fierce warrior. Since then they refused to have any more contact with civilization. They live far away now, completely isolated in the jungle."

"Who knows, maybe that was the best thing for them to do. They have a right to be 'uncontacted' and live however they like to live, don't you think?" Ernesto says, still trying to find out where this man's loyalties lie.

"The right, yes. But will they be left alone? I doubt it. There was talk of finishing them off in a pretty drastic manner."

"*Finishing* them *off*? How?"

"I'm not sure," says the man, averting his gaze and drumming his fingers on the table. "But they'll find a way."

Mr. Erikson orders coffee for two. He sees that his conversation has affected Ernest personally in a way that he does not fully comprehend.

"So, tell me about yourself, and Ernesto. What brought you to the Eastern Ecuador?"

Ernesto tells him his story or, that is, recounts his wanderings since leaving home, ending with his epic visit to the Huaorani center. He finally confesses to the man that he doesn't know what to do next.

"You mean to tell me you've been wandering from country to country and town to town because of your faith in a sixteen-year-old note written on a scrap of paper?"

"Yes, because of faith, and hope on a scrap of paper. You said it."

"Go home, Ernesto. It seems pretty unlikely, absurd, actually, that your biological mother would write, *I come from Esperanza*, instead of, *I'm from Peru*, or, *I'm from Ecuador*, or whatever country."

"Yes, I know," Ernesto agrees, his chin resting on a hand.

"If I may venture a hypothesis, it seems like the Esperanza your mother wrote about would be a little town just over the Mexican border, so small that maybe it's not even on the maps. If I were you, I'd go back to the United States and do the research with the Mexican consulate," Mr. Erikson counsels.

Ernesto sees the reflection of his disheveled hair in his coffee cup. The fact is, he has recently come to the same conclusion: that his search is ridiculous, and that his plan was based entirely on confused and incomplete information. Mr. Erikson's comment is a confirmation of everything Ernesto has been thinking. He buries his dreams for once and for all.

"But, back to the Huaorani," says Ernesto, "do you think the missionaries actually helped them?"

Having heard his two friends talk on the matter, and Rosa, too, he wants to know what the older man thinks.

"That's a tough question, Ernesto. In some cases, the missionaries eliminated certain practices that were ... well, not very constructive for the community, to say the least. They used to settle all their arguments with their spears. But when they shipped them off to their so called "protectorate" they got polio and started dying off from the white man's diseases. It was a badly planned and badly done project."

"Was that the evangelists' fault?"

"I think some of them are well-intentioned, but others sold themselves to the oil companies. I'm sure they justified it to themselves somehow. In any case, a lot of people think this tacit alliance between the missionaries and the oil companies is pretty fishy."

"Well what do you think?"

"I agree. And I think the missionaries' position was quite arrogant," he continues. "They told the natives: 'Your culture is obsolete. It's unworthy.' They tried to change them and mold them in their own image."

Ernesto remembers what Moipa told him when they were on the road, and his words now acquire another dimension:

They gave us a dream that wasn't ours, Ernesto. Do you understand what I mean? Wait, what am I saying? No. The truth is, they didn't give us a dream, they sold it to us! And we paid dearly for it. And now we see how bad it was for us.

Mr. Erikson continues, and Ernesto sees that he's making an effort to be objective: "The biggest problem with the conversion of the Aucas or any other group is this: they're exposed to the material goods of 'civilization', but not the means for acquiring these goods. So the upshot is they turn into beggars."

Someone comes to the table and tells him that his flight has been reserved. This reminds Ernesto that he has to make a phone call. With his passport in his hand, he goes to reception, leaving behind the strong smell of smoke from a Huaorani cabin that still impregnates his clothing. He tries several times to make a collect call but no one answers the phone. He leaves a message, then returns to Mr. Erikson's table and thanks him for dinner and for the advice. He grabs his now dry but still black-mud-encrusted boots and tells him that he's heading over to the *Los Capuchinos* shelter to get a bed for the night.

"Listen, I'm taking the last flight to Quito and my room is booked through tomorrow morning," Mr. Erkison says. "So you should stay in it."

"Oh! Did you pay for tonight?"

"Not me. Texapetrol, of course!"

Ernesto is grateful to have a bathtub that evening. He takes his clothes off, peels his socks off his feet, and the effluvium invades the bathroom.

He sinks into the bathtub to restore his body and his many aches and pains suddenly claim his attention. The blisters where his boots rub against his ankles have left the area skinned; one of his big toes has a split nail; the fungi that erupted in his armpits burn like hot coal; and the mosquito bites covering his arms like a miniature mountain range are inflamed.

Fortunately, Mr. Erikson has left a first aid kit with fungicidal and antibiotic creams, and a disinfectant soap.

"The jungle is a witch, my friend: if you aren't careful it'll seduce you before killing you," Mr. Erikson remarks while rolling his suitcase out of the room.

"Thanks so much!"

"Don't thank me," responds Andrew Erikson wryly, "this is also courtesy of Texapetrol."

Ernesto washes himself and then begins treating his bruises, jock itch, bites, scratches, and blisters. Finally, he washes his clothes in the bathtub and hangs them up in the window. He lies down but remains awake for some time, eyes glued to the ceiling fan. He watches the blades slowly turning and thinks of the wheel circling within himself: a circle without exit. He is done searching for María Moreno and there will be no more Esperanzas on his horizon, either.

II

In spite of the humidity, the monumental morning heat dried the clothing in the window. While dressing, Ernesto remembers his dream. His father's right hand is stained with blood, and no matter how much he washes, it won't go away. The only thing that can remove so indelible a stain, says his father, extending his hand to him, would be to take his son's hand in his. But the son refuses.

Right after breakfast—also courtesy of Texapetrol—he hits the street, buys a cheap pair of tennis shoes and dumps his old boots in a trash can, which someone behind him almost immediately retrieves.

266

On impulse, he buys a disposable camera to take pictures of the city. His father might want to see how it's changed. Ernesto is sure that it has indeed changed, and for the worse. He wonders what year exactly he father was there. He wasn't born yet, and his father must have been around 30.

He ventures down side streets lined with open ditches where human waste flows.

On a corner, an Indian is sleeping next to the ditch—that terrible sleep that is brother to death, the undeserved nightmare of the alienated poor who ends his day in an awful binge. Ernesto, out of respect for this man's misfortune, refrains from taking a picture.

Graffiti on a wall, however, merits his first shot. Someone has painted in red:

The oil flows. The jungle bleeds.

The word 'blood' conjures last night's dream. A bloodstain in the jungle … an oil stain on a hand … a river of oil in the jungle … a line of blood on a hand….

Submerged in this swirl of words that accomplish nothing more than deepening his anger and sadness, Ernest wanders the streets of Lago Agrio without paying any attention to the street vendors. Should he tell his father to his face that he was an architect of the disaster?

The dream image of his father extending his hand to him, and his refusal to accept it, has left Ernesto's heart sore. The internal implosion that began yesterday in the Sacha Oil Station has reached the depths of his being and his world collapses into the ruin all around him.

The bus to Quito is leaving. Ernesto is in the back above the wheel, but he doesn't care. The constant bounce and jostle of the road, ravaged by constant Amazonian downpours, is hypnotic, and the pounding music from the bus radio is just the anesthesia he needs.

After a three-hour journey along the Trans-Andean oil pipeline on Route 45 the bus enters the terminal of a small city, and the driver announces a transfer for passengers continuing on to Quito.

"Where are we?" Ernesto asks.

"Baeza," replies from a passenger who is getting off the bus.

"Baeza! This could be Rosa's village! Yeah, it definitely is!" Ernesto exclaims to himself. She mentioned it to him in passing, but the name remained hanging in his memory with a sweet resonance, because at that moment another Baeza flashed through his mind: a village not far from Jaén in the heart of Andalucía. And he loves Andalucía! How could he forget a name like Baeza!

He leaps off the bus. This place is not large. Surely someone here knows Rosa's family.

"Ask at the post office", the bus driver counsels him, "they might know something".

"Yes, there's a Huaorani family that has a farm," they inform him at the Post Office. "Don Pablo can give you directions; he's got a phone business and he has messengers."

Don Pablo is a well-known personage in these parts, and in a few minutes Ernesto is in his place of business.

"Yes, I know Rosa, and her family," says the man. "My son is just back from school. He can take you to see old Caento."

III

November 1.

The telephone rings in vain at the Ruizes. "Just when I need them most they don't answer!" the boy laments as he leaves the telephone booth. On the other side of the street he sees a sign proclaiming "Internet". It occurs to him that here in Quito, in the new center of this thriving city, petrodollars have brought new amenities. Cyber-cafes are proliferating.

He goes in and asks for a computer. He wants to send an e-mail to his parents asking them to buy him a return ticket. He'll pay them back, he assures them. He types in the email address and looks for the "at" symbol, which doesn't seem to be where it ought to be. He utters the English monosyllable that has become a universal epithet, and a girl on the adjacent machine explains, in English, that he needs to type "control shift 62." He thanks her and sends his email, which is short and dry. He knows that his parents, who have only recently begun to participate in the world of cybernetics, check their e-mail several times a day.

He turns to the girl next to him and thanks her again. Just as he's getting up to go to the airport for the night, or for whatever number of nights he'll need to spend on a chair in the waiting room, the girl strikes up a conversation. She's Brazilian. She clearly wants to practice her English, and Ernesto finds her efforts entertaining. She soon desists from her English and tries out a heavily-accented Spanish, partially learned in Irish pubs in the city of Buenos Aires. Ernesto finds this even more amusing.

Flattered by the boy's smile, she invites him to a cocktail party tonight in the saloon of the hotel where she is staying. There'll be lots of people his age, she tells him. Ernesto confesses that he hasn't showered in quite a while, that he's just arrived from the jungle, and that his hotel is a ways off, at the airport, and that he has no car. The Brazilian assures him that he can take shower in her hotel, since he'll be her guest. Ernesto points to his oil-stained jeans, but she says it's not a problem. On the contrary, it gives him an exotic touch. Plus, if he wants, she can get him a clean shirt. As she rises from her chair Ernesto notices how her jeans emphasize her buttocks, two perfect circles, and then his gaze wanders up to her swooping, flowered blouse. He feels an emptiness inside that he's been putting up with for too long, and accepts.

The girl's name is Conceição. She is in her early 20s.

The hotel, softly illuminated by indirect lighting, is full of people, some standing and others seated at the bar or on the various leather easy chairs placed around the saloon. Waiters wend through the crowd with platters of hors d'oeuvres and drinks, and a pianist absentmindedly plays arpeggios as a singer announces the next number.

Ernesto finds his new friend in a corner where the younger generation has congregated.

"So what's the occasion?" Ernesto asks, speaking into her ear after finishing off a couple hors d'oeuvres.

"There was an oil company conference this afternoon for firms working in Amazonia," the girl explains to him in Portuguese. "How did you like the Jacuzzi?"

"Oh, I loved it. Thanks," says Ernesto, thinking about the split toenail that broke off his big toe as he was drying himself. "And... I suppose Texapetrol is hosting the party?"

"No, no," she says in broken Spanish. "Texapetrol isn't the big boss anymore."

"What do you mean?"

"I mean, the Ecuadorian Amazon is also ours now, know what I mean?"

"What do you mean 'ours'?"

"I mean ours, not the gringos'. Petrobras, our Brazilian company! It's going to begin the exploitation of two blocks, which is why we're here, *of course*. See that girl over there? She's the daughter of a YPF executive. That's the Argentine company that just bought Maxus; and that guy over there is from Petroecuador, one of the national companies here. They're not all multinationals. Everyone wants a slice of the pie, so we've got to share, don't you think?"

"Yeah, you've got to share the wealth," says Ernesto with a smile. "Divide up the pie," he repeats, looking admiringly at the magnificent marble floor.

He feels a sudden urge to get out of there, followed, immediately, by the thought that it might be interesting to get to know the antipodes of the world he has just entered. What's more, he's starved, and without a single dollar in his pocket, he should at least hang around until he's dealt with his hunger. And his curiosity.

A young man from Petroecuador comes to the table to say hello and to find out who this *yankee* is that Conceição has invited. From the color of his skin, he doesn't seem anything like an American, although he speaks English fluently and is wearing very cool pair of jeans that are unavailable in these parts.

"Nice to meet you, I'm Raul Robledo."

Later someone notices Ernesto and his oil spots in his jeans, and tells a friend that "this guy is speaking Spanish with the Mexican girl, but with a peninsular accent, he must be from Repsol, the Spanish company that is negotiating a merger with

YPF. He might be a good source of information." He approaches Ernesto with a glass of wine.

"I see you've come from the Amazon," he says, pointing to Ernesto's jeans.

"Sorry, didn't have time to change. I just came from Lago Agrio."

"Ah, Lago Agrio! There you can smell dollars!"

The Brazilian, sipping a 'sex on the beach,' watches Ernesto, who handles himself well.

"He's so cute!" She whispers into her friend's ear.

"Conceição, isn't that boy too young for you?" says an elegantly made up Argentine who, before finding out that Ernesto was from the United States, wouldn't have given him a second glance. "Don't rob the cradle. He's not even 20 years old!"

"True. Do you think he's a virgin?"

"Conceição! You're a little slut!" says a Venezuelan girl who has been eavesdropping.

She tosses her hair and they all laugh with conspiratorial glee.

As the night progresses Ernesto circulates among various small groups that form and disband according to the laws governing social situations—those of giving and, above all, receiving, attention. He chats a bit, and when he gets bored quietly moves toward another circle, sipping his cocktail and noting snatches of sentences.

"And yesterday when I met this… We went dancing at Los Barriles ..."

From time to time waiters pass with platters of food and drink and Ernesto stretches out his hand to resupply himself with more throat-burning rum.

"I think the car companies have to come up with something totally different if they want to survive."

Ernesto moves off toward another group:

"She must've had some plastic surgery, don't you think?"

"Definitely. Everybody has!"

"Everybody? Who's everybody?" Ernesto asks himself as he places his empty glass on a table and springs for the fancy cheese and *foie* something... someone replenishes his cup.

"I asked my analyst. He says that it's an oral fixation."

Ernesto empties his glass and moves toward the bar, where several Argentines from YPF are talking and gesticulating like Romans. A Mexican has had the bad taste to criticize Argentine beaches and one Argentinean guy jumps on him like a Doberman.

"Bullshit! The problem is that you went to *La Bristol*! That beach is crap, that's where the poor folk go. Why the hell did you go there? Mar del Plata has other, much better beaches, *che*!"

Ernesto senses that the Doberman might jump on him at any moment. Meanwhile, the man's wife is giving their address to another woman with carrot-colored hair.

"We live in Olivos. You don't know Olivos? It's where the *Quinta de Olivos* is, where President Menem lives, that's our neighborhood."

Ah, the *quinta* ... the *farm*. Ernesto remembers that in his pocket he has photos of Rosa's house, which he developed at the bus station. He goes to an empty table in a corner to look at them yet again:

Here they are: Rosa's grandfather in the river showing off his canoe, the children bringing warm eggs from the chicken house, Grandma offering me a guayusa tea...and me riding Rosa's horse around the farm. If only Rosa knew I've been riding her horse! And that I put my name besides hers in the heart that was carved into the tree trunk!

In his memory's holograph, Ernesto sees the farm like paradise on earth.

A group of middle-aged men, evidently from the executive class, comes over in search of an available table.

"May we?" one of them asks as he brings up some chairs.

"Of course."

Ernesto puts his photos away. They are too out of place. In this petulant world where music sounds sweet and sweetness sounds false, poverty, even if it's in paradise, has no place. An air of exclusivity, of self-satisfaction, of self-confidence, of "look how well-off I am", although not articulated, floats in the air and emanates from every pore of the bodies present, each encased in a bubble of opulence. *We're doing well, aren't we? Look how good we have it! Isn't life grand?!*

Although he has moved away from the group, he hears a voice that interrupts his internal monologue.

"You can't dig wells there, not with the Tagaeri at war with us. You can't even do seismic tests there."

Tagaeri? Ernesto is startled into attention. This is worth listening to.

"These savages have no right to obstruct modernization, to the progress of the entire nation!" someone vociferates. "We offer them everything: schools, hospitals... and they don't want to hear of it. They need to get civilized or just disappear from the map!"

"I heard there was a proposal to send in the Air Force to bomb their villages."

For a few seconds no one knows what to say. Their mouths are shut in guilty silence.

"Are you sure?"

"Yeah, I'm sure. I have a cousin in the military."

"That seems a little ... drastic," another man says.

"Yes, but it would solve the problem once and for all, wouldn't it?" a third man opines.

"Well, at least they should be harassed and pushed to the other side of the border. Then let the Peruvians deal with them!"

Ernesto remembers what Mr. Erikson told him about the plans to finish off the Tagaeri, and the deep shadow that passed over the man's eyes at that moment.

He feels like telling these gentlemen that a third of the Ecuadorian Amazon has already been occupied by the infamous oil blocks, and that....

Conceição notices that Ernesto is alone. Nor does his expression escape her - a slight grimace of disgust. She goes to him with a glass full to the brim in order to remedy the situation, whatever it may be.

"You're not drinking anything?" she asks in Portuguese. "Are you trying to sober up?"

Ernesto tells her that he's already drunk too much, that his head is spinning, and that he would like a glass of water. "That's what I really need," Ernesto thinks, "simple water, like the water at Rosa's farm. Fresh, cool, innocent." If there's any place in the world he'd rather be right now it is there at the edge of the jungle, beside the clear water, to quench his thirst and cool the hot poker burning within him.

That authentic, fluid world, and this other hypocritical and usurping one that is all around him—that's the way he sees them—are two painfully different realities, so far apart that it seems reasonable to suppose that one or the other must be a dream. Or perhaps, would this be the case of one of those parallel worlds that they say at times collide with ours and, in a random quantum leap, throw us into confusion?

"Here's some water," says Conceição when she returns. She lifts the glass to his lips. "Would you like to lie down?"

A short time later Ernesto finds himself walking hand in hand with the girl toward her bed.

Eight hours later he wakens with a raging headache and the vague recollection of a party followed by the ephemeral delights of a night in which he became a man.

23. Absolution

I

November 1st

The court overflows with people and the audience is clearly divided into two sectors: pink faces, grave and indignant on one side; dark faces, proud and equally indignant on the other. After a brief recess, the case continues.

"The man on the right is the owner of a farm," whispers a member of the public in the ear of someone who has just arrived. "His name is Anselm Hilton. He's suing a woman who worked for him for years, for having passed merchandise to some middlemen without a proper invoice. Basically, she's accused of being an accomplice to robbery, and she was arrested. But around here everyone knows that the man who denounced her did it on the day she told him that she had cancer because of the pesticides used on the farm."

"So he was afraid she'd sue him because of the pesticide exposure, and this was all a preemptive strike?"

"Exactly. That's why he came up with this story of stealing merchandise. The defense lawyer has all the evidence; the farmer's denies it all, of course. Her lawyer is a good one, though."

"How did she get enough money to hire a private lawyer? Are you sure she really didn't steal?"

"There's an NGO around here that helps immigrants by getting lawyers for them. Well, they're coming in. That's the accused woman, in green. The other lady is the translator."

The prosecutor questions the farmer, who reiterates his story: the woman stole merchandise valued at 4,000 dollars. The judge calls the defense lawyer, who also questions the farmer, emphasizing that the accusation was made on the same day the woman informed him that she was ill, the 18th of last month, and not the day when the supposed fraud took place which, according to papers presented by his accountant, occurred weeks earlier. Why did he wait all that time? The farmer claims that he only discovered his employee's malfeasance on the 18th of November. His *lapsus linguae* is plain. The lawyer points out that today is the

275

first of November, All Saints' Day, and that he could hardly have travelled to the future. The left side of the room erupts in laughter.

"Order in the Court!"

The judge brings his gavel down hard on his desk and threatens to have any disorderly persons thrown out of the courtroom.

The defense lawyer whispers something in the woman's ear. She nods.

"With your permission, Your Honor. My client would like to testify and she requires a translator."

"Permission granted."

Alba Caento rises with some difficulty, aided by her lawyer.

"Thank you, Your Honor. I would like to say, first, that I've worked on his farm since I got to this country. I've always paid my taxes, because they told me I should, so that one day I could become a legal resident. Second, it's true that I bought a fake document, Your Honor, so that I could work, because my boss demanded one. And do you know who I bought it from? From Mr. Hilton's farm supervisor!"

Stifled laughter ripples through the audience while the interpreter strives to speak loudly enough to be understood. The judge bangs his gavel.

"And thirdly, which is in truth number one, because it's the most important, I could hardly have robbed anybody when I was lying in the hospital emergency room on that day. Here are the hospital admittance papers to prove it!"

The lawyer submits the document to the judge, who examines it under a magnifying glass.

"The rest of the story you already know, Your Honor. In the six years that I worked on the farm, due to my own ignorance, I sprayed pesticides without any protection. Nobody ever gave me any. And I didn't know what I was doing to myself. That's why I stand before you today with cancer."

In her sorrow Alba breaks down, then composes herself and continues: "I ask that you consider my circumstances, Your Honor, and be ..." – she stumbles for a moment – "even if not with me, merciful to my daughter ... She's traveling here. I asked her to come and take care of me ." She struggles to maintain her

276

composure. "But ...we lost touch," she continues, weeping. "She left almost two months ago, on and old fishing boat. I haven't heard from her since she got to Mexico! I'm sorry, Your Honor, the only thing I want is to find my daughter, and I ask you to be generous with her. Give her your protection. But I don't know," she says, looking at the public, "I don't know where my little girl is."

"I'm right here, Mom!" comes a voice clear as a bird's from among the audience, as two skinny arms rise into the air like a bird beginning to fly.

"Rosa, Rosita!"

Rosa's joyful voice opens heaven's doors for Alba Caento. She stretches her arms toward her daughter, but emotion overtakes her and her lawyer lowers her into her seat. The audience cries as one body, hundreds of eyes turn toward Rosa, and the excitement spreads like wildfire as the gavel begins to rise and fall.

"Order, order in the court!"

No one listens. The interpreter dries her tears on her sleeve while others rush to Alba's assistance. The fruit pickers in the audience throw their hats into the air. Chaos reigns.

"This Court is in recess, ladies and gentlemen. Recess!"

Rosa, having run forward, is in her mother's arms.

II

When Ernesto opened his email this morning in Quito, with a hangover still kicking inside his head like a herd of horses, a message from his father appeared on the screen: "We'll be at the airport. Bon voyage! Dad."

And there is a copy of his flight itinerary.

His father's messages are known for their minimalist style. Ernesto's mother thinks this is a holdover from the Morse Code system her husband learned in his youth. His own explanation is that he simply hates computers. As for Ernesto, what matters is that his parents received the call for help and came to his aid. That's what families are for.

The flight attendant shakes him lightly. Ernesto could swear she is the same woman from seven weeks ago. This time he fills the entry forms apathetically. He has had a repetitive dream in which his father, who has served at times as a Texapetrol consultant, tromps into Rosas's house with muddy, oil-soaked boots. This desecration has left Ernesto in a state of extreme distress.

Thank God it was just a dream! It's a relief to be awake.

But the truth is, reality has its own ghosts for Ernesto. He has the sorrowful feeling that he has moved away from this "man who raised him" and he is not sure if he will be able to approach him again with an innocent heart. It's as if he had discovered that his father was once a thief, or a murderer. In regard to his personal quest, he is harassed by a sense of failure. It is true that his experience in the arms of the Brazilian girl has strengthened his self-confidence, and today he feels older, but that feeling has in no way calmed his spirit. On the contrary, today more than ever he feels like the swallow in the song "in the regions of the lost and unable to fly."

Moreover, his body accompanies his soul's suffering because, in addition to the infamous mental nebula of his hangover, a violent tumult has suddenly unleashed itself in his intestines, perhaps due to his tropical journeys, perhaps from excess of alcohol, just as he is boarding the aircraft. He feels doubly humiliated.

Now, in the lobby of San Diego's airport, he strives to respond to the warm embrace of his parents with a happy face.

During the ride from the airport to the house he doesn't mention his trip to eastern Ecuador. This is not the time. He summarizes his visit to Mr. Moreno in Mexico, to the Moreno Xequijel in Guatemala and to Mrs. Moreno Quipe in Ecuador, to whom he must not delay in sending the promised pair of glasses.

"Ernesto, you have no idea how many sleepless nights you've caused us," says his mother. "And what a relief it is to have you back safe and sound!"

"I'm sorry, Mom. The worst part is that I didn't find what I wanted," he adds in a slightly irritated tone.

"That should've been our responsibility, dear. We're the ones who brought you home, remember?"

"Yes, I remember perfectly well! Even though I was only a few weeks old, right? My memory's awesome.

"Very funny, Ernesto. Now, listen. We can help in another way. When Rosa was here..."

"What Rosa?" Ernesto interrupts. But really he means to say: "What? Rosa? "

"The Ecuadorian girl, that friend of yours you sent our way."

"She's here? at our house?" Ernesto's dejected heart soars like a comet.

"She stayed a couple nights, about three days ago. Esteban, didn't you tell Ernesto anything in your e- mail?"

Three days? When I was on her farm?

It occurs to Ernesto that this could very well be one of those beautiful symmetries that life offers, because for every distortion and disharmony and degradation that occurs somewhere in the world, there must be, somewhere else, a harmonious and positive force to restore the lost balance, so the world does not end. He must have read about this somewhere he can't remember. Or did he just make it up? Or is it one of those eternal truths that are latent, imprinted in the dark cellar of the Self, waiting to be discovered?

"Well, you know how your father is with e-mail," Isabel continues. "As I was saying, we took Rosa to Oregon, where her mother was. That's why we weren't home when you called. The González family has lived there for years; they helped us find Rosa's mother. Rosa's a sweet girl. And through Mrs. Caento we met a lawyer from the Farmer's Union, who was her defense lawyer in the court. We'll tell you later on about the case. But for now let me tell you that this guy is great. He handles labor rights cases, but he also knows about adoption and family tracing. He said there are ways of finding out more about how you got to the convent; these institutions are required to release their files to adoptees.

"That's interesting. But, wait a minute. Rosa's mother is in trouble with the law?" Ernesto wants to know.

"Esteban, tell him the story."

Esteban Ruiz begins a long narrative, punctuated with exclamations and comments from his wife, from the moment when Rosa called them until yesterday in court.

279

"Too bad you missed the drama! When your mother saw Rosa and her mother hugging she cried like a baby."

"You weren't exactly dry-eyed either. I saw you hide your face behind your hat!"

"Alba won the case," adds Ernesto's father, without contradicting his wife, "because she had an irrefutable alibi. And she got a humanitarian visa, so she can stay in the country for the rest of her treatment."

"That's right," Isabel continues. "The lawyer made a brilliant defense."

"It would have been a terrible shame to deny her the treatment," says Esteban, "when her illness was caused by the toxic pesticides that her employer was using."

He stops suddenly. The silence in the car is dense.

"Did you say *toxic*, Dad?"

Esteban didn't mean to say it, but it exploded, in the same way that repressed feelings sometimes explode in dreams.

After a few long seconds, he says, in an anguished tone that Ernesto has never heard:

"We have to talk, Ernesto. I owe you an explanation about what you asked me on the phone."

There's so much I have to tell you. I need to ask you to forgive me, he tells Ernesto in a confession without words. *If I could melt the years frozen in time and sail back to the past, I would do everything differently, Son. But now I can only hope you'll forgive me.*

Ernesto sees his father's watery eyes and tired expression through the mirror; a face more worn by melancholy than by age. And he realizes that the man who is sitting there now is not the same Esteban Ruiz from the past, when he was barely 30 years old, living in a different world—when the indestructibility of the planet was taken for granted.

He thinks back to when he was buried in Palenque. He feels that life is charging him now for what he borrowed on that occasion, and that the time has come to settle his debt with destiny.

He'd like to tell his dad that he has already forgiven him. Because Esteban is his father as much as the other one is. Because he, Ernesto Moreno Ruiz, is not just a bunch of strands of DNA;

he is that, and much more. He is the receptacle into which his adoptive parents and grandparents poured their flow of humanity.

Who knows? Maybe it was the hand of fate, Ernesto thinks, that took him through these intricacies of life to ultimately face, not *his* past, but his father's past, to test him, to see if he could understand and forgive, to give him an opportunity to forgive. Because the path of the pilgrim is, after all, a path to his inner Self. And the Self is a surface to be polished until it becomes mirror.

And in this intriguing alchemy of the mind, where the rough can be transmuted into gold with a light touch of consciousness, Ernesto finds that his journey has not been in vain. Maybe he and his father, together, can undo what was wrong, or redo what was badly done. Perhaps his father needs him to heal his spirit, as he needed his father to cure his orphaned self.

A lantern is lit inside him, giving light and warmth; even the inside of the car looks brighter.

Isabel, who doesn't appreciate the long and stubborn pauses among the men, changes the subject:

"Ernesto, the lawyer is going to get us an appointment at the convent to go over your files, if that's what you want. He's interested in your case."

"Our case, that is," corrects Esteban Ruiz, coming out from his silence, "because we had something to do with it. Right? Oh, and don't go out tonight—Rosa's going to call. By the way, she can't be deported because she's a minor. That's the law now. She'll be able to enroll in school."

"That's great," says Ernesto, as if he's not that interested.

A feeling of epiphany flows through him.

24. From Esperanza

I

At ten to five in the morning, the Ruizes and their attorney are standing by the door of the convent. Although Isabel wears dark glasses, Ernesto knows that his mother has been crying. At ten o'clock they ring the bell. Then, a tiny window opens and reveals a big eye that moves from side to side. The window is closed, the heavy door opens and a nun, the owner of the eye, invites them in.

They go through the high-ceilinged hallway, yellow walls and long wooden benches on either side, leading to a large courtyard covered with colonial tiles.

A well with curbstone tiles, the Moorish style arcades with still blooming bougainvillea around them, and geranium pots on the windowsills or hanging from the window bars remind Ernesto that California used to be New Spain. He thinks again of the confluence of those two rivers flowing inside himself. And that the fact he was left in this place, so Spanish, seventeen years ago, is no coincidence, but another facet of what he calls the symmetries of his destiny.

The nun leads them to one of the rooms facing the courtyard. Despite the poor lighting, it is clear that this is the center of the monastery's records: the shelves are full of thick black binders with white labels, covered by cloister dust, undisturbed by the hands of the world.

The July 1978 files are already there, in a manila envelope on a table, available to this visitor.

"You cannot take the files with you" the nun says, "but they may be photocopied, if desired."

The Ruizes and their lawyer go to another room to fill out some bureaucratic forms that the nun places in front of them, expeditiously. Ernesto puts the papers on the table and reads:

June 20, 1978, 10am. A woman leaves a male baby a few weeks old with Sister Dora in Saint Joseph Church. She says that the baby is her son, and asks for the love of God to take care of him until she returns. Before the Sister could ask for an explanation, the woman runs.

At 9pm, the mother not having returned, Sister Dora brings the baby to the care of this institution. There, a note pinned to the baby gown is discovered. The baby's name is written, "Ernesto", and his mother's name, "María Moreno".

With a tightness in his chest, Ernesto observes the yellowish note that is attached to the files' first sheet. Despite the faded ink, the words are not difficult to read:

Name: Ernesto Moreno
Mother's name: María Moreno, de Esperanza.

None of this changes what he already knew, only that the paper does not say "take good care of him." Apparently the story that reached him was an amalgam of the written note and the spoken message. But at least it is true that he was left by his mother, even temporarily. "So, my mother was planning to come back to get me," Ernesto thinks. "Why didn't she do it?"

June 27, 1978. Mr. Esteban Ruiz and Mrs. Isabel Echeverria de Ruiz, both of Spanish origin and permanent residents of the United States, offer to have the baby "Ernesto" as a foster child while the attorney for the jurisdiction starts searching for the parents.

This information isn't new either. But the lawyer must have been a fool, Ernesto thinks, for there can't be that many María Morenos in a city. He tries also to imagine what his life would have been like if the lawyer had not been a fool and had found his mother. Would he be the same Ernesto he is now? Yes and no. He is one of the many possible Ernestos, one that became a concrete reality in the curve of a quantum universe of infinite (or almost infinite?) possibilities. But the Ernesto that became reality in this world, here and now, is *this* Ernesto and not another. He keeps reading:

December 5, 1979. Not having found baby "Ernesto"'s parents and the eighteen months stipulated by law having expired, the social worker has demonstrated to the juvenile court that the child has been abandoned, and the judge gives the Ruiz family the right of permanent adoption (see adoption papers attached), which ends the responsibility of the institution regarding the child.

"What was I like as a baby? How much of that baby is there in me now? Was I too impulsive even then, as Dad says I am now?" he wonders. The boy remembers that his grandfather Ruiz once told him: "Within you live the brave and the coward, the generous and the stingy, the humble and the arrogant. And something or someone makes one in the pair manifest itself, and the other fall asleep. And when you're young you have to watch them all, and feed the one you want to grow, and starve the other one!"

January 20, 1980. Mrs. María Moreno appears before this institution to claim her baby. She is informed that, in view of her prolonged absence, the baby has been considered "abandoned," and therefore, according to the law, he has been permanently given for adoption and that, under this same law, the name or address of the adoptive parents will not be given to her.

A feeling of sorrow and even guilt rushes through Ernesto. "You missed me by a few weeks, Mom." He knows that on January 2 of that year his family moved to Spain, that on January 6 he was celebrating his first "Reyes Magos" in Bilbao with his parents and grandparents Echeverria, and that he would not return to the United States until after his tenth birthday. "Why did my parents wait so long to look for me?" he wonders. He would like to jump to the end, but refrains from doing so.

January 21, 1980, 10am. A man who claims to be the father of the baby "Ernesto" appears before this institution in search of him. Again, and protected by the state legislation, he is informed that he has already lost custody of the baby because of neglect, and that no information about the child's whereabouts can be given.

At noon, the same man mentioned above breaks the window of the Mother Superior Heloise of the Cross, with a stone, and inflicts serious vandalism to the building. The Mother Superior decides not to involve the authorities in this sad episode. She states that it is "an act of God," where no one is to blame. Furthermore, the institution has acted according to the law, which mainly ensures the baby's safety and the privacy of the adoptive parents. But the man is warned that if he comes back to the institution, they will be obliged to report him to the police.

After that there are no more entries in the record. Ernesto shuts the folder and finds himself saying "Aha!" and laughing with satisfaction. "My dad broke a window! I have to see it; I have to see that window. The lawyer has to tell them to let me see it!" Only then does he realize a nun is watching him, from a corner, with disguised interest. No time to feel ashamed, because the woman says, pointing to the door of an adjoining room:

"There are some people who want to see you. This way, please."

See me? If it is the Mother Superior wanting to apologize or something, or the lawyer of the convent to cover his ass of any possible lawsuit, I am not interested. It is best to talk to Dad.

"They might want to talk to my parents or my lawyer, maybe? They are in the other room."

"No, no, it's with you they want to talk".

Ernesto goes into the little room and perceived the fragrance of orange blossom.

Sitting on a sofa, a woman and a man look at him, smiling.

II

"Finally, Son! We've been looking for you so long! Such a handsome boy!" says the woman, getting up from the sofa and extending her arms.

Son? Ernesto feels his heart burning in a cavern within. Did she say *Son*? The old longing beams in his eyes. "María Moreno?" Ernesto finally stammers.

"Yes, Ernesto, it's me. Please forgive me, Son!" the woman exclaims through her tears. "We have so much to explain!"

An ardent, heartfelt current flows through his whole body, and though he also wants to extend his arms and run toward her, his legs are too weak. He wants to smile, but he holds his lips tightly shut to suppress his desire to weep. When he finally takes his mother's hands between his, the smile she was waiting for erupts along with the tears.

His mother's black hair, falling in loops, frames the face of a woman not yet 40. It is a face like a full moon, with soft and harmonious lines and a broad, clear forehead. A beautiful face, with tiny wrinkles at the corners of the mouth and around the eyes, but still young. It is the color of wild honey and amber, golden auburn, like his, and with luminous, fresh skin, as fresh as the first grade teacher he remembers from elementary school.

"You look so much like your grandfather, Son!" says the man, also rising and extending his arms toward Ernesto.

"This is your father, Ernesto," says María Moreno.

Ernesto takes the man's hands between his. He remembers the episode of breaking a window with a stone, and smiles. And this man who has the same features as Ernesto, though carved in lighter skin and with graying hair and a lush mustache, smiles back at him.

"Please, sit down!" Ernesto tells them, with rapid breathing. He is fighting tears.

He brings another chair to sit closer to them and then, these two human beings who call him "Son" take his hands, one in each of their own hands.

It is a sweet, long, longed-for feeling. He wants to show manliness, but his mother wipes his flowing eyes with her hands. Her relaxed gaze comforts him.

"I'm sure you've wondered why we left you, Son. I know that must have hurt you a lot."

"Yes, I have always wondered. And yes, it did hurt me, a little. I don't know what your reasons were, but I never held it against you," he says quickly.

"Well, Ernesto, let me tell you the story: I worked in a daycare where I was allowed to take you, even though you were very small, just a few weeks old," his mother recounts. "Your father was still in Mexico, but he was planning on coming to join us. There was work here. One day someone lodged a complaint against the daycare because it had undocumented workers—I was one of them. Then there was a raid. When I saw them entering, I grabbed you and took off running from the *migra*. But I couldn't run with you in my arms; I found myself in front of the Church of San José, and I ducked in and left you there with a nun. I thought that she could take care of you for a few hours until I got away. You were wearing a little tag, with your name and mine, because that was the rule at the daycare. You know how babies can look so much alike."

"That's enough, Dear, now get on with the story," her husband urges.

Ernesto enjoys the sight of his father's mustache sketching the air as he speaks; it's not the drooping mustachio of a bandit, but a cheerful one, with a little upward swoop.

"As I was saying, I took off running, and when I got to the corner, they caught me. I told the officers that they couldn't take me to jail, that I had a baby to nurse. But they didn't care. They detained me and then they deported me. When Father went looking for me at the detention center they locked him too. They loaded us onto a bus and forced us to leave. I was crying so hard my face was drenched. And the milk was streaming out of me like two waterfalls, soaking me all the way down to my pants. Your father, enraged and grieving. I wept so much that night, and the following night and all the ones after that, until I had no more tears in me left to weep! Back in Mexico, we wanted to save our money to come back for you. But, as you know, a person proposes but God disposes. Your father fell off a scaffold. We thought he was going to die."

The man takes his wife's hand. That misstep on the scaffolding still fills him with guilt. The impossibility of going back for Ernesto hurt him more than all the ribs he broke in the fall, he tells them, pulling a gigantic handkerchief out of his pocket.

His father's large eyes, two jet black pools, require a handkerchief of extravagant dimensions. Ernesto imagines that his father has a bit of Moorish blood, because he has the enormous

287

eyes of a *cante hondo* singer that he once saw in Seville, and he never could forget the fiery expression of the man. Now he encounters it again in the intense gaze of his own progenitor. Perhaps he, Ernesto, also has Arabic genes woven in amongst the rest?

"Please forgive us, son," says his father, drying his tears.

Ernesto squeezes his hand and nods. His mother continues:

"Your father was in coma in the hospital for two months."

"In Esperanza?"

"In Aguascalientes. We were so happy when he came out of the coma. It was just a miracle he got well. I had to work and care for him. But all that time I was writing letters to the convent, with a translator. I told them I was your Mom. After several letters and calls, they finally wrote me. They said you were no longer there because it wasn't an orphanage, that you were in a family's home, and that was all they knew. Nothing more. When your father got completely well we decided to come back and look for you. Your heart breaks into a thousand pieces when you're apart from your son, your own flesh and blood. At that time it was still easy to cross the border without papers. So we rushed back here. They said the same thing they told us in the letters. They knew nothing!"

Ernesto observes his father and behind the boyish expression that cries and laughs in the same breath he divines an impetuous character that he knows well.

"In the end they told us to speak with the judge. But, of course, at that time we didn't have residency documents. The amnesty laws hadn't been passed yet, and going to the judge would've been like checking ourselves into the jail. And yet we did it. But it didn't help at all. The judge told us that it was too late, that you had been adopted and that they had taken you to Spain and he couldn't give us any more information. And then they deported us once again."

María Moreno looks at her husband.

"A while later we came back to the United States," the father continues, blowing his nose, "crossing over where people always crossed before they made that wall. This time we stayed in the States. Every year, we came back to the convent, religiously, to bang on their doors and ask for you. We were hoping to find a nun who would take pity on us and give us more information. This was our yearly pilgrimage."

"Yes, we were also hoping that someday, when you grew up, you'd come back to San Diego, and maybe you'd go to the convent to ask about us, if your parents told you that you were adopted, that is."

"I did go," said Ernesto, "several times, but they also closed the door in my face. They are not, or were not, allowed to give any information. Judges' orders, they said: The files are closed. That's why I decided to search for you. Now tell me, where is your village? I searched half a continent looking for all of those Esperanzas."

"Your lovely mother Isabel told me, Son. Yesterday she told us over the phone all about your adventures. But Esperanza is your father's name, not a village. We are from Aguascalientes, Mexico."

"That's right, Ernesto. I'm Julio Esperanza," his father explains while giving his mustache a twirl.

"What? But, I always thought ...look at what's written on this paper!" Ernesto points, showing his mother the legendary message. "Here it says, 'María Moreno, of Esperanza', see?"

"I think that your mother has to explain a few things," says Julio Esperanza, with a smile. "María, explain this business about the comma to Ernesto."

"It's because my writing isn't very good, Ernesto. I didn't go to school for very long, you know? I guess I put the comma in the wrong place.[13] I was so nervous on my first day of work at the daycare, I don't know ...So, everybody thought I was from a village called Esperanza, and not married to Esperanza! Ay ay ay! I can't believe all of the confusion that one little misplaced comma has caused!'

"You mean to say that the comma was an accident?" Ernesto asks.

---

[13] **Translator note**: The Spanish "de" after a woman's name means that she is married to the name that follows. But if there is a comma, the "de" means "from", that is, place of origin.

"That's right, which is why I always say it's better to avoid using periods and commas, one should write as one speaks. But that's how things are in this world: upside down and inside out."

"What do you mean?" Ernesto asks, suspecting that his mother has a philosophical bent.

"Because sometimes, a tiny thing is important, and what looks important is nonsense, and other times the most valuable is hidden in the most humble. And the smallest fact can lead to something enormous. Don't you think so, Ernesto?"

Ernesto agrees.

"A comma is as small as a fly's little foot," the woman continues in the manner of one who is speaking to a child, "smaller than a grain of sand, and look how it's made you travel over God's earth! Huge distances! And see how, in the end, we found each other in the same exact place where we separated. That's why I always say life is a circle."

Ernesto's mother hugs and kisses him, leaving lipstick traces on each cheek.

"You see, son, God works in mysterious ways," adds Mr. Esperanza.

The *divine disorder*, Ernesto thinks, evoking his grandfather Ruiz. '*I think the universe has a great design,*' the old man used to say, '*even though it seems chaotic and inscrutable; and if our lives coincide with this superior design, then we've lived for something. I think that Great Designer weaves our stories, Ernesto, and it's our task to understand and follow the pattern that is woven. That's the work of the true pilgrim!*'

"True. I never imagined I'd find you where I began!" says Ernesto, thinking about that circle on the map he always carried within himself.

He thinks about his grandfather's letter, about the meaning of his quest, parallel, perhaps, to that other one the old man referred to. And he feels himself a centimeter closer to the sacred place evoked by his grandfather, where memories of an Eden persist.

"Well, there are no more judges' orders to keep us apart, Boy! Let's go celebrate right now! You need to meet the rest of the family. Your grandparents, your aunts and uncles and, of course, your three little brothers and the two we adopted," says Mrs. Esperanza.

"Three little brothers? And you also adopted two more babies ???" Ernesto asks in surprise.

"Yes. One day the twins appeared in our doorway, in a bread basket. Imagine! They were babies, like you," says Mr. Esperanza. "Your mother said, 'This is a sign from heaven that one day we'll find our Ernesto.' And so we adopted those beautiful little girls and raised them as our own."

"That night, Ernesto," says Mrs. Esperanza, "I heard a voice in the dark telling me that I was going to find you at the end of a long journey. Journey? What journey would I take, with all these children to take care of? I asked myself. So I left it in God's hands. And it turns out that the end of the journey was *your* journey, not mine!" she continues, laughing.

"We'd better get going," says his father, "because this convent has a musty smell. And you know how Mexican families are: there's a big party waiting for you at home."

Ernesto feels that he couldn't possibly have a nobler lineage.

The Esperanzas leave the convent gloom, into the light of day, hand in hand with Ernesto. The Ruizes, proud of their son, and with tight-lipped smiles, follow along behind.

Epilogue

Ecuador (2011)

In a small court on the second floor of the Lago Agrio Commercial Center, lawyers for the Chevropet-Texapetrol Consortium face off against lawyers for the Ecuadorian villagers organization in history's largest environmental lawsuit ever. Thirty thousand members of various native Amazonian and colonist communities seek 27 billion dollars of compensation for damages caused during the decades of petroleum exploitation by Texapetrol, which was acquired by Chevropet in 2001.

In an adjacent office, an engineer, a geologist, and a human rights lawyer, members of the advisory committee of the plaintiffs, look with horror at the stacks of documents piled to the roof. There are 200,000 pages, they are informed, containing evidence of the crime and ready to present to the court. They prove that a third of the Ecuadorian jungle was affected by the operations of the petroleum companies, and that nearly 1,400 indigenous persons have died of cancer as a direct consequence of contamination produced by Texapetrol.

Chevropet's lawyers (a firm that, upon purchase of Texapetrol, inherited the lawsuit) reject the evidence and, with various maneuvers, prolong the process.

An official opens the door partially and sticks his head into the room:

"Esteban Ruiz?"

"Yes."

"Come in, Sir. Dr. Pablo is waiting for you.

In a corner of the office the other two are whispering:

"It's not a fair fight, Rosa. Chevropet has the best lawyers in the U.S., tons of money, and influence."

"I know, Ernesto. But don't forget that David defeated Goliath."